DEATH IN UPTOWN

A *PAUL WHELAN* MYSTERY

MICHAEL RALEIGH

DIVERSIONBOOKS

Also by Michael Raleigh

Paul Whelan Mysteries
A Body in Belmont Harbor
The Maxwell Street Blues
Killer on Argyle Street
The Riverview Murders

Diversion Books
A Division of Diversion Publishing Corp.
443 Park Avenue South, Suite 1008
New York, New York 10016
www.DiversionBooks.com

For more information, email info@diversionbooks.com

First Diversion Books edition February 2015.
Print ISBN: 978-1-62681-763-0
eBook ISBN: 978-1-62681-619-0

To the memory of Barney and Mary Raleigh

PROLOGUE

CHICAGO, 1983

The dead man in the alley had been small, almost childlike in appearance, with small hands and feet and a thick brush of straw-blond hair shot with gray that hung down over his forehead. The eyes were half open, as though he were struggling to rouse himself, and they were blue, pale blue, like a child's eyes. The yellow cast to his skin and the discolored whites of his eyes announced the last stages of cirrhosis. There was a gash over one eye and severe bruising across both cheekbones, and a cut on the bridge of the nose, another at the corner of one eye. His lower lip was caked black with clotted blood and the underside of the chin was bloody from where he'd landed on the pavement. The hair was matted dark over his left ear, and as though these injuries hadn't been damage enough, the tape-covered handle of a knife protruded from his sunken chest.

The dead man leaned against the wall of a garage, one hand limp across his lap and the other stretched out on the pavement, fingers out, pointing to nothing. Two uniformed officers crouched over the body and both turned at the approach of a car.

A gray Caprice pulled into the alley and stopped ten feet from them. From the passenger side, a tall thin man in a tan jacket emerged. A moment later a heavy-set man with a brush cut and a loud green plaid jacket got out from the driver's side. They walked toward the dead man, the heavy-set one hitching up his trousers as he walked. The taller one, an older man, stopped a couple of feet from the corpse and put his hands in his pockets as though no longer interested. His companion approached the body.

"Dave," he said, nodding to the older of the two uniforms.

"Hi, Al."

"What you got?"

"Not ours. Somebody buttonholed the meter maid and she called it in. We just got here. How'd you get here so fast?"

"We heard the call come in. We were over on Ashland. We got nothing better to do." He shot a look at his partner, who shook his head slightly and squinted up at the sun. The heavy-set man winked at the other cop, ran his hand across his brush cut and crouched. The dead man wore a flannel shirt over a T-shirt, and the heavy-set man pulled the flannel shirt open on one side to look at the emaciated body. Literally a bag of bones: the knees and elbows made hard points in his clothing.

"Lookit this." The detective encircled the corpse's upper arm with his thumb and forefinger. Then he let the arm drop. He looked at the face for a moment and then reached out and put his fingers on the dead man's cheek. He looked up at the two uniforms and saw that the younger one was frowning.

"You think I'm weird, right? Your partner thinks I'm weird, Dave. Somebody should always touch a dead man," he said quietly.

Emboldened by this direct address, the young cop gave a little shrug. "Why, detective?"

The detective's gray eyes held his for a moment and then the face creased in irritation. " 'Cause they just should, that's all." The detective looked up and down the alley. One block away he could make out the steel-and-glass block of Truman College. It was ten o'clock in the morning and summer classes were in session; young people in bright colors were entering and leaving the building. He stared for a moment, then looked at the body again and shook his head.

"Ain't this a bitch."

"You make it a strong-arm, detective?"

The man called Al rubbed his brush cut again and looked up at the young officer with amusement. He stood up and looked at the man's nameplate. Then he looked back at his silent partner.

"Jones!" He pointed at the plate. "Come look, honest to God. A white guy named Jones." He put his hands across his eyes and laughed quietly, then pecked out between his fingers at the other uniform.

"Davey, I tell you, I love this job. It's always something, ain't it? I swear. Every day it's something new. I been a cop for twenty-one years and this is the first time I ever met a white guy named Jones."

"That guy in Youth, used to work Shakespeare," the other detective said.

"No." The heavy-set one shook his head. "That wasn't his real name. He was Armenian or something. His name was… like, Josarrian or some shit like that. No, this here, this is the first one." He looked back at Jones. "So, Jones. This was a strong-arm robbery, huh? A mugging, eh? Somebody wanted this guy's gold watch, or what?"

The young cop went a deep purple, cleared his throat, made a slight wave with one arm, shuffled his feet, opened his mouth and could say nothing.

"Easy, Jones, easy. What's your first name?"

"Wayne."

"Okay, Wayne. Look, maybe you don't know me. Al Bauman's my name. I got a weird sense of humor. Just jerking your chain, is what I'm doing here. Look, this ain't a robbery. I'll tell you that much."

Rejuvenated, Jones nodded. "I didn't mean the victim had…uh, valuables. I meant somebody killed him for, you know, something he had in his possession. A bottle, maybe, or money."

Bauman looked at the young man with a grave expression, but the glint in his eye showed that he was suppressing the urge to laugh. He looked away. A fight to the death over a bottle of Richard's Wild Irish Rose. Vicious old derelicts, scourge of the city. He caught the older cop's eye, held his breath, but it was no use. He started to snicker again and was able to make a pretense of blowing his nose. By the time he was finished tucking his handkerchief away he was under control again. He looked up the alley for a moment. The cop named Dave, a red-faced Germanic-looking man, stepped in to save some face for his partner.

"So what do you make of it, Al?"

"I think somebody didn't like this guy and killed him."

Jones knelt down beside the corpse and nodded. "Somebody *really* didn't like him. Beat him half to death, then finished the job with the knife."

"No." Bauman looked at his watch and milked the moment.

"So what happened, Al?" the older cop asked.

"He was dead already. When the knife went in." He looked at Jones. "What would happen if I stuck you there?" He touched the young officer just under the heart.

"I'd bleed, and—"

"Yeah, you'd bleed. You'd *spout*, babe. There's almost no blood. There's no blood on the ground except a couple drops. Somebody beat this guy to death."

"Why would you beat a guy to death and then stick 'im, Al?" Dave smiled. "Who's got that kind of energy in this heat?"

"He stuck the guy to hide the fact that he beat 'im to death. That's why."

"Why would somebody do that?"

"I didn't say I understood. I just told you what I thought. He was dead when he got stabbed. And that's what the M.E. will say. You watch."

"Seems pretty complicated to me," Jones said. "I mean, it's a lot of trouble to go to over an old wino. Aren't we gettin' kind of carried away here?"

Bauman looked at him. Amazing, the recuperative powers of the young. "So he's a wino, so what? So it's okay that somebody whacked him and walked? What, that's all right with you?"

"No, I didn't mean it like that—"

"I knew this guy. He had a name. Name was Shinny. Shinny, that's what they called him. We useta call him 'the climber.' When he was younger, before he got…like this here, all fucked up on the bottle, he used to go through windows that were open six, eight inches. He could go between those wood slats they put on buildings to keep people out, he could go up walls, up drainpipes, he could get in heating vents. A fuckin' *artiste*. He was a thief but we used him a couple times to get in places for us." Bauman looked at the corpse again, noted the thick scabs on the knuckles and a dark hard patch on one ear, marks of earlier injury. "He wasn't bad people, though."

Bauman nodded to Dave and then to Jones and walked back to his car, followed by his partner.

"You gonna be on this one, Al, or what?" Dave called out.

"If they let me spin my wheels on a bum. Yeah, I guess. And if nobody gets in my way. Somebody always gets in my way." He gave his partner a quick look and then shrugged. They got into the Caprice and backed out of the alley. The older cop looked at Jones and clapped him on the shoulder.

"Hey, don't let him get to you. He likes to dick young cops around. It's how he gets his jollies."

"He's an asshole," Jones said, glowering at the departing Caprice.

"He's pretty strange, all right. But he's smart. He's real good at what he does. And I'd hate to be the guy that got in his way."

ONE

"You're in my way."

Paul Whelan, a lanky redhead in a Mexican cotton shirt, turned and saw a little man in a winter coat carrying a Jewel bag with what were presumably all his worldly possessions. Squinty and older than Genesis, the little man stared righteously at Whelan and held up one hand. "You are in my way, sir."

Whelan stepped aside. "Okay. Now I'm out."

The old man looked at him for a moment and then nodded. "Look to your soul, young man."

"Thanks. I'll do that." The little man launched into oratory, bellowing out biblical injunctions and citing scripture, and Whelan stepped out into Broadway against the traffic. A Checker cab came within six inches of him and the cabbie leaned on his horn and shouted something profane. The little man yelled that the cabbie was damned and the cabbie gave him the finger and the little man began running after him, and Whelan told himself that he lived in an interesting neighborhood.

On the other side of the street, a vacant-faced kid was passing out little blue leaflets. He handed one to Whelan without looking at him. The leaflet bore the picture of a woman in her fifties or sixties and proclaimed her to be "your guide to the spirits."

Whelan looked at the kid and smiled. "Oh, good. Fraud, my favorite." The kid looked at him, picked at his ear, examined whatever he found and looked away again. Whelan looked at the brochure.

It said the woman's name was "Madame Claire" and told him that she was "the most sought-after and internationally acclaimed clairvoyant and astrologer in the Western Hemisphere," and went on to give both her education—a degree from Florida Astrological Institute, plus various certificates attesting that Madame Claire was a sort of honor student among seers and clairvoyants—and her pedigree, namely her descent from "Gypsy royalty" of the fifteenth century. Whelan studied her picture: she had blue eyes and blond hair and it was clear that she was descended from the Norwegian branch of the Gypsy race.

Madame Claire was apparently a virtuoso among spiritualists: she knew the future, could communicate with the dead, even, the brochure claimed, "if they have been dead a long time," and spoke eleven languages fluently. Her specialty was her remarkable success at helping people pick winning lottery tickets; this success had apparently been limited thus far to the New Jersey lottery, because all her testimonials were from New Jersey residents. The pamphlet was filled with these quotes from happy New Jerseyites claiming to have made the Big Score on predictions from Madame Claire. She offered to tell fortunes, unravel family difficulties, explain life's mysteries and help people select careers. She accepted Visa and MasterCard and tossed in the time-honored freebie of all fortune-tellers: one free question.

Whelan looked at the kid. "You know this lady?"

The kid squinted, scratched his head and nodded. "My aunt."

"So you're a Gypsy too."

The kid looked uncomfortable and shuffled from one foot to the other.

"Hey, don't be embarrassed. This is America. It's okay to be a Gypsy. Listen, ask your aunt who she likes in the first race at Arlington. That's my free question." He tossed the leaflet in a trash can and walked on.

A few doors from his office building, just outside the el station, a pack of teenage boys had gathered to watch two kids fight. Just a half mile to the east, more sensible types were already filling up the beach or spreading picnic blankets in Lincoln Park, and a short mile or so to the south they were lining up for tickets to the Cub game, but this was ghetto life, in the multicolored ghetto that was Uptown. The streets were overrun with bored kids who hadn't landed summer jobs; most of them would be on these corners till Labor Day. A few, he knew, would stay here the rest of their lives.

One of the young pugilists was small and stocky and looked Mexican. The other was taller, very dark, heavy-lidded and smiling. He looked like Nino Valdez, a flashy Cuban heavyweight of the late fifties. Like most heavyweights of the time, his moment in the sun had passed when he fought Sonny Liston. After Liston stretched him, Valdez claimed he'd been fed a drugged orange before the fight. Valdez faded quickly from the public eye but the orange went on to become famous.

The two boys traded lefts and Nino wasn't smiling anymore. Whelan was about to stop it when a squad car rolled around the corner and the whole crowd vanished under the el tracks.

Sam Carlos came out of his grocery store and sat on a fruit crate in his doorway. He gave Whelan a little salute.

"Hey, Pablo. How's the detective business?"

"I'd rather be in groceries, Sam." Carlos laughed and surveyed his window. New hand-painted signs decorated the window and his door, and Sam's store now proclaimed itself a CARNNICERIA though it hadn't seen fresh meat since Nixon.

"Hey, you like? You like my signs?"

"You've got too many n's in *carniceria*, Sam. There's only one."

Sam turned on his crate to look at the new sign. He grunted and shrugged. "Hey, whaddayou know? You don' know Spanish."

"Yeah, but neither do you," Whelan said and laughed.

Sam Carlos was a source of amusement to Whelan. A short fat man who seemed to go out of his way to dress in the filthiest clothes, Sam carried more cash on his person than most people had in banks. He looked and acted broke, and he spent long hours after closing time ringing up false register tapes to feed his equally corrupt accountant, and he lied to everyone about everything. His store was a monument to the melting-pot culture of Uptown: he sold tripe and avocados, rice, garbanzos, catfish, buffalo fish and three kinds of greens; he routinely overcharged, hit the wrong register keys purposely and apologized profusely if caught, and took delight in giving short weight. If you paid for a pound of hamburger, you got thirteen ounces and the weight of Sam's thumb. Most fascinating of his poses and postures was his continuing role as Puerto Rican businessman. Sam was Armenian.

"Here. You look like sick man. Like you don' make no money lately." He tossed Whelan an apple and laughed. "I buy you breakfast in case you got important case today."

Whelan caught it and shrugged. "I'm not proud." He waved and walked on, biting into the apple. It was dry and mealy.

Across the street, the marquee of the Aragon Ballroom was being changed: BOXING: YOUNG JOE LOUIS VS. HERMINIO ESPARRAGOSA PLUS 8 BOUTS was being removed, letter by letter.

One of the Persians caught his eye and waved to him from the window of the A&W next to the Aragon. It was Rashid. The Iranian smiled, winked, nodded, secure in the knowledge that if he made no other sale today he'd still get Whelan's money. Whelan seldom had lunch anywhere else. For his part, Whelan was glad to be so predictable. He couldn't imagine eating anywhere else when there was a place of such unadulterated bizarreness at hand. He was certain that there was no A&W like this one anywhere in the world and possibly no eatery of any kind like it. Two menus, one Persian and Middle Eastern, the other American junk classics. The customer could choose not just between sandwiches but between worlds. A papaburger or shalimar kabob; the cheez dog or a shish kabob; felafel or a taco; chili, pizza, egg rolls, pizza puffs, ribs, chicken, gyros, Polish sausage and Italian beef. And Whelan had tried them all, every item on the menu except for the one that truly frightened him: he'd never had the ham and cheese. He'd never seen anyone order the ham and cheese, knew only that the ham, hard and red like the stones of the pyramids, sat there in a glass case and aged itself.

He pushed open the heavy door to his office building and

noticed the puddle in the corner of the hallway. He held his breath and went quickly up the steps—marble steps, and brass handrails to go with them, reminders of the time long since passed when the building and the entire neighborhood had been prosperous, a refuge for the wealthy from the rest of a dirty, noisy city. Now, it was one more office building holding a lot of empty space and counting the days before it became a parking lot.

He paused at the landing to the first floor and looked at the offices on both sides of the hall: a small travel agency whose continued existence puzzled him—no one he knew in Uptown took vacations; two social service agencies—the death sentence on any building was the day it was forced to rent its space to welfare agencies; a baby photographer; two small Korean importers; an old man who rented out theatrical props. Whelan counted the days for one of them to move out so he could be forever free of the hated second floor. Other than the Whelan Investigative Agency, the only other tenant upstairs was a nervous-looking accountant seldom there. The halls were kept in semidarkness by the penny-conscious owner, who lived somewhere in suburban Lincolnwood avoiding taxes and subpoenas, and all doors but the front were kept locked, including those to the restrooms. Whelan had to use the one on the first floor, and had to get the key from the baby photographer. The owner was rumored to be the landlord of an entire block of burned-out buildings on the West Side, and Whelan fully believed some morning he'd come in to find the building a pile of soot.

He opened the door to his office, picked up his mail from the floor and went in. If possible, it was hotter inside than on the street, and he opened the window quickly to let the fumes from Lawrence Avenue and the noise from the el come in. Across from his window, the Aragon marquee was undergoing rapid transformation: "FRIDAY NITE SALSA! three bands y un grande…"

He laughed at the familiar Creole employed by the management of the old dance hall and went through his mail. There were two carryout menus, one for a new pizzeria over on

Addison near the ballpark and another for a place calling itself Imperial Mongolian Majesty House and promising Szechuan and Mongolian cuisine. He filed both menus in his top drawer, with the rest of his collection. There were now over ninety, representing most of the cuisines of the planet Earth, and he intended to sample them all before he died.

There was also money in the mail. "Fat City," he said.

The money was a check from Kenneth Laflin for six hundred dollars. It was supposed to have been seven hundred and change, but Whelan by now understood Laflin's approach to his obligations, his grasp of math and his adversarial world view. The letter was an exact duplicate of all Laflin's others, just as Laflin was a clone of the fast-moving high steppers on La Salle Street, where lawyers bred and multiplied like the Gerbils from Hell but always seemed to find work for one another. Tall, perfectly dressed, with silver-fox hair, a year-round tan and the morals of Legs Diamond. And of course, successful. Dealing with him was an irritant, but Laflin was a major contributor to his income, and the relationship afforded Whelan the exquisite pleasure of occasionally telling a rich young attorney to go screw himself. The letter thanked Whelan for his professionalism, for his ingenuity and for his inventiveness, and expressed the hope that they would continue their professional association in the future. Whelan stared at the letter, annoyed that he'd have to come up with a new set of photocopies for his expenses, then looked at the check and felt better.

He sat clown at the gray steel desk, inhaled the exhaust coming in through his window and looked at the sports section of the *Tribune*. Art Shears was coming by around ten but he expected no other calls or visitors till then. He often had coffee and donuts delivered at ten-thirty from the greasy spoon under the tracks, just to give his hallways some traffic and himself a face to talk to. There was really no reason to be in the office now, but he willingly spent his mornings at the desk, for he believed it was the way he kept order in his life. Each morning he came in at nine, sat at his desk, wrote his reports to Laflin or other clients, drank coffee and read the paper column by column. Often he took the rest of the day off, but the mornings provided structure. If you let go of the structure in your life, you left yourself vulnerable to other things and you lost what you had, whether to sloth or drink or something worse. Whelan was fairly well convinced that if he were suddenly freed of the need to work to support himself, he'd go off the deep end.

At nine-thirty he called his service, normally a perfunctory call, brief and friendly. He was surprised when a new voice answered, not the whiskey-throated Shelley, whom he'd never met but envisioned as Lucille Ball at 275 pounds, but a man, a young man, and of distant origins.

"Hello-good-morning, this is the offices of Wee-Lan Investigative Sarviees," the voice sang.

"No. It's 'Way-lan.' It's pronounced 'Way-lan.'"

"He is not in," the little voice sang back.

"No, the name, *my* name, is Paul Whelan. It is pronounced 'Way-lan.'"

"Good morning?"

"Paul Whelan *speaking*, my friend."

"Thank you very much, sir. Mr. Wee-lan is not in. I am answering sarvice."

"I know that. You are *my* answering service."

There was a pause, indecision, perhaps a breakthrough. "Who is calling, please?"

He took a deep breath and said, "Paul Whelan."

"He is not in," the voice chirped, its confidence back.

Whelan took another breath. "Good morning, friend. And what is your name?"

"I am Abraham Chacko," the voice warbled.

"Hi, Abraham."

"Hello. Good morning."

"And, ah, where are you from, Abraham?"

"I am from India," he said excitedly.

"No kidding? Well, Abraham? I am Paul Whelan of Whelan Investigative Services. I am. The man to whom you are now speaking is Paul Whelan."

"He is not in."

17

A dull pressure, more of an ache, began to form behind Whelan's eyes, and he saw spots of white light. "Every day dozens of people are killed for trivial reasons, Abraham, did you know that?"

"Excuse me, sir?"

"Where is Shelley, Abraham?"

"She is not here."

"Yeah, that was my guess, too. Tell you what, Abraham. You call Mr. Whelan for me at his office in about, oh, ten minutes and tell him I'll see him later."

"Veddy good, sir."

He hung up and began fiddling with his desk clock, which had not worked since winter. In a few minutes there was a ring on the phone.

"Hello?"

"Hello-good-morning, Mr. Wee-lan, this is answering sarvice. You have but only just the one call and he is a Mr. Paul. He will see you later."

"Thank you very much."

The service was, in many ways, a waste of money, since the bulk of his calls turned out to be phone solicitations, wrong numbers, teenage jokers or weirdos fascinated by the notion of speaking to a private detective. Still, the phone brought occasional business and was a way for people to catch him. Or it had been till the appearance of Abraham Chacko.

At ten after ten there was a knock, followed by a cough and the sound of feet shuffling. Through the clouded glass of the door he could see the slightly stooped silhouette of Art Shears.

"Come on in, Art."

Whelan could see at a glance that Art Shears's life had seen changes and they weren't for the better. He hoped he could hide his shock. Art's hair was shaggy and going to gray, and it hung over his collar. He'd lost weight, more than he needed to, and his rumpled seersucker jacket seemed to be a size too large.

"Hey, Paulie. Long time no see."

Whelan nodded and got up to shake his hand. "Joe Konzcak's funeral."

"That's how it is now. Weddings and funerals, that's where we all see each other. When you're young, you think you'll hang around with your friends forever, that you'll never stop seeing them. Then it's just weddings and funerals."

"And not many weddings," Whelan said, laughing.

"No. Maybe yours, Paul. Got to happen some day. How bout it?"

"Don't hold your breath, Artie. I think you got married for both of us."

"Still seeing Liz?"

"No. And don't ask. How're things with you, Art? Sit down."

"Oh, super. Can't complain." Art Shears took the client's chair and Whelan sat down on the edge of the desk. There was a rash across both Art's cheeks and the bridge of his nose. Artie grinned and fidgeted and Whelan could smell whiskey.

"Sorry I'm late, Paul. I called to say I'd be running a few minutes behind and I got some guy from Pakistan."

"India. My answering service." He laughed and Art smiled.

"Some service. Hey, interesting location for an office, Paul. You love stuff like this. Soaking up the local color, or what?"

"I thought I was the local color."

"You ever think of writing a book?" Whelan shook his head. "Why not? You're a smart guy, you've seen a lot of interesting things up here. You ought to think about it, Paul. There's nobody who knows the street up here better than you. You've got your contacts and you know how to talk to the people, and I could give you a hand with it." Art seemed to be warming rapidly to his own idea and Whelan wanted to head him off.

"You were always the writer, Artie. So, how're Marie and the boys?"

Shears's eyes clouded but he answered quickly. "Oh, they're great. Matt's a junior at Gordon and Tommy's already got a job with the *Trib*, and he's not halfway through De Paul yet."

"Really? So he's going to be a newshound like his old man, Art?"

Art beamed and shrugged. "He could do a lot worse, right?"

"Sure. You still living over on Peterson?"

Now there was a hesitation. "No. I, uh, I'm over by the ballpark, Paul."

Whelan nodded. Not "we" but "I." Art Shears reddened and the blotches grew darker but he clung tightly to his smile. "Never could get myself too far from the old haunts, you know?" He looked around the room for a moment. "Marie and I...we separated just after the holidays. So she's still up there on Peterson and I've got a...you know, a little place on Wilton."

Whelan nodded. A little place. A furnished room, most likely. Artie put his hands together and let them hang between his knees. He looked down at his shoes. A man in distress, a man without prospects. Whelan was suddenly jolted by the thought that perhaps Art wanted him to do something in connection with the separation. Watch Marie. He squirmed in his chair and leaned forward.

Artie misunderstood and raised his hands. "Hey, Paulie, relax. I'm sorry, I know it makes people nervous but I don't mind talking about it. It's just temporary. We talk on the phone just about every day, we really get along as well as we ever did. We'll be back together in no time. I'm as sure of that as...I don't know, as sure as I'm sitting here." He shrugged.

He wanted to say something to ease Art's discomfort. "Good, Art. You've been together a long time and she's a great lady."

"Oh, she's the best, Paul. The best there is. Anyhow...I... it's my fault. I was having some rough times, you know how it is. Newspaper business is a bitch and I got to, you know, drinking a little too much and I did a couple things that I guess put a scare into her."

"Like...what? Anything you can talk about?"

"Oh, Jesus, no, look at your face." Art Shears's laughter was genuine. "No running around or anything like that. I don't get into fights or chase women. I just had some troubles at work, had it out with my boss. And I quit. I also lost a little bit at the track, which didn't help things any. You know how stupid you get when you're in money trouble and it comes without warning? You try to make it up in one day. And when you lose, you come right back to the ponies the next day. So…" His voice trailed off.

"You quit the *Trib*, huh? And you had nothing else lined up?"

"Nope." Art smiled confidently. "But I'll do all right. I'm on my own now, free-lancing. I'm writing my own stuff now." He leaned back in the chair and grinned.

Whelan smiled and hoped his friend hadn't seen him wince. He'd never yet heard anyone use the term "free-lancing" who wasn't on the verge of searching the want ads for tomorrow's employment. People who were waiting and paying the rent by it simply said they were writers. You were "free-lancing" when nothing had happened yet.

"So. Making a few bucks at it, Art?"

"Oh, a few here and a few there. I've been doing some reviews for a couple of…uh, community newspapers and I'm supposed to get together with the features editor of one of the big suburban papers. And I've got a lunch date with Bill Friedman next week, maybe do myself some good writing features with the *Times*. And besides, I've got a few bucks left from what they gave me at the *Trib*. Took my vacation in cash, plus I had a few dollars coming when I left."

"Sounds good to me." Sure. He'd sold "reviews" to a couple of papers with circulations under two thousand and he had appointments, including lunch with an old friend too nice to say no.

"But I didn't come here to blow my horn, Paul. I'm working on something else, something a lot better and much bigger."

"Oh? You gonna let me in on this?"

"Yeah, now that you mention it. I'm writing a book. A big book. I'm doing a book on the guys who live on the street."

"These streets? You mean the derelicts?"

"Sure, Paul. There's a thousand stories out there. Hell, you know a lot of these guys, right?" Whelan shrugged. "Now, I know what you're thinking, Paul. Somebody's done that already, about a hundred times for the sociology department of some college, but I'm gonna do it differently."

Artie loosened his collar button and pulled at the knot of

his tie. The tie looked clean, the collar wasn't, but Artie was growing excited now and Whelan realized he could finally relax.

"You going to keep me guessing, or what?"

"What sells books, Paul? Facts? A lot of facts? Uh-uh, no, *entertainment* sells books. People want to read something that's entertaining. I've read a lot of the stuff that's been written about these people and I can do it better. Nobody's going to buy a book about fifty hoboes when most of them have led pretty boring lives, and I'm not going to write about the stockbroker who lost it all in the Depression and became a juicer."

"Makes sense," Whelan said, just to be contributing.

"There's one guy out here on Wilson, over by the college, stays in that hotel and does day labor. He was a fighter in the forties and fifties, fought Billy Conn and knew Joe Louis, Jersey Joe Wolcott, all those guys."

Whelan nodded. "Barrelhouse Joe. Worked for a brewery a long time."

Art pointed a finger at him. "You know him, I knew you would. And I met this other guy, decorated in World War Two, fought at D-Day. And then I got one guy," and he began jabbing his finger excitedly at Whelan. "I got this guy, I think he's been on the run all his life for something he did a long time ago. All his life. I mean, I could tell the first time I talked to him, he had something he was hiding. He's always looking around, got these dark little eyes that flit back and forth constantly when he talks, like he's been looking over his shoulder so long he won't ever he able to stop."

Whelan nodded, glad to see Art happy about something and wondering where all this was heading.

"But I'm telling you, Paul, sometimes I feel my skin crawl when I'm down here."

"That's natural. It's not a safe place to be hanging around."

"It doesn't bother you," Art said, pointedly.

"I worked here a long time. Now I live here. I never got far away from it. I just inherited the family estate, which happened to be smack in the middle of it."

"Great old house, though."

"Yeah, it is that." Whelan's house was a sandstone building on Malden, a block gradually giving itself over to rehabilitation and respectability but still an island in the middle of blocks of burned-out and rundown buildings. You could drive to the Loop in fifteen minutes, you could go six blocks in any direction and find calmer, saner neighborhoods and typical Chicago life, but it was a long fifteen minutes, a long six blocks. He'd always loved the house, which his folks had bought when he was in high school. Upon his mother's death he'd moved in almost immediately. It had never occurred to him to sell and get himself something in a nicer neighborhood.

"Anyhow, I think this guy has a story. Lived out on the West Coast for a while, near as I can make out, came here about a year ago. But he's from here. He mentioned Riverview once, taking his kids to Riverview and taking them on the roller coasters and the parachute and all that stuff. I don't know…I can't figure out what he did, but he's on the run, that much I'm sure of."

Artie stopped and seemed to be waiting for a reaction.

"You were born out of time, Art. You should have been born back in the twenties or thirties, covered the Spanish Civil War, parachuted onto the Serengeti, something like that."

Art Shears laughed and his face looked younger for a moment, and Whelan knew his old friend was forgetting his troubles, at least for a while.

"Listen, I've got coffee and rolls coming in ten minutes. Buy you breakfast, okay?"

"Best offer I've had all day. I haven't eaten breakfast yet." He cocked his head to one side and watched Whelan for a moment, a sly smile on his face.

"So, aren't you curious yet?"

"What?"

"Don't you want to know why I came to see you?"

"I thought maybe it was a long-awaited social call. Shoot the breeze and all that fine stuff."

"I don't mind doing that, Paul, but I came here with a business proposition. I need your pro-fesh-un-al services." He wiggled his eyebrows.

"Now you have my total attention."

"I need you to come with me on some of these interviews. I need you to help me talk to these guys, some of them."

"Sounds to me like you're doing fine."

Art shrugged. "Maybe I am, maybe I'm not, but I'm not stupid, I know somebody who's good at getting people to open up would be getting more out of some of these people than I am. And Paulie, there's nobody who can do that like you can. I've never known anybody who could get strangers to open up, tell their stories, spill their guts like you can. Honest to God, Paul, sometimes I'm with a guy for an hour before I get anything I can use on the tape."

"You're recording all your conversations?"

"Yeah, I know what you're thinking. Yeah, it makes some of 'em nervous and others couldn't care less, but I give 'em a few bucks for their time and it seems to cut through a lot of objections."

"I bet it does."

"But I think you'd be better at the kind of thing I'm trying to do. These aren't…you know, these aren't Studs Terkel's people, exactly. A lot of these guys just don't like to talk, aren't used to it. Most of them, when they do talk to me, just answer exactly what I ask and don't give me anything more. I get a lot of one-word answers. I think you'd know how to get things out of them."

"Oh, I don't know about that."

"I do. It's what you've always been good at. Probably why you took to this line of work. And I hear you're good at it."

"At certain aspects of it, I am. I like to talk to people. I can find people, that seems to be my strong suit. I sure don't make a lot of money at it, though."

"I bet you make whatever you need. But Paulie, that's not the only reason I want you to help me." He laughed with embarrassment. "I think I need a bodyguard. I can talk to these guys during the day but I think at night, when it's dark and a guy can get a few cocktails into his system, I can get more out of them, but that's when I don't want to be roaming around by myself. I swear, sometimes I get the heebie-jeebies down here. I spent an hour one morning crouching down *in an alley* with an old burnout black guy, kept stopping in the middle of his sentences to stare at me like I was gonna rob him or something. And this guy, the one I told you about—"

"The guy that acts like somebody's after him?"

"Yeah, when I'm with him, after a while I start to feel like *I'm* on the run, like I'm being watched."

"You've got to be careful down here, Art. I don't know…" He wanted to be able to say something encouraging, even offer his help in some limited form, but he couldn't see spending his free evenings wandering around with Art and interviewing derelicts. "You see, Art, I don't really have a lot of time right now, and there's—"

"You're wondering about money, right. I know, but I could make an arrangement with you, share a percentage. And I could come up with some cash to give you till then, I know I could."

Art Shears looked off into a corner of the office for a moment, obviously running schemes through his mind, searching for the aforementioned cash.

"No, no, Art. I didn't mean money. I just meant, there's the question of time."

"Oh." Art looked puzzled and Whelan laughed.

"Surprised, huh? Doesn't look like I'd ever be busy?" He grinned and took out a cigarette. As an afterthought he held the pack out to Art who took one, eagerly.

"Thought maybe you gave it up, Art."

"You kidding? No, I just didn't get around to buying a pack this morning."

Art blew smoke and indicated the office with his free hand. "No, it looks like you're doing fine, Paul, I just thought…you're working on something, huh? For that lawyer?"

"No. At the moment I'm trying to figure a way to get him to quit paying me in little pieces. I don't really have anything else at the moment, but the problem is, I can't commit blocks of my time or even make anything like this a regular deal, you know?" Shears nodded slowly, disappointment coming into his eyes.

There was a knock at the door and Whelan said, "Come on in, Ricky." A young black boy came in with a white paper bag and set it on the desk.

"Two-oh-six, Mr. Whelan."

Art Shears made a move for his pocket. "Hey, I got this, Paul."

"The hell you do. You're my guest. I do this for total strangers, Artie. Why can't I do it for you?" He gave the boy $2.75. "Keep it, Ricky."

"Thanks, Mr. Whelan." The boy closed the door and could be heard skipping down the hall.

They sipped coffee and nibbled at the chocolate donuts and Whelan bought time with small talk while he tried to find a way out of Art's "project" without discouraging him. He stared at Art, saw how the man gulped the donut and the coffee and realized what a joke it had been for him to think of coming up with a retainer. He thought about Art's book and told himself this was not a way to run a business, not even a dog-eared one. It was unprofessional, it was irritating, it was an imposition. He watched Artie Shears wolfing down the donut. An inconvenience. No, a favor for my oldest friend on earth, who looks like he's run out of favors as well as luck.

"Okay, Artie," he heard himself say. "This is what I think I could do. You pick out a couple, three of what you consider tough interviews, stubborn folk, or just a couple times when you think you'd really want somebody with you. And I'll come along a couple times and we'll work together. I just can't make it, you know, a regular thing. Sometimes…sometimes a case comes my way and I have to put a lot of time into it, day and night for five, six, seven days in a row, a couple of weeks sometimes. And I get paid for it. I don't work often but when I do, it's worth good money to me, so I really have to keep myself available, you know? And I can't turn down a case if it's my type of case. I mean, I live pretty close to the edge, financially." There was a glimmer of understanding in Art's eyes and he nodded.

"I don't want to cramp your style, Paul. Just for the hell of it, what's a private investigator cost these days?"

"Oh, a big agency with a lot of staff and the latest technology will cost you your left nut. Me, I get two hundred a day and expenses."

"Two bills?" Panic showed clearly in Art's face, and he showed a lighter shade of pale.

Whelan laughed. "Easy, Art. Don't hyperventilate in my office. I'm not gonna charge you."

"Well, I gotta pay you something."

Whelan shrugged. "If your book sells, you can give me a few bucks. But I'll do this for old times. And you can buy me dinner when we do the interviews."

"Such a deal! How can I lose?"

"Don't see how you can."

They finished their coffee and made some more small talk about the heat, the Cubs, politics and old times, and at 11:15 ran out of conversation. Art Shears got up and shrugged. "Middle of the week? What do you think, Paul? Wednesday, Thursday?"

"Okay with me. Just give me a call."

"I'll call you tomorrow afternoon. I want to see how things go with these meetings I got." He took Whelan's hand. "I appreciate this, Paul, I really do."

"My pleasure. I think I'll get a kick out of working with a genuine writer."

Art pumped his hand again. "You're the best, Paul. I'll give you a buzz tomorrow."

He sat back in the chair and watched Art Shears leave. He waited a moment and then went to the window. Below him, Art cut across Lawrence and made his way toward the corner, a bony, disheveled man, a man running out of luck. He could just barely make out that Art Shears was smiling, and that had to count for something.

Two

A car backfired somewhere down near Wilson and he woke with a start. He had fallen asleep with the TV on again, almost a nightly occurrence. There was a movie on now, a wonderfully cheap monster movie shot in a few days, using filters to give the impression of night shots. He stared at the set for a moment, and the faintest trace of warning came to him, a split-second before the phone began its startling clamor.

"Hello?"

There was a hesitation, then a swallowing noise and then Marie Shears's voice. "Paul? Is that you, Paul?"

"Yeah, Marie. Marie, what's wrong?" His stomach began to knot up.

She began to speak and sob at the same time. "Artie's dead, Paul. Somebody killed him."

"Oh, no..." His voice sounded hollow, distant, and he was having trouble concentrating. There was some mistake.

"He was down there..." and she let go of it, gave herself over to her grief and it was thirty seconds before she could speak. The knot in his stomach turned to nausea and he forced himself to think about Marie, to do or say something helpful. He thought he'd never heard anyone so heartbroken and wondered if she cried for Art's death or for the beaten, hard-luck man, down at the heels and frayed at the edges, that he'd become.

She sniffled and swallowed and was in control when she resumed. "They found him in an alley up by Wilson and Broadway. Near the el tracks. Somebody hit him and fractured his skull. Then they went through his pockets. Oh, Paul, why would they kill him? He would have given them his wallet. Why couldn't he get a break just once?"

She began to cry again and he realized that very little of this was for herself; she was still the same class act she'd always been. He bit off the thought, and when she seemed to feel better he let her talk for a moment, then asked her some general questions to get a handle on what had happened. Her brother had gone down to identify the body. The police believed it was a simple robbery: Art's wallet was gone and when Marie told them he'd carried a small tape recorder, that clinched it.

He asked a few careful questions about the boys and her financial situation and she broke into the middle of one.

"We're okay, Paul. You can stop beating around the bush. We've been getting by on what I make and what we had in the bank, and Tommy pays board now. And when there's something major or unexpected, my dad helps out. He's a professional grandpa of Depression vintage. Wants the boys to have a million and one chances. Besides, you know, Paul…Art hadn't really made any kind of money for a while. We weren't looking for him to…support us or anything. We just hoped he could get himself straightened out." Her voice fell and he sensed her embarrassment at having to speak this way about her dead husband.

He sat there with the phone to his ear and told himself that Artie Shears was dead, that he'd never see him again. He remembered the other times in his life when he'd received phone calls like this, the call about his father, and he felt weak.

"He called me yesterday, Paul. Just yesterday." She sighed. "He said you guys had been in touch. I was glad about that."

"Oh, sure. We got together a couple of times," he lied. A harmless lie. "We talked about his book."

"About the derelicts?"

"Right."

She was silent for a while. When she spoke again, it was in a tired voice, resigned. "You know, when the police came, my first thought was, 'It was that damn book, otherwise he wouldn't have been down there,' but that's not true. He was just lost, Paul. He'd been drinking, and there was some gambling, and, lately, half the time I talked to him he was…you know, high. And other times he was in these incredibly upbeat moods, as if he didn't have a care in the world. He talked like he was about to win the Pulitzer or the...the lottery or something. You wouldn't believe it."

Whelan said nothing, but knew a man living off a bottle would have his moments when the world seemed to be his oyster.

"I think something was bound to happen to him sooner or later, Paul. Like he would get drunk and fall asleep in that little room of his..." she broke off for a moment and then composed herself. "...you know, fall asleep with a lighted cigarette and... that would be it."

He fought the urge to speak for a moment: better to say nothing than to say something foolish.

"You make the arrangements yet, Marie?"

"No, not yet."

"Will you need any help?"

"I don't think so, no, but I'll call you if I do, and I'll let you know when...everything's going to take place." She sighed. "We probably won't even find out who did it, you know? Yesterday he was alive and this morning he's dead in an alley in Uptown."

"Did, uh, the police say they have any leads?"

"No. The man I talked to was a Detective Bauman. He said it just sounded like a mugging that got out of hand."

"That's what it sounds like."

She thanked him again and he felt helpless and clumsy and was thankful when she hung up. He went into his kitchen to boil water for some instant and glanced up at the wall clock: midnight, and there'd be no sleeping till the wee small ones. He dropped two spoonfuls of coffee into a red cup and tried to understand that Art Shears was dead. And he acknowledged his guilt, not that he hadn't been with Art to prevent his death—he just wished with all his heart that, on the second-to-last day of Artie Shears's life, he'd been able to take him seriously.

The death of Arthur Shears was mentioned briefly in the *Tribune* the following morning. The news story gave the place as the alley behind 4540 North Broadway. The article said that the police had no suspects and that robbery was believed to be the motive. On the obit page there was a paragraph describing Art as a former *Trib* reporter believed to have been doing research for a book on "urban problems."

Whelan looked again at the little news story, read the address: an alley two and a half blocks from his office. He needed to see it.

A little before nine, as the streets filled with overheated people going to work and getting on with normal lives, he found it. The alley was a little dogleg between an appliance store and the back of a six-flat that had been cut up into a dozen or so apartments. The bend in the alley came just ten yards or so from Leland Street. There was nothing to see. No chalk outlines, no bustling technicians, no reporters, just a narrow strip of patched concrete over the old brick alley, lined on both sides with fast-food containers, mud-gray newspaper and broken glass, much of it the green glass of wine bottles. The alley saw little more than foot traffic these days, and weeds grew in cracks down the center and along the sides.

He paced up and down, searching the ground for nothing in particular, looking over his shoulder, walking faster as his frustration grew. He turned the corner at the angle of the dogleg and stumbled, literally, over a pair of legs. The legs belonged to a skinny gray-haired man who slept folded over in the bricked-over doorway to an old garage.

"Shit!" The man awoke with a sputter and swung his legs out in a rickety attempt to right himself. He pushed off the wall with his arm but couldn't hold his own weight, and when he tried to scowl at Whelan he couldn't focus his eyes.

"Sonofabitch."

"No, I'm not. Take it easy, babe. Relax." Whelan crouched down in front of him and held his breath as the man spewed muscatel fumes at him.

"Whoa! Been drinking our breakfast again, huh?"

"Who're you?" The man's head wobbled back and forth as though unmoored and Whelan shook his head involuntarily at the man's bony arms and legs. The blue shirt he wore bagged on his frame, and a good four inches of ankle showed from each pant leg.

"I'm a detective. I just need a little help."

"I jus' drank a bit." The man showed worry and wiped his mouth with the back of his hand.

"Lordy, you sure did that. Not a crime, though. And I'm not a cop, I'm a detective. You know a guy was killed here night before last?" The man nodded slowly.

"I heard."

"What did you hear? Remember?"

"Nothin'. Jus' some guy got hisself killed. Busted his head open."

"Hear who he was?"

"Jus' a guy, is all." The man's eyes began to focus now and he wet his lips continually. "Hot. 'S real hot."

"Yeah. Gonna get hotter." And you're thirsty already, Whelan thought. He shook his head and gave the man a buck. The wino struggled to his feet and went shuffling off toward Leland. Whelan walked a bit farther down the alley and knelt down beneath a brick wall with NO LOITERING painted across it in white. There was blood on the pavement. As far as he could tell, it was only in this place, this one place, and this was where it had happened. Art hadn't staggered around or run with his injuries. He'd just fallen. Here. In time the August sun would fade it and the city winds would scour it with grit and a gracious rain might wash it away, but right now it was here. Whelan forced himself to look at it and a series of unasked-for images came into his mind now, of the young Artie Shears standing at Whelan's door and asking if he wanted to go swim off the rocks, Artie Shears whacking away at a softball, Artie Shears and Paul Whelan passing the same dime bottle of R.C. back and forth behind Artie's house. Smiling, confident Artie Shears, who had always been a little bolder than Whelan, a little smarter, better-looking, more popular: an odd recollection now, for the grinning boy's face held no hint of failure or sickness or trouble, and certainly no foreboding that he'd end his life in an Uptown alley.

He looked around and a slight movement caught his eye; he looked up. In a third-floor window of the cut-up six-flat a man watched him. No derelict, this was an older man, perhaps in his sixties, with close-cropped white hair. He watched Whelan with unmistakable suspicion, and when Whelan stood up suddenly, the man disappeared behind a faded green curtain.

Whelan went quickly up the back stairs, stretched to get across a missing step and knocked at the door on the third floor. A couple feet away, the sun-bleached curtain moved slightly and the face appeared again. It was a tan face, the face of a man who has spent much of his life outdoors, and the man watched him through dark, heavy-lidded eyes.

"Yessir?" the man said through a screen.

"Sir, I wonder if I could talk to you."

"Depends who y'are."

"I'm a detective and I'm looking into the killing that took place here the other night."

The man stared at him for a moment, frowned and shook his head. "Already told you folks everything. Talked to you already 'bout this. You gonna worry me to death over this?"

"I just want to ask—"

"Didn't see no badge, either."

"I'm a private detective."

"Then I got nothing to tell you. You want my story, you get it from the other one."

"The police detective?" He fished for the name Marie had mentioned. "Bauman? That the one?"

"Yeah, Big one with a crewcut. They was two of 'em. Told 'em I didn't see nothing. Now I'm telling you the same thing. Now you gonna let me be?"

"All right. I'm leaving."

He went down the stairs and walked back up the alley toward Leland, and when he'd gone fifty feet or so he turned quickly. The green curtain moved back suddenly. He took a last look around him at the alley, shook his head and left.

He walked distractedly up Broadway, and when a tall black man accidentally jostled him, he realized his heart was pounding with anger.

Halfway up the block, in front of an African import shop

where he'd never seen customers, a small crowd had gathered and seemed to be watching an altercation. When he got closer he could see that some of the onlookers were amused and others appeared worried.

An old man was involved in a shouting match with a group of teenage boys. Whelan lost no time choosing sides. He'd seen the kids before, including once coming out of a gangway on his block. They sported denim vests over T-shirts, and the vests were covered with a mad amalgam of Confederate flags, Nazi insignia and military buttons. They were white, they were losing their long fight with acne, and they were having a fine time at the old man's expense. They were what Whelan had been looking for.

Not that the old man needed much help. He was small and stooped but he wore an old brown suit and his tie was carefully knotted, and in one hand he carried a reticule sort of shopping bag in which Whelan could see groceries.

"You're all a bunch of punks. You're…you're thugs. That's right, thugs. You got no respect for people, you think you own the world, tough guys, real tough guys."

"Fuck you, old man. We don't need your shit." The speaker was not as tall as his companions but was the most muscular-looking, a stocky kid who had shaved most of his head except for a little strip of fur down the middle. It wasn't enough to be considered a Mohawk yet but that was its obvious intent. The kid stared at the old man and then let his eyes wander over the audience.

"You got a problem, old man?"

"You, you're the problem. Pushing people around—"

"Aw, eat it, old man." He folded his arms and grinned.

"Excuse me," Whelan said. The stocky boy looked at him, still smiling but clearly surprised that someone was complicating his good time.

"Why don't you fellas leave this gentleman alone." He made certain it didn't sound like a question. Behind him, he heard a voice or two in uncertain agreement.

The kid shrugged. "Talk to him, man. We're not doing shit."

"No, I don't want to talk to him. What exactly was he doing? Walking on your sidewalk?" He looked at the old man. "Is that it? Were you walking on their sidewalk?"

"He was hasslin' us."

"Hasslin'. I see. You were *hasslin'* these youngsters, huh?" He took a quick head count. "All six of them. You were hassling these fine young men." The trace of a smile appeared on the old man's lips and Whelan heard a snicker from the crowd.

"Listen, sir. These young men and others like them, they serve a purpose, which is to terrorize the community. If people like you continue to hassle them, they might go elsewhere. Is that what you want?"

"Hey, fuck this guy."

He turned to see who had spoken but they were all simply staring.

"You guys are the Rebs, right? You're heavy. Didn't you guys just get busted for breaking into cars? Manly work."

The stocky one spread his legs. "You trying to jerk us around?"

"Trying? I thought I was doing a pretty good job. Did you want to do anything about that?" He wondered what he was getting into but seemed unable to stop himself.

The stocky one opened his mouth but could say nothing. His face reddened and he began clenching and unclenching his fists.

"Wait up, Ronnie, I think he's heat."

Whelan looked at the one who had spoken, a tall kid in a baseball cap. Then he looked back at the leader.

"Whatcha got in mind, Ron? I'm not an old man. You want to be embarrassed? Lot of people here. Your friends won't be able to help you and you can't use a weapon in front of witnesses. Be just you and me in the bright morning sun."

"You don't look like you can do shit, mister."

"I got surprises. I got a left you won't believe."

It occurred to him that he might not actually be able to take this nasty punk but he was fairly sure he'd mark the kid's face for him, and that would be enough.

"He's a cop, Ron. Let's go."

The one called Ron moved one foot back and Whelan knew there would be no fight.

"Bunch of thugs," the old man muttered. "Look at his hair."

"Ron" made a move as if to sidestep Whelan and go for the old man, and Whelan stepped in front of him again.

"Easy, kid. These old guys got no eye for fashion. I like your hair." The boy shot him a hostile look.

"No, really, I like it. Makes you look like a Trojan warrior." He heard laughter from the onlookers and knew the kid's moment had passed. He took the old man by the elbow and gently but firmly ushered him around the crowd. The old man still had a few things he wanted to say.

"Look at how they look. Look at that hair. Why do they do that to their heads?"

"I think it's a visitation from God," Whelan said. "And I think you ought to watch what you say to kids on the street, friend."

"I'm not afraid of 'em. But thank you for your assistance."

"My pleasure," Whelan said as they reached the corner and the old man turned to be on his way. But he didn't feel much better as he made his way to the office.

He threw open both windows and couldn't feel any difference in the temperature. He called his service and this time got Shelley.

"Hey, Shelley. Glad to hear that Lauren Bacall voice."

"Didja miss me, baby?" Shelley laughed her hoarse laugh. "I went on a little vacation with my new honey. Took me to Lake Geneva and we went out on his boat and drank martinis and did naughty things." She laughed again and said, "How'd you like Abraham, honey?"

"He's…different. He's got quite a phone manner."

"You should see him. Looks like Gandhi with hair. He's about five foot four and weighs about eighty pounds. I keep thinking I should take him home with me and show him how much fun a big girl can be."

"Turkish delights? Maybe you should show me."

"Baby, my new fella would have to hurt you. Abraham, he

wouldn't mind, but you—"

"Any calls for me?"

"Liz called."

"Oh. Anybody else?"

"That's all so far."

"Okay, thanks, Shel."

"Toodle-oo, baby."

He put off calling Liz. Instead he called Marie Shears, got her son, Matt, and learned that the wake would be that night and Thursday at Earhardt Funeral Home, with burial on Friday morning from St. Mary of the Lake over on Sheridan.

He called Area 6 and asked for the Violent Crimes Unit. Detective Bauman wasn't in, and he asked to leave a message with the detective who answered, a Detective Skronski.

"What is this regarding, sir?"

"I'd just like to talk to him about the Art Shears killing, that's all."

"Are you a member of the family, sir?"

"No, an old friend."

"The detectives are pretty busy, sir. Is there any information you'd like to add?"

"No. I really just want to know if they've got anything."

"Sir, if they do, they're working on it. It won't help anything to bother them now. Several members of the family have already called—"

"Look, I just thought I could be of some help."

"Sir, these are experienced detectives. They know what they're doing." He could tell that Skronski was being patient.

"Would it help if I told you I was a former police officer?"

"You know the answer to that already, buddy. It wouldn't change anything. Listen, leave the guys alone. They're good. Especially Bauman."

"I'd still like to talk to him."

"Fine. I'll give him your message. And if you're lucky, he won't call." Skronski laughed.

"Something I should know?"

"I don't ask Bauman about his cases, friend."

Whelan left his number and hung up. He was fairly certain that Bauman would greet this as civilian meddling, that he probably wouldn't return the call. But he knew there was a likelihood that Art Shears would soon be a statistic. He wondered for a moment if he was simply being stubborn or reacting from guilt or helplessness. But he'd seen the alley. Art Shears had died fifty or sixty feet from the alley entrance. He hadn't been dragged in by a mugger, and Whelan was left with a simple question: Why would a man who by his own account went around the streets of Uptown looking over one shoulder go into an alley at night? He turned it over in his mind, looked at it from each of its angles and found no answers. A robbery, they were saying. He shook his head and then thought of Art's tape recorder. The recorder would tell him if it was really a robbery. If it showed up somewhere, it was a robbery.

He looked at the clock, saw that the morning was passing him by, and picked up the phone.

She answered on the fifth ring, sounded hurried and distracted as always.

"Liz?"

"Oh, Paul." She said his name with that unique mixture of easy familiarity and irritation that made plain his status.

"You called me."

She gave an exasperated laugh. "I've been calling a *lot*. I kept getting some Indian guy I couldn't understand. Couldn't get you at home. Finally I got through to that woman who answers your calls." Whelan allowed himself a smile. Liz had always been put off by Shelley's voice and Whelan had never understood why it made a difference to her. A hard, fascinating creature, his Liz, former obsession, frequent fantasy, occasional "project" whose flinty shell he never quite succeeded in denting, and now a closed chapter in his life.

"So what's up?"

"Well, I've got your stuff."

"I know. We talked about it."

"No, I mean…I've got it *here*."

Whelan laughed, at both of them. "You mean you've got

my stuff in a box and it's—what, next to the phone? In front of the door? Did you put it on your porch, Liz?"

"You think this is easy for me, Paul?"

"Yes. Yes, I do. You've put it off forever and I think you're doing fine."

She sighed into the phone. "I'm late for work. Did you call just to—"

"Oh, knock it off. I called because you called me. You want me to come over and get my stuff, right?"

"Uh-huh. Whenever."

"Well, you're working today till—when, nine?"

"Yeah, but a couple of us are going out later."

"Tomorrow?"

"Sure, that'd be fine. Morning, afternoon. Whatever. I'll—I'll make you lunch if you want."

"Well, we'll see. How's Charlie?"

"He's fine. He—he's sending you a letter. I gotta go."

"Right. Bye." He hung up and thought of Liz's son, Charlie, an eight-year-old with his mother's dark hair. He was already missing Charlie, though Charlie was not his child and he'd been careful over the last couple of years not to allow himself to become too attached to the boy, a hedge against the day when Liz made good on her constant promise to get out of Chicago and make a start somewhere new. Now Charlie was in Wisconsin with his grandparents and Liz would soon be joining him.

He went home to check his mail. The sun was reaching its high point and people moved listlessly in the heat. Here and there old men shrank back into doorways to find shade and a clump of younger men passed a bottle back and forth in the shadow of the el tracks. A few feet away from them, oblivious to the men and all else, a pair of long-skirted Vietnamese women in sweaters went through the garbage and stuffed aluminum cans into a large green trash bag. Whelan paused for a moment and admired their work. All over Uptown at this very moment little groups of Southeast Asian women, Vietnamese or Cambodian or Laotian, were digging through the refuse of Chicago and scratching together a few cents by selling cans. Whelan knew a waitress named Tho at a small Vietnamese place on Damen called Little Home Saigon; Tho had once told him that some of these women digging through the alleys were less than two or three months removed from the terror of the open boats, that their quiet preoccupation gave no hint of the horrors they'd seen at the hands of the soldiers in their own country or from the ravages of the Thai pirates on the open sea.

He got home just as the letter carrier was coming down the warped stairs, stepping gingerly on the old planks. He waved when he saw Whelan.

"You ever gonna fix this?"

"No. And if I did, then I'd get a Doberman. Take your pick."

The mail carrier, a wiry young black man named Bruce, shook his head and laughed. "Don't fix nothin' on my account."

The home version of the mail was in no way superior to what he'd gotten at the office. There was an offer to join a record company, an offer from Ed McMahon to buy life insurance and an advertisement for a furniture store: it was written in Spanish.

He tossed the mail in the wastebasket and made himself lunch, a smoked-turkey sandwich with tomatoes grown in his desolate garden.

He watched the last part of the midday news and turned off the TV. After a while, he went into the living room, put on a Crusaders album and listened to a little jazz. He tried to force his mind onto other things, but the same picture insinuated itself again and again: the last moment he'd seen Art Shears alive, head down, walking up Lawrence and hoping his luck would change. He shook his head and wished he'd had a chance to say goodbye, a short visit in a hospital, maybe, a moment to say…what? That he'd always, every moment he'd known him, understood that Artie Shears was special, and that he couldn't say that about more than a handful of the people he'd known.

He thought of Liz, sullen and hostile and as attractive to him now as she'd been the day they met, eighteen years ago. He shook his head: no time for that now.

Later that afternoon, listless and uncomfortable in the growing humidity, he threw some water on his face and went back out. To save time, he took his car, a rapidly decomposing '76 Olds Cutlass that he called "the Jet." When he turned the key in the ignition, the Jet made a grinding sound and died. He cursed. He had a car that didn't start on cold days, on rainy days, in humidity. At that moment, he believed that he had the only car in Chicago that had trouble starting on a ninety-degree day. He pumped the accelerator four times, tried again, got a longer grinding noise. He waited a moment, tried again and the engine turned over. And died. On the fourth try it started and stayed with him. He drove up Lawrence, turned onto Broadway, made a left onto Leland and turned into the alley. He drove a few feet in, parked in front of a sagging cyclone fence and got out. He spent half an hour in the alley, walking slowly up and down, examining the ground, looking for something out of place, something different, something of Art's. He stooped down and stared at the bloodstain, already appearing faded in the midafternoon sun, losing color and outline, vanishing evidence of a murder of no significance.

He looked up and down the alley. At the south end, a pair of older men argued over a bottle in a paper bag. He looked up. In the third-floor window, the green curtain moved and the white-haired man appeared again. He watched Whelan for a moment, squinting. Whelan looked at him and then waved irritably. The curtain moved back and the man was gone.

He sat down on the dusty surface of the alley and had a cigarette. A pair of kids on bikes came shooting up the alley from Leland and he just looked at them. They stopped talking when they came near him, gave him an anxious look and went on their way. It began to cloud up and the humidity grew almost unbearable. He watched the darker layer of clouds move in from the west and was thankful for the coming rain. From the far end of the alley a group of people moved uncertainly toward him, a woman and two men. They staggered and chattered and argued; the woman pushed a shopping cart piled high with rags and cans and an odd assortment of objects. Occasionally she stopped, went over to a trash can, rummaged for a moment and came up with a new addition to the pile. Whelan watched them come closer: the primal unit, three sun-darkened faces, three aging, sickly bodies tramping through alleys hoping to find something to make tomorrow a little better than today. The woman and one of the men, an Indian, wore winter coats. The other man wore a T-shirt and an open flannel shirt, and a Cub hat.

They slowed when they noticed Whelan but kept coming. The Indian looked at him for a moment and then asked, "You all right?"

Whelan laughed silently and then nodded. I'm sitting in an alley and behaving irrationally and the old winos are worried about me.

"I'm fine, buddy."

The woman gave him a sidelong glance. "Any spare change, mister?"

She made it a statement, a perfunctory exercise of the required questions one asks a stranger.

He lit another cigarette. "Yeah, I got spare change."

"You got a cigarette?" the second man asked, apparently encouraged by a little friendly banter.

"Yeah. I got spare change and cigarettes."

The Indian gave him a sheepish look and smiled uneasily. Whelan read the look and shook his head.

"No, I'm not jerking you around. I can spare a couple bucks." He got to his feet, gave them five bucks and the remainder of his cigarettes. The woman grabbed the bill and tucked it quickly beneath her several layers of clothing. The Indian and the other man tore the top off the pack and pulled out cigarettes. Whelan lit them.

"Friend of mine got himself killed here the night before last. You hear anything about that?"

"Heard something," the Indian said. "Din't know 'im. Little guy, name of Shinny. That him, mister?"

"No. No, this was somebody else. Different guy. Thanks anyhow."

"Thanks for the smokes, mister." He looked dubiously at the woman. "And for the money, too." He grinned at her and they were off, moving a little faster this time, all smiles. Whelan watched them leave the alley and then went back to his car. As he was getting in, a gray car pulled into the alley mouth, stopped, backed out and went back toward Broadway.

It began to rain as soon as he was in his car, and soon it was coming down hard, a sky-darkening rain that overwhelmed the rotting blades of his windshield wipers and soon made it impossible to drive. Eventually he pulled over on Broadway and waited it out. He listened to the radio and the tattoo of the rain on his roof, and when it abated, he went on, window open all the way to suck in the cooling air and fresh smells that would be gone by morning.

The Earhardt Funeral Home was a small two-story limestone building on Montrose. It was just six-thirty when he pulled into the little parking lot behind the building and he was glad to see the half dozen cars already there.

Two men in dark suits paused in conversation when he entered the parlor of the funeral home, a crowded little room with several sofas and a half dozen or so armchairs crammed into its corners. He did not know the men, nor the two women sitting quietly on one of the sofas. One of them smiled slightly at him, a gray-haired woman, and he nodded, then looked down at his blue blazer to assure himself that he looked all right.

The actual viewing room was off to the right of the parlor, a long narrow room with folding chairs along both sides and, at the far end, the coffin. There were a half dozen people sitting stiffly on either side, and they looked at him as he entered. He recognized none of them but thought several of the men looked like newspaper types.

Marie Shears and her sons were at the far end of the room, a couple of feet from the coffin, and talking with a white-haired man. Marie turned away abruptly and came forward to greet him.

His heart skipped slightly and he was embarrassed. At forty, Marie was no longer girlishly pretty but was more eye-catching than ever. The flecks of gray in her dark hair gave her a regal touch, and the tiny lines at the corners of her eyes and mouth gave her face character. She was trim as ever, a slight woman who could take charge of a room simply by entering it. He'd known her longer than he'd known Liz, almost as long as he'd known Artie, and once, in the distant world of his youth, he'd been absolutely awestruck by her. At eighteen he'd given pursuit, lost out to Art and let it drop for good, but he knew he'd be attracted to her till the day he died. He wasn't troubled by the knowledge, believing there were people in the world who worked on your chemistry in ways impossible to analyze, and who retained that ability forever. He bit his lip, told himself some things just could not happen and held out his hand.

"Paul," she said, then slapped his hand away and hugged him. He inhaled the smells of cologne and soap, held his breath, patted her lightly on the shoulder and pushed himself gently away.

"The years are nicer to you than they are to anybody else."

"Baloney. I look forty and you know it."

"Yeah, but it's not like anybody else's forty, and *you* know it."

"I'm glad you—" She stopped herself and shook her head. "All these stupid things we say at wakes. Like you wouldn't have come or something."

"I know. It's why people dread them. You say stupid things all night and then you go home feeling embarrassed. Those are the boys, huh? Amazing."

"Isn't it?" She smiled proudly, then took him by the arm over to the boys.

She made the introductions and the boys shook hands stiffly, and he understood how miserable they were to be here. The younger one's eyes went back to the coffin several times as they made small talk. Tommy, the older boy, seemed to take more interest in him when Marie introduced Whelan to the white-haired man as Art's oldest and best friend. The white-haired man proved to be Bill Friedman of the *Sun-Times*, with whom Art had been scheduled to meet for lunch in a few days. Marie noticed a group of newcomers standing in the doorway and went to greet them, and Whelan moved between the boys as Mr. Friedman went over to have a seat.

"So how you guys doing?"

They said "Okay" almost in unison and then looked around uncomfortably. He looked over at the coffin and then at them. He remembered them both as very small boys, carried by a beaming Art Shears who seemed to have everything possible in life going for him. He remembered his envy of Artie, who had a noisy cluttered life and people in his house when he came home. They were good kids and he wanted to say something to help but knew there was nothing.

"It's a miserable time, isn't it." They nodded and looked at him.

"I had to do it for both my parents. All night people are gonna be saying stupid things to you, telling you how proud your dad was of you. All I can tell you is…it'll pass. You'll be all right. It'll take longer for your ma, though. You'll have to remember that, and be patient." Matt, the younger boy, looked down and swallowed.

"Anybody asks, you tell them your old man was a good guy, the kind of guy that attracts friends to him without effort. He went through his whole life being just that, a good guy. A special guy. I knew him for almost thirty years."

Tommy, the elder, looked at him, smiling slightly. No tears, a tough one. "Thanks, Mr. Whelan. He…he was having his troubles, you know? He—"

"Everybody has troubles. Some people never quite come out of them. It doesn't lessen their worth. It doesn't make them different people than they were all their lives. Troubles or not, he was the same guy." Whelan smiled at him. "Nothing personal, guys, but I knew him a lot longer than you did, longer than anybody who's likely to show up tonight."

Both boys were smiling at him now and Whelan suppressed the urge to say something more.

"Excuse me, fellas." He moved to the casket.

Art Shears was wearing a blue suit with gray pinstripes. With the heavily caked makeup and artificial shaping of the face, he didn't look much like either the boyishly handsome Artie Shears of Whelan's youth or the haggard, unhappy man in his office a few days earlier, regardless of all the lies people would tell his family tonight. But it was Artie, and for a long time Whelan could do nothing more than stare in disbelief. There was no sense to this, no fairness to it, and it made a difference to him that this had happened when the guy had been in a tailspin. He stared at the face and swallowed, and put his hand on the dead man's folded hands. Then he knelt down on the little cast-iron kneeler and said a prayer for an old friend whose hard luck was over. When he was through praying, he waited a moment for his eyes to dry.

He'd hoped to make a fast, quiet exit but the boys cut him off a few feet from the casket. They held out their hands and he shook with each of them.

Tommy looked at him in curiosity for a moment. "You're still a detective?"

"Yeah, that's what I do."

The boy nodded and looked at his younger brother. "Are the police going to find this guy?"

He saw that they didn't want to hear the usual bullshit.

"They might. They might not. But I think I might take a look, too. I know people down there."

The boys smiled at him and he moved on to their mother. They spoke for a moment and he noticed with relief that the room was filling up. There would be a crowd for Artie.

Marie watched the people filing in and seemed to relax.

"There'll be plenty of people here tonight, Marie."

"I know. It's not for me, Paul. It's for the boys. I want them to see that people…cared about Art."

"I think that's what they're gonna see. I don't know if I'll be here tomorrow night, Marie, but I'll be at the funeral."

She turned to him. "Paul, could you—"

"Be a pallbearer? I'd have been pissed if you hadn't asked. Yeah, I'll he there."

She squeezed his hand and he felt pity for her, now that her marriage wasn't going to have a chance to heal itself. He bit off the impulse to tell her he intended to look into Art's death. It was the last thing she needed to be reminded of. Right now, it was just a wake: the man in the casket was not the victim of violence, simply a dead man. He gave her a hug and left. Outside, it was raining and Whelan was pleased. His father had always said that rain at a funeral was a good thing, a proper thing. He'd never explained why.

THREE

He woke at five-thirty to the sound of someone leaning on a horn and couldn't get back to sleep. It was airless in the old house, and the day was expected to be a carbon copy of the three before it. Heat wave in Chicago. A muggy week in August in Chicago. He thought about Artie, pictured him shuffling down Wilson and up Clark in the heat, pursuing a book and a new life.

He turned on the radio to a jazz station and wandered into the kitchen to boil water for coffee. He caught the tail end of an old Wes Montgomery tune and then the weather report, confirming what he already knew. There would be a lot of uncomfortable people in this town today, and the ones in Uptown and on West Madison and other streets like them would be worse off than anyone: a derelict had no refuge from the heat. He'd watched them on Wilson, over by the college where they sat on benches or the lawns and stared numbly straight ahead of them till rousted, then moved on into the alleys looking for shade. Shade and water. Once, for the better part of an hour he'd watched an old man, an obvious veteran of the street, moving from a doorway to the shadow of a building, then into a gangway and a succession of halls, constantly on the move to avoid the sun and the occasional complaint of a resident, and Whelan had realized he was watching the man's daily routine to escape the sun. There was another, less successful routine for such folk in the bitter, gnawing cold of January and February, when dozens of them simply died in doorways a few feet from warmth.

He sipped his coffee and thought of Liz. Later he'd have to drop by and pick up his things, and he was in no hurry. If anything, he was cured of the notion that certain relationships are fated to be, for he'd wasted the past three years on this one, trying to resuscitate a dead one from his youth. At times it filled him with a dull ache, a hollow awareness of time slipping away from him. Time to find a new one, start something with someone new. He nodded. Sure, and just how did one do that? How did a man pushing the big four-oh meet women? Time to call Bobby Hansen, maybe, for whom women had never been a problem—at least not till he married them. Bobby, perennial ladies' man, had been married and divorced four times. Whelan laughed. Still, Bobby at least *knew* some women: Whelan knew Liz and the half dozen or so waitresses who took his orders.

He got up and went to the back window to look hopefully at his garden. "A moribund enterprise," Mr. Sterne across the alley had called it. Sterne was a speech professor at Loyola whom Whelan occasionally engaged in conversation simply to enjoy his slightly archaic turn of phrase.

Well, it was a moribund enterprise, this little square of Chicago dirt that his father had been able to bring bursting to life with a dozen kinds of vegetables and rows of gaudy flowers planted simply to please Whelan's mother. Under Whelan's stewardship it grew dead things, yellow things. It gave up the occasional cucumber, but Whelan knew even the dead can grow cucumbers; he'd managed a couple of medium-size tomato plants but most of his tomatoes were dead or dying, some of them burned yellow in the dry heat and intense sun, and the others eaten or simply clawed up by Mrs. Cuelho's cat. Whelan caught just a faint brown furry movement across the yard and opened his window suddenly. The cat leaped over the connecting fence without touching it.

Whelan nodded. "Later, asshole." And the cat probably understood, for Whelan now made daily attempts to connect tomatoes with fear in the cat's twisted psyche, showering the animal with pebbles whenever it appeared in his yard.

He showered and left the house, his hair still wet. He decided to head for air conditioning. The Greek on the corner of Lawrence and Broadway had an air conditioner that would chill the Gobi.

There was life on the street now. People were moving off to work and Mrs. Cuelho was on her porch—she was always on her porch, as though Mr. Cuelho had banished her there for unconscionable behavior. Whelan waved to her and she gave him a curt nod. Relations had soured since she'd caught him heaving a brick at her cat.

A gray Caprice was parked behind Whelan's car. It had been washed recently and gleamed in the morning sun. He took a casual look inside as he passed it. The backseat was alive with garbage: fast-food containers, crumpled napkins, empty cups crushed and tossed into the seat. Aftermath of a hot date?

At the Greek's he had the cholesterol platter: three eggs, toast dripping with butter and a side each of bacon and sausage. After he ate, he walked up Lawrence to the A&W to get coffee.

"Hello, detective," Rashid said. Rashid was the taller and thinner of the two Iranians, and was delighted to have a detective as his neighbor.

"Hi, Rashid." He sat at the edge of one of the stools at the counter. "I need a cup of coffee to go. The Greek has lousy coffee."

"The Greeks, they don't know about coffee. The Persians, we invented coffee, did you know that?"

"Can't say I did. Large, black."

From the door to the back room a head appeared, a large head with shaggy black hair that sprouted at strange angles from beneath the obligatory white cap. This was Gholam, Rashid's partner and cousin. He nodded and grunted.

"Hey, Gus. So what are you making today, Rashid?"

Rashid grinned and showed what seemed to be fifty or sixty teeth. "This one chicken biryani. You will like this guy."

"Biryani?"

"Yes, chicken biryani. This guy is spicy guy. You will like."

"Persian chicken?"

"Yes. Absolutely, yes."

"No." Gus came in carrying a box of frozen fish fillets. "Is not Persian. Is Pakistani food."

"No," Rashid said. "Is Persian food."

"No," Gus insisted. He looked at Whelan and grinned slyly. "You eat that shit, you get the runs. I don't eat that shit."

"No, *you* eat this other shit, this American shit," Rashid said. He stood with hands on hips and glared at his cousin. His head was thrust forward and he nodded, reminding Whelan of an angry vulture.

"I eat what I want."

"Yes, you eat this hamburger shit and these hot dog shits and these chili dog shits and I cook good Persian food and you make jokes." He looked at Whelan in exasperation. "He comes here, he forgets our country, where culture began, he wants to be American."

"He is already. So are you. Everybody is. It's easy," Whelan said.

Rashid shook his head and went back to his chopping and stirring, then buried his hands in a stainless-steel mixing bowl for a while. He seemed to be kneading something. Whelan looked around and wondered about his coffee. He looked up at the food signs.

"You know, Rashid, I think you guys have created an American original here. I don't think I've ever seen anything like your menu."

Rashid grinned over his shoulder. "I got new one, too. Besides this guy." He set down the mixing bowl and walked over to a large crock-pot. He opened it, stuck in a large fork and came out with a dripping mass of what seemed to be seaweed.

"See? For the black people. It is 'greens'. 'Colored greens' it is."

"It's...uh, collard greens, Rashid. 'Collard.'"

"Yes, well, they like this guy. So I gonna serve him up when they come in." He winked, the American entrepreneur making a score.

"Good idea. Listen, how about a cup of coffee?"

Rashid gave him a stricken look. "Oh, my God. I'm sorry, detective. I get him right away."

Whelan took his coffee, told Rashid he'd see him later for some chicken biryani and left. There were already a half dozen men outside the pool hall on the corner but it was too early for the kids that usually inhabited the block. Sam Carlos waved to him through the grocery window.

He had been in his office less than ten minutes when there was a knock on the door.

"It's open. Come on in."

Two large men entered the office, a tall thin man with a long Irish face and pale blue eyes, and a heavy man, almost as tall, with a red face and a dark brush cut. The thin man was in shirtsleeves; his companion wore an ugly green plaid sportcoat.

"Paul Whelan?" the heavy one asked.

"Yes, sir. What can I do for you?"

The man flashed a badge and put it away again in a practiced movement.

"Hey, better practice that, detective. I almost got a look at it."

"You saw it."

Whelan smiled. "Could've been tinfoil. Could've been, you know, some Guatemalan general's chest ornaments. Could've been—"

"It's a badge, sir," the tall one said, calmly.

"Anyhow," the heavy one said. "I'm Detective Bauman and this is Detective Rooney. We'd like to ask you some questions about, ah, Arthur Shears."

"Sit down. There's another chair over there." Rooney pulled over a chair and both men sat down. Whelan caught a whiff of Right Guard and thought he smelled cigar on one of them. He had a sip of coffee as they arranged themselves in the chairs. They exchanged a glance and Rooney cleared his throat.

"We know Mr. Shears was a close friend of yours and we're sorry about the way he died, and we're sure you'll want to help us out."

"Sure. I called you guys yesterday—"

"Yes, sir, we know that. Was there something in particular you wanted to tell us?"

"No, I just wanted to see if you had anything yet." He looked from Rooney to Bauman, who stared unblinkingly at him. Good Cop and Bad Cop, except that he had a feeling Rooney was always Good Cop and Bauman always Bad Cop.

"Mr. Shears's wife indicated that you were close friends. You grew up together."

"Right."

"And you saw each other often."

"Not as often as Marie thinks. We actually just talked for the first time in more than a year last—"

"He had your card on his body," Bauman said, leaning forward. He straightened for a moment, then leaned back. He was sweating visibly and Whelan decided he was a drinker.

He held the detective's stare for a moment and nodded. "Do people that see you every day have your business card? We hadn't seen each other in a while and I gave him one of my cards."

"For what purpose?" Bauman asked.

"Wasn't any particular purpose. I just had new ones made up." He grabbed the little plastic wallet the printer had supplied and shoved it across the desk. "Help yourself."

Bauman held his gaze. "No, thanks. I don't get much call for private detectives." Bauman tilted his head to one side and squinted. "Now why would he have your card on his body? Was this a business meeting or something?"

"I guess. He was writing a book down here."

"What type of book, sir?" asked Rooney, the Good Cop.

"Oh, he had a notion to do a sort of Studs Terkel kind of thing about the men who wind up here on the streets."

Bauman shook his head. "Did he know how close he was to winding up on the street himself?"

Whelan stiffened. "Meaning what? You talk like this to his wife?"

"No, we didn't, sir." Rooney shot a glance at Bauman. "Of course not."

"No, we don't talk that way to somebody's widow," Bauman said. His cheeks were mottled red, and Whelan guessed most of it was his natural coloring. "I just made a comment. We did some checking and the guy was…he was having his troubles.

And he was a drinker. I could tell that by looking at him."

"That something you know a lot about?" He was surprised at himself and tried to calm down, but there was something in the fat red face he didn't like.

Bauman opened his mouth and then shut it; his attempt at self-control was visible.

"Okay, so we caught you on a bad morning or you don't like me or you're feeling worse than we realized about this thing. Awright, I'll give you that one. I was outta line. It just seemed… from what we heard, that he was kind of a…" He went fishing for vocabulary and came up empty.

"He was a loser," Whelan said calmly. "There's no polite word for it that I know of. When you're in school, they call you an 'underachiever' but once you're on your own, you're a loser. Yeah, I guess that's what he was. Near as I can make out, he drank himself out of his job with the *Tribune* and his marriage and he…he had this idea that he was going to straighten it all out down here. He just had an illusion that he was going to write a book and get back on his feet. And everything would be fine. He was a mess and I didn't know what to tell him so I was biding my time."

He looked out the window and shook his head at the sudden image of Shears's face across the desk, smiling with self-delusion.

"Good guy?" Bauman asked.

"Yeah. He really was. He always was. You would've liked him. You and I aren't getting along so well but you would've liked Artie."

Bauman shrugged. "Couldn't have been a bad guy. His wife, she's a real nice lady. Anybody can see that. Kids in good schools, how bad could he be? Who knows, maybe one of us is not far behind, eh?" Bauman looked at Rooney and raised his eyebrows. Rooney simply shrugged and looked uncomfortable, and Whelan caught a whiff of a man nearing retirement.

Bauman looked at Whelan and smiled slightly. "Okay, Whelan. I'm sorry if you thought I was popping off about your friend. This is what we got and we want to know what you got, if anything. Art Shears had been seen for several days interviewing different people on the streets with a small, you know, tape recorder. On the night of his death, he was seen coming out of the liquor department of the Walgreen's on Wilson and Broadway with a bottle. About seven-thirty or eight, this was. Sometime later that night, probably between nine and ten, according to the medical examiner, he was killed in what was probably a robbery attempt. Maybe for drug money."

"A user? Why a user?"

Bauman shrugged and Rooney leaned forward. "He was killed by several blows to the head, sir. Wouldn't have taken that much to knock him out. Your average drug user gets a little carried away sometimes. Some of 'em are a little crazy."

Whelan thought for a moment. "Why would he have been in an alley?"

Bauman shrugged again, smiling slightly. "Well, you know… to have a couple pops. He bought a bottle, right?"

Whelan shook his head. "Uh-uh, not Artie. Not in an alley. If he was in an alley, *any* alley, there was another reason. He wouldn't he drinking in an alley."

"How do you know that?" Bauman asked irritably.

"The reason he came to see me was to get company on his little expeditions up here. He was nervous about it. He didn't mind it so much in the daytime but he was getting a little spooked at night. He was afraid of the neighborhood and some of the people he talked to made his skin crawl. A guy like Art wasn't about to go lurking around in alleys."

"So he wanted a place to drink in peace." Bauman forced a small smile.

"Fine, he would've gone into a doorway. Or he would've gone into the john in some greasy spoon and had a taste. Or he would've poured it into his Seven-Up and walked around with it. He used to do that once in a while. But he wouldn't go into an alley in Uptown at night. Not just to drink."

Bauman leaned back and looked at Whelan. Rooney sighed.

"His blood alcohol was pretty high, sir," Rooney said. "We got the results yesterday. He drank his bottle, sir."

Whelan looked around his office and a thought struck him. "You find the bottle?"

Bauman sat up and opened his mouth, then looked at Rooney, and back at Whelan.

"Well, shit, I suppose so. Yeah, I guess we did. We found *all* the bottles, Whelan." His cheeks seemed to be a little redder.

"The alley is full of bottles, sir," Rooney offered.

"I know. I was there."

"We know," Bauman said, and smiled happily.

Whelan looked at him and nodded. "Gray Caprice, lot of crap in the backseat."

Bauman nodded curtly and Whelan felt his own face reddening slightly. "Not bad. But if you didn't find a bourbon bottle in that alley, then he didn't go there to drink. He was there for some other reason."

"What?" Bauman blinked and tugged at his collar.

"Some guys go down hard, they fight it. All the time I knew Artie, he never drank anything but bourbon. Turned his nose up at anything else. If you told him he was an alcoholic, he would've laughed at you because he drank nothing but good whiskey and he had this idea that a guy who can be fussy can't have much of a problem. I hadn't seen him much lately but I can't believe he'd change about that. So if you found a half pint of Beam or Early Times, or maybe Old Forester if he had a couple bucks on him, then maybe I'm wrong. But I was in that alley and all I saw was wine and vodka. If he went in there, he did it for some other reason."

"Such as?"

"I don't know. Somebody talked him into it. Or…or he was looking for somebody, I don't know. But you guys don't either."

Bauman wet his lips. "Okay, smart fella. We don't know. But we're trying to find out."

"I could give you a hand."

"No, thanks," Bauman said, getting to his feet. "Just wanted to see if you had anything interesting to say, Whelan." The room seemed to be filled now with his scent of sweat and deodorant and tobacco.

"I was a police officer."

"Yeah, we know," Bauman said, his back to Whelan.

"That's why we'll expect your complete cooperation, sir." Rooney bit his lip and stared at the wall for a moment, then turned back to Whelan. "So you never actually went out on the street with Mr. Shears? To work on his, uh, book?"

"No. He asked me if I would and we agreed to talk about it later. But I never—It never happened."

"Know if he was talking to any users? Anything like that?" Bauman raised his eyebrows.

"No. I don't think so. I'm not sure he would've known."

Bauman opened the door.

"Have a nice day," Whelan said, deadpan.

Bauman paused and gave him a long, hostile look and Rooney shook his head at Whelan. They left.

FOUR

By eleven o'clock he'd sweated through his shirt. The digital thermometer on the Community Bank building told him it was 101; the one on the college said it was 99. The truth was somewhere in between and it didn't make much difference. There was the faintest pawing of breeze in the air, and maybe later the lake would send a wind, but at the moment it wasn't doing a thing. The previous night's rain had left no trace of itself but a few puddles that already looked stagnant, as though things might be growing there.

He pounded pavement, buttonholed strangers, had cigarettes with winos and made small talk with a couple of neatly dressed black kids from the college, and it all got him nowhere. Several of the street types told him they remembered Art, and he actually believed one, but the man could tell him nothing more than that he'd seen a man with a tape recorder.

The young man in front of the Walgreen's could have been the prototype for all the Jehovah's Witnesses Whelan had ever seen. He was very young, wondrously clean-cut, earnest, impervious to scorn, criticism or the mocking glances of passersby, and persistent. He wasn't a Witness, though, for he wore no tie and his neatly pressed blue shirt was long-sleeved and he called attention to himself by wearing the sleeves buttoned, western style. Whelan felt hot just looking at him.

He stopped and watched the dark-haired young man speaking to a trio of drunks collected around a fire hydrant. His impassioned gestures were impressive, as he waved his arms, beat his breast and covered his eyes with his hands. The three drunks looked at each other and laughed. Whelan could see that the young preacher was growing impatient. Finally, just as Whelan neared the group, the young man leaned over and heatedly said something to one of the men, who leaped up and took a roundhouse swing at him. The punch caught nothing but air and the young man jumped back, visibly stunned by this reception to his fresh-air ministry. The three drunks moved off and the young man watched them. Then he noticed Whelan looking at him.

"Hello."

"Hi. Rough morning, huh?"

"I guess so."

"What was it you said to him?"

"I just…I wasn't thinking. I just forgot myself. I asked him what his mother would think about the way he's turned out."

Whelan laughed and looked away to minimize the young man's embarrassment.

"Did it ever occur to you that his mother might be dead and that maybe she didn't have such a good life herself? These guys don't want to hear about their mothers, pal. Is this your, ah, first…mission?"

The young man put his hands on his hips, struggled for nonchalance, and nodded. "Yes, sir, it is. I suppose I've got some things to learn, but—"

"We all do. Where are you…do you have a church up here?"

"I'm working under the direction of the Reverend Charles Roberts." He beamed, as though he'd just mentioned Billy Graham. "Do you know Reverend Roberts?"

"No, not personally. He's headquartered just up the street, right?" The young man nodded. "But I don't know a lot of the local clergymen personally, Reverend."

The young man gave him a sheepish look. "Oh, I'm not *Reverend* yet. I'm still studying and…it's just plain Don. Don Ewald."

Whelan held out his hand. "Paul Whelan. So you're a seminarian?"

Don nodded eagerly. "Exactly. Only here, on the streets, I'm called an 'intern.' The Way Mission has four summer interns, from all parts of the country."

"Where are you from, Don?"

"Bakersfield, California."

Whelan smiled. "Got anything like this in Bakersfield?"

Ewald looked up and down the street and shook his head slowly. "No, and I couldn't have imagined this many poor people, this many alcoholics, this many runaways, homeless people…you know, Bakersfield isn't heaven but the scope of this is incredible to me. The Lord has his work cut out here."

"He does that."

"Well, I should probably get back to my ministry." He smiled. "Perhaps you could stop by the Way some time for coffee."

"I might do that. You folks might be able to help me with something."

"Help you, Mr. Whelan?"

"I'm trying to get some information. A friend of mine was killed up here a couple of nights ago, and I'm investigating his death. I'm trying to find anyone who may have talked to him before he died."

The young man's eyes widened. "You're a police officer?"

"Nope. Private investigator."

"Really?" A childlike grin spread across Don Ewald's face. He looked like an altar boy. "I've never met a private investigator."

"Well, you have now. Not so impressive, is it?"

"Well, sure it is! Wait'll Tom hears about this. Aw, he'll be so jealous. He reads detective novels all the time. Oh…" His face grew serious. "I'm sorry to hear of your loss, Mr. Whelan. If there's anything—"

"Thanks. Who's Tom? Friend of yours?"

"My roommate. We usually work together but he's got a cold." He tried to look somber but lost control again. "Are you actually looking for his killer?"

"Yeah. Yeah, I am. So are the police, but they don't have the manpower to put people on something like this full time. They think it was just a robbery that got out of hand. I thought I'd poke around in it awhile. My friend's name was Art Shears. He was medium height, thin, and he was starting to lose his hair. He would probably have been wearing a light blue summer sportcoat and he was using a small tape recorder and interviewing some of the derelicts around here. Remember seeing anything like that?"

"No. Do you know of any of the people he was interviewing?"

"Not really. He didn't mention any names, so I'm kind of stuck there."

Don Ewald thought for a moment. "Well, I didn't see him but I can ask the other interns. One of them might have seen him. You know, between the four of us, we cover quite a bit of ground every day." He sounded hopeful.

"I'm sure you do. Well, maybe I'll stop by sometime."

"Come by during the week and I'll ask everybody."

"I'd appreciate it. And I'll look forward to that cup of coffee."

"Great." Don held out his hand and they shook. "It was real nice to meet you, sir."

"My pleasure," Whelan said.

He had lunch at the A&W, where Rashid and Gus were arguing when he came in. Several customers walked out without ordering. The subject of debate seemed to be the approximate age of the Italian beef. Gus held that it was fresh, Rashid seemed to think it posed public dangers. As Whelan took a seat at the end of the counter, Rashid held the plastic container to his nose.

"This one is old." He sniffed, wrinkled his nose and said "Peuu...this guy is bad. Flies won't eat this guy."

"Goddamn!" a young black man at the counter said, and walked out, shaking his head.

"You're losing business, guys," Whelan said. "I'll save the franchise. Give me a Shalimar kabob and onion rings and a Coke. Quick, let people see me eating."

"No chicken biryani?"

"Tomorrow."

"Serve the detective his food, Rashid."

"You are a pig," Rashid said to his cousin, and his eyes implored Whelan to agree with him. Whelan busied himself with a cigarette and tried not to laugh.

"You are a pig, Gus," Rashid told his cousin's departing form. "You leave old shit food all everywhere, make fucking people sick." He put his hands on his hips, hung his head and became the portrait of aggrieved authority. After a moment, he looked at Whelan, snapped his fingers and grinned.

"Shalimar kabob for the detective! Oh, you gonna like this one."

"I always do. Just don't ever tell me what's in it."

"It is only good Persian food."

"Good Persian food, hah!" Gus called out, shouldering open the kitchen door. He plopped a large white box on the counter directly in front of a thin man in glasses. The man's A&W basket jumped and a few fries escaped. He looked at Gus and shook his head as he retrieved his potatoes.

"You don't know nothing about Persian food."

"I'm the *cook*!"

"Bah. You call this cooking?"

"These are the recipes of my mother." He held Gus's gaze and dared him to insult his mother.

"Your mother is no cook. She is no chef, for sure."

Rashid's face darkened. *"Your* mother, she—"

Gus straightened slightly and looked over at the back counter, where a cleaver was resting on the stainless-steel surface.

Gus's large stomach heaved with his emotion. "Say something about my mother."

"Your mother…is Assyrian." Rashid's face burst into a delighted grin, the grin of victory, a conqueror's grin. He turned to Whelan and pointed to Gus.

"He is only half Persian. The other half is Assyrian."

Whelan looked at Gus, who was clearly imagining the sudden death of his cousin.

"I thought your people killed all the Assyrians," he said.

Rashid shook his head. "No. We got a million Assyrians. We got Kurds, too." He shrugged apologetically, as though Kurds and Assyrians were a blot on the good name of Iran.

"You gonna kill each other or serve me some food?"

Rashid slapped himself across the head. "Oh, shit. Yes, yes, yes. He's coming right up!" He glanced at Gus, who was still staring malevolently at him. "Ah, is okay. Assyrians are okay. They just don't know about Persian food."

Gus grunted and resumed his duties.

"You know," Whelan said. "I keep hearing that the national pastime in Iran is chess or backgammon. It's not, though, is it?"

"No," Rashid said. "Not chess. Not the backgammon, no."

"It's arguing, isn't it."

With his back to Whelan, Rashid laughed, putting together a bright red A&W basket of Shalimar kabob with its spicy sauce, a few fries, and a handful of onion rings, a meal, Rashid told him, "fit for the kings."

He got nothing from a couple of old-timers he knew, and he was driving up Broadway when he saw Bauman talking to a couple of men outside the schoolyard at Broadway and Sunnyside. He pulled over and parked for a moment, till Bauman got into the Caprice. When Bauman went on up Broadway, Whelan pulled out and followed him.

He was delighted with himself. There was no certainty that Bauman would do any better on the street than Whelan had been doing, but there was a certain undeniable satisfaction in tailing the detective, and it might end up saving him some energy.

Five times in the next hour he parked and watched Detective Bauman at work. It was plain that Bauman was getting nowhere, but Whelan was mildly surprised to watch him go through his drill. The hostile detective was obviously at ease among the winos and old men, and surprisingly patient in his questioning. It seemed to bother him not at all when several of the men refused to talk to him, looking away or even walking in the other direction when Bauman asked questions. A couple even began walking away when Bauman approached, and Whelan laughed: Bauman might as well have been wearing a sign. He was wearing his green horse-blanket jacket and had that 1957 haircut, and on a street filled with tiny Asians and cadaverous winos and street people, he stood out like Lady Di. And had no idea.

Whelan had seen this lack of self-awareness before. In his early days as a police officer, he'd become friendly with an undercover officer named Shealy. Most of the time Shealy did well in camouflaging himself: he dressed plainly, in dull colors, usually wearing a hat. It was the summer that was Shealy's undoing. Pink-skinned and scrupulously well groomed, as well as twenty pounds overweight, Shealy chose gaudy T-shirts for his summer costume, often with trendy slogans. And when he walked down the street, people gave him a wide berth and he never knew why. He was simply the type of man who would never be seen in public in a T-shirt, like the cardinal or the mayor.

In front of the bank Bauman buttonholed a tall thin man with pale blond hair and Whelan parked up the street. He got out and went into the Subway Donut Shop under the tracks on Broadway, got a cup of coffee and took a window seat. He could see Bauman perfectly. The conversation took several minutes. After a while Bauman seemed to tense up, leaning forward in more aggressive body language and the thin man took a step back, shuffled a bit, shrugged, shook his head and said something. Bauman nodded, said something, then turned and walked back to the Caprice, which was parked in a bus stop. Whelan was about to get up when he realized that the thin man was headed for the donut shop.

Hot damn. Great detective work.

A black man lounging near the door said, "Hey, Woody," as the thin man entered. A fat white man standing at the counter nodded and said "Woodrow." The thin man nodded to them and went over to the glass donut case. He ordered coffee and a day-old donut from the young Greek behind the counter, who paused while turning ham steaks on the grill, poured the coffee, picked a donut out with a piece of wax paper, took Woody's money and spun around back to the grill, where he began spreading a handful of hash-browns. An artist at work.

Woody was a little older than he'd looked, perhaps fifty-five. He brought his donut and coffee over to the window and took a stool near Whelan. He sat hunched over the coffee, holding it in both hands as though warming himself on the cup. He poked around in the ashtray with a shaking finger and muttered to himself. Whelan took out a smoke, made a production of lighting it, blew out the match, took a deep drag and exhaled noisily. He looked at Woody, did a double take, then slid the pack along the four feet of empty space between them.

"Help yourself, babe." He tossed the matches after the pack.

Woody nodded and reached for the pack but did not look up. Whelan sipped his coffee and studied the foot traffic on Broadway. A pretty young Vietnamese girl walked by and he pretended to watch her as Woody fished a couple of extra smokes from the pack.

Woody puffed away, still shaking, and Whelan went fishing. "Little cold in here, huh?"

Woody nodded. "Shit, yeah. I'm cold. Dunno what they need air conditioning for. It ain't that hot out. You can get sick from too much air conditioning."

"I've heard that, too." It was a clammy seventy-five inside the donut shop and this man was chilled to his bones. Woody had shaved within the past few days and still had the nicks in his cheeks to prove it. The day-old donut lay untouched as he sucked at the cigarette. His skin was pale and there was some sort of rash across the backs of his hands. A strand of the thinning blond hair fell across his forehead and Whelan was reminded briefly of Artie. Time to stop jerking this guy around.

"How well do you know Bauman?"

"Who?"

"The cop with the crewcut. Name's Bauman."

Woody shrugged and looked away. "I seen 'im around."

"He ask you about that guy they found in the alley over the other side of Broadway?"

"What's that to you?" Woody gave him a belligerent look.

"I'm investigating the same thing he is. It's a little more personal with me, though. That guy who was killed was a friend of mine and I want to find out who killed him. It was probably somebody out here on the street." Woody shrugged indifferently but there was a look of intelligence in his eyes now.

"He was asking you about that. About my friend."

"Maybe he was, maybe he wasn't. I talked to him already, I don't see no reason to talk to you." He looked sullenly out the window.

"I'm not a cop. I'm a private investigator and I'm gonna find out who killed my friend. I think I can do some things the cops can't do. Also…I don't know that they give a good shit what happened."

"It don't make me no never mind."

"Come on, Woody. He was a friend of mine. He never hurt anybody. He was a writer, he was interviewing people for a book he was—"

Woody turned, nodding. "Yep, asking a lot of stupid goddamn questions, goddamn fool, sticking his nose in people's business. Ain't no great wonder he got hisself killed."

Whelan leaned over and grabbed the cigarette pack. "Listen to me, asshole. I'm trying to find out who killed my friend because I don't think anybody else will. The police think he was just a drunk and got killed for no particular reason. I think different. So I'm here trying to find things out and I'm willing to pay for information, and I'll listen to a man that's got something to say but that doesn't mean I've got to sit here and inhale shit from some old clown that just wants to tell me what an asshole the guy was. Tell you what, Woodrow…maybe when you die, some other guy'll sit here and tell folks what an asshole you were. Get your own smokes." He got up and left. He turned up Broadway and lit another cigarette and it was a block before Woody caught him.

"Hey, mister." Whelan stopped and looked at him. Woody was wheezing and huffing.

"Yeah? Got some more free personality analysis for me?"

"I'm sorry, mister. I'm sick, and I get tired of people asking me about all this shit. Your friend asked me all kinda questions, never even gave me a smoke. He didn't belong down here. Didn't know nothing 'bout living down here. I'm sorry 'bout your friend, mister. I sure don't wish nobody dead. He didn't do nothing deserved killin', far as I can see."

"Take a walk with me, Woodrow." He handed Woody his cigarettes. "Keep 'em."

"Thanks, mister." Woody tucked the pack inside his shirt and seemed to squeeze it into a small space under his arm.

"You're gonna bust 'em all up, Woody."

"Nah. I flatten 'em up a little, but they's still smokes."

They began walking up Broadway and soon they were just fifty yards from the alley where Art Shears had died.

"Woody, I need to know who he was talking to. I don't really have a place to start, just hunches." Woody nodded. "He told me he was talking to one guy in particular, just a day before he was killed. He seemed to think this guy was, I don't know, a little different from the other ones he talked to. Said he thought this fella was on the run or something like that."

Woody shook his head. "Don't know nobody that's on the run. Not down here."

"Something else, then. He said the guy was a little different. Maybe…I don't know, better educated or something. Did you see him actually talking to anybody? Was he talking to anyone that you know of, anyone that was an educated man?"

Woody nodded. "I saw 'im talking to Sharkey. Sharkey's an educated man. Hear him tell it, he was important once, but people will tell you all kinda bullshit. But he seems like an educated man to me. And he never bragged on it, said it like he was ashamed. Said he made some money, big money. Had a good job, bank job, something like that. I think he took to the drink and just run away. Had a family and a house, too. So he said."

"Seen him lately?"

"Nope. Hector, neither."

"Who's Hector?"

"Sharkey and Hector stay together. Hector kinda looks after Sharkey. Shark's kinda small. Hector ain't. People don't bother Hector much. He's Indian, Hector, half Indian and half Tex-Mex."

"When's the last time you saw them?"

"Four, five days ago."

"Can you give me a description? What am I looking for?"

Woody smiled. "Won't have no trouble pickin' 'em out if you come across 'em. Sharkey's kinda small, like I said. Wears a blue raincoat kinda thing. Hector's a little bigger than you and he's pretty good built. He's got a busted nose and one of them lips that sticks up like this." He pushed a finger into the center of his upper lip.

"He's got a harelip."

"I dunno what you call 'em."

"But you're pretty sure I'll find 'em together?"

"Yes sir. Sharkey don't like to be on the street by hisself. He's like that, and Hector, he needs the company. Can't read. Not a word," Woody pronounced gravely.

"Where would I find them? Where do they do their drinking?"

"Up around here mostly. No taverns, though. No money for it." Woody shrugged and laughed. "Who the hell has money?"

"You don't know where they flopped?"

"Nope." Woody shivered.

"Seen a doctor lately?"

"Been over to that place up the street. That health center place. Stood in lines, sat in a chair, waited. Nothin' wrong with me. I just ain't been eating right lately. And I drink some."

"What do you live on, Woodrow?"

"I got a little pension from the Illinois Central Railroad. And sometimes I stand out there in front of that Allhelp place. They always find something for me, they know I'll give 'em a day's work, no matter what. I ain't no bum, mister. I stay on the street 'cause that's how it's worked out for me, but I ain't no bum." Woody looked him in the eye and nodded.

"No, you're sure not. You probably have a steadier income than I do. Got a place?"

Woody nodded. "Got me a little room over a tavern. Ain't much, but it's somethin'." He gave Whelan an odd look. "What kinda money can a fella make in your line of work?"

"Not much." He laughed. "Not much at all. I do some work for some lawyers and I do a few things on my own, but it just barely keeps me afloat."

"You seem like a smart young fella. There's gotta be other work you could do."

"I'm sure there is but this is the only thing I've come across where I don't answer to anybody."

Woody seemed to reflect on this for a moment and then nodded. "I can see that, all right."

A thought occurred to Whelan. "Woody, do you ever eat at the Salvation Army place up here on Sunnyside?"

"Oh, sure."

"Ever see these guys there?"

Woody smiled. "Sooner or later, you see everybody there. Yes sir, they eat there sometimes. You might try there."

"Thanks, Woodrow. Take care of yourself."

"You do the same, son."

He walked back up Broadway, bought a new pack of cigarettes from the convenience shop inside the el station, then stopped at the corner and bought a *Tribune* from the genial Pakistani who ran the newsstand. The man took his money, folded his paper carefully, grinned at him and wished him a good day, head bobbing all the while. Whelan had been buying his paper at the stand for fifteen years, most of those years from an old white-haired man named Dutch, an inexhaustible source of trivia, gossip, street rumor and tips on the ponies; his specialty was the trotters. They were easier races to fix and he seemed to have excellent sources, and until the racing commission cleaned up harness racing Dutch was making a good buck on the side. Dutch was dead now and Whelan had no illusions about the little Pakistani man ever becoming a source.

His forehead was wet and he could feel the perspiration on his scalp. The sun seemed to be stuck overhead. On the corner across from the Salvation Army Center was a schoolyard, and here, despite the heat and their barren surroundings, a group of children, perhaps twenty of them, were playing baseball with a heavily taped ball and a ragged collection of gloves and bats.

He stopped to watch for a moment. There was no shade anywhere, and the sun glinted off shards of broken glass on the asphalt surface, and Whelan thought it was the most unpleasant place a kid could find to play ball. But no one had told the kids, who seemed to be having a wonderful, sweaty good time.

To his left, Whelan heard a familiar jingling, and he turned to see a Mexican in a green baseball cap pedaling a little white cart into the schoolyard. The hand-painted sign on the cart proclaimed him to be the representative of *Azteca Paleteria* somewhere on the south side. Below the lettering, there were gaudy, primitive little paintings of the *paletas* themselves, the homemade popsicles that were found nowhere else. A paleta might be strawberry, it might be watermelon or mango or guava or lime, but whatever the flavor, a paleta was an experience, sweet and juicy, often thick with pieces of fruit, and Whelan's mouth was watering. The Mexican grinned at the children, jingled his little bells at them and nodded.

At that moment, from the other entrance to the schoolyard, different jingling sounded, and the vendor turned suddenly, as did the children, to see another vendor pedaling in. This one was an Anglo, a skinny, blond, hard-looking man in a visor, and the sign on his cart proclaimed him to be *Mr. Popsicle*. Mr. Popsicle yelled something to the kids and pedaled toward them. Mr. Azteca hopped on his seat and began motoring over to get there first. Mr. Popsicle pulled up a few feet away from the Mexican and called to the kids, then yelled something Whelan couldn't hear at the Mexican. Mr. Azteca then dismounted and said something back. Mr. Popsicle gave Mr. Azteca the finger and got off his little three-wheeler and Mr. Azteca grabbed his crotch in response and began to yell at Mr. Popsicle. They walked toward one another, pointing fingers and screaming, a couple of hot, sweaty men trying to scratch a few bucks out of the city and having a bad time of it. The children were no longer playing baseball but standing in a tightly packed, excited group and watching two businessmen compete for a market.

The two vendors were almost nose to nose now digging deep into the wells of profanity to come up with insults so vile that the moment became a learning experience for all who witnessed it. Whelan couldn't hear it all but was able to make out a few words. The gist of it seemed to be that Mr. Popsicle was a *puta* and that his mother slept with dogs in the alley, and that Mr. Azteca had relations with all the women in his family for several generations, and in no time at all the two were exchanging wild roundhouse punches. Like most street fighters, they weren't very good at it, and after several misses on each side and an occasional accidental success, they grappled, got somehow into twin headlocks and hit the pavement. There they rolled and swatted at each other and gouged, to the delight of the children. They screamed and cursed and rolled over and over on the pavement, covering themselves with dirt and broken glass. Finally Whelan decided to stop the fight, but someone else did it for him.

As he started to walk across the schoolyard toward the belligerents, he became aware of another tinny jingling in the distance. The children turned and Whelan looked up to see a third vendor entering the schoolyard. This one was much older than the other two, a sunbrowned old man with shaggy white hair and a toothless smile, and he pushed his rickety cart rather than rode it, and as he looked at the warring vendors rolling on the ground, he nodded and began to laugh. He looked at the children, wiggled his eyebrows at them and pointed to the gleaming rows of bottles on his wooden cart, then at the pristine mound of ice: a snow-cone salesman. The children looked at the lovely line of syrup bottles and imagined themselves slurping at little cones of colored ice, and the two men rolling in the dirt were forgotten forever.

The fighters seemed to realize they were no longer the center of focus, and they rose to a seated position and watched their ancient competitor dish out a dozen and a half snowcones. Whelan watched for a moment and then walked away, laughing.

Across the street outside the Salvation Army Center, they were lined up halfway down the block waiting for a meal. Most were men but there were several dozen women, of all ages, and some had small children. All of God's races seemed to be accounted for.

Near the door to the center, a tiny man in a blue uniform

was struggling to pull a man twice his size off the curb. The big man seemed to be talking to him but his eyes were closed. A couple of the men stepped out of line to help the Sal Army officer but they weren't much help, and after a moment, the officer gave up and stood, hands on his knees and panting. It was a few seconds before he noticed Whelan watching him.

He was a blond fair-skinned man in his thirties with a scholarly face, a short goatee and wire-rims that framed a pair of remarkably candid blue eyes. The body of a twelve-year-old was tucked into the blue uniform. He was a good deal smaller than any of his "flock," and Whelan wondered how anyone so obviously overmatched had drawn Uptown as his assignment. Somebody down at Sal Army headquarters had a sense of humor.

The little man smiled slyly. "It's pretty comical, huh?" A touch of pink came into the pale cheeks and the faintest trace of irritation into the eyes. Perhaps not so overmatched after all. It was Whelan's turn to redden slightly.

"No. I couldn't get him up either. Do you really want to?"

The little man laughed. "I have to. He wants to come back to our program."

"Detox?"

"Yes. He has good intentions but he can't walk."

"I can give you a hand."

"I could sure use it, if you don't mind. My security guard is busy at the moment."

"No trouble at all. I was coming to see you anyway."

The little man looked at him. "All right. Let's get him on his feet. Come on, Archie. Help us out."

Whelan got down and put Archie's arm over his shoulder, the officer did likewise with the other arm, and they both pushed and grunted and Archie seemed to be singing, but eventually they had him on his feet. Archie immediately began to sag again, but the door opened and a tall thin black man in his forties emerged. He was wearing a dark blue guard's uniform, and his gaze took in everything as he walked toward the officer.

"I'll take him now, captain." The guard nodded at Whelan.

"We're glad to see you, J.B. He's all yours."

The guard grinned and showed several gold-capped teeth. He put a shoulder under Archie's arm and grabbed him around his waist, and Whelan watched in amazement as the guard walked off with the heavy drunk.

"You going to put him on the dumbwaiter, J.B.?" the captain asked.

"Next time, captain," the guard said, and disappeared inside.

"In-joke?" Whelan asked.

The captain gave Whelan a puckish look. "Sort of. The men's quarters are upstairs and some of these fellows are pretty big, like Archie there, and we always joke about putting them on the dumbwaiter—which we use to get food to the upper floors. But one night we had a fellow who must have weighed two hundred seventy-five pounds, and J.B. was off duty, so my wife and I stuffed the man on the dumbwaiter and sent him on up, and then we ran up the stairs after him and rolled him off. So now it's an emergency course of action."

"How come J.B. doesn't have the same trouble carrying him that we did? Magical powers?"

"Boy, I don't know. I've seen him swimming, so I know there's no secret mass of muscles hidden under his uniform. He's amazing, and all he has to do when there's trouble or somebody gets out of line is put one of those skinny hands on a man's shoulder. Like putting someone in a vise. Let's have a cup of coffee."

"Sounds good."

The captain led him inside and opened a door just past the staircase. Whelan followed him inside. A chubby, cheerful-looking woman in a Sal Army uniform sat at a desk and smiled as they entered.

"Hello, Doug. Good morning, sir."

Whelan looked at the officer. "I know I'm 'sir' so you must be Doug."

The captain laughed. "This is my wife, Eunice. She hates her name but you can use it anyway. I'm Doug Wallis."

"Paul Whelan. Should I call you 'captain'?"

"No, Doug is fine. I've been Doug a long time. I've only

been captain for three years. Come on into the lunchroom. That's where the coffee urn is."

"I know. I've been here before."

"Oh?" The captain looked at him with interest.

"When Captain Salley was here. He helped me find a young woman I was looking for. She had been in your women's program for a while."

"You're a police officer, then?"

"No. I used to be. Captain Rogers was here then. Now I'm a private investigator."

"Really? How interesting."

"Probably not as interesting as running a service center in Uptown. I notice business is booming, by the way."

The captain smiled and led him to the coffee urn. "Yes, it is. We're feeding thousands of people a week now. The Detox program is actually beyond its planned capacity, and we have more young women on the third floor than we've ever had before. We'll never go out of business. How do you like your coffee?"

"Black is fine."

The captain poured him a cup of coffee and led him back to a private office.

"So, you said you were coming by to see me. What can I do for you, Mr. Whelan?"

"I'm looking for someone. Several people, actually."

The captain broke into a youthful grin. "I've never met a private investigator."

"I'm glad you're amused. You should see the impression I make on the police."

"Who are you looking for?"

"I'm not sure. A friend of mine was doing a series of interviews of men living on the street. During the course of his work he came across one particular man who seemed, at least to my friend, to have something to hide."

"Who doesn't, down here?"

"Well, that's how I felt. But Art was convinced that this guy had a story and he thought he could turn it into something.

Anyhow, he was following this man around, trying to get a line on him and a few other people. He asked me to sort of team up with him. What he really needed, I guess, was somebody to watch his back door. I just thought it sounded like a guy grasping at straws. I didn't really think there was a book in it. We were supposed to talk about it in a few days and I...I was going to go along with it. Humor him, I guess. Now I don't have to. He was found murdered in an alley Tuesday."

"I'm sorry, Paul." Whelan found himself being studied by the blue eyes. "You feel responsible for his death. In a way."

Whelan looked into his coffee, then focused on a city map on the far wall of the room. "Not really. At least, I'm not aware of it, if I do. What I really feel is...that I could have been a little more, I don't know, decent, maybe. A little better to him over the last couple of years the few times we talked. He was my best friend, my oldest friend. I wish I could have done something for him to make him feel a little better about himself. He was a doomed man the last time I saw him, and I was shocked. He had a drinking problem and his marriage was on the skids and he'd lost his job. I don't feel responsible for his death: I feel like I could have done something for his life. I only saw him a couple of times over the last few years but all those things were probably in progress and we just...I didn't have any time for him."

"This is my line of work, Paul. I know about these things. You couldn't have arrested these problems of his. His family couldn't. And the last time you saw him, you said you'd help him?"

"Yeah."

Captain Wallis shrugged. "Then his last recollection of you would be of an old friend who was going to do something important that he asked you to do." He folded his arms across his chest and nodded.

"You're pretty good at this work, huh?"

Captain Wallis shrugged slightly and smiled. "Paul, I assume the police are looking into your friend's death. Why are you?"

"Hard to explain. First of all, the detectives assigned to the case don't inspire me with confidence. I also think they've got Artie pegged as a bit of a derelict himself. Once they run out of gas on this thing, they'll let it go. I won't. And I've got some advantages: I know the neighborhood, for one, and I know some of the people who work up here and a few on the street."

"So can I be of specific help?"

"Yeah. Tell me if you know somebody named Sharkey and an Indian or Mexican named Hector."

"I know both of them. They eat here regularly. So did Shinny."

"Shinny." Whelan drew a blank for a moment, then remembered hearing the name from the three people in the alley. "That's the man that was killed last week?"

"Yes. He was stabbed to death in an alley not far from here."

"And Shinny knew these other men?"

"Yes. They were together often. Shinny was a little bit of a loner but he was often in their company. He was small, like Sharkey, and Hector looked after the two of them."

"Did they ever stay here?"

"They were never in Detox. I think Sharkey would have made a good candidate. I'm not sure whether Hector had that serious a problem. I never actually saw him intoxicated. And the Indians are more comfortable with their own program over on Sheridan."

"I know some of those folks. I'll have to pay them a visit."

"But I can't say I've seen either Hector or Sharkey recently. Not in at least a week." He picked up the phone and buzzed J.B. on the com-line, asked the guard about the two men, listened, then shook his head. "Sorry, Paul."

"No, you've been a lot of help. A couple people mentioned this other killing but I wouldn't have known there was a connection."

"You think there is a connection?"

"Two men who knew a third man are both found dead in alleys a few days apart. Sure, there's a connection. You betcha."

Captain Wallis pulled at the blond hairs of his goatee and then looked at him. "Well, stop in again, Paul. Just to chat and have some coffee."

"I'll do that," he said.

Liz was brief and distant over the phone but said to come over. He immediately felt self-conscious and debated whether to go home first and shower and change, then decided to get it all over with. He drove up Clark to Roscoe and parked in front of Sammee's, a Korean restaurant where they'd eaten often in better times. He walked down the surprising slope of Roscoe—Clark Street ran along a prehistoric ridge, the ancient shore of Lake Michigan, and these east-west streets ran downhill all the way to the lake—and climbed the steps of the three-flat where Liz had lived for more than ten years with her son.

She must have been watching from the window because she was standing in the open door when he got to the second-floor landing.

"Howdy," he said, feeling awkward and gritty and now wishing mightily he'd gone home for a shower.

"Hi," she said, a little breathlessly. He felt somehow relieved that she wasn't resorting to the casual persona she often adopted. It wasn't a time for being casual.

"Don't get too close. I've been out on the street all day."

She stepped back to let him in. "You didn't tell me about Artie Shears. I found out from Shelley. I just missed you at the wake. You're working on that, aren't you." She let it fall as a statement.

"Yeah. And I'm getting nowhere fast. But I'm probably doing better than the police are."

He took a few steps into the dining room, looked around and saw that she had packed dozens of boxes and had them stacked along the walls. The pictures were gone from the walls, the bookcases empty.

"Well...getting close, huh?"

"I guess." She leaned against her dining-room table and folded her arms. She was wearing a long blue T-shirt and cutoffs, and her hair was pulled back and she wore no makeup. He knew from long years of experience that she thought she looked dreadful at the moment, but he thought she looked wonderful. There was no point in saying it, though.

"Do you want something to drink?"

"Water. A lot of water." She smiled, bustled off to the kitchen, and over her shoulder shot back, "You wouldn't be thirsty so often if you stopped smoking."

He laughed and threw himself down on her sofa. Then, embarrassed to be sitting where they'd several times made love, he moved to an armchair by the window. Liz came in with a tall glass of ice water and he drained half of it at a gulp.

"So what do you hear from Charlie?"

"I just talked to him an hour ago. He's fine. He misses some of his friends but my dad's been taking him around, showing him turtles and ducks and deer and all that stuff, and he's rapidly becoming a little Wisconsin boy." She looked at him for a moment. She was sitting on the other armchair, leaning forward, chin cupped in her hands. For the first time in the long grueling months of the dissolution of their relationship, he could see her sadness.

"Do you want to talk about Artie, Paul?"

"No. The more I talk about him, the more it hurts."

She seemed to take a breath. "Do you want to talk about …us?"

"Can I change your mind with anything I might say?"

"No." She smiled slightly.

"Then, no. I'm not trying to be…I'm glad I'm here. I'm glad to see you."

"I'm glad you're here, too." Then, after a moment, she asked, "How do you feel, Paul?"

"Oh, I'm better. I'm not…I've had some other things to think about lately…so I'm doing okay. You?"

"I feel terrible. I know this is not what you want to hear, but…you're my oldest friend."

"You're right, it's not what I want to hear. Eighteen years and I'm your friend. What an accomplishment. Can we be pen pals?" He felt himself growing angry and took a long drink of his water to calm himself.

"There was a time when it would have worked and we…our timing wasn't right."

"Timing? You got married, for Chrissakes."

"You didn't want to get married, Paul."

"I was ten months out of the service, Liz, I was still seeing Cong snipers in maple trees." He put his face in his hands, shook his head, then looked at her.

"I'm sorry. This is no time for this sort of thing. Let's just…I don't know what."

"Are you hungry?"

"No, I'm not hungry," and then he laughed, at Liz who always wanted to offer him food when she was uncomfortable, and at himself and the hopeless picture he thought he made, and at them, at people who dance around in little circles for eighteen years and still can't quite pull it off. He stood up.

"I have a small speech." She smiled ruefully and he went on. "For eighteen years, more or less, you've been the woman in my life—"

"Among others," she said.

"Let me finish this, will you? And I understand how it is between us and I don't like it, and I'm not sure it's right, but I accept it. I'll write you letters and if you don't answer them, I'll just write Charlie letters. I think he'll answer. So…good luck." He smiled slightly. "That's it. That's my speech." She got up from the other armchair and came over and put her arms around him, and they stayed together for a long time, and then they broke it off. She took his hand as they walked to the door and he picked up the small box of clothes and personal articles he'd left here over the years. At the door he nodded to her and left. On the street, he took a quick last look at the house on Roscoe that he hoped he'd never see again, and walked back up the street to his car.

He stayed home that night and busied himself with what was, for him, an elaborate dinner. He made cornbread and a small salad with bleu cheese dressing and broiled two and a half pounds of country ribs, smothered in a hot sauce and covered in the broiler with sliced onions. He let the ribs cook till the sauce was candied and the fat on the meat was charred and caked and the onions were sweet and soft. It was the meal he'd cooked most often for Liz. He made a long, lingering exercise of his dinner, then sat in front of his TV set and nursed three bottles of dark Augsburger while the Cubs started a four-game series with the Astros in Houston. Here he could predict the future: like his garden and his relationship with Liz and his career prospects, a four-game Cub series in Houston was a "moribund enterprise."

The Cubs lost 7–zip and he took a long bath, reading old *National Geographics* in the tub. Then, unable to take any more of this day, he went to bed.

He didn't so much hear the noise as feel it, a subtle scratching, a tool against metal, someone working at his lock. He sat up in bed, looked at the glowing face of the clock and saw that it was 1:48. He slipped noiselessly out of bed and pulled on his pants, then crept out to the hall. The noise was coming from the back door. He padded quietly to the rear of the house, holding his breath and listening to the pounding of his heart, which now seemed to be lodged somewhere in his throat. At the door to the kitchen, ten feet from the back door, he paused and listened to the person breaking in. He came silently across the room, slid open the cutlery drawer and felt around in the dark. He pulled back his hand and saw that he'd come up with the "ginsu." It was ugly, it had a cheap-looking plastic handle, and it had a blade a foot long. It looked like a *kris* or something out of some Arabian fairy tale, and a TV ad had talked him into parting with $19.95 for it, a knife that would remain sharp forever. In a house filled to overflowing with cutlery, with his father's carving knives and the dozens of dangerous little daggers his mother had used to slice and pare and cut, the ginsu had seen little use, but Whelan now realized its worth. He had the longest, most unlikely kitchen knife on earth and unless the guy outside had a field mortar, Whelan had the edge.

He swallowed, listened to the tinkering, jumped when the

invader began to throw his weight against the door and then said, "Come on in, pal. I got something for you." There was silence and Whelan rushed at the door.

"Come on, asshole. You want to see me?" He fumbled at the old lock and finally managed to yank it open in time to hear the man's heavy footsteps going quickly down the back stairs. Whelan rushed out onto his back porch hoping for a glimpse of the intruder and heard his gate scrape open and shut. He ran back through the house to the front door, yanked it open and ran out onto the front porch. Whoever it was had been moving pretty well.

He stood for a while looking up and down his street. For a moment he had the feeling that his intruder was still somewhere up the street in shadow, watching him. Pulsing with anger, he came down the street and began to walk toward Lawrence, peering into gangways and the spaces between cars, and finding nothing. Eventually, when he was nearing the corner and almost a block from his house, a car full of teenagers passed him, and he saw from the looks on their faces that, as far as the rest of the populace was concerned, there was a shoeless, half-naked madman wandering Malden Street with a butcher knife.

He returned to the house, tossed the knife inside the hall and went in to get his cigarettes. He came back out and sat on the stairs and smoked. As he looked up and down the street, he tried to assess his feelings. In addition to the fear he'd felt, there was something else, something deeper. A sense of release, almost a giddiness. The pounding in his heart masked it, but it was there. He thought for a moment and understood. He needed to be immersed in action, in some kind of action.

What I really need is a mugging.

He realized that in the morning the idea of a home invasion wouldn't be so appealing, but right now, it was something. He sank back onto the stairs. The smoke and the cooler night air calmed him, and he spent another twenty minutes there. Eventually his thoughts turned to Liz.

FIVE

He woke at six, showered and had a quick cup of instant and was out of the house by six twenty-five. Two and a half hours till the funeral, a lot of time to work with. He drove up to Wilson and parked in front of the college.

The morning was cool with a soft breeze from the lake. The sun hadn't yet cleared the rooftops, so the air held an illusory promise of a break in the heat. And Uptown was rocking. For the people of the streets and gangways, he knew, there was no such thing as time, and in the coolness of this summer morning the streets were noisy and overrun with people—people standing and chattering, people dragging their bodies from one place to another as they'd done half the night and all the previous day, people talking to themselves, people dancing. Dancing. In front of the college a group of street people bounced and bopped to a small radio cranked up to its limits, and a few feet away, not one of their party but joining in anyway, a small dark-haired woman shuffled her feet and sang scat to the music. A couple of old men sat on a concrete bench a few yards from the music and stared dull-eyed at the dancers. The people beyond time, Whelan thought.

He cruised the streets, not certain what he was looking for, then returned to his parking spot and got out to walk. A group was gathering in front of the day-labor office between the Wilson Men's Club Hotel and the Wooden Nickel, and he attracted some notice as he neared them. One tried to stare him down, a blond boy, maybe nineteen. Whelan looked away and smiled. Not me, kid. I don't fight in hot weather. He decided to go up to the newsstand and get a paper. He was under the el tracks when he saw the familiar figure, weaving slightly and asking passers-by for change. A familiar figure and Whelan was disappointed to see him. The young man smiled agreeably at him, not recognizing him at first, and casually brushed his long dark hair out of his eyes.

"Hello, Wade."

"Hey, Mr. Whelan. Hey—"

"I thought you were leaving town."

"Naw, not yet, man. I just—"

"That's what you told me, Wade. You said you were going home. That was back in June. Jesus, I don't know if I'm glad to see you or sorry."

Wade shuffled slightly, half turned and shrugged, watching a bus move down Wilson. "Like, it's hard to get it together, you know?"

"You told me you were all set, you said—" And he caught the look in the boy's eyes, the resistance, and stopped himself. "Aw, what do I know. I'm glad to see you, Wade."

"Hey, it's cool, Mr. Whelan. I just thought—I think I'm gonna stay up here till the cold weather, get a little coin together, right? Then I can go back with something."

"You talk to your ma?"

"Yeah." He held up one finger. "I called her once. I did. I just don't wanna go back, you know, with nothin'."

"Right." Whelan looked around and tried to think of something to say. Wade Sanders had been his project for years. Whelan had picked the boy up one Friday night in response to a call that two youths were breaking into a pawnshop. And so they were. Two "youths" barely fifteen, Wade and an Appalachian kid named Terry Grimes, who was destined for bigger things. Orphaned at thirteen, Terry Grimes became a constant presence in Uptown and the various Northside lockups till his death by stabbing at the age of eighteen. That night, he and Wade were demonstrating how inept a pair of child burglars could be. Whelan and Jerry Kozel had caught them hammering away at the bars on the backdoor of the pawnshop, whacking away with a claw hammer and a tire iron and making enough noise to alert the Navy. As they pounded and swore at the bars, they were watched by a dozen people from surrounding apartments and a trio of old drunks sitting on a discarded sofa in the alley and passing a bottle. Wade had cried on the way to the station. He was from Ottawa, Illinois, and had come to Chicago with his father, who had died within the year, leaving the boy to live with a nineteen-year-old cousin. The cousin had left town and young Wade had found himself on the street. Wade's mother had remarried, and the young man and his stepfather loathed one another. Whelan made the boy his project. Over the next six months, he got Wade into a group home and into an alternative high school on Montrose where he was able to complete school; he'd gotten him summer jobs with the Park District, helped him find a studio apartment and had given him money on several occasions. Wade was a good kid, smart and streetwise and well liked. He was optimistic about his future, convinced that he'd eventually get into a vocational program, learn a trade and return to Ottawa to show everyone he was respectable. He was just short of his twentieth birthday and, Whelan believed, an alcoholic.

"Buy you breakfast, Wade?"

"I just had a donut, Mr. Whelan. I'm looking for a dude that owes me a little bread."

"Take a rain check, then. We should get together, since you're staying for a while. Right now, I think you could help me. It's worth a couple bucks to me."

Wade smiled. "Man, you don't have to pay me for helpin' you. What do you need?"

"I'm looking for someone. A friend of mine was…killed. Beginning of the week, over in the alley there behind Broadway."

"Shinny or that other dude?"

"The other one."

"Hey, I'm sorry, man."

"He was working on a book and interviewing people, and I want to talk to one of the guys he was interviewing. I think his name is Sharkey, and I think he runs with an Indian named Hector."

Wade nodded. "Hector I know. He's okay people. I like

Indians, you know?"

Whelan laughed. "Wade, you like everybody. Do you know Sharkey?"

"Not to say nothing to, you know, but we had a few pops together."

"Seen them lately?"

"Nope. Not in a while. I could ask around, though."

"I'd appreciate it. You working at all?"

"I been doin' a little of this and a little of that. Working for the place down the street here, and doin' some stuff for the guy that owns the Nickel."

"Good," Whelan said. Day labor with the old men, porter at the Wooden Nickel. "See you soon, Wade. Call me if you hear anything."

"Will do, Mr. Whelan."

He went back to his car and cruised for a while longer, then returned home and dressed for the funeral. He had a cup of coffee and listened to the news, then called his service.

"Hey, Shel."

"We're up early this morning. How's tricks, sweetheart?"

"Same as usual. Listen, Shel, if I get any calls this morning, tell them I'll be in the office in the afternoon. I'm going to a funeral."

"You got one call already, hon."

"Really? What kind of hours do they think a detective puts in? Who was it?"

"A Miss Jean Agee."

"I don't believe I've had the pleasure."

"Sounded about eighteen, lover. You picking them young these days?"

"These days, I'm not fussy. But I don't know this lady."

"She said she'd call again."

"Okay, Shel."

He drove to the funeral home and was early. There was a short procession over to St. Mary of the Lake and a Mass that was surprisingly well attended. After the Mass, Whelan drove several of Marie's friends to the cemetery. There was a brief graveside prayer and the casket was placed on a frame, on which it would he lowered into the grave later. Then the funeral of Art Shears was over. The sky was a whitish blue and there was a haze to the air, and Whelan's dark blue jacket felt like tent canvas.

Marie Shears broke away from a group of people and came over to him. She put her arm around his waist and hugged him.

"Thanks, Paul."

"Thanks for asking. It was an honor to be his pallbearer."

"Want to come by the house? We're having, you know, a little lunch. Nothing fancy, just sandwiches and salad and things like that."

"I've got to go back to work. I know that sounds humorous, but I do."

She looked at him for a moment, inclining her head. "You're looking into this."

"The boys tell you?"

She smiled. "No. I know you. Can I help?"

"Maybe. For now, did Art tell you the name of the man he'd been interviewing, the last one?"

"No. He said he was talking to a lot of different people. He just said one of them was a little unusual. A small man that hung around with an Indian man." She shrugged. "That's all."

"That helps."

She gave him a little squeeze and looked at him candidly. "He always thought you were something special, Paul Whelan. He said you were the most dependable person be ever knew. Maybe that doesn't sound like much of a compliment, but I know how he meant it."

"I'll take it." She went back to her people and he walked out to the parking lot and got into the car.

He went home and changed into a loose cotton shirt and white painters' jeans, then went out, leaving the car behind. He grabbed a quick cup of coffee at the New Yankee Grill on Wilson, chatted with Eva, the perky little Tennessee waitress, paid his money to the fat sullen woman at the register and left.

He called Shelley from the office.

"I'm here, Shel, but not for long."

"You've been popular. Miss Agee called again, and a Detective Bauman."

"He's a charmer, isn't he?"

"Oh, aside from the fact that he hasn't got any manners, he's not so bad. He tried to make me."

"It's that voice, Shel."

"I think he can tell what goes with it."

Whelan laughed. "Listen, if these people call again, tell them I'll be back in the office around one-thirty, two, okay?"

"Miss Agee requested an appointment."

"Tell her she's got one. Talk to you later."

There were an estimated twelve thousand Indians in Chicago, and most of them eventually made their way to Sheridan Road. St. Augustine's was on Sheridan, less than a mile in a straight line from Wrigley Field; it was a social service agency for Indians, run by the Episcopal Church. It was housed in a beautiful old brownstone building that had once been a funeral parlor. A woman stood on the porch of St. Augustine's. She was perhaps sixty-five, plump, fair skinned and dour, and a chain-smoker. Whelan knew her to be the daughter of a Stockbridge tribal chief and one of God's toughest creations.

" 'Lo, officer."

"Hello, Abby. You know I'm not a police officer anymore. How're you?"

"Got bronchitis. And I'm old. Other than that, I'm fine. Lot of people doin' worse. What brings you here?"

"Looking for somebody. His name is Hector and I think he'd be with a white man, older fellow, named Sharkey. Don't know the Indian man's last name. At least I think he's Indian. Might he Mexican."

Abby nodded. "He's both. He's half Mexican and half Pima. All the same, though. Mexicans are Indians anyway. They just don't know it."

She sagged against the column of the porch and took out a pack of Camels. Unfiltered Camels. "You want one?"

"Sure. So you know these guys?"

"Oh, we know 'em. Hector comes here to eat. Brings that other one, too. Hector Green, that's his name. Goes to Bo' Jou Nee Jee, too."

"He goes where?"

"Bo' Jou Nee Jee. That's the alcoholism program we got up the street."

"I know the place. I just didn't know it by that name."

"Ojibwa. Means 'welcome friend.' "

"So you've served the other guy, too. Sharkey."

"Sure. We don't turn hungry people away. We're civilized." There was open amusement in the dark eyes. He grinned at her. In his time as a street cop, Whelan had seen this woman handle drunks twice her size. If she didn't want them inside her building, they just didn't get in. She sent them off to sober up. She'd be firm and impassive. Only once did he ever see her lose her temper, a hot afternoon when she'd chased two young Indians down Sheridan and finally whacked one across the back of his head for calling her a "fat old white lady."

"Seen these men around lately?"

"Nope. Try down the street, They might've seen them there. Try the War Bonnet, too."

"You think they'd have money to drink in a tavern?"

She shrugged. "Somebody in there might know where to find 'em." She puffed on her Camel. He took a deep drag on his and the unfiltered smoke seared his lungs. He patted her on her shoulder.

"Thanks for the smoke."

"Don't mention it."

A small group of Indian men were eating soup at a wooden table inside the double storefront that housed Bo' Jou Nee Jee. In a far corner an Indian woman sipped lemonade, and Whelan realized how dry he was. He stood just inside the door; no one looked up. After a moment or two he was approached by a small, dapper man with curly brown hair going gray and the widest, most innocent-looking green eyes he'd ever seen.

"May I help you?" The man smiled at him, still wide-eyed, as if he'd seen God.

"I'm looking for someone. My name is Whelan. I'm a private investigator and I'm trying to locate a man."

"I'm Harold Ludwig. I'm the staff psychologist here. The man is an Indian?"

"I'm really looking for two men, a white man named Sharkey and an Indian named Hector Green."

"We know Hector here. We know his friend Sharkey, too. Why are you looking for them? May I ask that?"

"Sure. I think they were among the last people to see a friend of mine who was killed in an alley less than a block from here."

"Oh, that poor man that was robbed?"

"Yes."

"I'm sorry." He looked at Whelan for a moment, as if wrestling with something, then nodded. "I'll ask some of the men." He excused himself and went over to the table and spoke to the Indian men. Two shook their heads, one did nothing and a fourth looked lip briefly, glanced at Whelan and spoke. Dr. Ludwig nodded and returned.

"Joe Browndeer says he saw Hector on Friday or Saturday and hasn't seen him since." Dr. Ludwig smiled. "He thinks it's because Hector owes him money."

"Thanks."

"Do you think Hector killed this man?" The doctor's gaze was direct, a challenge.

Whelan looked around the room and shook his head. "No. No, I don't guess I do. There's…" He shrugged, groping for a concrete way to explain his suspicions. "There was something deliberate about this, something planned. I don't think he was robbed and I don't think he was killed by somebody like these men."

"We read that he was robbed," the doctor prodded.

"Any number of things could explain that. A kid could

have come along and robbed the body. The killer could have taken Art's things to make it look like robbery." He looked at the doctor and smiled. "Not a simple world."

"No, it's certainly not."

"So you tell me: is this something Hector Green could have done?"

Dr. Ludwig's eyebrows jumped. "Good Lord, no." He looked over at the table full of Indians. "They drink too much, they live too hard. But they're not killers or thieves."

"I didn't think so. Look, I'm really looking for the other man, for Sharkey. He's the man my friend was talking to. Can you have some body give me a call if either one turns up? I won't get anybody into any trouble, if it can be avoided."

"We wouldn't think of withholding information."

"Yeah, you would, doctor. I can hear you thinking." Dr. Ludwig smiled and Whelan handed him a card. The psychologist studied the card with undisguised amusement.

"I know, you've never had the business card of a private investigator, right?"

A touch of pink came into the little man's face. "I've never met one. I thought they existed only in the movies."

"Check out the Yellow Pages. We're everywhere."

Dr. Ludwig laughed and tucked the card into his pocket. Whelan waved to him, nodded to the Indian men watching him and left.

The first face he saw in the War Bonnet was Geronimo's. The poster was yellowing with age and showing rips and tears along its edges but was still perfectly positioned so that a customer entering would see the Apache chief in his most famous pose, kneeling and scowling, his Winchester across one knee.

The face behind the bar belonged to Charlie Bodie, "Choctaw Charlie," and the faces lining the bar were all Indian, mostly younger men. They looked up when the door opened, studied Whelan, marked him for a cop and looked back down into cans of Blue Ribbon.

Charlie was loading a case of Hamm's into the far cooler and Whelan studied the decor while he waited. Early Hostile, he decided. Bold but tasteful. Directly over the register and highlighted by the bare bulb a few inches above it was the famous and outrageously gory Budweiser print of "Custer's Last Fight." There were prints of Osceola, Sitting Bull, Tecumseh, and Cochise, and a dramatic sketch of Pontiac with forts burning in the background. There were crossed plastic tomahawks above the mirror, and toy bows and arrows were taped to the liquor cases, and a bumper sticker echoed the Indian writer Vine DeLoria's *Custer Died for Your Sins*.

"Oh, Paul. Didn't mean to keep you waitin'."

"It's okay, Charlie. How are you?" He extended a hand and they shook. Charlie was a thin old man who wore his white hair in a crewcut. The cataract had completely taken over his left eye now and Whelan wondered how long the right would last. Long-sleeve shirt, collar and cuffs frayed, and burn holes in his shirtfront. Charlie was one of a handful of old ones who could still speak the old Choctaw tongue. He smiled at Whelan and showed bad teeth.

A young Indian in a red headband came to the bar, pool cue in hand, holding out a buck for change. He gave Whelan a slow look, then turned away, too polite to make his hostility obvious.

Charlie took the dollar, made change, nodded to Whelan. "This fella's a friend of mine, Warren." The young Indian pursed his lips, nodded. He looked at Whelan.

"Shoot a little eight ball?"

"Not well enough to play with you, I bet."

The young Indian laughed and went off to the table in back.

"He's a pretty good boy," Charlie said. "Just can't see why whites want to drink here. So how you been, Paul?"

"I get by."

"Still a detective?"

"Sure."

"Runaways, still?"

"Seems to be what I do. Right now I'm doing something else, though. For myself. You heard about that guy they found in the alley up there between Leland and Broadway?" Charlie nodded. "He was an old friend of mine. I'm trying to find people who can give me information about him. I don't think the police are going to turn anything up."

"What can I do for you?"

"How about something cold first. And one for yourself."

"What kind?"

"I'll have what you're having."

Charlie reached into the nearest cooler and came up with two cans of Dr. Pepper. He held them up and laughed.

"Dr. Pepper, Charlie?"

"I give it up, the booze. It was makin' me sick to my gut, every day. Now I'm okay. Figure I can live a few more years this way."

"Good for you. It's too early in the day for me, anyway. Dr. Pepper it is. Charlie, I'm looking for a guy named Sharkey, and a guy named Hector Green. Know 'em?"

One of the Indians to Whelan's right looked up and then away. Charlie opened his mouth and then closed it again.

"Charlie, I'm just looking for Hector because of the other guy. My friend was talking to this Sharkey just a day or two before he was killed."

Charlie considered and nodded. He looked to the Indian closest to Whelan.

"George? Can we help this fella out? He's an old friend of mine. Got my nephew Alvin out of jail twice."

George looked at Whelan and nodded, then smiled shyly. "That Alvin sure was trouble. You a cop?"

"Used to be. Now I'm a private investigator with a problem."

"Everybody got problems. Hector in any trouble?"

"I think the trouble is the guy he's with, for some reason."

He nodded. "There's a building over on Sunnyside, had a fire there last winter. They boarded 'er up but there's lots of folks stay there. Hector and them other ones, they stay there sometimes."

"Other ones?"

"Sharkey and that Shinny that got killed."

"Oh. You know, there's a lot of burnt-out buildings up that way, George."

"This one's kinda red. Bout the same color as me." He smiled. Whelan bought him a beer, had a cigarette with Charlie and drank some Dr. Pepper. When he got up to leave, he dropped a ten on the bar.

"Get the boys a round, Charlie. Keep the rest."

He found the building with no trouble. It was one of three on the same block, one of scores in the neighborhood that had made "absentee landlord" a white-collar crime rather than a real estate term. There were three entrances leading to perhaps eighteen apartments. His work was simplified by the fact that two of the three sides of the building, entrances and windows, were totally boarded up, and in this heat no squatter would spend a night in an airless apartment. The main entrance had once had a glass door; now the pane was shattered. The boards from windows to two of its apartments bad been pried off. Whelan nodded to himself, muttered, "Shit" and clambered through the man-size hole in the glass door.

The smells of squalor inside the hall were almost overpowering, the air heavy with the ammonia smell of urine. He moved quickly up the silent, airless staircase and stopped at the first-floor landing. A knock brought him nothing. He tried the knob and the door opened. Within, he found the skeleton of a human habitation. Bare, dirty walls, curling linoleum, broken windows, cracked plaster and peeling paint, all of it lead-based and toxic. A place that had not seen maintenance for years before its abandonment. The fire had gutted the rooms in the back, and the charcoal smell and odors of burned wood and cloth hung in the air. The living room seemed to have escaped the flames, and it was here that some wanderer had made a temporary home. Fast-food wrappers and bread crusts littered the floor, and an empty green wine bottle lay on its side in a corner. Whelan squatted down, staring at the primitive surroundings and trying to make them tell him something of their inhabitants. He touched an old hamburger bun: brittle and hard, days old. He poked around a bit longer and then gave up. He left and went across the hall to the opposite apartment. This time he didn't bother to knock. The second apartment promised less than the other one. Fire had demolished the floor in all but one room, and the windows were still boarded up. Airless and dark, no one slept here.

He went upstairs to the second floor, reached for a doorknob and froze when he heard a sound just inside the door. He waited a moment, then grabbed the doorknob, turned it and threw the door open.

Movement in the room, someone moving away from the door. No time to think about it. He rushed in, turned the corner and found himself in a living room, facing a terrified woman in her seventies.

"Oh, Jesus. I'm…I'm sorry. I was looking for somebody."

She stared at him in open-mouthed terror made more pitiful by the fact that she wore glasses. One lens was gone, giving her a wall eyed appearance. She was sun-browned and filthy and couldn't have weighed more than eighty pounds. The hem of her skirt was torn and hung down in back to her shoes, and the black sweater she'd draped across her shoulders like a shawl was full of holes and festooned with loose threads. She seemed to be clutching a bag of some sort to her breast.

"I'm sorry, lady. Ma'am. I won't hurt you. I was just looking for a man named Sharkey. Do you know Sharkey?"

Without realizing it, he took several steps toward her and the little woman retreated to the farthest corner of the room. The air was heavy with her stench and her fear and he wanted to be gone. Then he caught himself and stooped down, resting on his haunches, and lit a cigarette. Made thus smaller, he gave her breathing room and she seemed to relax a bit.

"Cigarette?"

She shook her head. She stared at him, breathing noisily through her mouth.

"I know. Shitty habit. I'm really sorry I bothered you. I'm leaving." He put three singles on the floor and got up. "Something for your trouble." When he was at the door, she spoke. He was surprised at the loudness of her voice.

"Downstairs. He stays downstairs, with that dark man. But I ain't seen 'em. I think they're gone. Thanks for the money."

"Don't mention it."

He took the stairs two at a time and when he got down to the ground floor he burst outside and inhaled deeply. It was ninety-four, the air was suffused with the dirt and dust and exhaust fumes and acrid smells of a neighborhood coming undone, and to Whelan it was perfume.

He had lunch at the Subway Donut Shop, a little grease and saturated fats for his pains: three eggs over easy, side of bacon, toast and hash-browns. He ate at the counter and watched the young Greek work his grill. The Greek would walk away for a few moments, talk to a customer without looking at the food on the grill, then return to flip ham steaks, burgers, eggs, bacon, grilled cheese sandwiches and cube steaks, all of them done perfectly on one side. He was good, all right, though not the best. The best was an old black man named Leon, who ran a grill at sixty-third and Woodlawn and could do anything this Greek kid could do and more, cutting the potatoes as they were ordered, standing over his grill and slicing paper-thin disks of potato onto the grill with an evil-looking knife and singing to his radio as he worked.

A couple of men nursing coffee in the coolness of the shop were men he'd questioned earlier. One nodded to him, the other looked away. There was no sign of Woodrow. He ate, dawdled over his coffee, had a smoke and waited to see if anyone he knew would come in. Eventually he grew restless and left.

He didn't really consider it a sixth sense but something close: he knew when someone was waiting for him upstairs in his office. Perhaps it was the rarity of the event, or perhaps he sensed some subtle change in his environment, but he could tell as he came up the stairs, he could always tell. In this case, there wasn't much of a mystery, and the change was in the air and it wasn't subtle. It was Right Guard, oceans of it, on a fat sweaty body.

Bauman was inside the office. His beefy form was jammed into the guest's chair and he had one foot on Whelan's desk.

"Oh, good. Company. You pick my lock, detective?"

Bauman shrugged. Slowly he turned in the chair. He raised an eyebrow, smiled slightly and sank back, folding his arms across his chest. Whelan walked past Bauman and sat down behind his desk.

He stared at Bauman and said nothing. Bauman stared back, a slight smirk on his face. He was dripping sweat. Whelan was conscious of the trains pulling into and out of the el station half a block away.

Bauman smiled and Whelan raised his eyebrows in question.

"What, you don't feel like talking, Whelan?"

"It's my office. You talk. I'll listen politely."

"Okay, we'll talk. Anything you wanta tell me?"

"Nope. Where's Rooney?"

Whelan thought he saw Bauman's lip curl at the name.

"Forget Rooney."

"Why?"

"Rooney's an old lady. He's got a cold. Summer cold, he says. He's six—no, five months away from retirement."

"And what can I do for you, detective?"

"Like I said. You can talk to me. I'm lonely."

"It's your deodorant."

"Shut up about my deodorant. Least I use one. Come on, Whelan. Let's talk."

"You made it pretty clear you didn't want to have anything to do with a private investigator, remember? You guys said my help wasn't needed."

"Yeah, I did. And you didn't listen." Bauman leaned forward, hands clasped in front of him. "You been a real busy guy."

"You know what they say, Bauman. You want something done, you have to do it yourself."

"What, you think we're not good at our jobs?" Bauman was smiling.

Whelan leaned forward now. "I don't know what to think,

pal. He's been dead almost a week. We put him in the ground this morning, Bauman, and you guys don't have any suspects."

Bauman's face flushed and he straightened up. "No, huh? We don't have suspects? Listen, Whelan. You know something? You give me a pain in my ass. I can't figure out what it is you do for a living. I don't like your stinkin' office, I don't like the way you talk, I don't like the way you look at me. Look how you dress, you look like a goddamn Filipino."

"And I'm wild about your clothes, Bauman. I could hear your jacket a block away. I got a rug on my kitchen floor with that same pattern."

Whelan thought he saw the trace of a smile on Bauman's face.

"Where do you get shirts like that, Whelan? I mean, I see the Mexicans and P.R.'s wearin' them but I wouldn't know where to find one."

"Wouldn't find one your size, Bauman. There aren't any three hundred pound Mexicans."

Any trace, any chance of the smile faded. Bauman nodded. "Yeah, I'm carryin' a few extra pounds, but I can still do what I got to do, Whelan." He shrugged and forced a smile. "But I didn't come here to put the arm on you."

"Could have fooled me. Why did you come here?"

"To find out why you think you have to nose around up here, do my job for me. Makes me curious, Whelan."

"I told you. I get the impression nothing's going to happen."

Bauman inclined his head and stuck his tongue into his cheek. "I don't think that's it, Whelan. I think you know we're lookin'. Maybe not the way you'd like us to but we're doin' it. I think you got some other reason for wantin' to have your nose in this, that's what I think."

"I think ten years from now, you still won't have a suspect."

"No, huh?" Malice in the small gray eyes now. Bauman nodded, sat back, crossed his legs and showed a hairy ankle above blue socks. "Well, now. Now, why's that? 'Cause I'm, what? Fat and stupid like all the other cops, right? No suspects. Well, my friend, you're wrong there, you know that?" He feigned a friendly smile and pointed a fat finger at Whelan. There was almost palpable tension in him and Whelan wondered if Bauman was about to come over the desk at him. He found himself planning his strategy: move to his left, hook to the body, uppercut to the head. No, better yet, hit him with the ashtray and run like hell. It might work. He relaxed when Bauman let out a gust of air and held up two fingers.

"Two, babe. I got two."

"Two? I'm impressed. Who—" and the identity of the first hit him. "Oh, yeah, of course. That's why you're here. It's why you came the first time."

Bauman shrugged. "Makes sense to me. Your business card, you knew the guy, nobody knows what kinda deal the two of you had going. The guy's wife said you two were good buddies, you tell me you didn't see him all that much. Then you go around asking questions about this guy your friend was talking to and—I assume—asking about me, about who I was looking for. How am I doin' so far, Whelan?"

"Not bad at all. It makes a kind of sense. Except—well, you don't know me, so I suppose it fits better to you than it does to me. If you knew me, you'd know…I'm not what you'd call a violent person."

"You were a police officer. We're all supposed to be violent." Bauman looked at him coldly for a moment, then waved a hand at him. "Aw, we know about you, Whelan. And I don't really think you whacked your pal or this other poor fucker we found. Shinny. You didn't know about Shinny when you started asking around. Which puts you out of it. And you helped me out a little. I didn't know I was looking for Sharkey till you started asking people about him. I used to know Shinny but I didn't know he was runnin' around with these other two lately"

"Is that when you saw the connection?"

Bauman smiled and shook his head slowly. "I look at two stiffs a week apart, both of 'em killed the same way, I don't need any help makin' connections."

"Shinny was stabbed, I thought."

"Stabbed after somebody beat 'im to death."

"Would Sharkey be capable of that?"

"Naw. Jeez, sounds to me like he's one of those guys, he's afraid of the dark, for Chrissakes."

"Hector, then?"

"The Indian guy?" He looked up at the ceiling, frowned, apparently at the cobwebs dangling from the light fixture. "Swell place, Whelan." He grinned. "No, I don't think so. He's a pretty good size boy, this Hector, but he's just a big, easygoing guy, likes his wine, likes Sharkey, don't let nobody get near Sharkey. But he wouldn't kill nobody, from what I know."

"What *do* you know? How do you know enough about these guys to—"

Bauman looked away. "I just know, is all. I know some of 'em. I spent a little time up here. I seen you before, Whelan." He made a pistol of his fingers and pointed it at Whelan. "I seen you around here. You like these guys."

"I know some of them from the old days."

"When you were a cop."

"Right."

Bauman waved his arm, taking in the office. "Why would you quit for this? To do this stuff? I mean, didn't you like being a cop?" Whelan almost laughed at the genuine puzzlement in Bauman's face.

"Sometimes. But it's not for everybody."

"You lose your nerve? That happens to some guys."

"I just got tired of it."

Bauman shook his head. "I know lotsa guys leave the force but they usually do it for money. You did it—what, for this?"

"Not exactly. When I quit I wasn't sure what I'd be doing. I just kind of fell into this. But I like it."

"C'mon, Whelan, you can't be making anything at this."

"I make enough. I don't have a lot of overhead." He laughed and Bauman smiled. "I also don't pay rent or a mortgage. I've got a house. And I make pretty regular money doing odds and ends for a couple of lawyers."

Bauman made a grunting sound. "I hate lawyers."

"I'm not wild about some of them but they're overpaid and sometimes they send some of it my way."

Bauman didn't answer. He looked around the room and appeared to be thinking of something else.

"So what do you really want, detective? I'm not a suspect anymore, right?"

"You? Nah. You're one of those guys—you probably voted for McGovern, right?"

"You betcha."

"That's what I figured. No, you're no killer. I just want to know what you know. Anything you want to tell me?"

"I don't know anything. I know I'm looking for a guy named Sharkey because Art Shears was talking to him, trying to get him to open up about his past for some reason."

"His past." Bauman chewed on his lip. "He say anything about Sharkey's past?"

"He told me Sharkey was from here originally, and he thought Sharkey was on the run from something."

Bauman snorted. "They're all on the run from something."

"Well, he's running now."

"Yeah, he sure is. He's trying to stay alive."

"But you're sure he wouldn't be the killer."

"No, but I think he knows who whacked Shinny and your friend and he don't want to be next."

Whelan looked out the window. "And you've got a suspect, you said. A real one" Bauman smiled and said nothing. "So you're ahead of me, detective."

Bauman got to his feet. "Guess so. You just don't talk to the right people, my friend." He walked toward the door. "See you around, Whelan. And if you hear anything, I want it, hear?"

"Sure."

"Don't gimme that 'sure' bullshit. You don't know me, either, Whelan, or you'd know I'm good. I'm real good and I'll find this fucker if he's still around." He nodded curtly and left.

Whelan pulled his chair over to the window. For a long time he watched the street traffic, the el and the cars and the men standing in bored groups by the pool hall, and gradually it came to him. He saw the pale, frightened face in the window above the alley and realized the difference a badge sometimes makes.

Six

After a while he went out for cigarettes. He made a circuit of Lawrence, Broadway, Wilson and Sheridan. In front of the Popeye's Chicken on Broadway he saw Don Ewald talking earnestly to a heavy-set woman with a shopping bag; the woman seemed to be looking for a way around him. Behind Ewald, a taller young man with sandy hair seemed to be adding a few words to the conversation. Whelan turned the corner quickly but Ewald saw him and waved. He waved back and thought he saw the other young man give him an odd look.

A young woman was standing at his office door when he got back. Even before he reached the second-floor landing he could hear her nervous pacing. He heard her sigh and took the last few steps in a hurry.

"Hi. Are you waiting to see me?"

The young woman turned quickly. "Are you Mr. Whelan?" She was slim and dark-haired and very young.

"Yes. You must be Miss Agee." She nodded and smiled. He fumbled for his key, fumbled putting it into the lock, dropped it on the floor and laughed at himself. He opened the door finally, held it for her, closed it behind her and dropped his cigarettes.

"I like to make a good first impression. Cool nonchalance is what I try to cultivate." She laughed nervously and he decided he liked her already. "Have a seat, Miss Agee."

The office suddenly seemed dusty and smoky and he opened the window wide.

"Were you waiting long?"

"Oh, just a minute or two." He could tell she'd been out there awhile; probably all the time he was strolling through the neighborhood, she'd been pacing in his dark, airless, foulsmelling hallway. A bright sheen of perspiration covered her face and neck.

"I got your messages, Miss Agee."

"My first name's Jean."

"Jean, okay. Paul Whelan." He stuck out his hand and she shook it. She sat back and looked around for a moment at his office.

"I've…I haven't been in the office much lately, so it's kind of dusty."

"Oh, that's all right." She turned around in the chair and looked back out through the clouded glass door to the hallway. "Are…are all the other offices empty?"

"There's an accounting firm down the hall." The jittery accountant had just become 'an accounting firm.' "And the first floor's full."

"Oh. I just didn't see anybody else on this floor."

"No, they're all on vacation, I think."

"It would scare me to death to sit up here all alone," she said breathlessly, and laughed.

"It scares me sometimes. I don't come in to work at night very often." And he found himself laughing. He looked at her. No one would ever call her beautiful, perhaps not even pretty. But cute. Terminally cute. Short dark hair framed a round face, with large brown eyes, a pug nose, a small mouth with full, swollen-looking lips. When she smiled, a dimple puckered one cheek. She wore a denim skirt that stopped a modest inch above the knee and a sleeveless white tank top. She was small-breasted and athletic-looking and she reeked of sunshine and fresh air and seemed wondrously out of place in his office. In Uptown, for that matter.

"What can I do for you, Jean?" He thought his voice had suddenly developed a reedy quality, and he cleared his throat.

"I'm trying to find my brother."

"I see. And how did you hear…how did you come to me?"

She flushed prettily. "Well, actually, I called another… agency. That I found in the, you know, the phone book. The Jacobsen Agency."

He nodded. "Good outfit. Very high tech."

"And they recommended you."

He tried to hide his surprise. "That was neighborly of them. They say why?"

"They said they were completely tied up, that all their… people were, you know, busy with another operation. That's what they called it, an operation."

Whelan laughed. "And they didn't say their 'people.' They probably said 'resources.'"

She laughed a little. "They did. That's what they said. All their resources."

"It's how they talk over there. But they're busy, all right. They specialize in debugging. About a week and a half ago, surveillance devices were found in a booth in a downtown restaurant. Nice place, fancy place, that caters to politically prominent people, and this particular booth is the favorite of a group of our fine public officials believed to have ties with organized crime. The Jacobsen Agency was called in to do a sweep of the restaurant, and when all the other high-stepper-type restaurants went into a panic about bugs in their booths, every joint in town wanted the Jacobsens to do a sweep. So they'll be busy for a long time. And they're going to be very rich very soon."

She smiled. "They said it was your specialty, anyway."

"What?"

"Finding missing people. Missing persons, I mean."

"I guess it is. You want to tell me about your situation?"

"Well, I'm from Hope, Michigan. Do you know Hope?"

"Oh, sure. Been through Hope a few times," he lied. He was surprised at himself, but only once before had a female client ever come to the office, a much older woman. The sunlight coming through the window picked out reddish highlights in Jean Agee's hair and he was conscious of her perfume. "Nice little town," he embellished.

She took out a Kleenex and wiped along the sides of her nose and he straightened.

"Listen, Jean, it's kind of hot here. Let's go down to the coffee shop and get some coffee. We can talk there."

She seemed to be relieved at leaving the office and he prayed that the little cafe under the tracks would have its air conditioning cranked up. They went out and Whelan waved to Gus and Rashid, who made strange Persian gestures toward Jean Agee and rolled their eyes.

The greasy spoon, a tiny, nameless restaurant that could seat two dozen people on its best day, had a small menu, decent coffee and a wonderful air conditioner, and a wall of cold air struck them as they opened the door. He heard Jean Agee make a little moaning sound.

There were five booths, four of them taken, and he slid the girl into the last one. He waved at Rickey, the delivery boy, and a chatty woman in her fifties took their order, coffee for Whelan and iced tea for Jean Agee.

"So, Miss Agee…Jean, you're looking for your brother. And do you have reason to believe he's in Chicago?"

"Yes. He moved here. I mean, eventually, he came here. He wrote us—my mom and me—from here. He said he was going to find work here."

"When was that?"

"March. Late March."

"And that was the last time you heard from him?" She nodded. "No calls, letters, nothing?" Another nod. "And he made contact with no one else?"

"Nobody I know of."

"All right. Tell me about your brother. Let's start with a name."

"Gerry. His name's Gerry. Gerald, really. He's three years younger than I am. So he's twenty-two."

Whelan nodded. She looked younger than twenty-five. "What else can you tell me?"

She frowned. "He's very…serious. He's sensitive, he takes things very hard, and he's been having trouble, ever since he got out of the service. He just…" She shrugged. "He didn't seem to know what to do with himself. He tried a number of different things in Hope, just to please Mom, really, but he was miserable. He started drinking—no, that's not true. I think he was drinking in the Army."

"Lots of people drink in the Army."

"Well, he started drinking really heavily. Sometimes outside the house, in taverns and places like that." Places like that. She sounded as though she'd never been in one. "And then at home. We kept finding bottles under his bed and in his closet, and in his drawers under the clothes. And he got into some, you know, some trouble. Just like any other young guy, really."

"Well, what kind of trouble? Did he murder anybody?"

"Oh, no, nothing like—Oh, you were joking. Okay, you're right, he's my brother so I assume everything he did is normal." She blushed prettily and Whelan swallowed. "He got into some fights, he and some friends of his. In the taverns. You have to understand, Mr. Whelan—well, you've seen Hope, so you know there isn't a lot to do there. Gerry is very intelligent and he's a very…complicated person and I think he should have gone to college. Instead he went into the Army because most of his friends were going into the service or into trades."

"So after he started getting into trouble, then what? He left town?"

She nodded. "He was giving Mom some money every month but he still managed to put some away for himself, so he left and said he was going to try to get into construction, get some experience and maybe get into a trade union. He said he wanted to use his hands, wanted to get into something where he could travel around the country and, you know, be able to find work, be employable. So he came here. And it, I don't know, it just didn't work out for him."

"How long did he…How long has he been here?"

"He got here in the fall, in September."

Lousy timing for anyone who wanted to get into construction, Whelan thought, but held his tongue.

"He called at Christmas and told us things were working out real well for him, but they really weren't."

"Where was he living?"

"The YMCA." She smiled and he could tell that she thought she'd just given him vital information.

He sighed and said, "Which one?"

She blinked, opened her mouth and then closed it abruptly.

"We have...a lot of YMCAs, Jean. Do you know which one?"

"I've been there. I went there to find him. It's very big. And it's on Chicago Street. Chicago Street in Chicago, Illinois. Gerry thought that was funny."

"Chicago Avenue. That's the Lawson YMCA. It's the flagship. The big one. I used to eat in their cafeteria when I was a police officer. My precinct house was just down the street from there."

She brightened visibly. "You were on the police force?"

He laughed. "Yeah. Why, does that make me a better detective?"

"Well...doesn't it?" She was serious.

"Whatever gives the client confidence," he said. "Okay, your brother was staying at the Lawson Y till—when? Do you know for sure? What did they tell you when you went there?"

"Our letters started coming back in March. They couldn't forward them, the people at the YMCA. The last one Gerry wrote us was from March, March seventh or eighth, and he was still there then."

"And you had no one here to call, no family or friends?"

"Nobody. I think that was part of the appeal for Gerry." She leaned forward. "He was really starting to think of himself as a washout, you know? He wanted to get a new start somewhere but it had to be a place where no one could watch him. In case he, you know—"

"In case it took him a couple of tries to get it right." She smiled and nodded. "Okay, so what did you find out when you went to the Y?"

"They couldn't give me an address or anything. They said he just left to move to a new neighborhood, to get closer to construction projects."

"They say which one?"

"This one."

He nodded and took a sip of his coffee. To buy himself a

moment, he looked around the restaurant. A cabdriver he knew was just getting up from the counter and they waved to each other. When Whelan looked at the girl again, her eyes were clear and there was an expectant half smile on her face. Why bullshit the girl?

"No address up here, huh?"

"No." Her eyes read his and the smile began to fade.

"Jean, people don't move into this neighborhood looking for work. This is not what you'd call a big...you know, a big construction area. There isn't much of that going on here. New buildings don't go up very often around here, old ones get burned down. Uptown is a—" He fumbled for a polite way to describe the neighborhood. "—sort of a low-rent district. Do you understand what I'm saying?"

She nodded hesitantly. "It's one of your bohemian areas. A lot of artists and people like that, like the Village?"

He looked away for a moment to keep his face straight. Uptown, haven for struggling artists.

"Not exactly. There are a few people up here who just live here because it's cheaper, but the general population is just poor. It's a port of entry for a lot of people—a guy from Mississippi might come up here with his wife and kids in the family beater, looking for work, and more than likely he'll wind up in Uptown. And with a fairly good chance he'll wind up *living* in the beater for a while. There are a lot of homeless people, hundreds of derelicts, runaway kids, new immigrants from Southeast Asia and a lot of other places. There are also a lot of drug addicts and disturbed people, people generally down on their luck. It's not a nice place and not a safe place, and I'm telling you these things because if a young guy from Hope, Michigan, came into town with a few bucks in his pockets last fall and wound up here six months later, it's not because he found a ground-level spot in the construction industry but because he's in trouble. You told me he has a history of drinking trouble, well, this is the place for men—and women—with that kind of trouble. If Gerry's up here, he's not in such good shape. I might be wrong but that's what I think."

Her face seemed to stiffen and there was something odd about her color, and Whelan suddenly realized she was holding her breath. She looked just past his shoulder and he saw her bite her lower lip, and he looked away and sipped his coffee and didn't look back till he heard her sniffle.

She was not the first person whose naïveté he'd been forced to stomp on. It was always necessary at some point but never easy, and there was a pain in the brown eyes that made him wince inwardly.

She straightened in the booth and did nothing to wipe away the tears that ran in twin tracks down her cheeks; her lips formed a swollen little pout but her eyes were frank and challenging.

"Mr. Whelan, when he told me he was moving to Chicago I was sick to death, I knew it wasn't the place for him, I just knew it. I told myself it could work out for him, it might be the best thing for him, but when he left I could have just died. But I came here to find him, and that's what I'm going to do. I don't care if this is a nice neighborhood or not, but…could you find him for me? Or just find out if he's alive."

He smiled at her. "I never had a sister. I would have liked one just like you. Well, I can try, but there are a few things you should know. One is that I'm involved in something else right now, something important to me personally, and quite frankly, it doesn't appear to be anywhere near finished. So I couldn't promise you anything like full time on this. It might even be best for me to recommend another detective."

She pointed a finger at his chest. "I want you to help me."

"Any special reason?"

She looked slightly flustered, shrugged and said, "I don't know. I just do."

"Okay. Next thing is, if Gerry's still here, he won't be easy to find. It's hard enough to find somebody on the street, but there's a good chance that Gerry's taken some steps to make sure he doesn't *get* found. He might not even be using his own name."

She gave a little shake of her head. "Gerry is my best friend. My brother and my best friend. He wouldn't hide from *me*."

"If you were that close, all the more reason why he wouldn't want you to see him living in a place like this. You've got to understand that he's probably living in a dump, he's working some menial job if he's working at all." She opened her mouth to debate further but he stopped her with an upraised hand. "But there are ways to look, some steps we can take to determine whether he's living here in a normal pattern."

"Normal pattern?"

"Sure. We can find out if he's got gas, electric or a phone, like a normal person, or if anyone else knows anything about him, any of the state or city agencies. The V.A., since he was in the service, Public Aid, Unemployment."

She smiled. "Is it that easy to get information from all those places?"

"Hell, no! It's illegal, some of it." The waitress looked at him from the next booth and gave him a little smile, and he lowered his voice. "It's illegal now for the utilities to give out information about who has service. But I know a guy at the gas company, and a woman I did some favors for works for the phone company. With Commonwealth Edison, I'll have to use my boyish charm."

"Your serenity, maybe."

"What?"

"Your serenity. You seem to be a very…serene person."

He laughed. "Actually, I'm having a very bad week."

She smiled sympathetically. "You hide it well."

He shrugged. "Anyway, I know people at the government agencies, and they don't have to withhold information from me, so maybe we'll turn up something that way. But I'm still not optimistic about your situation. I think you have to be ready to accept the fact—"

"That he's dead."

Trying hard to be tough, and he liked her for it. "No, Jean, I don't think he's dead. *That*, you might have heard about. He'd have some kind of identification with his belongings and the authorities would somehow have gotten a hold of you. It doesn't always happen that way but the odds are fairly good that you would have heard. What I was going to say was that he might have left town. He could be anywhere in the country."

He watched her eyes widen and saw that the thought had never occurred to her that he might have kept on moving, might literally have gone underground.

"I want to get all the unpleasant stuff out of the way, so I want you to understand this: he could be in Seattle, he could be on a dirt road in Texas, he could be in Mexico. And if that's the case, he'll be real tough to find unless you have other resources."

She composed herself. "Speaking of which—what are your…rates, do you call them? Your charges?"

He sighed. "Like I said, I won't really be putting full time into this for a while, so I don't see how I could really charge you a normal fee or anything like it. And if nothing turns up around town, there wouldn't be any point in taking your money."

"But you'll still be spending your time."

"Some. I can do some of these things over the phone in a half hour. I can do most of it out of my office."

"It doesn't seem to me that you'll ever get rich, Mr. Whelan."

"Something I've never wanted to be. Time's a lot more important to me than money. Now, down to business. Do you have a picture of Gerry?"

She grinned and went fishing in her bag. With a couple of deft movements she pulled out a snapshot.

"It's not, you know, real recent."

Whelan groaned. "Oh, Lord. A graduation picture?" He looked at the photograph and shook his head. "Not real recent, huh? You have a gift for understatement."

"Well…we had a few others but they just…they weren't very good. We had one, it was taken at a wedding. Gerry was drunk. You wouldn't even recognize him."

"How am I going to recognize him from this? You know what this is? It is a creature unique to this society, a genuine artifact of American folk art, the graduation picture. Think about it—did yours look like you?" She shrugged and looked sheepish.

"Mine sure didn't. Made me look like Gary Cooper. The idea is to produce for each family one shot, just one shot, of the little darling they want, the way they want the world to see him.

You have a clever photographer, tricky lighting, an airbrush, and he takes two dozen shots to increase his odds. He checks out the kid when he comes in, wearing a tie that's crooked and his father's suitcoat. With the proper slant of the head and the right amount of savvy from the photographer, you get miracles: a profile shot and nobody'll notice that Johnny's left eye is two inches lower than his right eye. You get Johnny to look up at the camera, like an angel trying to make eye contact with God, and nobody sees that Johnny's got no chin. And teeth, you want nice teeth for Johnny? No problem, the photographer's an artist, an unsung artist. Out go Johnny's bad teeth and in go Burt Lancaster's. No cowlick, straighten his nose, brush away the creepy sideburns he's wearing, wipe off his attempt at growing a mustache. Maybe Johnny's got ears like a fruit bat, so Ma and Pa ask the photographer to go that final yard and give Johnny nice ears. The result is one of these." He flicked the photograph with his nail and Jean Agee laughed. It was not a nervous laugh anymore, but husky, throaty and rich and had the sound of something used often.

"It's a nice picture, Jean. It just probably isn't Gerry the way I'd see him. Tyrone Power, maybe, but not Gerry. I wish I had the drunk shot."

She gave him a rueful look and pointed to the picture. "This is how I like to think of him, though. Sorry."

"It's okay. Maybe it'll do what it's supposed to do. Okay, I'll make a few calls and do a little marching and we'll see what happens. Is there somewhere I can reach you? I assume you're staying at a hotel."

"I'm at the Estes Motel." She wrinkled her nose and Whelan laughed.

"Interesting choice. You get to experience the Magnificent Mile without paying top dollar." The Estes was one of several small motels at the south end of Michigan Avenue, out of the "action" but close enough to reach it. There was nothing remarkable about any of them, and a tourist with money wouldn't give them a second look, but you could stay in one and tell your friends you had a room a block or two from the Hilton.

"Did you plan it that way, Jean?"

"The cabdriver took me there from the train station. I told him I wanted to stay in downtown Chicago without spending a lot of money. It was his second choice. First he took me to a place called the Quality Inn. There was a nasty-looking tavern right across the street from it."

"Have you gotten to see any of Michigan Avenue?"

"Oh, it's gorgeous. I really had no idea a big city would look like that."

She looked over her shoulder out at Lawrence and he read her thought.

"But this is more like what you pictured, right?" She smiled and nodded. "Well, okay, Jean. I'll give you a call in a day or two and report on what I've found." A thought struck him. "You know, I may not be able to reach the people I need to talk to till Monday. People have a way of disappearing from the office on Friday afternoon in the summer."

She smiled and pursed her lips and the dimple reappeared. "I know I should just go back to Hope, but I can't leave. I've been here three days and it's driving me crazy already. I've called my mother twice long distance."

"Long distance on a hotel phone?"

She looked away. "I've got some money. I was going to go to Mexico with two of my girlfriends in September, so I've got that much to spend looking for Gerry. And that's why I'd feel better if we could talk about money. Isn't there a…couldn't I leave a deposit? Or something?"

"A retainer. A retainer is customary. You can give me a hundred dollars if that's convenient, Jean." She smiled, fished in her purse, came out with a wallet and drew a crisp hundred-dollar bill from it.

"A word of free advice: don't carry big bills, don't carry all your money on you, don't carry all your money in one place on your person when you go out."

She laughed and looked embarrassed. "That's some 'word.' I'm breaking all the rules at once, right?"

"Not all of them." He signaled for his check, paid the bill

at the register, then went back and left the waitress half a buck.

Outside on Lawrence they stood in front of the restaurant and watched traffic for a moment and he realized he didn't know quite what to do next. She looked at him and nodded.

"I'd better be going."

"I left my car at home, or I could give you a ride."

"That's okay. I can take a cab."

He flagged a Checker just pulling away from the pool hall and the cabbie hit his brakes and left a layer of tire on the pavement. He took her across the street to the cab, opened the door and helped her in. As she tucked her legs under her, the denim skirt rode up her thighs and he looked away as she fought with it.

"Driver, the lady would like to go to the Estes Motel on South Michigan."

The driver, a Nigerian-looking man in his fifties, nodded curtly. He looked at Jean Agee. "I'll be talking to you, Jean."

"Just give me a call and let me know what's going on, Mr. Whelan. Maybe you could even come down and I'll buy *you* a cup of coffee. Or lunch, even." She smiled and tried to look casual.

"Best offer I've had all day," he said, and closed the cab door.

He struck out with the utilities: no one had any record of Gerry Agee or Gerald Agee under any spelling. He went out. Late afternoon and the people of the street were running out of gas. On Wilson, where he made a quick stop at the Wilson Men's Club Hotel to show Gerry's picture, the dancers weren't dancing anymore. The neighborhood was parboiled and the boogiers had gone off in search of doorways. The street was still crowded with strolling groups of kids, Vietnamese women, students emerging with a groan from the air conditioning of the college into the lung-searing air of the street. No one at the hotel recognized the young choirboy type in the photograph. On the corner by the newsstand, he showed the picture to a couple of old men who ignored it and asked him for change. He gave them each a couple of quarters. A well-dressed man in a light blue summer suit stopped and stared angrily at Whelan.

"Don't you realize you're helping them buy more poison?"

"They eat sometimes," Whelan said, walking away.

"You're just poisoning them," the man persisted.

"Mister, you're out of your league here." He walked up Broadway. Across the street, in front of the Walgreen's where Art Shears had bought his last drink, a young dark-haired cop was flirting with two pretty Vietnamese girls. The cop waved to him. Whelan returned the wave. He no longer remembered the cop's name and told himself to take a look at the nameplate next time they were close.

Near Leland, where the el tracks made a gray curve across Broadway, an empty storefront bore a new sign:

SOON HERE
KAMPUCHEA RESTAURANT AND GROCERY
CAMBODIAN & CHINESE FOOD

He wondered what Cambodian food would be like and guessed it would be somewhere between Thai and Vietnamese, which made it a winner. "Hot damn," he said to himself. Then he realized he'd be trying this one by himself, more than likely. In the past, he'd tried out the new restaurants, the new cuisines, with Liz, who liked to eat almost as much as he did. He wouldn't be taking her to this one.

A drunk was urinating against a telephone as Whelan entered the alley. The man wobbled slightly and sprayed the area for several feet in each direction.

"Hey, don't let me interrupt," Whelan said.

The same somber face watched the alley from the third-floor window. Whelan waved and went up the back stairs calmly, making no effort to be quiet. When he reached the third floor, he saw the sun-bleached curtain move and banged on the screen door. When no answer came, he banged some more, louder, rhythmically, for perhaps half a minute.

"Lemme alone!" came the voice, louder than he'd heard it before. Angry and frightened.

"I just want to ask a couple questions. You don't even have

to let me in. How the hell can that hurt?"

"I don't want no trouble. I'm by myself here. Some of these goddamn people are crazy."

"Yeah, right. And they killed a friend of mine right down here in your alley and I want to find them."

"I talked to the cops. Talked to you, too. You said you weren't a cop. Now get outta here."

Whelan took a deep breath to stem his rising anger, told himself that this was just a bleached-out old man living his last days in a place that terrified him. "Okay," he said to himself. "Time to bring out the big guns."

"Hey, buddy. Look out your back window for a second." The curtain moved slightly, then moved a few inches, till Whelan could see the old man's pale blue eyes and the old man could see the twenty-dollar bill he was holding up to the window. The eyes seemed to latch on to the bill for a moment, and then the old man surprised Whelan by laughing, a high-pitched wheezing laugh but genuine, and the old man shook his head.

The curtain fell back and he heard shuffling footsteps in front of the door and the old man's voice muttering, "This place is like a goddamn movie." The door opened and then the screen door, and Whelan found himself staring at a slightly potbellied old man of medium height. His white hair was thin and worn short but hadn't been cut for some time: it was beginning to cover his ears and his collar. He wore a faded flannel shirt with the sleeves rolled up over his elbows. He smelled musty, a stew of old cotton, body odor, mildew and cooking smells.

He looked Whelan over briefly and then stepped back from the door. "You come on in. I don't need nobody knowin' my business."

"Thanks." He entered the apartment. The old man moved back a few steps and stood in the center of his little kitchen, unsmiling, and watched Whelan look around.

"It ain't exactly Buckingham Palace, is it."

"Nothing wrong with it," Whelan said, looking around. A battle was being fought here, a time-honored, familiar battle, and the old man was losing ground. The place was dusty and there were dirty dishes in the sink—a plate and a bowl and some silverware—but this was not a dirty apartment. There were a couple of hanging plants on the curtain rod over the back window and there was a vase of some sort on the kitchen table holding a few sprigs of dried flowers. He pointed to the vase.

"My ma used to keep dried flowers on the kitchen table," he said to establish some common ground.

"Habit I picked up from my wife," the man said. His late wife, Whelan knew. He could smell the ancient yellowing linoleum and the dry wood around the doors and windows and the tired dusty padding of the old man's furniture but could tell that this was a man who made a daily effort to stave off loneliness by keeping busy around his place, to fight off disorder and eventual surrender by keeping things together. Somewhere in the background Whelan was aware of a metallic voice, a radio.

The old man shrugged and said, "Come on into the front. I like to sit there. It's cooler."

Cooler it was, dark and almost comfortable. The stained shades were pulled down and there were more plants, in heavy stands in the various corners of the room. There was a short green couch and a heavy armchair, into which the old man sank. On the table beside him there was a yellow clock radio that made a jarring contrast with the forestlike darkness of the room. The old man saw him looking at the radio.

"I like to keep it on. Listen to the news. I got a TV there," he said, pointing to a small black-and-white on a folding table on the far side of the room. "I don't look at it much, though. I like the radio. It's what I grew up with." The pale eyes studied Whelan for a moment and then he looked at his radio.

"It's a nice one."

The old man's face brightened. "Five bucks. At that pawnshop over on Wilson."

"Got yourself a deal."

"You gonna stand there all day? Take a load off." Whelan sat on the sofa. "You like radio?"

Whelan nodded. "Yeah. I watch a little TV but I listen to the radio a lot. Some things radio just does better. Ballgames."

The old man nodded. "Yeah, I like the ballgames on the radio."

"And fights. There's nothing like listening to a big fight on the radio. I remember listening to them with my dad, late fifties, early sixties: Marciano and Archie Moore, Patterson and Moore, Patterson and Johanssen, Clay and Liston. There isn't any way watching a fight on TV can touch that kind of suspense."

The old man's eyes narrowed. "Marciano and Archie Moore? You don't look that old."

"I'm thirty-nine."

The old man nodded. "I heard 'em all on the radio, as long as they been puttin' 'em on the radio. I heard Dempsey."

"*You* don't look old enough."

"Yes, I did. I was seven or eight. Heard the first and second Tunney fights. Like yourself—I listened with my old man and my grandpa."

Whelan leaned back on the sofa. "Dempsey, huh?" The old man nodded and looked around the room and Whelan tried to get him back. "Cub game tonight."

"I know. Nine-oh-five from Houston. I'll listen for a while but they just can't play there in that place with the roof on it."

"You have a nice place here."

"I like it fine. It's what I got, so I'm satisfied. A lot of people my age, they're in homes or on the street. And I got a place of my own."

"You all right? I mean, around here?"

A smile came to the old man's face. "Are you nuts? Who's all right up here? Nobody belongs in a neighborhood like this, but it's the way things are."

He looked around his living room for a moment and Whelan tried to plug the silence.

"Look, why don't we go up the street, get a sandwich and something cold to go with it. And if you feel like it, you can tell me—"

The old man snorted. "You think you got to feed me?" He looked at his furniture. "It ain't much, is it. No, I don't guess it is. Seems like something to me, though. It's clean…well, a woman wouldn't think it was clean, but it's probably as clean as *your* place—am I right?" Whelan laughed and nodded. "And, anyhow, I lost my woman fourteen years ago. That's when I moved into this place. Makes more sense for one person to live in a small place. But at least I got a place. I ain't living in a cardboard box like some of these poor bastards. And the rent's paid, yes sir." He jabbed a knotty finger at Whelan. "Oh, I know what you thought. You thought for twenty dollars I was gonna do cartwheels and piss in the wind. Well, let me tell you something—"

"I didn't think anything like that at all, I was out of ideas. I was desperate to talk to somebody who could help me, that's all. There was no insult intended."

The old man appeared to be mollified. He nodded slightly and tapped his fingers on the worn arm of the chair.

"You're a private detective, you said. That last time."

"Yeah, but this isn't a case for me. This guy was a friend of mine and I want to see somebody's ass in storage for it."

He realized he had suddenly leaned forward and started to raise his voice, and he sank back onto the sofa, slightly embarrassed. The old man raised his eyebrows.

"Not as slick as you like to let on, are you?"

"Nope. Guess not."

"You any good at this kind of work?"

"Mostly I find runaways. And, yeah. I'm good at that. I don't exactly know why, I just am. But like I said, this isn't a case."

The old man nodded. "You got a name or did your people just send you out on the street?"

"Paul Whelan."

"I'm Tom Cheney."

"Pleased to meet you, Tom. And I like your place. I really do. It's better than mine."

"Well, now, young men don't usually have the time nor the inclination for housekeeping, and I lived with a pretty fair housekeeper for thirty-eight years, my Betty."

"You've got a twang, Tom."

Tom Cheney shook his head. "*You* talk funny. I speak the

king's English. At least, the way I was taught in school."

"Where was school?"

"Greybull, Wyoming." He smiled.

"What's a fellow from Greybull, Wyoming, doing in Chicago?"

Cheney shrugged. "In the thirties, everybody was movin' around. People'd go all across the country to find work. I came here, made some money, went back home and got married. Wasn't much for me out there except cowboyin' so I come back here, worked in the stockyards and for the railroad, made me some money. Sent a lot back home to my folks and Betty's dad and my brother. He's still there. Earl."

"You never see him?"

"Haven't had the money to go back, not since my father's funeral. Nineteen sixty, that was." Tom Cheney's attention drifted for a moment, and Whelan wondered if he was thinking of the great windswept vistas of Wyoming and the irony of living his last years in such a place.

"So, what did you want to know?"

The question startled Whelan, and he shifted on the sofa. "This is gonna sound odd, but I'd like to know just what you told the cops. Especially the fat one."

"The one with the crewcut? That one?" Cheney gave him a little smile. "Now he's something, that one. Smiled and called me 'sir' like they do but he's about as patient as a moose in rut. Kept that smile on his face like it was plastered there." Tom Cheney leaned forward and looked Whelan in the eye.

"Now, why do you want to know what I told him?"

"I think you gave him a suspect. Whether you meant to or not. And...I'm not sure—I just don't know what to make of him."

"You think he's a bad cop?"

"No, not really. I'm just not sure how seriously he's gonna take all this. He's a strange one, and I think he's got a hard-on for me and I'm not sure it's going to help him see this thing clearly. I've got a better chance to find something than he does."

"Why, 'cause you're smarter?"

"No, he's smarter than he looks. A lot smarter."

"Be hard *not* to be smarter than he looks."

"Yeah. But he's just too much of a hard case. He'll scare off more information than he'll collect. So. What do you think, Tom? You want to trust me with what you told him? Tell you what, once you tell me what you've told him, I'll be happy. I'll have exactly what he has and he can't do anything about it. And if you don't trust me, you can call him and tell him. And he'll be at my door in five minutes."

Cheney rubbed his hands on his pants and nodded. "This is pretty interesting, isn't it?"

"That's one way of looking at it."

"What in the world was your friend doin' down here?"

"Oh, Jeez. He was…things weren't going real well for him and he was trying to start over. He was going to write a book, had this idea to write a book about the streets up here. He'd been talking to some of these guys that live around here, in particular to an old guy named Sharkey, who he thought had a 'real story.' He thought this guy was on the run. Ring any bells?"

Tom Cheney pursed his lips. "Nope. I don't know nobody out there, Whelan. Only people I know is people who live in houses. I ain't no gentry but I don't have much call to talk to somebody that lives in an alley."

"I can understand that."

"I don't know this Sharkey. Same name as the fighter, huh?"

"Same name."

"Almost beat Dempsey, you know."

"Read about it. Thought he was getting hit low and complained to the referee while the fight was still in progress and Dempsey cold-cocked him."

Tom Cheney nodded and sighed. "I'll tell you what I told that big one. And it ain't much. You're gonna think you wasted your time. I heard something that night. Heard somebody talkin'. Somebody angry or scared or something. Two voices, I guess. And I heard noises like people fighting, and I heard a garbage can go over. And I went to my window there and I saw…two men. One of 'em was down too close to the wall for me to see clear but the other one was over near the, you know, the entrance to the alley."

"Near Leland?"

"Yep. And he was close to the streetlight, so's I saw him clear. I saw him real clear. He was young, with kinda long hair, red, it looked to be, and he was real skinny."

Whelan thought for a moment, excitement mixed with disappointment. No description of the man beneath the window, but this other man, the young one, fit no description he'd heard so far and he realized he'd already made his first mistake, that of anticipating what a witness would say.

"The man beneath the window—was he doing anything you could see?"

Tom Cheney looked down for a moment, rubbed his hands on the tops of his legs again, then looked up at Whelan.

"He was goin' through the pockets, I think. Couldn't say for sure."

A faceless man going through the pockets of the dead Artie Shears. He felt sick, chilled. For a moment he could say nothing. Finally he took a deep breath.

"But you couldn't tell anything about him."

"Nope. And I'm sorry."

"It's okay. And the other guy, the young one with red hair, what about him? What was he doing, exactly?"

"He was watching. He was kinda leanin' forward, looking into the alley."

Whelan thought for a moment. "You think they were together?"

"No. This young one, he took a step or two into the alley, then he froze, like. Then he started moving backwards, real fast, and then he took off runnin'."

Whelan got up from the sofa.

"You gonna go?" Tom Cheney's disappointment was obvious. "You don't want a cup of coffee?"

Whelan was about to plead a heavy schedule but heard himself say, "Sure, I'll take a cup of coffee. And here, for your trouble." He took the twenty from his shirt pocket.

Cheney looked at the bill, waved it off and started for his little kitchen. "Shit, I don't want that. I was only gonna take it if you turned out to be an asshole."

Whelan laughed. "And I didn't?"

"Not yet, anyways. How do you like your coffee?"

"Black."

"Good, 'cause that's how it's coming."

SEVEN

He walked back to the office and on a hunch called Jerry Kozel.

"Sergeant Kozel," the voice droned, and Whelan laughed.

"Hey, sarge, now you sound like all the other desk sergeants. They send you to school for that?"

"Oh, hi, Paul. How you doing?" He didn't sound interested.

"I'm okay, Jerry. Am I calling at a bad time?"

"No, no. No problem," Jerry said but didn't sound convinced.

"I won't keep you," he said, surprised at the reception. "I want to know if you can tell me anything about—"

"Al Bauman," Jerry Kozel said, and now he laughed.

"You reading minds these days, or has he been asking about me?"

"You say something to piss him off?"

"Not that I know of, unless you count my existence, which seems to piss him off. What did he say?"

"He wanted to know, did I know you well, why did you quit the force, are you honest, did you ever take as a cop. Uh, let's see, did you have anything going on the side, were you dangerous, ever take anybody out in the line of duty, were you a drinker, ever gamble. Like that."

"I'm flattered to be the object of his lust. We're both interested in the same case."

"Art Shears."

"Yeah. And Detective Bauman's got a hard-on about me. Can't make up his mind whether I'm a suspect in his case or just meddling in it. What he's sure of is that he doesn't like me, and I can live with that. I don't like him either. Is he a straight cop?"

"Oh, he's straight all right. Don't fuck with him, Paul. He's bad, he really is. These other guys that run around playin' John Wayne, they're just pulling on their dicks, you remember how that is. But Bauman is just what he looks like. A tough fucker with not much of a sense of humor and no patience. Thinks he's a one-man avenging army. He's had five citations and been suspended once. Undue force."

"Somehow that doesn't surprise me. What about his partner, this Rooney?"

"The Odd Couple. Rooney's a short-timer, wants to be home at his place in Wisconsin catching walleyes and Bauman wants to go to war. They don't care for each other much."

"Anybody who likes Bauman?"

"His ma did but she's dead."

"When he gets on a case, is it his custom to go a little bit crazy about it?"

Jerry Kozel laughed. "Yeah. He's got his share of nicknames, but the one that tells it all is 'C.C.' Constant Cop. He don't let go for nothing, Paul."

"But he's straight?"

"You mean is he on our side or the other side? He's ours, far as I know. And Paul? You never talked to me. He asks you, you haven't talked to me since last year."

"Okay, Jerry. Thanks."

J.B. showed him into the captain's office. Captain Wallis was looking at what appeared to be a budget and laughing. Across the room, stuffing envelopes, Eunice laughed with him. Whelan wondered what their secret was. The captain looked at Whelan over the tops of his glasses. "You're growing fond of us?"

"I'm growing dependent on you. More questions."

"Have a seat. Coffee?"

"No, thanks. I've had about seventeen cups already. I won't sleep again till Sunday."

Whelan took the side chair and straddled it. He laid the picture of Gerry Agee on the captain's desk. "Know this kid?"

The captain looked at the picture for a moment, then shook

his head. "No, I don't. How about you, J.B.?" The guard paused at the door and came back. He looked at the picture for a second and shook his head.

"He live up here, he don't look like that no more," the guard added.

"Is this boy involved in your…problem?"

"No. This is something else. Family's looking for him. He came here in the fall from a small town in Michigan and the city swallowed him."

"Sorry. Wish we could help."

"That's okay. I've got another one. All I have here is a description and not a very complete one. Young guy, very thin, with long red hair."

"That sounds like Billy." The Captain wasn't smiling anymore.

"Billy?"

"Billy the Kid," J.B. said.

"Billy the Kid, huh? Is he the local desperado?"

The captain shrugged and looked at his papers for a moment, then looked up at Whelan. "He's certainly one of the more volatile people around here. He's wild and quick-tempered and very…youthful."

The buzzer to the outer door sounded and J.B. left.

"Can you tell me something about this kid?" Whelan asked. "I take it…you know him pretty well. Is that what I'm picking up here?"

"He's a sort of special case for me."

"He's your project. I've got one too. Kid named Wade Sanders."

The captain raised his eyebrows and smiled. "I know Wade. I guess *everybody* knows Wade. Well, then you understand. The young ones are always sadder cases, it seems to me."

"Does this Billy have a last name?"

"Not one that he's telling. Most of the people he seems to associate with are older, so it was a short jump from Bill to Billy the Kid. He's a very tough kid. He came to the center one night when he'd been in Chicago for six months or so and it had dawned on him that he was a man in free-fall. He's from Missouri. Where, I don't know. He came to see me and he was drunk and babbling and lonely, and sick to death of this city, and he sat there in his black T-shirt with his homemade tattoos and he cried his heart out to me." Captain Wallis looked at Whelan for several seconds. He made a little gesture of helplessness with his hands and then let them drop. "I'll tell you, Mr. Whelan, I've never been so moved to help anyone in my life. It's not so much that he was helpless because every minister on earth has seen someone truly helpless. It's more that he…he spends every waking hour acting a part, the tough, hardened street kid who'd just as soon crack your skull open as look at you, and it bears no resemblance whatever to the scared country boy within."

"Who does he hang around with?"

"Oh, it varies. He has no particular set group of companions. My Lord, in a neighborhood of lost, lonely people, the poor boy doesn't even have a circle that he fits into." He gave Whelan a frank look. "And why, Mr. Whelan? Why are you looking for Billy? Do you think he might have killed your friend?"

"No. I think he saw it. I think he's a witness. I have information that puts him there at the time of the killing, and I think he saw the whole thing. Which makes him the best lead I've got, and probably the best lead I'm going to get."

"I see." The captain appeared to be struggling with something. "When he has money, he takes a room at the Wilson Men's Club Hotel."

"So does Wade."

"They may know each other, Mr. Whelan." He looked away and shook his head. "I've done everything I can to keep Billy here, to get him into detox and get him into a stable environment, just to put a roof over his head. I've even hired him a couple of times, just to keep him where I could see him. But the idea I have, the one that recurs over and over again, is to get him drunk and put him on a Greyhound for that little town in Missouri. Any little town in Missouri, because that's where he belongs. I know it's not my role or my business, but that's what I think."

"Maybe he'll turn out all right."

The captain thought a moment and shook his head slowly. "No. He's too explosive, too violence-prone. He thinks he has to fight to maintain his image. He'll fight over anything. In a small town, it would just get him thrown in jail. Here, it would get him killed. He doesn't even have Wade's prospects."

Whelan watched him for a moment. "You're not exactly a typical Sal Army officer, are you?"

"So they keep telling me downtown. My supervisors are wonderful people but they have trouble figuring me out." He smiled archly at Whelan. "And you had better be on your guard if you go looking for Billy, my friend. He's a very hard young case and if he finds that you're looking for him, he's liable to let you find him. Don't get into a street fight with Billy, Mr. Whelan. You don't want that to happen to you."

Whelan laughed. "I have every intention of avoiding violence, captain. But thanks for the advice."

He got up to leave and Captain Wallis came around the desk. "Mr. Whelan, I take it you heard about Billy from someone else. May I assume the police are looking for him as well?"

"Yeah. They probably don't have a name yet, but they have what I have. That a tall skinny redhead was there."

Captain Wallis nodded slowly and looked resigned.

He blew off another hour and a half on the street. Doorways and alleys and vacant lots. Vacant stares, half-truths, outright lies and occasional hostility. Several of the men he questioned knew Hector and Sharkey but hadn't seen them recently. The clerk at the Wilson Men's Club Hotel knew Billy but said Billy hadn't taken a room in weeks. A couple of older ones simply told Whelan whatever he wanted to hear. The high point of the afternoon came a little later.

His shirt clung to half a dozen places on his body and his feet burned, and he retreated into the cool darkness of a little Guatemalan restaurant on Wilson. The lone customer, he ordered *carne asada* and a chicken taco on the side. The carne asada was a little mountain of food, a dark spicy heap of carefully trimmed beef atop a hill of rice, and the taco came neatly wrapped in wax paper to hold it together and give the diner a fighting chance: there was a healthy portion of chicken inside, and lettuce and diced tomatoes and a few pieces of onion, but the crowning glory was the huge dollop of sour cream slathered from one end to the other. He took a bite and shut his eyes and moaned, and wondered how many Guatemalans died of heart disease. The hot sauce was an ordinary bottle of La Victoria but perfection would have made him suspicious.

He watched the street as he ate and was soon rewarded for his day's labors. Bauman loomed into view, horse-blanket coat flung over one shoulder, and Whelan watched with delight as the detective questioned a pair of very drunk old men that Whelan had talked to earlier. They had lied shamelessly to Whelan and were now giving Bauman the same treatment. As he watched, Bauman went through a series of poses and gestures, and his body language bespoke volumes. He scratched his bullet-shaped head, waved his arms, poked the men with his fat fingers, shook his head and at one point put a hand over his eyes. Finally he asked a question and one of the derelicts pointed east, toward the lake, and the other pointed due west. Bauman stalked away fuming and Whelan laughed happily. The Guatemalan woman came out from the kitchen to ask if there was anything wrong with the food.

He killed time at his apartment, waiting for darkness. He had coffee, smoked a couple of cigarettes and noticed that the pack he'd bought that afternoon was almost gone. He couldn't remember smoking that much and hoped he'd given away more cigarettes than he remembered. At nine he turned on the Cub game from Houston. Rick Reuschel was pitching and in three innings he registered six strikeouts. What the Astros were able to hit, they hit on the ground. Unfortunately, the Cub infield couldn't catch any of it, and at the end of three, Reuschel had a one-hitter and the Astros had a 3-0 lead. At a few minutes to ten, he left and walked once more to the red-brick building where the Indian in the bar had told him Hector and Sharkey stayed. He passed the vacant lot at the east end of the block and drew stares from a group of young whites in T-shirts sharing a six-pack. They leaned against a pair of rusted cars with Rebel-flag decals on the bumpers. He took a quick look to see if any of them were the kids he'd had words with on the street earlier in the week but recognized no one.

In the front courtyard of the building a pair of older men passing a bottle froze when he approached. He nodded to them and looked straight ahead and they moved off to one of the side doorways.

He stopped a few feet from the center door and looked up at the second-floor window and as he did so, something moved, quickly. He swallowed and went on, through the broken door, up the dank, foulsmelling staircase, past the first-floor landing and up to the second, and as he climbed, the air around him seemed to grow more humid and his breathing became more labored and his heart raced, and he knew he hadn't been this frightened, not even close, since Vietnam.

He paused at the second-floor apartment, debated whether to crash through and maintain surprise or knock and then go in. He listened at the door. For a moment, there was total silence; then, gradually, he became aware of breathing, of a heavy, wheezing sound somewhere away from the door and then a shuffling noise and the creak of old floorboards, and he realized that whoever was inside was about to leave the back way. He turned the doorknob and the door opened and then caught on its chain. He heard the shuffling sound more clearly and wanted to call out, then put a shoulder into the door. The chain did not give at the first impact and he swore and hit it again and the chain broke. As he entered the apartment he was aware of the sounds of a door opening in the back, and then he heard the wheezing again. There was the smell of sweat and sweet wine close by, and he had just fixed the source of the smells somewhere to his right, when, as he turned, a heavy blow to the side of his head knocked him against the wall. Another punch caught him just below his left eye and he smelled the man's breath and dirty clothes. He swung out of instinct, caught nothing but air with his left but landed a glancing right to the man's ear and was rewarded with two body shots that dug deep into his stomach and made him groan.

Great, I made him mad.

He felt himself sliding down the wall and stopped trying to punch back, covering his head tightly with his arms. A foot caught him in the side just as he hit the floor. He fell over on one arm and was kicked in the shoulder. He rolled onto his back and was about to roll over onto his knees when a shoe caught him in the side of his face.

"Oh, shit."

He lay back and listened to his own gasps. Somewhere just beyond his line of vision, the other man panted and gulped air. Whelan heard himself groan.

"You leave him be, hear? You come back around here, I'll bust your ass good." The man's voice trailed off to a gasp at the end as though he didn't have the wind for such a sustained speech. Whelan lay on his back and hoped the man wouldn't kick him anymore. He heard the man stagger from the room, heard the sound of a backdoor slamming, heard voices outside, then silence.

The left side of his face throbbed, all of it, from jawline to socket, and his ribs hurt and there was a dull pain just above his ear, and for a moment he thought he would vomit. He had a sudden recollection of a similar moment twenty years earlier, on another hot summer night over in Hamlin Park when he'd gotten in the way of the local crazy and spent half the night lying in the bushes with a closed eye and a fat lip.

Yeah, this brings back fond memories.

He lay there for what seemed to be a long time, gradually becoming aware of the noises of the street, sounds that a normal man would not notice or be aware of, the drone of cars going by down Wilson, the seemingly random, patternless conversations of passersby or the men in the vacant lot, or the old ones having a cocktail in the doorways. He heard a quarrel over money and negotiations over a bottle of wine, and from an apartment somewhere, a woman screaming obscenities in a voice filled with pain, and the sounds of glass breaking. In the background, far away, sirens and the low rumble of the el, the screech of tires and the whine of bad brakes. He was aware that he was beyond the fringe of his own world, that he could die in this rank airless place and no one would know for a week. He was making mistakes, large ones, and he counted himself lucky that he hadn't paid more heavily.

He got to his feet and leaned against the doorjamb to pull himself together. He looked around in the blue glow of the moon coming in through the window, tucked in his shirt, brushed dirt from his trousers, ran his fingers through his hair and left.

Outside, the streetlights seemed glaringly, gaudily bright and the courtyard was alive with activity. A new group of men stood in the open doorway of the side entrance working on Friday night's bottle. A pair of teenagers leaned against a beater parked out front, and across the way from him, a skinny, dark-haired man with what looked to be dried blood on his cheek muttered to himself and drew back into the doorway when he saw Whelan.

He took a breath and tried to walk casually out through the front gate, as though he'd just popped in for a look. He looked calmly around when he reached the old brick gateway, then turned onto the street. He looked up and down the sidewalk and headed north on Dover. A few feet ahead, a large shape separated its shadowy bulk from the trunk of a huge cottonwood.

"Hey, snoop. How 's the detecting business?"

Whelan stopped abruptly. Another law of life had proved to be true: at such moments in life, one can expect to meet the last person one would want to see.

"You don't have a home, huh, Bauman?"

"You're walking kinda funny there, inspector. You start partyin' early, or what?" Bauman squinted at him, grinned, craned his head forward and pretended to be having difficulty seeing in the glow from the streetlight.

"Hey, what happened here? You got an owie, Shamus?"

"I met with what they call 'foul play.'"

Bauman came closer and examined Whelan's face. He grunted and raised his eyebrows. "Who'd you run into, Marvin Hagler?"

Whelan hesitated for a moment, half wondering if Bauman already knew what had happened to him, then decided he was simply being paranoid. Bauman grinned amiably, tilted his head to one side and made clucking sounds.

"Nice work," he said, and Whelan felt a sudden, delicious urge to paste him one in the mouth. Another time, maybe. And it would have to be a sucker punch.

"How come you can never get a cop when you need one, Bauman?"

"You got one now. So talk to me."

"I believe I've found these guys, and I think I just made the acquaintance of Hector."

"Yeah? In there?" Bauman gestured with his chin.

"Yeah. It's where they've been staying, I guess."

Bauman gave him a short appraising glance, "How'd you know that?"

"You gotta know who to talk to, detective."

Bauman surprised him by laughing, and the laugh was genuine.

"Ah, I ain't so surprised, Whelan. I heard you were pretty good. You got your ways, I got mine. So you got a line on 'em, huh? This is their flop, huh? Or it was till tonight." He laughed again.

"Yeah. I guess I flushed them now."

"Do us any good to look around? You were in there awhile, they're probably long gone by now."

"How would you know that?" Bauman gave him a stiff shrug and looked away.

"Should we go in and have a look, Whelan?"

"Waste of time. I heard them leaving."

"*Them?* You sure?"

"I heard the sounds of two men. One jumped me. Pretty big, he seemed. Pretty good, too. I think I landed one and he landed about twenty. Smelled of muscatel. He warned me off."

Bauman looked at him. "What'd he say?"

"Said, 'Leave 'im be.' Said if I came back he'd bust my ass good. Seemed sincere, too. I heard somebody else leaving just before this guy belted me. I figure it was Hector watching the door and Sharkey leaving." He looked at Bauman closely. "You were out here all the time. Tailing me."

Bauman shrugged.

"So where's your partner?"

Another shrug. "I'm on my own time here. I'm, you know, doing my own thing. Got nothing to do with him."

"On your own time."

"That's right", Bauman said. He looked away, uncomfortable for the first time.

"You need a hobby, detective."

Bauman smiled slyly. "This is my hobby, Whelan. It's what I do for a living, it's what I do for kicks. It's me, babe."

"You're a piece of work. I'll give you that."

Bauman nodded curtly. "You're right. I am. Come on, let's go get you put back together. I'll give you a lift to your place. That where you want to go?"

"It'll do." The Caprice was parked in front of a hydrant at the far end of the block. Bauman put in a call on the car radio to get the beat cops watching for Hector and Sharkey. Then he drove Whelan home. He followed Whelan in, looking around the place with interest.

"This is nice. Great old house. Dogshit neighborhood, though."

"Hey, the yuppies are moving in. A couple of houses across the street were just sold to young couples with money and delusions of grandeur. This was my parents' house. I moved in after my ma died."

Bauman looked around and nodded absently. "Mine died a long time ago. Long time ago."

"Sit down. There's beer in the fridge. And pop."

"You got an ashtray?"

"On the mantel."

He went into the bathroom, turned on the light, looked in the mirror and laughed. Hector, if that was who it was, was a very efficient bodyguard. There was no blood to speak of, except for a cut at the top of his ear, but one cheekbone was swollen and already a deep purple, and there was a blue bruise along the side of his right eye. The bridge of his nose was pink and swollen and there was a dark abrasion along the left side of his face where Hector had kicked him. That one would be darker by morning. If none of the swelling or discoloration went away, he'd be damn near unrecognizable tomorrow.

"Jee-zus. This guy did a nice job."

He heard Bauman laughing in the next room. "I was afraid to break it to you," he called out. "Your career in pictures is through."

Whelan washed, got ice from the refrigerator and wrapped it in a towel, then came into the living room and sat in the armchair across from Bauman, holding the ice to his injuries for a minute or two apiece.

Bauman puffed at a small, thin cigar and looked at him for a moment, then burst out laughing.

"Yeah, I'm a million laughs, Bauman."

"Naw, naw. I'm not trying to be a prick. It's just that…well, it just occurred to me, I prob'ly got to take you off my suspects list now." He laughed again and, after a moment's hesitation, Whelan joined him.

"I understand you've been asking around about me."

"Who told you? That Kozel?" Whelan shrugged. "That's who told you."

"He used to be my partner, Bauman. Don't get pissed at him. He's not your friend, he's mine."

Bauman nodded. "Fair enough. I just wanted to get a line on you. Figure out what kinda guy you were, 'cause you were stickin' your beak into this stuff so deep. I wanted to find out who you were."

"So now you know."

Bauman smiled and shook his head. "Not hardly, babe. All I know is you're honest and you were a straight cop. That's all

I know. And far as it goes, I got nothing on you that says you'd be a killer."

"We talked about this already. We both agreed I'm not a killer."

"You never can tell, though. Never can tell who's gonna turn killer."

"No? Well let me help you out there. You can shorten your list. Take me off."

"If I do, so what? Don't mean a thing, don't mean you're not involved."

"Come on, Bauman."

"I got too many questions about you. So how come you're not a cop no more? You like it, I can tell you like it. You were a straight cop, you got citations—"

"It was too much. *This* was my beat. I got sick of it."

"This?" Bauman frowned. "How'd you get a beat in your own neighborhood?"

"I didn't live here. My folks did. I lived up on Armitage."

Bauman raised his eyebrows and grinned. "Ooooh, trendy."

"No, not then it wasn't. The Young Lords had their headquarters in the church across the street from my house. On a hot Friday night there were fights all up and down Armitage. Cook in the local restaurant took a knife to one of the gang kids and the restaurant got firebombed. The local liquor store was burned out three times in three years."

"Montoya?" Bauman's smile widened.

"Yeah. You know Montoya?"

"Oh, sure. That was *my* beat when I was a uniform. Sure, I know Montoya. I got the call on all three of those fires, Whelan."

"Ever find out who did it?"

Bauman shut his eyes and began to laugh. "Montoya."

Whelan laughed and Bauman nodded. "It's true. Couldn't prove shit. All the Fire guys could prove was that it was arson. Witnesses saw a Latin guy setting one of 'em. Montoya said it was this other Mexican, named Ruiz. Owned a liquor store up the street, but we think it was old Montoya, playin' the persecuted businessman and collecting on his insurance."

Bauman's thoughts seemed far away for a moment, then he looked pointedly at Whelan. "So how come you left, really? You got a citation the month before you left."

"That was the reason. Not the citation, the way it happened. It was just the last in a long line of things. That day, the one I got the citation for, you know what happened?"

"Yeah, I do. You and Kozel responded to a call, stopped a robbery, Kozel got hit—"

"Yeah, Jerry got hit."

"And one of the perps."

"Yeah, by Jerry. And I hit the other guy but he lived. So Jerry got hit, and both of these guys, these two young clowns that thought they were the Daltons, coming out of this liquor store at us with their guns going. And they got hit, and a guy across the street got hit and a woman inside the store took a stray round, and the squad car took a half dozen rounds and caught fire and I just stood there looking around. There were five people down and a car on fire, and for a moment it was like I was in a chopper above it, looking down at the bodies and the flaming car, and I could see Jerry on the sidewalk, not moving and his eyes kind of staring up at me funny, and I had this… pressure in my ears. I couldn't hear for a minute, and I thought for a second I was back in Vietnam and I think I was pretty close to losing it. And that was it for me. No more cop."

He was looking down at the rug, and when he looked up again he saw the surprise in Bauman's face.

"You were in 'Nam?"

"Yeah."

"And you saw action?"

"You could say that. I was a medic. I never shot anybody but I saw all the same shit."

"I thought you said you voted for McGovern."

"I sure did. I would've voted for him twice but that tradition seems to be dying out. Yeah, sure I voted for him. Anybody who could have gotten some of those poor fuckers out in one piece, I would have voted for."

"A medic, huh?" Bauman nodded slowly.

"Yeah, a medic. I don't kill people. So take me off your list. The guy you're looking for lives in an alley someplace—"

"No." Bauman pointed a tobacco-stained finger at him. "It's *not* one of these guys. It's an outsider. It's somebody who don't live here. These guys don't kill like this. We got two people dead and a couple guys lyin' low so they don't get whacked, and you can't tell me a wino is behind it all, you can't. It's an outsider."

Whelan looked at Bauman for a moment and decided that it all made sense, solid sense. Unless someone out there living on the street was not what he seemed.

"So tell me, Whelan. Why are you a private eye?"

"I'm not sure I can explain it. I don't work for anyone else, for one. I don't punch a clock, I decide when I'm going to work and for whom. I do things that interest me—I only take certain kinds of cases. Runaways and missing persons, mostly. I work for people that need help. I provide a service, I don't follow somebody's wife around or anything like that."

Bauman gave him an amused look. "I had you wrong, Whelan. You're not a sleaze, Whelan, you're a weirdo!" He laughed and flicked a long gray column of ash at the ashtray.

Whelan pointed a finger at him. "But you are, too, Bauman, or you wouldn't be wandering around here at night on your own time."

Bauman took a puff on his little cigar. "What else I got to do? Might as well do something useful."

"You do this for every case, or just this one?"

Bauman stuck his chin out. "All of 'em. All of 'em. Specially if the department drops one. I stay with all of 'em. I mean, eventually I got to let go of an old one and pick up on something new. But I stay with 'em. You never know what'll turn up if you keep the pressure on."

"So we use the same advanced, scientifically proven method. The dog method."

"What's the dog method?"

"You know, you sink your teeth in and clamp 'em down and shake the thing till the meat falls off."

Bauman nodded. "Yeah, that's what I do. And also I play

hunches. Lot of hunches, since I got a lot of time."

"So what is it about this case? You guys were giving out that robbery line five minutes into it and I don't think for a minute that you bought it."

Bauman wrinkled his nose. "Department does. They got a hundred open homicides any one time, a lot of 'em the kind that get into the papers, so—"

"So a couple down-and-outers aren't such a big deal in the greater scheme of things. So why does it make a difference to you?"

Bauman blew smoke. "They're all the same to me. It's just that these ones aren't gonna get solved unless somebody goes out of his way."

"Which is what *I* was doing."

Bauman gestured at Whelan's face with the cigar. "Yeah, and I'm real impressed by the results you got."

"Is that right? Well, I got a name to go with the guy you're looking for."

Bauman stared at him for a moment and Whelan was amazed at how quickly hostility replaced self-assurance in the face.

"Come on, Bauman, ease up, huh? You're gonna have a stroke in my house and they'll think I killed you. Go have a cardiac somewhere else, okay? I'm in this one. He was my friend and I want to find the person who killed him, and more than that, I want to know why he had to die. And you can't keep me out."

Bauman leaned forward and put his hands on his knees. His face was red, his eyes wide, and a vein was standing out just below the hairline. "You listen to me. If I want you out of this. I'll get you out. Whether you want to or not. You might have an accident."

"Sure, Dempsey."

"Hey, look what a wino did to your face."

"What makes you think you're as good as he is? Besides, I'd have to scream 'police brutality' and we'd both be out of action."

He watched Bauman smother his anger. His jaw worked

and his breathing was audible. A walking explosion, a land mine in a loud jacket.

"And anyway, Bauman, you don't have a partner. At least, not one you can count on."

Bauman looked away and expelled his breath. "Aw, Rooney's all right."

"You told me he was an old lady. Your exact words. And I asked around about both of you. He's looking for a soft place to land."

"Aw, you know how some of 'em get. He's afraid something's gonna happen his last week as a cop. I suppose, I was in his shoes, I'd be wantin' out like he is. He's got his wife to come home to and they got grandchildren now, little ones, and they got a place in Wisconsin, talking about moving there. Me, I got time, oceans of it." He looked around Whelan's living room.

"You got a nice place, though. You like it?"

"I like it a lot but I don't like staying in it much. It's too big for one person, so I'm not here much."

"It's clean. You keep it clean. My joint, it's got—whaddya call 'em, the gray things you get under furniture?"

"Dust balls? Dust monsters?"

"That's it, dust monsters. I got 'em three feet long. I'm just there to sleep." Bauman looked around again.

"I know some facts about you, Bauman, but I can't quite put them all together. You told me you spend some time up here, you know some of these people. You knew Shinny, you said. Why is that?"

"I already told you—"

"No, I don't mean about this case, I mean in general. You hang around the streets a lot, you said you know the people. Why is that? Are you from around here originally?"

Bauman shifted in the chair. He moved his shoulders as though his jacket were too tight. "You a drinker, Whelan?"

"I like a cold beer now and then, particularly after I've just had the shit kicked out of me. Why? You thirsty from all this talking?"

"I'll buy you a beer."

"Fine with me." Whelan changed shirts and dabbed at his face one final time with the washcloth and Bauman drove them over to the Alley Cat, a lounge on Broadway not far from Whelan's office. Bauman parked his car in the bus stop.

Whelan ordered a Beck's dark and Bauman ordered a draft and a double shot of Walker's Deluxe. He sighed as his drinks were put in front of him. Whelan looked at the shot and beer.

"You take your drinking seriously, huh?"

Bauman sipped his whiskey. "Looks that way, right? You said I needed a hobby. This is my hobby." Whelan laughed and Bauman shook his head. "No shit, Whelan. I'm serious. This is what I do when I'm not…" He inclined his head to indicate the street. "I don't go out much. I really don't pay much attention to sports. I watch a fight now and then but that's about it."

"I had you pegged for a football man."

"I hate football. I couldn't play when I was in high school, so I wouldn't watch it."

"How come you couldn't play?"

"Practice started in July. I had a summer job every year and I couldn't quit till Labor Day." He looked around the bar. "So this is what I do with my time. Lot of guys, they drink 'cause they got nothing better to do with their time. I'm one of 'em. But I like taverns, I really do. Some of 'em, they're beautiful." He sipped at his whiskey and took a swig of beer. "So what about you, Whelan? You ever married, or like that?"

"No."

"Got a woman?"

"Thought I did but she's leaving."

"Leaving to go where?"

"Wisconsin."

"Everybody's goin' to Wisconsin. Why's she leavin'? She, ah, tryin' to *find herself*?" Bauman smiled and made a face.

"No. She's not an airhead, Bauman. She was married once and it was a bad one, and now she's not the most trusting or patient woman in the world. Besides, she's got a kid." Bauman nodded as if this explained a move anywhere. Then he frowned.

"Jesus, you're having a run of luck, huh? Your friend winds

up dead, your broad is leaving, and you get the shit beat out of you. Tomorrow's got to be a better day, huh?" He laughed hoarsely and shook his head.

"God, I hope so. I'm thinking of staying inside all day." He sipped his beer and watched Bauman.

"How about you? You ever get married?"

The detective shook his head curtly. "I had this…this one I was seein'. But…" He made a little wave in the air. He looked away and Whelan read his body language.

"It happens. They say there's more out there, though."

Bauman drank his beer and belched. " 'Scuse me. Yeah, they're out there. I just think I'm getting a little—what do they call it? Long in the tooth. Yeah, I'm getting a little long in the tooth to be 'dating,' you know?"

"I never liked it much myself."

Bauman looked past Whelan's shoulder out the window and grinned. "Lookit this one." An old man wearing a heavy jacket and wool cap despite the heat was rooting through the trash can on the corner a few feet from Bauman's car.

"Watch. He's gonna find dinner now. See?" The old man pulled out a fast-food bag, lifted the half sandwich inside, sniffed at it and wrapped it. "He's gonna put it in his pocket and save it for later, eat it in privacy." Bauman smiled and winked at Whelan. Whelan watched the old man tuck the sandwich in a coat pocket and search in the garbage for more food. "See? I like him. Name's…uh, Bennie. That's it, Bennie. He's about a thousand years old."

Whelan watched Bauman and smiled. He shook his head slowly. "*Why* do you know his name, Bauman? Why do you know his habits?"

A wariness came into Bauman's face. "I just do. So what?"

"But how?"

"You know how it is, you spend some time out there, you get to know things. You know some of these guys yourself. What're you making a big deal out of it for?"

"I don't know if I know them the way you do. And I still can't figure out why."

"I like 'em." He looked at Whelan challengingly. "I do, I like 'em. I talk to 'em, they're okay. They beat the fuck out of each other sometimes but they're okay. A lot of 'em, it ain't their fault they're out here. And they all got a story, every one of 'em."

"Just bums to most people."

Some of the red returned to Bauman's face and Whelan found that he was enjoying himself.

"They're not just bums. And fuck 'most people' anyway, all right? I know these guys. I'll tell you something, Whelan, some of 'em are better people than your asshole business types that make their living screwin' people."

"Calm down and drink your drink."

"Don't tell me what to do."

"Why are you getting so worked up?"

"I didn't like what you said, okay?"

"Just wanted to see how you'd react. Now I see."

Bauman studied him for a moment. "When I was a kid, it was just me and my brother and my ma. We didn't have shit. My brother and me, we had jobs, one job after another from the time we were nine or ten. My old man died when I was maybe five. Anyhow, he had a brother. My uncle Ray. I can't tell you much about my old man because I was too young to know much but I can tell you about Ray. He was the nicest, most generous guy I ever knew. He was good as gold to us. He lived in Milwaukee and came in to see us every month or so. I didn't know it at the time but he was comin' in to look in on us, give my ma a few bucks, make sure we were all right. Didn't have no wife or family of his own, just a job. I'm tellin' you, Whelan, his visits just lit up our fuckin' lives, my brother Joe and me, just lit up our lives. He brought us stuff, toys, candy, model ships, and he took us places, he took us to ballgames and the movies and museums and out for pizza and Chinese food or whatever. And at night when I was in bed I just kept wishing he'd marry my ma and become, you know, my father. And he'd just go back to Milwaukee and do what he did. And what he did was work. That's all he had, his job. And this." Bauman nodded toward his whiskey.

"You gotta try and picture this man, Whelan. He wasn't real

smart and he got through maybe eighth grade. He was kinda short and he was, you know, kind of a homely guy. And he just didn't have any kind of social life. Drank like a fish. I didn't know about it at the time but he really had a problem. Eventually, sometime when I was in my teens, he hit bottom. Started to get sick, lost one job after another, went on disability, lost that, lived on part-time jobs for a while, wound up on the streets. My ma went up there once to look after him, then she went up there after he lost his place, to try and find him, but she couldn't. Not that he woulda wanted her to find him. Anyhow, he died in the County Hospital at the age of fifty-two. And I look at these guys around here, these guys that stink like the alley and have pimples and shit all over their faces, and I see him, I know he was like this. So I try and spend a few minutes shootin' the breeze with 'em." He looked at Whelan, shrugged awkwardly and then looked away. He leaned almost imperceptibly away from Whelan and finished his whiskey, then took a deep drink of his beer. When he looked at Whelan again, his eyes were hostile.

"So…you said you had a name for this guy I want. Gimme it."

"Ask me nice." Whelan signaled the bartender and ordered another round. The bartender brought the drinks, stared for a second at Whelan's face, then took his money.

"Don't fuck with me, Whelan. I want this guy's name."

"Don't be so hostile or I'll make you beat it out of me."

Bauman stared for a moment and then gave a short bitter bark of a laugh. "Jesus, I dunno who's worse to work with, you or Rooney."

"Rooney. 'Cause I'll stay with this till it's finished. And way down deep inside, I don't care which one of us figures the thing out."

Bauman looked at him for a moment and then nodded slowly. "You're a slick one. Does everybody just get diarrhea of the mouth around you, or what?"

"I'm a good listener. I listen to everybody. They talk and I go with it. All my life people have been using me as a sounding board."

Bauman looked down at his drinks. "I guess so. Okay, Whelan, just give me the name. I'll buy you a drink.".

"I don't need any more drinks. You bought me one already. You can buy me lunch some time. Billy the Kid."

"What's that? A hot dog stand or something?"

"That's the name you want. Billy the Kid. Tall, skinny redhead, young guy with long hair. Twenty years old, maybe, good with his hands, short fuse. And probably not our killer anyway."

Bauman gave him an irritated look. "I don't need you to figure stuff out for me. I already told you, I don't think this was street people. Billy the Kid," he repeated. "Okay, Whelan. I owe you a lunch."

Two young women came in and sat at the bar, close to the door. They were in their twenties, both brunettes, both attractive, slender and tanned, and wearing loose white blouses to show off tanned arms. Whelan looked at them and at Bauman. The detective studied the two women, shook his head and lit one of his little cigars.

"The scenery here is beautiful," Whelan said.

"Yeah," Bauman said, looking back at the women.

"Should we buy them a drink?"

Bauman gave him an incredulous look. "What, are you crazy? I got nothing to say to them. Maybe you do—till they get a look at your new face—but I'm…shit, I'm old enough to be their father. They'd go home and tell their friends about the fat old guy in the funny clothes that hit on 'em." He puffed at his cigar and stared at the bar mirror. "They wouldn't want nothing to do with me."

Whelan laughed. "Thanks for the pep talk, Bauman. I feel a lot more confident. I think I'll be taking off. I've had a busy day."

Bauman laughed noiselessly. "You wanna ride?"

"Nah, I'll walk."

"Bad neighborhood," Bauman said, grinning.

"I'll have to chance it. How long are you going to stay?"

Bauman looked down at the bar. "Who knows? I might close the joint."

"See you around." Whelan left the bar. The air outside

seemed close and gritty. He took one last look in through the window. Bauman was staring down at the cigar he held in his big hand. There was no one on either side of him for ten feet, and Whelan had the impression that Bauman didn't even notice.

EIGHT

He awoke at a quarter to seven after dreaming that he'd fallen down an immense staircase. He hurt in many places: ribs, nose, jaw, the side of his head and his ear. The news from the mirror was no better: everything was discolored or swollen. He looked like a fighter in desperate need of retirement. He took two aspirin and made coffee and wheat toast. The toast hurt his mouth. It was at least eighty in his apartment, and he turned on the radio in time to hear the disk jockey predict that it was going to be "another hot one, folks."

To pamper himself a little he drove to work. Warm air seeped out of the vents when he turned on the air conditioning.

You are a fine car, he told the Jet. He parked outside a narrow storefront at the corner of Montrose and Broadway. A homemade variety of lettering proclaimed the storefront to be THE WAY MISSION. Just below the name, a small brochure, listing services and prayer meetings, was taped to the window. There was a tiny air conditioner above the door, whirring away with the sound of overstressed belts and unlubricated metal. He opened the door and was pleasantly surprised: the little relic worked and he was in cool air for the first time that day.

Don Ewald was sitting at the desk inside the storefront, poring over a *Chicago Street Guide* with the same young man Whelan had seen the previous day. Taller and with lighter coloring, he cut his sandy hair the same way and facially he could have been produced from Ewald's genetic material. Same tailor, too: specializing in plain blue shirts and dark slacks. Ewald looked up when he heard the door, smiled and got to his feet quickly. He looked at Whelan, poked the other young man, and said, "Hello, Mr. Whelan." To his companion he said, "Mr.

Whelan is a private eye." Whelan winced.

"Mr. Whelan, this is my friend and colleague, Tom Waters." Whelan shook hands with Tom Waters. He looked at the nameplate on the desk that read REVEREND CHARLES ROBERTS. Roberts and Waters—at least Ewald was slightly Germanic, but he had a suspicion that such gloriously Wasp names were commonplace in the Way movement. These names were now fashionable, with Messrs Meese and Watt and Deaver and Baker and Bush. You had to lop a couple of syllables off your name if you wanted to get anywhere in government, that was clear, and if your name ended with an "A" or an "O" you were dead in the water.

Tom Waters gave Whelan an uncomfortably intense stare to go with his meat-grinder handshake. Whelan noted the razorlike creases in his shirt and the perfectly combed and parted hair, and knew Waters was one of those people who chewed each mouthful twenty-one times.

"Really a pleasure to meet you, Mr. Whelan. Don was telling me about his conversation with you. You're looking for a couple of men on the run down here."

"Well, not exactly. They're not really on the run in your, ah, John Dillinger sense. They just seem to have gone underground and I'm trying to get some information from them, basically. They might be avoiding me…"

Waters was no longer listening. Whelan could have launched into filthy Army songs or pornographic poetry and Waters wouldn't have noticed. He looked at Ewald and saw the same look: they were both studying his facial injuries with a kind of awe.

"What happened…were you in a fight, Mr. Whelan?" Don Ewald spoke for both of them and Waters nodded.

Whelan sighed, knowing he'd be giving variations of his explanation for the next couple of days. "I went poking around somewhere I shouldn't have. The guy I ran into didn't like it. Take a lesson, guys."

"Good gosh," Tom Waters said, clearly stretching his street vocabulary to the limit. He shook his head. "You're looking for an Indian and a short white man, right?"

"Well…yeah. A fellow with mixed blood named Hector and the other guy's name is Sharkey. And I'm looking for a couple of other people too. For one thing, I'm looking for a younger guy, white, red hair, tall and skinny. Goes by the name of Billy the Kid."

Waters shook his head and Don Ewald blinked, screwed his eyebrows into a bunch and demonstrated intense mental activity. Waters seemed about to say something but stopped with his mouth opened and frowned, which made him look addled. A couple of streetwise guys in Uptown.

Ewald's face returned to something like its basic shape and he looked at Whelan disappointedly.

"I just don't know anybody like that, Mr. Whelan."

"Neither do I, sir," Tom added.

"Well, don't feel bad. I haven't run across him either. But if you see anybody like that, give me a jingle." He reached into his shirt pocket and pulled out a couple of business cards, handing one to each of them. They looked at the cards admiringly, smiled at each other and nodded simultaneously. They grinned at him: an adventure. *The Katzenjammer Kids Meet a Detective.*

"This guy shouldn't be hard to pick out in a crowd, Mr. Whelan," Don said, putting as much nonchalance into his voice as he could manage.

"Should be easy," Tom added. He put his hands on his hips and looked out the window, trying mightily to look world-weary.

"I'm glad you guys are so interested in this stuff. I've got another puzzle for you. This fella's family wants me to find him" He took Gerry Agee's picture from his wallet and let them each have a look at it. "Try to imagine him with a little dirt on his face and maybe a week's growth of beard."

Both young men leaned forward and produced more intensity, and Whelan suppressed the urge to laugh. After all, these were his colleagues now. Tom Waters inclined his head to one side. "Seems to me…I could be wrong, but I think I've seen him." He looked up at Whelan. "But he looks different now, just like you say. He's going bald in front. And he's…he looks a lot older, in his thirties."

"No, Tom. This kid is your age and he's still got all his hair, at least to my knowledge."

"Oh," Tom said, crestfallen. Don Ewald was squinting at the photo.

"It's okay, guys. Just let me know if you see anybody like him, or if you run across this red-haired kid."

Ewald looked at him, blinking. "You're looking…for a lot of people."

"Yeah, sure seems like it to me."

"This Billy the Kid," Waters said. "Mr. Whelan, is this guy…you know, that name and everything…"

"You mean, is he a hard guy? Well, don't try to hold on to him till I come. He's a handful, they tell me."

Tom Waters frowned slightly. "I'm not afraid of any of these men, Mr. Whelan. You can't do the Lord's work in a place like this if you're afraid."

"I can see that, Tom. Just be careful. You don't want a face like mine."

They both laughed nervously and Whelan left.

He spent the rest of the morning and the early part of the afternoon hitting all his contacts again. He stopped by St. Augustine's and this time talked to Father Collins, the slender Episcopal priest who was the actual administrator of the Indian center. The priest was a different type of source than Abby, and a conversation with him was a chess match. Shrewd and thoughtful, and said to possess a wondrous memory for faces, the priest was also intensely protective of his Indian clients. Whelan knew that when the priest looked at him, he still saw a blue uniform. Whelan accepted these limitations on his questions: the priest was a good guy, the Indians could use all the help they could get, and if you pumped your source for information he wasn't inclined to give you, you lost a source. There were few things dumber that an investigator could do. Whelan asked him about Billy—whom he said he knew but hadn't seen since Billy had scuffled with a couple of Menominee boys a few weeks earlier—and about Gerry Agee. Father Collins studied the photograph, shook his head and said simply, "Poor small-town boy like that will never know what hit him."

Whelan popped over to the Public Aid office on Broadway, tried the day-labor places and a rooming house on Lawrence and Gino the barber on Racine. Then he hit the taverns: the Wooden Nickel and the Red Rooster, and the Golden Goose, a striptease bar where the girls gyrated to jukebox music and provided their own quarters for their music. No one could tell him anything. Outside the Goose he saw Bauman and Rooney. They were parked across the street. Rooney leaned against the Caprice and Bauman blocked off the sidewalk and they took turns asking a pair of wobbling old men the same questions Whelan had been asking all day.

Why not? he thought and crossed the street toward them. Both of the detectives looked around as he approached, and Bauman nodded slightly.

"Afternoon, gents. How's business?"

Bauman shrugged and Rooney gave him a sour look, shaking his head at Whelan's new face. The two old men took this opportunity to waddle off and Bauman boomed out, "Hey, you two!"

The old men stopped as though shot. Bauman stalked over to them. "I ain't done with you yet, so don't go shufflin' off the first time I turn my head. You see these people, you get in touch with me, you hear? Call me at the number I gave you or leave a message with the Greek in the coffee shop. Awright? Now, go on, get outta here."

The taller of the two old men gave Bauman a look that should have withered his halls and Bauman laughed. "You don't like me, huh? Well, okay, fair enough." He grinned at them and then turned to face Whelan.

"So, Shamus. How's your face? Lookit his face, Roon. He was out boxin' last night. Right, Whelan?" Rooney pursed his lips and looked away, shaking his head again, an aggrieved pro in the presence of amateurs.

"He's not much good at this part of the work, our boy. Are you, Whelan?" He caught the malice in Bauman's eyes and read the message: Friday night was an aberration, this is reality.

"Guess not. Not like you professional law enforcement officers. Making a lot of progress, are you?"

"You doing any better? You're looking kind of sweaty, Whelan. No air in that beater of yours? Better wring that fancy shirt out, guy."

"I don't know about you, detective, but I don't wring mine out. I wash 'em. I'll put on a clean one if I decide to go out dancing."

"What's that mean? You wash 'em. Meaning what? Like I don't?" Bauman took a step in his direction and Whelan stood his ground.

"What's the matter, Bauman, I thought English was your native language. You have a problem with English?"

"No, no I don't. I don't have a problem with English, asshole. You got a problem?" Bauman's lips parted slightly and a thread of saliva hung from the upper lip.

"Detective Bauman, sir, fuck you and the horse you rode in on."

Bauman looked at him for a moment, and Rooney muttered, "Jesus," and then Bauman surprised him with a laugh.

"It's hot, Whelan."

"Yeah. It's hot and I've been out cruising all day. I've had all the sun I need for a month."

Bauman nodded and looked around idly. Halfway up the block, horns blared and a pair of motorists got out of their cars, apparently intent on doing battle.

"Lookit this. Lookit these two assholes," Bauman said. The motorists, a Latino and a Korean, gestured violently at each other, yelled, indicated stoplights and the relative merits of each other's driving, questioned each other's parentage in three languages and were about to come to blows when Bauman yelled out in a voice that could have brought down buildings. "Hey. HEY, YOU TWO!"

They turned and he held up his badge and walked a few

steps toward them and gestured angrily.

"Get back in your cars and get the hell outta here. Get in your cars, you assholes, or come with me." He kept walking till both men slid back behind the wheels of their cars. He kept yelling and brandished his badge as they drove by, and Whelan could see both drivers crouching down behind their steering columns for protection from the wrath of Albert Bauman. Bauman laughed as they drove off. At the next corner the Korean blew past a stop sign and Bauman laughed hysterically.

He walked back toward Rooney and Whelan, still laughing.

"Summer in the city, eh, Whelan?"

"You throw yourself into your work, Bauman. I'll give you that."

"Aw, I just like to have a little fun." He tucked his wallet back into a jacket pocket.

"So how about some help, Bauman?"

The detective looked at Whelan and frowned. Rooney gave a little irritable shake of the head. Bauman was right: Rooney would drive anyone crazy.

"You're shaking your head, detective, and you haven't even heard what I want yet."

Bauman laughed. "He wants ya to go through channels, Whelan. Right, Roon?"

Bauman looked at his partner. Rooney curled one side of his lip and Bauman laughed again.

"Okay, Whelan. So whatcha got, huh?"

"Got a case. A real one. With a client and a fee and the whole enchilada. Missing person."

"Family report it?"

"It's nothing like that. There's no evidence of foul play or anything like that. As far as I can make out, the guy was a drinker and ran into trouble and just dropped out."

"Went under, huh?" Whelan nodded. "You know he prob'ly don't want to be found, right?"

"Sure. I've got a picture. Sort of." He handed Bauman the photograph and the detective let out a whoop.

"Oh, lookit here, a choirboy. Whelan, this ain't a picture. It ain't a picture of anybody, you know that?" There was genuine mirth in Bauman's eyes.

"It's his mama's impression of him but it's all I've got."

"Lookit this, Roon." He showed the photograph to Rooney. "This guy prob'ly don't look anything like this. He's probably got warts and buckteeth and an Adam's apple like a pumpkin, and look what comes out of the darkroom. Shoulda seen my graduation picture. I looked like a priest. Your picture look like you, Roon? Oh, what am I sayin', they didn't have cameras when Rooney was a kid."

Rooney gave him an irritated look. "Yeah, they had *cameras*, for Chrissake, Bauman, they had cameras a hundred years ago. Mathew Brady—"

"Aw, fuck Mathew Brady, Rooney, I was just makin' a joke. Don't be such an old lady." He looked at Whelan. "He's got no fucking sense of humor." He handed the photograph back. "I never seen anybody remotely like this. How old is this guy?"

"Early twenties."

"Nah. Haven't seen him."

"Thanks, anyway."

"Don't mention it." As Whelan walked away, Bauman called out to him.

"Hey, Whelan. I been doin' some thinking. Maybe I'll look you up in a day or so. Pick your brain a little about this stuff."

Just what I need, he thought. "Anytime" is what he said.

Whelan parked at a meter that still had a half hour on it and walked east on Chicago for a block till he came to the Lawson YMCA. The desk clerk was a young man with a Wyatt Earp mustache and bright blue eyes. He gave Whelan's face a quick once-over, smiled and said, "Howdy."

"Hi, My name's Whelan and I'm a private detective."

"Outstanding!" the young man said, and Whelan laughed.

He explained his investigation, allowed the young man to scrutinize his license, and asked him if he remembered Gerry Agee.

The clerk nodded. "Oh, yeah, I remember Gerry. Okay guy. Real quiet, stayed to himself, you know? Lot of the other men here are older guys." He consulted the registration record and nodded. "Yeah, here it is. He split in April. April fifteenth, he paid up to. Then he took off."

"What else can you tell me about him?"

The clerk looked off into a corner of the room. "Not much. Like I say, he was real quiet. Just a nice guy. Seemed like, I don't know, a small-town guy. Country boy, you know?"

"Hope, Michigan."

The clerk laughed. "There you go."

"Did he have any places he went for fun? A tavern? Any friends among the men staying here?"

"Not that I know of. Listen, if you want, you can go up those stairs to the second floor. Turn left and you'll find the lounge. There's usually a couple of guys watching TV and one of them might be able to tell you about Gerry."

"Thanks. I appreciate your help."

"No problem."

The lounge was a wide room filled with dark furniture and dominated by a large color TV. The air was blue with smoke and there were a half dozen men sitting around the room in various degrees of involvement with the TV. The Game of the Week was on, Dodgers at St. Louis, and no one looked up when he came in. One of the men was fishing surreptitiously in a large standing ashtray for smokable butts. Whelan crossed the room and sat down beside him.

"Have a smoke?"

A worried-looking man in his early fifties, he nodded eagerly and Whelan held out his pack. Whelan took one himself, lit both and took a lungful of smoke. The older man took a puff, gave the cigarette a funny look and then broke off the filter. He took another drag, exhaled, sighed contentedly, said, "Thanks," and looked back at the TV.

"Gerry Agee," Whelan said quietly.

The man looked Whelan up and down, studied the bruises. "You're not a cop—right?"

"Right. Private investigator. His family wants to find him." He placed his pack of cigarettes on the wooden arm of the man's chair.

The man looked Whelan in the eye. "Could be he don't want 'em to find him, you know?"

"I know. But they hired me to do a job and I have to give 'em a break. I took their money, I have to make an honest effort to find the kid. You remember him?"

"I remember him," the man said, looking at the TV. "Younger than anybody else here. Didn't talk to nobody. Just sat over there in that green chair and read the papers. Looked at street maps all the time, tryin' to learn how to get around. You could see he didn't know the city. Not from around here at all."

"Can you tell me anything about him?"

The man shrugged. "He was just kind of a strange kid. Never said more than a couple words. Didn't seem to do much except walk around. Took walks a lot. I used to see him sometimes, walking around. There's not much I can tell you about him, but you could ask Harvey over there about him. He had the room next to that kid. He thought the kid was kinda crazy, he told me."

Whelan looked across the room and saw a tall sunburned man with thin blond hair. The man seemed to feel Whelan's gaze: he looked at Whelan for a moment and then looked away.

"Thanks. Here, take a few more smokes." He opened the pack and pulled out half a dozen, leaving himself three. The man mumbled his thanks and took the smokes eagerly.

Whelan went over and sat down on the couch next to Harvey. The blond man turned, took his time looking over Whelan's facial injuries, and looked away. Whelan was slightly uneasy. This was a man who did not take a lot from people. He held out his cigarette pack.

Harvey shook his head without looking at him. "Got my own," he said, with a slight twang.

Whelan watched the game for a moment, biding his time. The Dodgers loaded the bases and the Cardinal pitcher, the eccentric, perhaps even disturbed, Joaquin Andujar, hit the next

Dodger batter in the back. A brawl ensued, the Dodgers had a run and Andujar was warned for throwing at batters. He walked the next man on four pitches.

"Aaaah, shit," Harvey said, and fished a cigarette out of a pack in his shirt pocket.

"Cardinal fan?"

"I'm from Missouri." He shook his head. "Whyn't they take that guy out? Everybody could see he was losin' his head, that one."

"Yeah, well, your team's still better than my team."

Harvey looked at him with a small smile. "That's a fact."

"Fella over there says you knew Gerry Agee."

Harvey raised his eyebrows. "Friend of yours?"

"No. I'm a detective. His family hired me to find him. They haven't heard from him since March, when he was staying here. What can you tell me about him?"

Harvey looked back at the screen and shook his head, then looked back at Whelan. "He's a strange one." He tapped his temple. "Something missing up here. I don't know as I'd want him back, if I was his kin."

"Why? What did he do that was strange?"

Harvey shrugged. "Never talked to anybody down here but you shoulda heard him in his room. Had real interesting conversations in his room."

"In his room? With who? You mean with himself?"

Harvey smiled and tapped his head again. "All by his lonesome. Arguments, he had arguments. And you know what the spooky part was? He did the voices."

"The what? The voices?"

"The voices in the argument. He'd do both people, and his voice would get real deep when he was the other one."

Whelan thought for a moment of the cherubic photograph and tried to imagine that face contorted by madness, stalking a narrow room and imagining confrontations with faces from his past. He suppressed a shiver, blew out a long sigh.

Harvey smiled tightly and nodded. "Yeah, imagine wakin' up in the middle of the night and hearing *that* comin' through the walls."

"Was he...did he drink a lot before these episodes?"

"We didn't socialize, mister." Harvey allowed himself a smile. "Oh, I heard the sound of a bottle and a glass now and then but that guy wasn't just drunk. I'm telling you, he was crazy." He leaned forward and held Whelan's gaze. "That wasn't just liquor I was hearin'. That one's crazy."

"Do you know why he left?"

Harvey shook his head. "Didn't ask. Good riddance."

Whelan stood up. "Well, thanks."

Harvey looked up. "Sorry I can't give you nothing good to take back to his people."

"It's all right. It's important, all the same."

He went downstairs to the clerk.

"Did you get what you need, Mr. Whelan?"

"I got an earful. Tell me, when Gerry left, did he give you a reason?"

"No. But he talked a couple of times about trying to get into construction. He said somebody told him there were two big projects going up in Uptown."

"I live there and there's nothing going on that I know of. Did he have money?"

"Couldn't have had a lot or he wouldn't have been staying here."

"But, to your knowledge, was he in money trouble when he left here? Could that have been his reason for leaving?"

"No, I didn't get that impression. I think he just wanted to get out and find work. I told him he wouldn't like Uptown, though. Told him there were a lot of winos down there, that he'd just be seeing a lot of people he wouldn't like."

"He had a problem with winos?"

"Like I said, he was a country boy, you know? He just thought all the winos were dirty, lazy...you know, scumbags. He never gave anybody here any trouble, but the old guys would come in off the street to nurse a cup of coffee in our cafeteria, and Gerry didn't want anything to do with them."

Whelan looked around the lobby and then nodded. "You've

been a lot of help and I appreciate it."

"Hey, no problem."

He stepped out from the cool darkness of the lobby and the heat sucked his breath away. As he walked back to his car, he nursed a growing unease and realized that Jean Agee's case had gotten a little more complicated.

He drove east on Chicago to Michigan, eased the Jet into the barely moving traffic on the Magnificent Mile and allowed himself to watch the pedestrians—tourists, many of them—business types and stunning young women out shopping. He thought of Liz, and something tightened in his stomach. He got onto Lake Shore Drive and cruised past Oak Street Beach where the scenery caused him to lurch out of his lane and nearly into a Porsche. The driver gestured angrily with a car phone and Whelan ignored him. He allowed himself another look at the hundreds of young women sunning themselves shoulder to shoulder or playing volleyball; there were young men with many of them and Whelan couldn't remember ever having been a part of anything like it. For him, the lakefront had always been a place to take long walks and think.

He had told himself he'd wait till he had something positive to report to Jean Agee before calling her, but it now looked as though that wouldn't be anytime soon. He went back to the office to think. Across the street they were changing the marquee of the Aragon again. The Salsa Revue was apparently off to visit other ports, and Monday night there was to be BOXING: ROMEO VS. TILLIS 10 RDS.

He called Shelley.

"One message, baby. Miss Jean Agee." Shelley chuckled.

"And the message, Shel? Before you convulse yourself."

"No message, doll. She just asked if you were in and giggled a little and got nervous and said to forget about it."

"She's kind of lost in the big city, Shel."

"So you gonna show her the sights?"

He laughed. "No, she's a little young for me. There are laws, Shel."

He fiddled around with his desk for a while, paged through

the phone book looking for a mechanic to have a look at his car's air conditioning system, and finally found himself calling Jean Agee at the Estes Motel.

"Hello, Jean, this is Paul Whelan."

"Oh, hello, Mr. Whelan. I, I called you this afternoon..."

"I know, that's why I'm calling."

"I know this is probably irritating of me, I know you said you'd be in touch and keep me, you know, posted, but I thought I'd call and see if you had any, um, leads yet." She stopped for breath. "And I had some ideas," she added quickly.

"It's no irritation, Jean. I'm just a little embarrassed that I don't have anything to report yet. I've made a number of inquiries at places where I have contacts, and I made calls to the utilities and, basically, no one seems to have seen or heard of him. Also, I went up to the Lawson Y, asked around there."

"You did? The YMCA?" There was a tiny doubt in her voice that Whelan couldn't read. She said, "Uh-huh," and then it occurred to him that this wasn't what she'd expected to hear. She'd already been to the Y and this probably didn't seem like the most impressive detective work.

"You're thinking I spin my wheels on unnecessary things, right?"

She laughed and he could almost see her embarrassment. "You read minds, Mr. Whelan?"

"No, but I know the way most people view the work, and it's not really the way it is. Follow a police detective around if you want to understand monotony and wasted time. No clues, Jean, just people and their observations and recollections. All you've got, usually."

"No clues at all?"

"Oh, sometimes there are, but mostly it's a matter of covering the same piece of ground from every angle, asking the same questions of a widening circle of people till something turns up. And I just haven't turned anything up yet."

"Oh. Well, I'm sure you will—did you find out anything new at the YMCA?"

"Not really." No reason yet to tell her that her brother

might already have gone off the deep end, that he held enraged debates with himself, that he'd probably land in a padded cell before long.

She said, "Well…" and stopped. "I just thought I'd call and…" She wanted to talk.

"So," he said, and went fishing. "Are you getting to see any of Chicago?" Then he felt embarrassed: he'd asked her almost the same thing at their first meeting.

"I…I take walks during the day. *Lots of walks,*" and she giggled. "And I stay in my room. I don't know what else to do. I can't really go out at night by myself so I stay in and watch TV. I was in the park—Grant Park, right?"

"Across from you and down the street? Yeah, that's Grant."

"It's so enormous. I walked around there this afternoon." She stopped and before he could fill the gap, she sighed and said, "I was wondering…Maybe, maybe you could come down sometime, and I could buy you dinner and we could talk more about Gerry."

"Oh, well…anytime," he heard himself saying.

She laughed again and said, "We could do it tonight." It was more of a question than a statement.

"It so happens that I'm free," he said, and laughed with her.

"Is this…am I imposing?"

"No, not at all. My evenings are particularly unplanned these days. I'd be happy to come down, and we'll talk."

"I feel so stupid. I guess…I'm just not used to spending this much time alone, and I'm sure not used to being alone at night."

"Do you still live at home?"

"I did till about eight months ago. I've got two roommates now."

He was going to force conversation further but realized there was no need.

"Why don't I come by around seven? Too early?"

"No, no, that's fine. I'll be starving by then anyhow," she said, and laughed. He hung up the phone and listened to the conflicting signals he was hearing from himself: discomfort, just slightly, and excitement.

. . .

She opened her door smiling but the smile took a dive when she saw his face.

"My God, what happened to you? Oh, Mr. Whelan, if that happened while you were looking for Gerry, I'm really—"

"No, no, no, nothing like that. I overstep sometimes, and that's what happened here. I went somewhere I didn't belong and I had to take a few lumps. It's not as bad as it looks—most of it I got falling down some stairs," he lied.

He left his car in the parking lot of the Estes Motel and they took a long, slow walk over to State Street. The Loop was emptying out and there was a cool breeze coming in from the lake that brought the smells of the beach and the rocks and the harbor, the old fishing smells of his youth.

Amid the dark wood and bustle of the Berghof they ate sauerbraten and Wiener schnitzel and she spoke of her life in Hope, Michigan, and of her brother Gerry, and it was clear to Whelan that this young woman's world would never look the same if anything were to happen to her brother. He got her to talk about her lifestyle, about her two roommates, Linda and Karen, about her job as receptionist and sometime assistant to a very busy young dentist. He made a few disparaging remarks about dentists and their gouging prices and she laughed, and told him he had no idea at all, and went on to talk about the prices her employer commanded.

"My jaw hurts already."

"Your wallet would hurt when Dr. Walling was finished with you."

"I'd just tell him I couldn't afford to have teeth anymore."

"Oh, no, you wouldn't get off that easy. He's got more payment plans than a furniture store. He could get ten dollars a month from you for the rest of your life." And she threw back her head and laughed heartily.

He found himself questioning her, subtly probing for her personal history. She was single, had never married, had been "close" once. That there was no steady man in her life he assumed already: a girl stuck in a strange town would be calling her boyfriend, not strangers. He had her on the verge of launching into an account of that last serious attachment and then she appeared to catch herself in midthought. She gave her head a little shake, forced a smile and said, "That's old history."

"Old war stories, I call them."

"Don't you ever talk about yourself?"

"I don't know…I just…I don't try to conceal anything." He shrugged and realized he was slightly embarrassed.

"Not that it's any of my business," she said quickly.

"Oh, I don't mind—"

"It's just that all I know about you is that you were a policeman. You said that."

"Right. I was a police officer for a long time."

"And before that?"

He laughed. "Before that, I was in Vietnam. Actually, Vietnam and college—a couple of tries at college. Once on the G.I. Bill."

"You live alone?" she asked hesitantly.

"Yeah."

"Ever been married?" He frowned and she wrinkled her nose. "Come on, you asked me."

"You're right, I did."

"And I'm being nosy, I know I am. I won't stop where you did."

"I've never been married. And I don't really mind talking about myself, honest."

A seriousness came into her eyes. "You don't really have to tell me anything. I just want to talk and I think…I have this feeling that you're a very…unusual person. And I want to know why. If I'm prying, we can just talk about something else."

"No, you're not prying."

"Have you lived alone all this time?"

He laughed and fell back in his chair and she went a deep red and then joined him.

'I'm sorry, it just came out."

"It's all right. No, I had the usual male roommates a guy

has and then I started living alone. And your next question, if you actually get around to asking it, will be whether I had any women in my life during all this time I've been a bachelor." She nodded. "The answer is yes, several. One in particular that I've been...that I was seeing off and on for a very long time."

"And recently," she said, catching the change in tense.

"Right. Up till just recently. We met when we were kids and then we ran into each other later and got...involved. And broke up. And I got drafted and went to Vietnam, and when I got back I ran into her again and we started it up again and she wanted to get married. Her life had been going on at a normal pace, you see, while mine had been suspended. And I just wasn't ready to get married. Mentally I wasn't in the greatest shape, Vietnam didn't *improve* anybody. So we broke up again and a year or so later she got married to somebody else. Her marriage wasn't a good one, they couldn't work a life out. They even had a kid eventually, and I think it was a last shot at doing something that might make their marriage work."

"That's a shitty reason to have a baby," Jean said coldly.

"It's a stupid reason, but she turned out to be a good mother. It didn't help her marriage any, though." He looked around for a moment. "She'd been divorced a couple of years when we ran into each other again. One thing led to another and we started seeing each other, but I had a feeling that this time it was doomed from the beginning. I was just as interested in her the second time around, but her marriage—or the clown she was married to—took something out of her. She wasn't quite the same person. She wasn't as trusting, for one thing. And she was no longer desperate to marry Paul Whelan. So we saw each other for a long time and dated other people along the way and we just finally put an end to it. She's moving to Wisconsin." He shrugged and didn't know what else to say.

"Now I know I'm prying, and I'm making you uncomfortable. Want to tell me about being a detective?"

"Sure. Why not?" She sat with her elbows on the table and leaned forward slightly as he spoke. Her yellow summer dress set off her tan, her walks in the park had sunburned her cheeks and nose, and he was conscious of her perfume. She listened intently as he spoke about a couple of his cases and then began to reminisce about his days as a police officer. He sipped at a glass of Berghof dark and chattered and was aware that a pair of well-dressed young men at a nearby table were having trouble keeping their eyes off Jean, and he was pleased.

And eventually it surprised him not at all to find himself talking about Art Shears. He hadn't felt this much release talking to anyone in years.

"*That's* the other case you're working on?" She looked horrified.

"Yes. Why?"

"Oh, I feel terrible. I'm taking your time from something really important to you. Oh, Lord, Paul. I had no idea."

"It's all right. Basically I make the same rounds, ask the same people about Gerry and…the other people I'm trying to find. Besides, I'm not getting very far on that one, so it's good for me to have another situation to concentrate on."

"But how did you get hurt?"

"Poking around an abandoned building at night."

Her eyes widened. "An abandoned building? Oh, wow. My God, do you do this kind of thing all the time?"

"No. I'd have given it up long ago. It's *not* an exciting job. But two of the men I'm looking for were staying in this building and I tried to catch up with them there. And I guess I did." He laughed and she joined him.

"And I screwed up royally. They won't be back in that building again now that they know I've found their place."

"Now where do you look?"

"Who knows? Another building, the parks, I'm really not sure. It's the kind of situation where I need time or luck. Enough time passes, they'll come out and somebody'll see them. Or I've got to get lucky"

"Maybe they'll leave town."

"I doubt it. How would they leave town?"

She opened her mouth and shut it suddenly, and he took a stab at her thought.

"Take Amtrak, huh? No, these folks have pretty limited mobility, in general, and the two I'm looking for aren't kids anymore. One of 'em is probably in his fifties or sixties. His days of riding boxcars are long gone."

"Why can't they go to another neighborhood?"

"In another neighborhood they'd stand out. In Uptown a man can sleep in the alleys or in a doorway or in the park or in a burned-out building, or in a packing carton in a vacant lot, and nobody says anything because the neighborhood is a wreck and because there are thousands of people doing the same thing. And anyway, I'm not all that sure they ever have the luxury of thinking that far ahead." He looked at his watch. "Right now, most of them are close to where they'll bed down for the night, and a lot of others are looking for a place to sleep. They'll sleep in all those strange places, and tomorrow, they'll wake up trying to figure where to get food or money, where to get a drink. It's gonna be ninety-five or so tomorrow, so they'll spend most of the day trying to figure ways to stay in the shade. That's their life: looking for food, looking for a drink, looking for water on a hot day, looking for shade, trying to keep whatever they find from somebody who wants to take it from them."

"What do they do in winter?"

"A lot of 'em die. Usually, that first really frigid night of winter, there are a couple dozen people who die in Chicago. Most of them are these people that live on the street. They just die."

She looked at him for a moment without blinking, then swallowed and looked down at her nearly empty plate. "That's horrible," she said quietly. "What a…terrible way to end your life."

"Yep. I've always thought so." Jean looked away and a moistness appeared in her eyes and he took another whack at mind reading.

"But your brother's not out on the street, Jean, or I would have heard. I've asked in a lot of places and he's just not out there. He might have a room somewhere, and maybe he doesn't come out except to eat or…I don't know, look for work. And based on what I've found out about him, he's not a talker, he's not somebody folks are going to remember because he doesn't say anything to anybody. But it's more likely, I think, that he's not around here at all. There's no evidence that he ever was. Only something somebody told us at the Y. You know, it wouldn't take long for a smart kid to realize that there wasn't any work to be had in Uptown."

"What about your…you know, your contacts with the utilities?"

"Nothing. No record of him."

"I had an idea."

"Yeah, you said. Let's hear it."

"If you got all the records of people that just had utilities turned on in, let's say, April or May—"

"His name wouldn't be there."

"No, but maybe something *similar* to his name would be." She straightened and gave him a little half smile, proud of her newfound street savvy.

"Not bad, farm girl, but all I can do is try names on them. We'd have to come up with a probable alias and people would check it out for me. You can't get the kind of information you're talking about, it has to be subpoenaed, and that means a court can get it but a private investigator can't. A guy with clout probably can, a high-level cop, maybe, but not me. Besides, it would probably be a waste of time. If Gerry's out there, which I'm beginning to doubt, he's got a small place, a room somewhere or a little furnished place. Something like that."

He told himself he believed what he was telling her, but behind it all was the residue of what people had told him about Gerry Agee, and other, darker possibilities. "And like I said, there's a good chance he's gone. That he's in…California." Her eyes widened and she smiled. No, you don't think he's gone, he told himself. You hope he's gone, and for her sake, you hope he's been gone for weeks.

"Maybe he's gone back to Michigan."

She shook her head. "If he is, he hasn't made it there yet. I talked to my mom this afternoon. She calls me all the time now.

Afraid the big city's gonna gobble up her little girl."

"Well, she's already afraid it gobbled up her son. Who can blame her?"

She stared at him for a moment, waited till the waiter cleared away their plates, and then leaned forward, putting her hands on the table. "You really don't think he's here, do you?"

"I honestly have no idea. I'm almost certain he's nowhere I've been asking about him."

"But you haven't been able to find the other men, and you still think they're in Uptown."

"Yeah, but *they* know people are looking for them. *They're* hiding. Besides"—he pointed to his bruises—"I *found* them."

She smiled and shook her head. "So you'd probably rather stop looking for Gerry."

"Well, not exactly. I can give it another shot. And if it seems pretty certain that he's not around there, then we'll have to talk about the next step."

"Which is?"

"Looking all over the city for him." She smiled and he jabbed a finger at her. "And *that* will cost you." He gave her a wolfish grin and she laughed.

"And if it comes to that, Jean, you probably should go back home, and I'll report to you there. Save yourself some money." He sipped at his beer. He was glad he'd said it; it was the only honest thing to tell her.

"I appreciate what you're trying to do for me, Paul. Thank you."

She hadn't seen Buckingham Fountain at night and he thought no one should ever visit Chicago without seeing it. The night was actually almost cool and the sun had finally set, and the fountain's lights exploded on the night in all their gaudy glory. City of the Big Shoulders, maybe even City of Poor Taste, but an original, one-of-a-kind place. In another city, the fountain might be smaller, the lights more subtle, perhaps all of one color, but here, the fountain was a party hat. Jean was dazzled.

"It's wonderful, it's like a Christmas tree! I think I'll stay here all night." Whelan had a cigarette and said nothing. He remembered other nights here, long ago, himself and Liz.

After a moment, she turned to him. "Do you mind this? I mean, I've taken up your whole evening. Would you rather get going? I know this is an imposition."

"Hell, no. When I get back home tonight, it'll be hot in my house and I'll be thinking about this other thing. No, I'd rather be here."

"Are you afraid at all? I mean, about your case."

He considered for a moment. "I don't think so, at least not in general. On specific occasions—like last night when I got caught in that abandoned apartment and knew there wasn't anyone around to help, I was shitting in my pants, if you'll excuse the expression. But in general, I don't think about it. Lately, I mostly think about how badly I'm screwing this up and how the police aren't even doing as well as I am."

"The two old men you're looking for—do you think they're the ones that killed your friend?"

"No. I think they know something about it, though. I think if I could get them to stop running long enough to talk to me, they might tell me why somebody had to kill him."

She gave him a little frown. "Why don't you think they killed him? Because they're too old?"

He laughed. "Hell, no. One of 'em did all this good stuff to my face. He's not *that* old. But I've got a couple of reasons why I don't think it was them. There was another killing a week earlier, a little wino named Shinny who was a buddy of theirs. Derelicts don't kill people. They don't kill each other, especially. The police involved in this think the same person killed Art Shears, and for once I think they're right."

She nodded. "So you look for these two old ones because you haven't got any information about the real killer. How am I doing?"

"Not bad. It's where I started, basically. But I've got someone else I'm looking for now, a young one."

"And he's the killer?"

He hesitated because he wasn't sure what would come out, and then let it out.

"Maybe, maybe not. I don't know what to think, but I can place this guy at the alley at the time Art was killed."

"Did anyone see the actual killing?"

"Someone saw this street kid at the alley. It's possible he was a lookout, but I think he was just there by coincidence. I think he saw it all go down."

"You mean maybe he watched your friend being murdered and didn't try to do anything?"

"Maybe he knew he couldn't stop it. Maybe it was already over when he happened along. Who knows? Besides, this is the big city, Jean. People don't always behave the way you'd expect civilized, sophisticated beings to behave."

They began to walk back toward Michigan Avenue. After a while, he realized she was shuddering.

"I didn't really mean to talk about this kind of thing. Give you nightmares."

She laughed. "I'll be all right." She walked in silence for a few moments and then looked up suddenly, smiling. "Want to go watch TV?"

The question blew away Whelan's equilibrium and he laughed long and loud.

"Is that what the girls in Hope, Michigan, do on Saturday night?"

She stopped walking and squinted at him. "It's what girls everywhere do, Paul. They sit inside and watch TV or play records or read, and wait for some conceited jackass to work up the nerve to pick up a phone. And it's what I do when I'm feeling a little…nervous. The TV's like a person in the room. I keep it on when I'm ironing and doing housework, too."

"Okay, let's watch TV. I was going to offer to buy you a cocktail somewhere."

"I have wine," she said brightly.

"Wine's fine," he said.

*   *   *   *   *

It wasn't the Hilton but it was better than he expected. It was a decent room, a good deal bigger than she'd have been able to afford at another Michigan Avenue hotel. There was a double bed, a large color TV, by a manufacturer he'd never heard of, a desk and chair, a small armchair and a bed table. It was cool and had the sterile institutional smell of old motels, suffused just slightly with her scent. He stepped inside the door, nervous and a bit giddy, lightheaded, like stepping out of a dark tavern into harsh sunlight. He realized he hadn't been inside a woman's room, other than Liz's, in years. It's not a date, he told himself.

Jean walked a few paces into her room and then stopped, unsure what to do with herself.

She's going to say, Well, this is it, he thought.

"Well, this is it."

"It's nice. And cool. So what's on TV?"

"I don't know. Is there a ball game on, maybe? Do you watch ball games?"

"Sure. There's nothing as relaxing as a ball game. Next to sleep, that is."

She went into the bathroom and came out with an ice bucket. There was a bottle of white wine in it, sloshing around in melting ice cubes.

"I'll get you a glass."

"Are you going to have any?" he asked.

"Sure."

He took the remote from the top of the TV set and sat at her desk chair. The remote was a novelty to him: he'd never had one of his own. The Cubs wouldn't be on for another half hour but the motel had cable and that meant the White Sox. He shook his head: baseball had always been a poor man's game, and a man who had no money could always count on seeing his Cubs or his White Sox on TV. The White Sox, however, were under new ownership—slick, energetic, visionary types,—and their first official act had been to take the Sox off regular television and plant them on a cable station they owned. Now, for the first time in years, the Sox were winning while the Cubs were looking for a soft place in the canvas, and you couldn't see them.

He flicked the remote and searched for the orphaned White Sox. On the far side of the room, Jean bustled about, looking for the spare plastic cup the Estes Motel had provided. She located it, held it up to look for dirt or fingerprints, rinsed it in the bathroom, tossed six ounces of wine into it and filled the other glass. He found the Sox eventually, playing Cleveland and pounding bloody lumps on them. He stole a glance at Jean, who caught him looking and smiled. He looked away and focused on the game. I am thirty-nine years old and I'm in the room of a pretty young woman in her twenties who probably goes out with young guys that can dance and look good in T-shirts. He calmed himself: you're not on a date, asshole. She needs the company. Everybody needs company.

She came over to him with the wine and sat at the foot of the bed, tucking her tanned legs under her. He refused to look at them. He sipped at his wine and his nervousness made him gulp. He was halfway finished before she'd gotten a decent swallow out of hers. In a couple minutes his was gone and she noticed.

"Here, there's plenty more." She brought the bottle over, poured it into his glass and then frowned when it ran out. There were about three ounces in his glass. "Oh, dear. I wonder if I can get more."

"You can probably get some from the motel, but don't worry. I don't drink a lot of wine. I just tend to gulp it. I have some rough edges, Jean—you couldn't take me to a proper French restaurant and expect me to blend in with the ambience."

She leaned back on one arm and sipped her wine and he wondered how it was that women could assume the simplest positions and radiate sensuality. He shifted positions in the little wooden chair every thirty seconds. The ball game helped puncture the tension, for the Cleveland Indians were a bad ball club and their ineptitude was catching, and by the seventh inning there had been a total of seven errors, nowhere near the major league record but sufficient to generate comedy. He was sorry to have missed the early ones. As he watched, the Cleveland center fielder collided with his right fielder and both were helped off the field. While new players took their positions, scores from other games were flashed on the screen. The Detroit Tigers were beating the Yankees 11 to 0.

"Oh, the Tigers are winning!"

"You like the Tigers, Jean?"

She gave a little shrug and a rueful smile. "I don't follow them much myself."

Whelan nodded. "But Gerry does."

She nodded and looked down.

"Jean, I'll find your brother or I'll get you some outside help that will, if he's already gone from here. But you can't let it take over your mind or you won't be able to function. It's not healthy. We've got...there's no evidence that anything has happened to him."

"You're a very kind man." She smiled. "And do you mean to tell me there are *better* detectives out there?"

"Oh, you bet. There are some real hotshots operating around the country. There's a man in Texas who's about the best there is at tracking people across the country. And for your slick types that have the wherewithal to change their identities and set up new lives and new bank accounts and new businesses, there are two agencies that do incredible things with computers, do most of their tracking from a desk. There's a woman in the suburbs here who finds people mainly by using a collection of phone books and a wonderfully accurate knowledge of human behavior. So cheer up: if you strike out with me, there are other detectives who might be able to do better."

She wrinkled her nose at him and looked back at the TV. "Somehow I think you're the person to have on this." A moment later, she gave her head a little shake. "I just think... you know, Gerry could be going off the deep end somewhere. He could be sitting in a little room—like this, even, and drinking his life away."

He watched her for a moment. "Gerry's drinking...it's a little worse than you told me, isn't it?"

She looked at him quickly. "Well...I don't know. What do you mean? Do you mean, is he drunk all the time and not responsible for what he does? I don't think so. He wasn't so bad at home, but who knows? I saw those people on the street yesterday, drunk and falling all over the place in the middle of the afternoon, and maybe Gerry's like that now, but…who's to say?"

"Well, we don't have to assume he's in the gutter yet. Sometimes personality problems exacerbate the situation. I know you told me he was having trouble adjusting to things, but…did Gerry have any other kinds of problems that you know of?"

"What kind of problems? Do you mean with girls, like that? He wasn't gay, if that's what you want to know." She was leaning forward on the bed, aggressive: big sister defending little brother, and Whelan smiled.

"No, no, nothing like that. I was just trying to see if there are other factors that I'm not aware of yet. No outward signs of major conflicts, then, other than drinking and general aimlessness and a few fights with his friends."

"That's right."

"And what about them, the friends? Have you talked to any of them?"

"Oh, sure, but I knew it would be a waste of time and it was. He was never very close to the guys he was running around with and he sort of stopped talking to them a few weeks before he left. The ones I talked to didn't even know he'd gone to Chicago. They haven't heard from him and I doubt they will."

She stared off into space for a moment, chewing on the inside of her cheek, and he watched her. Whether Gerry had kept his troubles concealed from his family or they had surfaced after he'd left home, it was clear the girl had no knowledge of her brother's darker side.

"Should we see if there's a movie on?"

"Don't you want to watch the ball game?"

"It's not a matter of life and death, and it's a pretty bad game, so…

She smiled and took the remote from him. On one of the local channels there was a 1940's movie, a British tearjerker.

"Hot damn, Jean, here we go. When movies were movies. I've seen a hundred of these and without knowing which one this is, I can tell you the plot, which is totally irrelevant to the enjoyment of the movie."

"Okay, let's hear it."

"First, the Germans try to take over the world and they almost pull it off except for the Sceptered Isle, which fights them nobly. Second, a pair of unhappy lovers, who are both married to other people, meet, separate and are drawn into different branches of the service. Each one loses his mate to the war effort; the woman becomes a nurse, the man becomes a fighter pilot or commando or something and does manly deeds in the great tradition of epic heroes. Eventually he is shot full of holes and sent to a hospital behind the lines. There, he is nursed back to health by his long-lost lover, who hasn't cracked a smile since Dunkirk. He survives, they become lovers again, the Germans are defeated, largely through the courage and brilliance of the British, peace returns, Churchill gains weight and the world is happy again."

She laughed and pointed to the screen. "Oh, God, look, you're right, the woman's a nurse."

"And all the male actors are named either Alistair or Leslie, but in the movie all the men are named John."

"You're a movie expert, huh?"

"No, I've just watched a million of 'em and I go back a little further than you do. A lot further, in fact." He looked at her frankly and was glad he'd gotten it out.

She gave him a matter-of-fact look and shrugged. There was a gleam of amusement in her eyes and for the first time he wondered if loneliness was her only motive for inviting him up. His pulse quickened.

"You don't seem to be falling apart, Paul. You don't strike me as old at all."

"I'm thirty-nine."

"Big deal."

"You're—what, twenty-five?"

She grinned. "But it's an old twenty-five," and she laughed.

For a long moment neither of them said anything and he looked back at the TV, uncertain and tense. Finally he looked at his watch.

"I should get going." And he realized he meant it. This was no place for him to be, and he'd never allowed himself any involvement with a client, not even wishful thinking. He stood up and she uncoiled herself from the bed.

"If you have to—"

"Yeah, I do. I've got some things to do tomorrow, early."

"Even on Sunday, huh?"

"Yep, even on Sunday." He walked slowly toward the door and she walked beside him, putting her hand gently on his wrist. Her fingers felt warm on his skin and he tensed a little.

"Thanks for coming down tonight, Paul," she said, and there was unease in her voice. He wanted to laugh: she was as nervous about it as he was.

"My pleasure. I'm an opportunist. I saw a chance to have dinner with one of Michigan's finest-looking women and I jumped at it."

She laughed delightedly and put herself directly in his path with a neat little spin on her heels. She was standing no more than six inches from him and he could breathe nothing but her perfume.

"Thanks for the dinner and the company, Jean."

"I needed the company more than you did, Paul." She raised one hand as if to touch him, stopped with the hand in midair, gave him an exasperated look and suddenly put her hand to the back of his neck and drew his head to her. Her lips touched his lightly and he felt his throat thicken. He met the pressure and then her mouth was open and her tongue found his, and he was conscious of her slight, warm body pressing against his. He was surprised at the tightness with which she held him and realized that her eagerness was loneliness. He put his arms around her tightly and when she continued to press her mouth to his, began to move his hands across her body. His right hand went down to the top of her hips and she drew back, kissed him lightly, and shook her head.

"Oh, what am I—" She smiled in embarrassment. "I got a little carried away, I'm sorry."

"Me, too."

"I should never drink wine," she said, and sighed.

He fought a sudden impulse to tell her he'd call her tomorrow.

"I've got a few more leads to follow Monday morning. If you haven't heard from me by late afternoon, give me a call."

"I will."

"But I'll probably call you first," he said.

"You can call just to say hello, you know."

"Okay." They said goodnight and he left her room.

Outside, the dirty air of downtown Chicago, the air of a million exhaust pipes and factories and barbecues was doing battle with the cool breeze from the lake, and it seemed more like spring than summer. Michigan Avenue was seething with Saturday-night life and traffic, and he told himself that there were times when this was the greatest of towns, particularly when you were under the influence of a woman, any woman.

NINE

He woke early Sunday and drove out to St. Joseph's Cemetery. He spent a few minutes at the graves of his parents, pulling up a couple of weeds that had sprung up between the small gray headstones. He picked up a few pieces of paper that the wind had strewn in the grass covering the graves, stood in the hot sun for a moment, then nodded at each headstone and left.

He had a sudden impulse to visit Artie's grave, then thought better of it. A new grave was a desolate sight, and somehow he didn't want to visit the grave till he'd accomplished something in this investigation. Nothing to report yet, he thought.

On the way back he listened to jazz and thought about Jean Agee, going over every moment of the previous evening to assure himself that it had happened. He remembered her kissing him and shook his head. What is happening here, exactly? And then he remembered the time long ago when he'd had this same excitement, with Liz, and he grew uncomfortable.

He spent an hour roaming the neighborhood on foot and turned up nothing. In the afternoon, he went for a long drive and knew he was trying to keep himself busy so he wouldn't call her. He thought again about the difference in their ages and told himself he was going off the deep end.

So what? What else is there in my life?

It was almost three when he got back home, and he called her almost immediately. There was no answer, and when the switchboard operator asked him if there was a message, he ran out of nerve. He mumbled thanks and hung up, wondering where she was. More than that, he wondered if she was thinking about him.

He watched a couple of innings of the Cubs game and

turned it off when they were down five runs.

At five-thirty he took the car out again, cruised the streets without getting out of the car and finally decided to have dinner. As he drove west on Wilson he looked in his rearview mirror and saw a gray Caprice fading back into traffic a block behind him.

"Aw, give me a break, Bauman. Jesus, on Sunday?"

He went to Cho Sun Ok on Lincoln, sighed when the air conditioning hit him and was pleased to see a dozen or so Korean faces look up from their food as he entered. As usual, he would be the only Caucasian in the place.

The waitress, a tall, elegant woman, led him to a small side table and handed him a menu. He sank back and allowed himself the enjoyment of watching Koreans eat. Some of the tables were shared by families, others by groups of young men in dark suits, but at each table was an explosion of food, a riot of colors and smells: plates of dark, spicy *bulgogi*, platters of condiments and hot *kimchee*, huge bowls of Korean soups he'd never tried, clear liquid surrounding pyramids of Korean noodles and vegetables. At the tables of the young men, little bottles of Korean vodka seemed to evaporate before his eyes. A tall, dignified-looking Korean man of middle age entered and was greeted effusively by the owner, who emerged, panting and sweating, from the kitchen. After exchanging greetings and, apparently, a few howlers in Korean, the owner accepted a small key from the man, opened one of the beautiful little wooden liquor cabinets behind the counter and took out a bottle of Chivas. In almost every one of the locked compartments was a bottle of good scotch, and below each one, a nameplate indicating whose scotch it was.

For openers he had the fried dumplings called *Mandoo* and sampled each of the condiments the waitress brought him, particularly the turnips soaked in vinegar and peppers, and the kimchee, hot and almost red from the peppers that the cabbage had been marinated with. Then, mouth still afire from the kimchee, he attacked his main course, a large steel bowl of *bibim bop*, his favorite and, for his money, one of the most bizarre dishes ever invented—four or five kinds of vegetables, including shoots, sprouts and cucumbers along with a garnish of carrot and several types of plant life he had yet to identify—and a good helping of bulgogi, the succulently spicy broiled beef. To one side of the bowl was a small, unprepossessing dollop of the bright red "barbecue" sauce that would breathe fire and personality into the otherwise harmless mixture, and atop it all, like someone's idea of a joke, was a fried egg. He heaped steamed rice onto his plate, mixed the ingredients in the bowl so that egg and sauce mingled and permeated the other elements, and spooned it all onto his plate. Then he took a deep breath and fell to it. Strange-looking or not, it was a wonder, and with its garlic and hot peppers compounding the odors from the kimchee, it was a meal guaranteed to stop one's social life in its tracks. It was not for nothing that a patron in a Korean restaurant was usually presented with chewing gum when the bill was brought. Whelan worked his chopsticks into the mound of food.

I am a Korean at heart.

He went home with a fire in the roof of his mouth and a gentle contented rumbling in his stomach, and his breath would have withered the flowers in Mrs. Cuelho's garden. He opened his door, gasped at the stagnant heat in his place, shut the door behind him and then stopped dead at the entrance to the living room.

Someone had been here. He stood still for a moment, making no sound, and then turned on the overhead light. He went quickly into the dining room and did the same there. At the door to his darkened bedroom he paused, then reached around the doorjamb and flicked on his light. He shook his head: it was nothing he could see or even explain, but he knew someone had been in his home. He walked toward the kitchen, paused at the hall closet: the knife was at the far side of the kitchen, so he settled for an old baseball bat from the closet. In a half crouch, he slid quietly into the kitchen—the light switch was halfway across the room, an aberration that had been a constant source of irritation to his mother; his father had never gotten around to rewiring the room. He paused and listened. His hands felt sweaty on the bat handle. Then he crossed the room quickly and flicked on the switch. No one.

The backdoor was ajar and he pulled it open quickly. There was a small cut in the screen. He looked at the heavy wood door and saw that the chain had been broken. A matter of simple laziness: the chain had always been enough, so he'd gotten out of the habit of using the key. Now he'd have to use it. He shut the door and was about to search the rooms to see if anything had been taken when he saw the "evidence." There was a piece of bread crust at his feet. On the kitchen table, at the very edge of it, was a small piece of ham, already turning dark. Beneath the table was a small portion of sandwich, bread rolled hastily around ham.

He went to his bedroom and saw that the top two drawers of his dresser were open and the clothes had been tossed. The change he normally kept on the top of the dresser was gone. He walked slowly around his apartment: the TV and the stereo were still there. Some burglar. Change and a little food; the logical, reasonable side of his nature told him that a teenager had burgled his place. The intuitive side said two attempted break-ins in the same week were not coincidence. The intuitive side said a guy hungry enough to jam a piece of ham into a slice of bread during a burglary would take it with him, even if he was startled by something. No burglary. He'd been paid a visit.

After a while he went next door and asked Mrs. Cuelho if she'd seen anyone prowling around his backyard. The old woman, now an implacable enemy as a result of his bellicose treatment of her cat, answered him in monosyllables. No. Hadn't seen anybody. Nothing. When he told her his place had been burglarized, she was horrified. As he went down her front stairs, he heard her throwing the bolt and putting the chain across her door.

He tried Jean Agee again and was told she was out. He left no message. Awhile later it occurred to him that, message or not, she'd be told she had calls and that the caller was the same man each time, and he was embarrassed. He didn't try to reach her again that night, spending the rest of the evening watching TV and reading a couple of his father's gardening books.

His face looked better on Monday morning: much of the discoloration was gone and the swelling was down. He decided he looked more like an accident victim, a condition slightly more respectable than being the loser in a street fight.

He went out for groceries and then went to the New Yankee Grill for coffee. He tried to read the paper but found himself on a stool between two old men, each poking at a plate of biscuits and gravy and arguing about whether Roosevelt had ruined the country. Eventually he gave it up, finished his coffee and left.

For an hour and a half he drove or walked the same streets and alleys he'd covered the week before. This time he focused on the two young ones and by the middle of the morning Jean Agee's photograph was beginning to wilt. No one had seen Billy the Kid or the all American boy in the picture except for one ancient drunk sitting on a curb on Wilton, who believed he'd known the boy in the picture back in Tempe, Arizona, just before the war.

He stood on the corner of Wilson and Broadway and took a long, slow look at the neighborhood and its traffic. Four men, all of them probably within four blocks of where he was standing, and not a soul seemed to know where they were.

I ought to be able to find these guys. There's something wrong here. Maybe it's just time to find a new line of work, Whelan.

He went back to his car and sat there, listening to the radio and watching the pedestrians. After awhile he took out the photograph and studied it for a moment, trying to fit the picture with what Harvey had said about the young man. A picture gradually came to him, a picture he could not shake off for a time, of this promising young man, face contorted with rage at imagined injuries, standing over a stricken man and beating him to death.

He drove over to Sunnyside and parked for a while in front of the building where Hector had taken him apart. A squad car pulled up beside him and the officer on the passenger side asked him what he was doing there.

"Probably the same thing you're doing, officer. Looking for

a couple of old guys that were staying in there." He showed the cop his license. The officer looked at it, then at Whelan's face, and smiled.

"You Al Bauman's friend?"

"I never thought of it that way," he said, and the cops both laughed and drove off. He drove away, without a particular plan or destination. On Beacon, a block from the building where he'd been jumped, was another, almost identical, apartment building, this one built of yellow brick. A fire had put this one out of action, too, and boards covered most of the doorways and windows. Most, but not all. He drove by twice, first at normal speed and then slowly, and the more he thought, the more likely it seemed that a man run out of one building would seek a similar one. He shook his head: he would have to check this one out at night, too.

They only come out at night, he said to himself. Shit.

At his office he opened the window to exchange hot street air for hot stale air. There was no mail. He called Shelley.

"Well, I was beginning to think you retired, baby."

"Just a slow starter these days. What do you have for me, Shel?"

"Phone call from the President. He said to keep up the good work." Shelley laughed and cracked gum in his ear.

"My idol. I've always admired world leaders who wear makeup. What else? Anything?"

"Just one call. Nice old guy named Tom Cheney. He was calling from a pay phone, said he had some information for you, to stop by his place."

"And that's it, huh?"

"That's all you got, Hon." Nothing from Jean Agee.

He called the Estes Motel and was told that there was no answer in Miss Agee's room. He hung up, feeling unsettled. He sat and studied the cobwebs on his ceiling and saw a young woman from a small town, sitting at the edge of her bed, mortified that she'd kissed a seedy stranger twice her age and telling herself to have nothing more to do with him.

He left the office and decided to walk over to Cheney's. As

he walked up Broadway he saw Captain Wallis across the street, laughing and gesturing with a tall gray-haired Catholic priest. In front of Solomon Brothers' Shoe Store, a pair of shifty-looking young white boys trying mightily to look streetwise attempted to sell him a Sony Walkman and a pair of running shoes. He told them he already had an extensive collection of stolen goods and they took off running. Near the corner of Broadway and Leland, a pair of young drunks, one white and the other black, were engaged in the ritualized combat of the inebriated: the white one stood rigidly in a parody of a boxing stance while the black one went through the poses of some sort of homemade karate. A few feet beyond them, an elderly woman dug through a garbage can and ignored them.

He paused at Leland. Halfway up the next block, the twin angels of the Way Mission had found another customer. This one was not quite conscious and was attempting to pull himself up onto the curb he'd fallen off. They had him surrounded, Tom Waters was bending over him and speaking earnestly while Don Ewald shook his head and looked around. There was a distant look on his face and Whelan could almost feel his yearning for the clean streets of Bakersfield, California. Whelan waved and Don caught the movement, grinned and waved back. He started forward and Whelan quickly turned the corner. I have groupies, he thought.

He went up Tom Cheney's back stairs and knocked. The curtain beside the door moved slightly and a moment later the door opened.

"Hi, Tom. Thanks for the call."

"Come on in, young fella. I got some information." Tom Cheney was torn between a grin and an expression of profound seriousness, and the grin eventually won out, if only for a moment.

"Come on into the living room and sit down. Want some coffee?"

"No, thanks. Next time."

"I seen 'im," Cheney said before Whelan had fully settled into the chair.

"The redhead?" Cheney nodded. "You sure?" Another nod. "Where?"

Tom Cheney nodded toward the front window, east. "Down at the park."

"Clarendon?"

"Yep. I go down there some nights, before it gets real dark. It's cooler, and I like to look at the ballgames down there. Softball games, you know."

"Where'd you see him?"

Cheney laughed and shook his head. "He's a pistol, that one. He was in that little parking lot they have next to the field house. Tryin' all the car doors, goin' through the ones that was open. Saw 'im take a couple things out."

"He get caught?"

"He got *seen* but not caught. Couple of the softball players saw 'im and started chasin' him with bats. Big potbellied guys, couldn't catch me." He laughed at the image. "That kid, he took off soon as he heard 'Hey you,' didn't even look back, like, like—"

"Like he's done it a thousand times and bolts as soon as he hears a voice."

"Yep, that's it."

"And you're sure it was the same kid you saw at the mouth of the alley that night?"

Tom Cheney nodded and looked proud of himself. Whelan smiled and then a thought struck him.

"He see you, Tom?"

Cheney shook his head. "If he did, he didn't make no connection. That night in the alley, he wasn't lookin' up at me. He was lookin' at…at what was goin' on down there. He don't know me."

"That's good," he said but his mind was already working. It was a big park, there were literally miles of it stretching along the lakefront, with Clarendon simply a tiny section squared off for softball, and a man could hide down there for a long time in warm weather; it was cooler than the rest of the city, and Whelan knew that a number of men slept on the benches on any given night.

He made small talk with Cheney for a while, suggested that they have a couple of beers together some night the following week and said he'd stop by. Then he left.

The street was white with the heat and if it was ninety-eight in the air it was ten degrees hotter on the pavement. He thought of the walking he would do later that afternoon, of the pointless questions he'd be asking, of Jean Agee and his own blundering vulnerability to any woman who smiled at him, and he wanted to escape from it all.

He compromised and went to lunch.

There were a half dozen customers in the A&W already. Several young black men munched at Polish sausage sandwiches and a white guy in a tie had a hamburger. No one was eating anything foreign. It was a time for boldness.

"Hey, Mr. Paul. You gonna try this new guy? You gonna like him. He's spicy, just like you like them."

"What have we got today, Rashid?"

"Felafel. My own special recipe. Persian felafel. I make him spicy, not like the other kind."

Gus stuck his head out of the back room. "It's all fucked up, too. Rashid fucked it up. It's too hot. Felafel not supposed to be hot. He put jalapenos in the fucker. Rashid thinks he's Mexican. Have the Shalimar kabob. I made it, it's good. You like."

"I'll have a Shalimar kabob and a felafel."

Rashid grinned and Gus shook his head. Whelan heard a couple of the customers laughing.

Rashid nodded. "You're a smart guy. Diplomat guy. You should be in the government."

"And you two guys are artists. Give me a large root beer with that, too."

The door opened and Bauman filled it. He stood just inside the door, hands on hips, letting the hot street air in, and looked around the room, seeking and getting the attention of everyone in the place. When he was finished bogarting, he walked over to Whelan.

"Well, Sherlock, having an exotic lunch?"

"Yeah. Want to expand your horizons or are you afraid of anything that's not roast beef?"

Rashid brought Whelan's basket of food, two pocket pitas overflowing with their odd contents, and Bauman stared at it.

"Root beer looks good, anyway." He peered closely at the sandwiches. "So what is all that shit?"

"It's good, Bauman. Something different, at least. Lunch ought to be interesting."

"What's that green pasty shit? Some kinda sauce?"

"Yeah." He bit into the felafel, chewed, wiggled his eyebrows and winked at Rashid. "Good, Rashid." The Middle East meets Mexico.

Rashid grinned confidently. He raised his eyebrows and looked at Bauman. "How 'bout you, mister? You want to try Persian food?"

"Anybody ever die here?"

"Not yet," Rashid said happily.

Bauman looked at the pictures of A&W's more traditional food, shrugged, looked again at Whelan's lunch and said, "I'll have what he's having. A root beer, too."

Bauman looked around the room and then leaned against the counter and watched Whelan eat. Whelan stopped in midchew and looked at him.

"You always stare at people when they eat?"

Bauman gave him a little half smile. "I like to jerk your chain, Whelan." Then he chuckled to himself. "Actually I can't help it. I'm starving."

"Where's Rooney?"

He waved irritably in the approximate direction of Area 6 headquarters. "Ah, he brings his lunch. He eats in the cafeteria out of a brown bag. This guy gonna take long?"

"He doesn't have to send out to Iran for it."

Rashid came over with a basket and put it on the counter in front of Bauman.

"Here you go, mister."

Bauman looked at his food, then at Whelan. "You sure I'm not gonna die if I eat this stuff?"

Whelan looked at Bauman's stomach, resting atop the counter. "They don't have microbes in Iran that can handle anything that big."

Bauman sat heavily on the stool next to him and stared for a moment. "You keep making smart-ass remarks, Whelan. You think I'm in lousy shape? You wanna run around the block with me a few times? You wanna box, babe? You wanna—"

"Aw, eat your food. It was a joke."

Bauman bit into the felafel sandwich. "Hey, this is good," he said through a mouthful. "Hot, though. Supposed to be this hot?"

"No. The chef gets creative sometimes. Don't talk with your mouth full, all right?"

"Aw, fuck you, Whelan." He picked up his Shalimar kabob, bit into it and said, "Hey, all right." He turned and winked at Whelan. "Hey, Whelan, aren't you afraid these guys'll take you hostage? Ain't that their, uh, tradition?"

He looked back quickly to see if Rashid had heard but the Iranian continued to work.

"Not enough money in hostages, Bauman. These guys are entrepeneurs."

Bauman snorted and went back to eating. They ate in silence for a while, listened to the bustle around them, watched in amusement as Rashid got into it with a pair of young blond boys in dago T's who were apparently trying to convince him they'd already paid for their food. Rashid's manner grew more agitated, his speech more rapid, and then he began cursing in an impressive mixture of Farsi and English. Gus emerged from the back room with a cleaver and Rashid looked at Whelan.

"Detective? Mr. Detective Paul? We got troubles here."

"Aw, fuck me," one of the young guys said, and tugged at the other's arm. The second one threw four singles on the counter and grabbed his A&W bag and they left, mumbling and tossing hostile looks over their shoulders at Whelan, Rashid and Gus. Whelan noticed that neither one looked at Bauman. At the door, one of them called the Iranians "Camel jockeys."

Gus came over to Whelan and Bauman. "You know

something? There's no camels in Iran, not one. Okay, maybe in the zoo, but otherwise, no. No camels. The Arabs ride camels, not us. We ride…what do we ride, Rashid?"

"Fords," Rashid said, and they both laughed.

"I like this joint," Bauman said.

"It's an interesting place."

"You go to places like this all the time?"

"Whenever I can. I look for little out-of-the-way places all over the city. What kind of food turns you on, Bauman?"

Bauman thought for a moment and shrugged. "All kinds. I like hot food. I don't…I don't know much about the different kinds but if it's, you know, if it's got a little bite to it, I'll like it."

"Thai food?" Bauman shrugged and shook his head. "Try that. Or Korean. They're both pretty spicy and they're both cheap."

"I don't give a shit about that. I got nothing else to do with my money."

Whelan finished his food and had a cigarette. Eventually Bauman finished and took out one of his little cheap cigars, and Whelan waited for him to light it and take a couple of puffs before speaking.

"So. Why are we here, Detective Bauman?"

Bauman gave him his sly smile. "Thought we'd compare notes, see what we got."

"You mean, you thought you'd come around and put the arm on me, see if I had anything to give you."

"Is that what I meant?"

"What's the matter, didn't you find out all kinds of great stuff following me around yesterday?"

Bauman blew out smoke and gave him a long slow look, and Whelan decided it wasn't a look he'd like to see in an alley.

Bauman sighed. "I just tailed you for a couple blocks, is all. I wasn't followin' you. Didn't look like you were doing any good so I took off."

"You don't take Sundays off, huh?"

"What's that to you?"

Whelan let it go. "I'm getting shut out, Bauman. I'm

looking for these guys and I'm going in circles. I flush Hector and Sharkey but I lose 'em right away. I don't believe how this is going for me. I thought...I thought you guys would come up with something."

Bauman flicked ash into his A&W basket. "I got every uniform in Uptown lookin' for these guys, I got a car cruisin' that building where Hector kicked your ass—"

"He didn't kick my ass. He took a narrow and disputed decision."

Bauman laughed. "He kicked your ass. You didn't see your face, Whelan. I did. It was the face of a guy that just got the shit kicked out of him."

"Fine. I prefer my own version. And I've seen your guys."

"They ain't come up with nothin' yet. And we got guys looking on foot, the whole shot." He shook his head and a look of tired frustration crossed his face briefly.

"And we still got what we started with, couple of guys, a little wino and a guy a little down on his luck, and both of 'em wind up dead in alleys a couple blocks apart."

Whelan caught the softened reference to Artie Shears and allowed himself a smile. "Theories, Bauman?"

"Well, both of these guys...the killer wanted it to look like something else. Stuck a knife in Shinny, turned a couple pockets inside out. Took your friend's tape recorder."

"Fine, but if it's not the obvious thing, then you've got to supply the motive."

"Sharkey's the connection, Whelan."

"That's a connection, not a motive. Where's your motive?"

"Okay, smart guy. You tell me."

"I don't know. Somebody wanted...I don't know. To keep them away from Sharkey, it seems to me."

Bauman thought for a moment, then shook his head. "Nah. Something else. I got an edge here, Whelan, 'cause you didn't see Shinny. Guy that killed Shinny hit 'im in a lot of places you wouldn't hit somebody if you were trying to kill 'im." He held up his big red hand, knuckles toward Whelan, and patted his ring.

"Ring marks, lotta ring marks. Got hit backhanded a bunch

of times. Ring marks and cuts all over his face. Why would *you* hit a guy backhand, huh?"

Whelan took a last puff of his cigarette and ground it out in a little aluminum ashtray, then thought for a moment. "To frighten him. No. To get something out of him."

Bauman made a little shooting motion at him with his thumb and forefinger. "There you go. Not bad. Least, that's what I'm thinking. I think somebody was trying to get something out of Shinny. Information. See, everything I got says Hector and Sharkey went under a few days *before* Shinny got it. I think this guy was looking for Sharkey and Hector, probably just Sharkey, and tried to get Shinny to tell him about it."

"And Artie Shears had been talking to them."

"That's right, whoever killed Shinny thought your pal could give him something. Also, takin' the tape recorder was a nice touch, 'cause he probably listened to the tape, to see if the tape would give 'im anything." He grinned and Whelan wanted to laugh.

"Pretty pleased with yourself, huh?"

Bauman pursed his lips. "I'm gonna get this prick, Whelan. And if I get to him before anybody else. I'm gonna kick the shit out of him." The color rose in Bauman's cheeks and he nodded repeatedly and took a nervous puff at the stub of the cigar.

"Watch your blood pressure, Wild Bill. I'll buy you another sandwich."

Bauman blew out the smoke and coughed. He picked tobacco from his lip and seemed to be lost in his thoughts for a moment. Then he turned very slowly and looked at Whelan.

"You figure me for a weirdo, right? Or what? Rogue cop? Bum cop, is that it, Whelan?"

"I don't quite know what to make of you, Bauman. To tell you the truth."

"I'll make it simple for you. Twenty-four hours a day, I'm a cop. Nothin' else. And anything comes my way, I jump into it. And some things…some things make me a little crazy. You see, you didn't get a look at Shinny or your friend, right? The body?"

"No, I didn't."

"You wouldn't have liked it."

"I bet."

"I don't like any of it. Once you see the body, Whelan, they're not just cases anymore, at least that's how I see it. Other guys, they think I'm a little strange about it, but I don't think so. I think I get closer to the thing, I got a better shot than they do at closing it. And these poor schmucks on the street, they got no protection from anything, and when somebody takes one of 'em out, something senseless like this—"

"I know. You explained how you feel about them, and I think you're right."

"But the guy that killed Shinny and your friend, he thinks he's just about home free by now. He took out a couple bums and nobody gives a shit. Doesn't know me, though. I never let go, Whelan. Remember that guy they found on South Wacker back at the start of winter?"

Whelan thought for a moment, then gave him a surprised look. "The crossbow thing?"

Bauman nodded and puffed at his cigar. Whelan had no trouble remembering the killing: it had been just bizarre enough to make the evening news on all channels and in both papers. A derelict had been found in the dark tunnel of Lower South Wacker Drive with a crossbow bolt in his chest. He appeared to have been killed in his sleep, and there had been the suggestion of random selection, of thrill killing.

"Well, I looked for that fucker, Whelan. I'm still looking and you know that ain't anywhere near my beat. It wasn't my case but I went down there at night, had a few pops at Billy Goat's and then just kinda wandered around, hoping some asshole would aim a crossbow at me so's I could break his arms before givin' him Miranda. And you know what? We got leads on that one now', and one of 'em came from me, just from me walkin' around down there where I got no official business, from me standing on corners and beatin' my meat and waiting for somebody to tell me something."

The detective puffed at the now tiny stub of the cigar, shook his head, seemed to mumble something to himself and looked around the room.

"Bauman, I've got something for you. Not much, but it's something. An old guy I talked to said he saw Billy the Kid down at the park last night."

"Which park. Clarendon?"

"Yeah."

"Would this guy know?"

"Yeah. He described him to me."

"Where in the park? He say where?"

"By the softball field. Well, in the parking area. Going through the cars."

Bauman gave him a slow smile. He closed his eyes and gave his head a little shake. His cheeks puffed up and his face looked even rounder than usual, and for just a second Bauman looked positively jovial, the Oliver Hardy of the police.

"And you were gonna go down to the park and—what? Make the collar, right?"

"I was going to look for him. That's all."

"And then what?" A wide grin, the pro interviewing the amateurs.

"Who knows?"

"You were gonna strut your stuff and let me read about it in the papers."

"Look, you've told me from the beginning, you guys don't know anything about this officially. You told me they've even got you working on something else."

Bauman shrugged. "We got a couple homicides we're looking at. Couple druggies got popped, we got a good shot at it, so we're spending some time on 'em. But I'm busting my ass up here on this one, Whelan. And you know that." He crushed the cigar butt into the basket. "So you better not keep anything to yourself, 'cause I'll fucking have you in a lockup faster than you can piss, Jack."

"I love your simple but direct use of the language. And you didn't threaten to yank my license."

"I don't give a shit about your license. I'll kick your ass if you screw this up." He expelled breath and stretched. The paper in his basket was on fire. "But thanks for the tip." He smiled and winked. "And you're still gonna go down there and look, right?"

"I like to go down and watch softball once in a while." He poured the watered remnants of his A&W root beer into Bauman's A&W conflagration. A little cloud of smoke and steam hovered over the counter. Rashid came over and gave them a puzzled look.

"You blow this and I'll stomp on you."

"He'll make you from five hundred yards, Bauman, you or any other cop."

Bauman laughed, got to his feet and pointed at his smoking basket.

"This is good stuff." He looked at Rashid and reached into a pants pocket. "Good stuff, babe."

"Here, Rashid. The gentleman is my guest." He handed Rashid a ten and looked at Bauman. "Next time, you can buy."

"No problem."

"And we'll go someplace expensive."

He took his change, nodded to Bauman and left.

At the office he called the Estes once more and was told by an irritated switchboard operator that she was out, that Miss Agee had been out all day. He hung up and stared out the window and told himself he would hear from her again because she'd need his report. And then it occurred to him that she could quite easily get it over the phone. He sighed and turned slightly in his chair, and then noticed the two shapes outside his door.

"It's open. Don't be shy."

The door opened slowly and he whispered, "Oh, Lord."

Don Ewald and Tom Waters shuffled in a few steps and stopped. Ewald seemed to be bothered by the open door and tried to push it shut, but they weren't far enough inside and the door hit Waters, who then took a nervous couple of steps to one side and stepped on Ewald's foot.

"Sorry, Don."

"No problem, Tom." Ewald finally managed to get the door

closed and they stood there like children taking punishment, hands at their sides. They moved from one foot to the other, stuck their hands in their pockets and looked at one another.

"Hi, fellas," Whelan said, and smiled to ease their load. "Come on in and make yourselves at home." He indicated the two chairs in the room. Waters moved the extra one from the wall and put it beside the client chair and they sat down almost simultaneously. Whelan wondered if they drilled together in the morning.

"So. To what do I owe this rare privilege?"

Don Ewald rubbed his nose and smiled and Tom Waters made a little noise in his throat that could have been a giggle. They looked at one another again and Ewald leaned forward.

"We…we wanted to offer you our help."

"Oh. Well, you guys have been pretty helpful already."

Tom Waters shook his head. "No, we mean…we could do some actual work for you. You've asked us to keep an eye out, but…you know, Don and I, we cover a lot of ground each day, in the course of our work—"

"A lot of ground." Ewald said, nodding.

"Oh, I bet you do. I can imagine."

"And we thought, you know, we thought we could do some leg work for you. You just tell us where to go and we'll go."

He looked from one to the other and held his breath and prayed that he wouldn't laugh. He nodded slowly and glanced out the window as if thinking it over. Was this how Nixon felt when Elvis offered his services as a government agent? He could send them to the farthest corner of the neighborhood and get them truly out of his hair—maybe send them up to Argyle Street and have them look for a Vietnamese woman with one blue eye. Better yet, have them follow Bauman and Rooney. Good clean fun for everyone. He looked at the open, honest faces and felt a twinge of guilt.

"What did you have in mind, exactly?"

Don Ewald opened his mouth, said "Well…" and looked to Waters for help.

"We thought you could give us the…the boundaries, you

know, the…uh…" Waters shrugged.

"Parameters," Ewald suggested.

"That's the word, parameters. The parameters of your investigation, and we could work those streets into our work. The Reverend Roberts doesn't care where we go to do our work as long as we give—"

"Full measure. That's the term he uses," Ewald said. "Full measure."

Whelan nodded. "Well, it seems to me that the mark of a good investigator is to know how to deploy what he's got. And I think—I'll be honest with you guys. I've been using you already. It's no coincidence that I keep running into you, or that I stopped in to see you at the Way. I knew you'd be familiar with the streets I'm working. So I guess what I'm saying is, you're already working where I most need a couple extra pairs of eyes and ears."

They both bought it. Don Ewald blinked once and Tom Waters nodded.

"You expect to find these men…up around this part of the neighborhood?" Waters asked.

"Sure, it's where everything happened."

"But wouldn't they leave? Wouldn't they go off somewhere else?" Ewald asked.

"Go where? Where do these people have to go? No, I think they'd just go under and, eventually, come out when they got tired of hiding. And if they do, you fellas will see 'em. No, you guys are already helping me a lot." As an afterthought, he took out the picture of Gerry Agee.

"And maybe you'll be able to give me something on this guy. Nothing yet, huh?"

They frowned and craned their heads forward, again in unison, but could tell him no more about the picture now than they could the first time.

"It's okay, guys. It's not a very good picture, and I'm not at all sure he's anywhere around here." He thought for a moment. "Tell you what: when you're making your rounds, if you happen to hear there's anybody new camping out in one of these old buildings, let me know."

They looked at each other and then Tom Waters nodded knowingly, and Whelan wondered if either of them had the faintest idea what he was talking about.

"We'll keep you posted, Mr. Whelan."

"My name's Paul. Call me Paul."

They grinned and looked at each other again.

"See you soon, guys." They nodded and got up and bumped into each other and laughed and reshuffled his chairs and finally left, and he let out a deep breath. He looked out the window at the marquee of the Aragon and thought about going to the fights to get his mind off other things.

He sat back in his chair and stared at the calendar on the wall. Idly, he picked up the picture of Gerry Agee and took another look at it. After a moment, he got out his wallet and called Captain Wallis's number.

"Hello, Mr. Whelan. How's the detecting business?"

"Complicated and unsatisfying, and it pays badly. And the social services business?"

"Oh, about the same," Captain Wallis said and laughed, a delighted cackle, and Whelan smiled to himself. This was a guy who didn't get out of bed groaning in the morning.

"So what can I do for you, Mr. Whelan?"

"Just a quick question. When did Billy first get here? When was the first time you saw him?"

"About this time last year."

"You're fairly sure of that?"

"Fairly sure. I can tell you with certainty that he was here for Thanksgiving Dinner. I remember that he was the youngest person at his table."

"Yeah. That's about what I thought. You said you'd known him awhile. I was just fishing." And doing it badly, he thought. A long shot, trying to simplify what could not be simplified. Gerry Agee was not Billy.

"Is there anything else you can tell me about Billy, Mr. Whelan?"

"He was seen the other night down at Clarendon Park.

That's all I know."

"And the police are still looking for him?"

"Yes. But he's not necessarily a suspect. Just someone everybody needs to talk to."

There was a slight pause on the other end and then Captain Wallis said, "Well, if I can be of any further help, just let me know."

"Sure. And…if I hear anything about Billy, I'll be in touch, captain."

"Thank you, Mr. Whelan."

"Sure. Talk to you later, captain."

"God Bless."

TEN

Late in the afternoon he tried one more time and a new receptionist or clerk told him that Miss Agee was not answering. Time to stop feeling embarrassed and to start worrying, maybe. A woman alone in a strange city, gone for an entire day and most of the next. It hadn't occurred to him that anything might be wrong, and his stomach made a little flutter. He had a sudden afterthought and called his service. He winced as the voice of Abraham Chacko volleyed into his ear.

He calmed himself, composed a greeting carefully and turned it loose. "Hello, Abraham."

"Hello, Good evening, sir, yes, sir."

"Do you have any phone messages for Mr. Paul Whelan, Abraham?"

"Yes, sir," Abraham cantoed. "I have the phone message," his little Indian flute of a voice intoned.

There was silence. That was all Abraham was prepared to give. He swallowed and suppressed his irritation. "And what is that message, Abraham?"

"Miss Jean called. She is calling to tell Mr. Paul that she will call tomorrow for Mr. Paul's report."

"Tomorrow. Ah." He felt the color returning to his face. She was all right, she was speaking to him. He thought for a moment. "And how long ago did, ah, Miss Jean call, Abraham?"

"Three-oh-four she was calling, sir."

Three-oh-four and it was now 3:55. All right. If he'd stayed in his office awhile, he could have talked to her. Damn. But he felt a giddy relief that she was all right and he would be talking to her in the morning. He felt a sudden wave of affection for old Abraham, who was absolutely the worst answering service employee on God's earth.

"Well, thank you, Abraham. You are a fine telephone operator."

"I am thanking you quite nicely, sir. Very kindly."

He went back to his apartment and sank into an armchair and knew he would not be able to spend much time here tonight. He wanted to jump into his car and tear down to South Michigan Avenue and catch her just as she came back from a walk in Grant Park or as she stepped uncertainly from a cab, and grab her and say, "Let's cut out all the b.s. and go get something to eat," and knew he could not, that this was a young woman whose responses he couldn't predict. And he wondered again, as he'd been wondering most of his adult life, if there was anyone who misread women as often as he did.

He put off calling Marie Shears till he was just about ready to go to the park.

"Hello?" She sounded good, composed.

"Hello, Marie. Paul Whelan."

"Hello, Paul. Nice to hear your voice."

"How's it going, Marie?"

"We'll make it, Paul. But thanks for asking."

"That's good, Marie, but I never had any doubt about it. I wanted to ask you something. The guy Artie was talking to just before…just before. Did he tell you why he was so interested in this guy?"

There was a pause at the other end. "Paul, you wouldn't be asking something like that if…if it was just a robbery."

He hesitated, then could see nothing wrong with the truth. "No, Marie, I wouldn't. I don't think it was a robbery."

She paused again for a moment, then said, "Oh, my God," in a quiet voice.

"I know it makes it worse, Marie."

"It's just a shock, Paul. It's so hard to believe that anybody would intentionally…But he's still dead, either way." She sighed. "All right. The little derelict. No, Paul, all he said was that the man had a story behind him."

"Yeah, he told me the guy was on the run. Acted like somebody was looking for him."

"Right. For something he did."

"But he didn't tell you anything more specific, Marie?"

"No. He said the man was drunk when they talked, Paul."

"Yeah, that figures."

They talked for a moment about the boys and he told her he'd let her know if he turned anything up.

The lights had gone on at the softball field but there was still an hour of daylight. It was apparently a playoff game and the two teams had drawn a good crowd for a softball game. There were a couple hundred people, and the teams, primarily men in their thirties, were good, and very intense, as all Chicago softball players were. In other parts of the country men hung up their spikes and baseball gloves when they got a little wide at the waist and a little thin on top. In Chicago, they had sixteen-inch softball, with short base paths and underhand pitching and a ball apparently modeled on the grapefruit, and they could play forever. Some did—the pitcher on the mound at the moment was at least forty-five, maybe a well-preserved fifty.

Whelan watched the game with some interest, just because of the fervor of the crowd of wives, girlfriends and family. Occasionally, casually, he surveyed the stands, the area just beyond the field where three old black men passed a bottle and the small parking lot beside the field house. There was no sign of a skinny red-haired street boy.

He watched the game for a couple of innings and then noticed Rooney and Bauman at the farthest end of the stands on the third base line. Bauman had changed into a mustard-colored knit shirt for the occasion and stood out like a wart on a centerfold. He seemed to survey the crowd, focused on a couple of young blond women in halter tops a few rows away, for a moment, then looked back toward the street. Rooney squinted and moved restlessly and seemed to be in the grip of an attack of acid indigestion.

A tall black-haired woman arrived, tan and slender and tightly wound into a white tube top and hip-hugger jeans, and there wasn't an eye on the ballgame. Whelan looked across the field and laughed: Bauman had picked her out fifty yards away. Whelan watched Bauman until the detective turned in his direction, and looked right at him. Whelan waved; Bauman nodded and looked back at the woman.

At the end of the next inning, Whelan descended from the stands and walked around the backstop to the end of the third-base seats.

"Evening, gents."

"What's happening, Whelan?" Bauman cocked an eyebrow and seemed in a jovial mood. Rooney simply nodded curtly and stared out at the field.

"Nothing much."

"These games draw a lot of women."

"They do that. See anything you like?"

Bauman gave him a shrewd smile. "I like 'em all. All shapes and sizes. All colors, even. All the various colors."

Bauman seemed to he amused at his own remark. He looked at Rooney, who shook his head but refused to meet Bauman's eyes.

"You see, Rooney and I, we got differences of opinion about that. He don't believe in, uh, mixing the races. Me, I'm a liberal." He grinned at Whelan.

"That's just how I had you figured. Well, since you guys are here to serve and protect, I think I'll go on break."

Bauman laughed and nodded. "You do that, Shamus. We'll take this shift."

Whelan nodded, took a last, amused look at the dyspeptic Rooney, and left.

He told himself he had plenty of time to kill and took off southbound on Lake Shore Drive, past the dying crowds on the beach, past the boathouse on North Avenue beach that was built and painted to look like a beached ocean liner, past stretches of the calm lake inhabited only by lifeguards. He followed the Outer Drive to the Field Museum and eventually made his way over to Michigan Avenue and found himself driving slowly past the Estes Motel and hoping now she wouldn't see him. He was caught by a red light directly across from the motel and felt foolish. When the light changed, he gunned it and didn't look back.

Back in the neighborhood, he drove back to the burned-out building on Beacon and parked there for twenty minutes on the far side of the street. He saw the usual street types scuttling in for shelter and a solitary mumbler who stood in front and alternately conversed with and screamed at faces only he could see, and just off to the side of the building, he watched a minor drug transaction. It's only a hunch, he told himself. Then he took a look at the windows where boards had been removed.

I think you're in there. And then he drove off.

The park was a changed place now. The ball field was empty and the banks of lights were dark, and the emptiness made an eerie contrast with the cheerful noise of the crowd that had occupied the spot just a few hours earlier. He climbed up onto the grandstand, moved to the top row and stared out over the field and the surrounding park till his eyes adjusted to the darkness.

Just past the stands on the third base line he could make out three benches, each ten yards or so from the next. A man was sleeping on one of them, from this distance little more than a mound of rags with an arm dangling almost to the sidewalk. He heard voices to his rear and turned to see three young black men getting noisily into a car just outside the park. It was a genuine beater, and coughed its life out before they got it started and it pulled out with a heavy grinding noise and the birdlike whirring of cracked or broken bands beneath the hood. The noise made him uneasy, for it blocked out any chance of hearing other noises, and his heart began to beat faster. All right, not my best idea.

But he stayed there another twenty minutes, watching the sidewalks and the parking lot and the street just outside the park. He forced himself to remain motionless, to make no sound, to be receptive to the smallest change in the darkness beyond the softball diamond. And then he heard a sound behind him.

He held his breath and listened and the sound came again, and stopped. A man walking, then stopping. Whelan listened and the noise resumed; he began to count to ten and then the footsteps came faster, someone running. He turned and stood up in time to see a dark form turn the corner around the field house. He ran down the grandstand, taking two steps at a time, jumped the last three and hit the ground running. He made for the other side of the field house, hoping to cut the runner off behind the building.

He ran across the grass of a smaller baseball diamond, his street shoes slipping on the waxy surface of the weeds, and rounded the corner of the building, and the crystalline voice of reason asked him what he planned to do when he caught the runner.

Shit, I don't know.

He came out behind the building and knew instantly that he'd lost him. He couldn't get the idea out of his head that it had been Billy. Whelan panted and wheezed for a moment, then had a cigarette. Two puffs and he was hacking again. He walked back toward the grandstand, wondering what to do and then he saw that something in the landscape had changed. He looked around slowly, taking in every detail, and then realized that the sleeper on the bench was gone.

He moved across the ball field till he reached the bench. The sleeper had left his bedding behind: a plump, trash-filled paper bag he'd used as a pillow and the sheets of newspaper he'd covered himself with against dew and the night air.

Whelan looked back toward the field house and down at the empty bench and shook his head. Great detective work: flushed out another one. He sat down on the bench to think.

From the corner of his eye he saw the dark shape emerge from the bushes a few yards to his left and stood up. The man stopped short, planted his back foot and cocked his right, keeping his left low. Whelan stood up, sidestepped into the dim light over the sidewalk and took a good look at him.

He was young and thin and over six feet tall but couldn't go more than 150: welterweight posing as a light-heavy.

"Hello, Billy. Now what?"

The boy moved a little closer and to one side, just to the edge of the little circle of light. Whelan sidestepped with him and brought his left up and his right to his chin and wondered how he'd get inside those long arms. The boy licked his lips and Whelan realized that the kid was afraid.

"Do we really have to do this dance?"

The boy sneered but the fear never left his eyes. "You wanted it. Now you got it."

"I don't even know you, kid. We don't have to do this."

The boy nodded slowly. "You know me. Thought you was heat. You ain't no cop. You been askin' around about me, followin' me. I saw you here tonight. Now you're fucked, man."

"Won't be as easy as you think, kid. Come on, let's save us both some trouble. I just want to talk to you, that's all. Just talk to me for a minute. I'll even throw in—" The kid surprised him with a long looping right that he blocked. Whelan threw a left at the air, just to keep him honest, and when the kid stuck his left out and pawed in Whelan's direction, Whelan smacked him with the right. The punch caught the kid just below the eye but there wasn't much behind it; enough to sting, not enough to drop him. The kid touched his cheekbone, took a step to one side, nodded once and threw his left and got nothing, a right that Whelan slipped, and another left that Whelan took on his forearm.

And then he walked into the kid's foot. It seemed to come up from out of nowhere, quick and hard and sure, and dug deep into Whelan's midsection just below the rib cage. He expelled breath, fought nausea and lost his balance, and the kid threw a combination that caught him in the side of his face as he went down.

He hit the sidewalk with both hands and one knee and was attempting to get to his feet when the boy's foot dug into his stomach again and Whelan thought something would be ruptured.

He collapsed on the sidewalk and covered the side of his face with his arm. Above him, he heard the boy panting and then he could feel and smell the kid's breath on his arm. He waited for more. There was the sound of a car turning a corner somewhere in the background and then he sprang up at the kid, caught him around the knees and brought him down hard on the pavement. He scrambled up onto the kid and sat his weight high up on the boy's back and then relaxed. Billy jerked his body suddenly and Whelan fell forward, stopping himself with a hand against the sidewalk. Then Billy bit him on the wrist, and Whelan yelled and straightened up, and the kid bucked him off. They both scrambled to their feet and the kid was off into the darkness like an alley cat. Whelan ran after him but knew within a half dozen steps that he'd lost the boy for now. He stopped, hands on his knees, bent over with exhaustion and hurting in half a dozen places, and waited for the air to come back into his lungs. He heard the sound of a car door somewhere back near the field house, then heard the car start. He looked up briefly, saw a small dark compact pull out of a parking space just outside the park entrance and watched it move away.

He walked tiredly back to the field house parking lot and lit a cigarette as he slid in behind the wheel. He started the Jet, backed up and felt a strange but immediately recognizable lurching to the left. He backed it up a few more feet and heard the loud flopping of flaccid rubber and stopped the car. He rested his forehead for a moment on the steering wheel, then got out to verify what he already knew.

Both tires on the driver's side had been slashed.

I am having a very bad evening.

He leaned for a few minutes against his trunk and finished his cigarette. He'd have to get an early tow or the city would tow it for him, to a city pound conveniently located in a burned-out neighborhood somewhere at the outer edge of the solar system, and if he didn't get it out in time, it would be a skeleton when he saw it again.

Add the cost of a tow to the price of two new tires, and his wallet was taking as bad a beating as his face. He started walking toward Lawrence and eventually caught a cab home, where he had a couple of beers and soaked himself in the tub for half an hour. He looked at the late news for a few minutes, heard nothing to cheer himself up and decided the only way to improve his day was to end it. He went to bed.

It was hot and airless in the room and he twisted and tangled himself in the sheets till he began to drift off. He was dreaming, a dream in which many people were chasing him up and down streets he didn't recognize, and as he ran a ringing sound filled the air, and he woke to the sound of his doorbell. He looked at his alarm clock: 1:15. He'd been in bed for perhaps forty-five minutes.

There was a pause and the ring came again, long and insistent, and he pulled on a pair of pants and went to the front door. Through the small window in the door he could see a person moving around the front of the porch and apparently peering into his front window. He grabbed an umbrella from the hall tree, pulled the door open and stepped directly out onto the porch.

"Something I can help you with?"

Jean Agee let out a yelp and nearly fell backward over his banister.

"Jesus, Jean, what are you doing here at this time of night? Do you know what these streets are like at night?"

She seemed to have trouble catching her breath, and her eyes went to the dark object in his hand. He held it up.

"It's just an umbrella. I didn't know who was out here. I had a little trouble earlier tonight and I thought you were the fella I had my trouble with, come calling again. And somebody broke in over the weekend."

"Oh, dear. What kind of trouble did you have? Were you hurt again?"

He winced at "again" and smiled. "Not much. I got at least a draw this time. The other guy took off. I was doing pretty well till he kicked me." He pointed to his midsection, saw her look down and realized he was wearing no shirt.

"Oh, it left a mark." She took a couple of steps forward, raised her hand but did not quite touch the long red abrasion just below the ribs. Whelan swallowed.

"Well, come on in and tell me what you're doing here."

Inside, he sat her on his couch, went to his bedroom and put on a clean shirt.

He came out buttoning it. "Get you anything? I've got some beer."

"Will you have one if I have one?"

"Sure. I'm a perfect host." He fetched a couple of the dark Augsburgers and she made a sour face when he came in.

"Dark beer. I don't know if I can drink dark beer." She laughed nervously and took a beer from him.

"Glass?"

"No, this is fine." She took a long pull and gulped some of it down, and he knew she was trying to guzzle the whole thing without tasting it. She looked around his house. "This is...*nice.*"

"Why is that so amazing?"

She smiled at him and there was high color in her cheeks. "'Cause I've seen your office." She laughed.

Whelan laughed and wondered why he was so nervous. "I don't live in my office. I live here, so it's got to be decent." She nodded and looked around again and sipped at her beer, still holding her breath as she drank.

"You want to tell me why you're here at this time of night?"

She nodded and picked at the label of the bottle. "Yes. But give me a minute, all right? Would you tell me how you got hurt?"

"I got a little daring and went down to the park to see if I could find...one of the guys I've been looking for." He noted his own hesitancy and realized that, despite what Captain Wallis had told him, he was still trying to make Gerry Agee out of Billy the Kid. He thought for a moment and it struck him that the captain and J.B. hadn't *seen* the street boy he was looking for: they'd reacted to Whelan's very sketchy second-hand description.

"Jean, how tall would you say Gerry is?"

Her eyes widened and a new look came into them, and he repeated, "How tall?"

"Taller than you. Six-one or six-two. Why?"

"In the picture, his hair looks blondish. Would you call him blond?"

She hesitated and then said, "It's sort of brown but it's really a reddish-brown. If you see him in the sunlight, you can see all these little red highlights…Why do you want to know about that? You think the man you had the fight with…you think it was Gerry?" She was incredulous.

He looked at her before answering. She was sitting rigidly at the far end of the couch, body language screaming mistrust at him. He saw that her powder-blue sweater clung to her breasts and that she'd put on eye shadow, but there was nothing for him in her eyes at the moment.

"I'm not even saying…" And then he nodded because it was the truth. "It's…there's a possibility, that's all."

"A possibility of *what?*" Openly hostile now.

He sighed and shook his head. "A possibility that your brother is the young guy I've been looking for."

"You've seen the picture—is it him?" She leaned forward a little, challenging him to make some sense.

"I don't know. It didn't look like him, but you know what I think about that picture. And it was dark, and this kid had a couple weeks' growth of beard on his face, and his hair was hanging in his eyes and he was throwing punches. But his hair was red."

"Gerry's not a redhead. Nobody's ever called him a redhead." She watched him and he saw himself from her vantage point, a beat-up private eye with a seedy office in a lousy neighborhood, a guy given the simple assignment of finding her brother and then turning it into something hateful and insulting.

"I only said it was a possibility. I'm looking for a bunch of people I don't know, people I haven't seen, for the most part, and I'm trying to make sense of what little I know. Maybe it wasn't Gerry tonight. Probably wasn't. But there are a couple of things I haven't told you…about Gerry." He sighed and wanted her to leave, wanted to be back in bed.

"Like what?" Posture said defiance, eyes said something else.

"At the YMCA they told me a couple of things that I didn't think necessary to tell you. I didn't want to worry you unnecessarily unless I...Shit. They told me Gerry was frequently heard talking to himself in his room."

She gave him a smirk, eyes still worried. "A lot of people talk to themselves. I do. You probably do. What's the big deal?" She shook her head slowly and bathed him in contempt.

"These were conversations," he said bluntly. "He was talking to other people and...they were talking to him. They were angry conversations, Jean, confrontations with people, and they made him angry and he was heard bellowing at these people and speaking in different voices."

Her mouth opened and the anger drained from her face to be replaced by shock. She tried to speak and began to breathe audibly through her mouth and she started to shake her head.

"He was always so sensitive. Things *got* to him that didn't bother other people. And his drinking—is it possible that all of this was because of his drinking?" She looked to him frankly for insight that would soften this portrait of her cherished brother.

Whelan looked at her and saw a girl who'd long suspected that her brother had lost it and he was bitterly angry at having to confirm it all.

"I don't know. Maybe. But if you're asking me to give an opinion, no, I don't really think so. But there was something else that bothers me. He had a...a thing for these guys on the street. The derelicts and winos. He really disliked them." He shrugged to himself and looked down at his bare feet.

She began to cry, softly at first and then louder, and he made no move toward her. He held himself rigidly and refused to allow himself to touch her. She covered her face in both hands and let it all out, and only an idiot would have thought she needed somebody's hands on her.

Whelan looked down at the rug and waited, and when she was done crying he looked at her. She was facing him on the sofa, cheeks wet and red and tears still running out of the corners of her eyes and making dark smears of mascara. She sniffled, straightened, fished in her purse for a handkerchief and came up empty, and he bounded up to get a Kleenex, relieved to be doing something useful, to be moving. He handed her a couple of tissues, waited till she'd wiped her face and dabbed at her eyes. She smiled at him and there was shyness in it, awkwardness.

She looked at the makeup smeared on the Kleenex. "I bet I look like something out of a horror movie."

"Not to me."

She smiled again, said, "Thank you," and looked down at the rug.

"I'm really sorry about all this," he said.

"I know you are. And it has nothing to do with you. You're a kind man and you—well, you're very honest. I'm grateful for that. You don't really think I'm as naive as I sound, do you? I knew there was a good chance you'd find out that Gerry was dead, or that he was living in the gutter like these poor old men, or that he was in…well, jail or something like that. I knew that. It's just that I don't want to know he's been responsible for something terrible like this. I just can't face it, and I sure can't take that home to my mom. I'll make something up if I have to but I won't tell her something like that about her son. I won't."

Somebody else probably will, he thought, but said nothing.

"Look, there's also a chance, a good chance, that he has no connection with any of what has happened. If we look at the facts, we don't have much. A couple of guys at the Y said he had some problems, and they're apparently things you weren't totally aware of. It doesn't mean he's killed anybody. I just want you to be aware of the possibilities."

"But what you said about him…in his room. That was true?"

"Yeah. That was true."

She looked down. "So we can say he came here and lost his mind. That much seems to be true."

"We're not doctors. Maybe he has moments when he has trouble telling the difference between reality and his own…He needs help, wherever he is. That's the way you should probably think about it."

And I hope that's all it is.

When she seemed to be composed, he lit a cigarette, waited a few moments and then leaned toward her.

"It might be time for you to think about heading back to Hope. I can always call you there with my reports. I don't see what can be accomplished by your staying here. You'll spend a lot of your money and waste your time."

He started to say more but stopped, shrugged and took a puff on his cigarette.

She looked at him for what seemed to be a long time and then smiled. "You're really a nice man. I feel like I'm complicating your work. But you don't have to worry about me."

"It's none of my business, Jean, but you're making me nervous. I've been trying to get ahold of you for…all day, and I called you once or twice yesterday." He felt his face redden. He hadn't intended to tell her that if she didn't ask.

She nodded. "I know. I knew you were trying to get in touch with me and I knew I was acting crazy. Behaving strangely. I knew I was. I just didn't want to talk to anyone."

He cleared his throat and looked down as he spoke. "Look, if I was out of line the other night, if I offended you—"

She laughed. "Oh, you weren't out of line. I think *I* was, probably. And I felt a little strange about it the next morning, but it never occurred to me that you were the one that was at fault. I just felt a little weird about it, you know? So I didn't want to face you right away, at least not till I'd had some time to think about everything. But that wasn't why I didn't want to talk."

"Feel like talking about it?"

"Sure. I woke up yesterday morning and couldn't shake the feeling that Gerry's dead. That he's dead and he's been dead for months and we didn't know it. So I just went out and tried to have something to eat and couldn't. I started walking. I must have walked for two hours, I have no idea what neighborhoods I went through. At one point I must have been in a poor neighborhood: there were a lot of vacant lots and some abandoned buildings and all the people were black, and they were staring at me like I was a crazy woman. Then I realized I was crying and had tears in my eyes and everything.

"Then I was in this strange place where everybody was shopping, there were blocks and blocks of stores and it was really kind of neat but it smelled awful, it smelled of onions, the whole neighborhood smelled of *onions*."

"That was Maxwell Street. You covered some ground, girl. That's a far piece from the Estes Motel. It's kind of a Chicago landmark, Maxwell Street. You probably missed some bargains—and you should have stopped and had a Polish with grilled onions, then you wouldn't have noticed the smell."

She laughed and covered her eyes with her hands. "I had no idea where I was. Then I found a phone and called my mom just to hear a familiar voice but I couldn't talk to her for more than five minutes because I started thinking about how much all this could hurt her. When I was finished, I got a cab and had him take me to a museum."

"Which one?"

"The one with the elephants in the fighting pose, and the dinosaurs."

"The Field Museum."

"Then I went and sat on a bench near the lakefront, where the boats are parked."

"Moored."

"Whatever. I sat there in the sun and got all sweaty and felt sorry for myself. I'd probably have stayed there all day but this repulsive man came over and sat down next to me and started saying gross things to me. I got up and walked away and when I looked back, he was saying something to some young boy riding by on a bike."

Whelan laughed. "Hurt your ego, huh?"

She laughed with him, buried her whole face in her hands and laughed till her body shook. When she calmed down, she took a sip of her beer, made a face and looked at him.

"I just don't know how to deal with your city, Mr. Paul Whelan. I don't understand it. It scares me and it's fascinating, and I think half the people in it must be lonely and I think I've seen twenty or thirty people on the street who are just plain crazy. And the real reason I didn't talk to you yesterday was that I really wanted to, badly. I wanted some human contact."

He felt suddenly embarrassed and tried to joke it off. "What about the man in the park?"

"Very funny, but not what I had in mind. I—well, do you still want to know why I came here?"

"I guess I know. You're scared and you feel alone. You—" He shrugged. She finished her beer and looked at him, and just to be doing something he got up and took it from her. She stood and took his hand and pulled him to her and he was surprised at her strength. She put both hands around his neck and kissed him and he dropped the bottle. He pressed against her, felt the firm young body against him, felt her nudging against his crotch. He could smell her perfume and soap and the smell of sweat and her tongue was in his mouth. She broke it off and kissed him again and bit him, and he could picture the perfect little white teeth, and he ran his lips across her neck. His hands moved up and down her back and down to her hips and then his fingers were under her sweater, touching her skin. He moved his hands around to her stomach and she stepped back a little to allow him to lift up her sweater. When his fingers touched her breasts she groaned and he heard himself gasp.

"Been as long for you as it has for me?"

"Yeah," he said through clenched teeth, and led her to his bedroom.

She bent over the bed and kissed him on the forehead.

"What time is it?" Then he noticed she was dressed. "Now where are you going?"

She laughed. "To my room, to get a shower and put on fresh clothes and go shopping. I ruined the past two days. Today I'm going shopping at your famous stores."

He got up on one elbow, suddenly self-conscious about his unkempt self and unwashed body. She looked perfect and he could smell her perfume. When she kissed him, he smelled his mouthwash.

"Wait—" She paused at his door. "Are you gonna let this get to you like—"

She laughed. "No. No way. Call me tonight." And she left.

He stared at the alarm clock till its features came into focus: 6:30. He sank back onto his pillow and his nostrils were rewarded with the scent of Miss Jean Agee of Hope, Michigan, and he decided to lie there for a while.

ELEVEN

The mechanic told him the tires couldn't be saved. Whelan asked him to look at the air-conditioning system, too, and the guy said the car would probably be ready by noon. He took a Lawrence Avenue bus to the office.

They must have parked the Caprice around the corner so they could surprise him, and they did, stepping out of the doorway of Sam's Carniceria just as Whelan passed it. Bauman blocked his way and a pedestrian behind Whelan tried to pass and said, "Excuse me," and Bauman barked, "Go around!" and the man did. Rooney stood a little to one side, near the curb, and Bauman flashed his badge and this time held it long enough so that passersby and even gawkers from the bus would know that Whelan was being rousted.

"You're a prick, Bauman. That's the longest anybody's ever seen your badge."

"Good morning, Mr. Whelan. We'd like a word with you."

"What's going on now, Bauman?"

Bauman looked at Rooney. "His office, okay?"

Rooney shrugged and looked distastefully at the building.

"C'mon, Roon, it ain't gonna bite."

"I'll even order coffee," Whelan said, and Bauman gave a short flat laugh, then took his elbow and gave him a little shove toward the building, a shove they both knew was unnecessary.

Inside the office, Whelan called the coffee shop and ordered coffee and some donuts. Then he put down the phone and said, "Now what, boys?"

Bauman looked at Rooney and raised his eyebrows. Rooney frowned.

"You were at Clarendon Park last night, Mr. Whelan.

Correct?"

"That's a safe bet, Detective Rooney. You *saw* me."

"Can you give an accounting of your movements the rest of the evening?"

Whelan gave a truncated version of his bizarre evening and had their undivided attention when he described his encounter with Billy.

Bauman leaned forward and made a show of examining his face. "No fresh ones, huh? Musta done pretty fair, eh, Whelan?"

"About a draw. I landed a shot but he was better with his feet. We rolled around on the sidewalk a little bit, then he booked. He's fast, I'm not. He got away."

Bauman scratched his check and said, "Lemme see your hands."

Whelan held out his hands, knuckles out.

"Got a boo-boo there, Shamus. That one's swollen."

"Like I said, I landed one. Nothing fancy. Smacked him a good one just under his eye but that was about it. I'm no street fighter."

Bauman nodded and looked at Rooney. "Well, he ain't gonna get no rematch now, is he?"

Rooney ignored him and looked at Whelan with his sad, rheumy eyes. "Mr. Whelan, this street punk, this Billy the Kid, was found dead in the park this morning by a jogger."

Whelan felt the nausea uncoil in his stomach. "How?"

"He was strangled. He was beat up pretty bad, too, but I talked to the M.E. and he says cause of death strangulation," Bauman said. "Pockets pulled inside out and all that good shit." He stared unblinking at Whelan.

"Know when it happened?"

"Not for sure."

"No, we don't," Rooney said curtly, and Whelan decided to ignore him whenever possible.

Bauman inclined his head to one side. "The M.E. guy took a wild guess and said around midnight. Or pretty soon after." He smiled. "Now when did you say you were there, Whelan? Like that Sinatra song? 'In the wee small hours of the morning'?"

"No, I was home by then." And I've got an alibi, he thought, but held it back, his hole card. Then a thought struck him. "And you're pretty sure I didn't do it, or we probably wouldn't be here. We'd be down at Area Six." Rooney squinted and looked as though he would debate the point but Bauman grinned.

"Maybe so, Whelan, maybe so, but you gotta admit you don't look so good on this. And while I'm at it, you want a piece of advice?"

"No."

"It's free. Give some thought to, you know, finding something else to pay the rent, okay? You got your ass kicked—what, twice since Friday? Great record."

Whelan ignored him. There was a knock on the door. "Here's breakfast, guys." He went to the door and paid the kid for the coffee and donuts and handed the bag to Bauman.

"Could I see the body?"

Bauman sipped his coffee, burned his lip, said "Goddamn. What for?"

"I have a client. She's looking for her brother."

"You told me. So what? What's that got to do with this?"

"So there's a little nagging voice I been hearing that says her brother might be Billy the Kid."

"You saw 'im."

"It was dark. I want to see him in the light."

Bauman bit into his donut, tore away a third of it in one bite and mumbled, "Why not."

He suppressed the urge to hold her and forced himself to stand with one hand in his pocket as the morgue attendant opened one of the compartments and pulled out the gurney. He could almost feel her stiffen, saw the utter terror in her face and saw Bauman watching her with interest. The detective studied her face intently but still found time to give her body a careful once-over. The attendant looked at her, then at Whelan. He was a young man, in his early twenties, and it was obvious he hadn't worked here long. There was no color in his face and he continually wet his lips and blinked. He seemed to sense that the appointment was Whelan's and finally said, "You wanna view the, uh, body now, sir?"

Whelan looked at the girl and nodded. The attendant pulled the covering back from the upper half of the body and stepped back.

The breath went out of her and her eyes bulged and her mouth worked, and she began shaking her head. She looked at Whelan and shook her head again and turned to grab his shoulder.

"It's not him, is it?"

"No." She buried her face in his shoulder.

Whelan looked at the face of Billy the Kid and realized how little resemblance there was between this dead boy of the streets and the face of youthful promise in the photo. Grasping at straws. In death, Billy's face took on a different aspect; it was not the face of a hardened street fighter but a boy's face, the face of a young one who would always be a little confused, always kept a little off-balance by the world, always losing. He saw the small bruising beneath the right eye and felt a pang of remorse. He looked closer, saw the red marks on the throat, the deep marks half hidden by the red hair, where the boy had been struck. He looked at the attendant and shook his head.

The young man covered up the face and slid the body back into its compartment, clearly as relieved as anyone that the process was over.

Outside, Whelan helped her into the taxi and looked at Bauman. The detective was still watching Jean. He looked at Whelan.

"So who is this broad?"

"I told you. She's a client. Looking for her brother. It was a long shot, but I thought maybe…" He shrugged and looked around.

"So he's a runaway, or what?"

"He's running, all right, but he's not a teenager. I think he's out on the street somewhere. He's a drunk, for one thing." He thought for a moment, then pulled out the picture. "Want to take another look?"

Bauman glanced at the picture. "The choirboy. No, I don't need to take another look. If I see him, I'll let you know." He looked back at the girl. "That's a nice piece. Real nice." He looked at Whelan with surprise. "You layin' her?"

"We're gonna take up a collection, Bauman. Send you to charm school. No, I'm not."

"But you'd like to. I'd love to get next to something like that. But that broad's half your age, am I right?"

Whelan looked at Jean. "Yeah, she's half my age."

They said little as the cab took them back to the Estes. He wanted to talk but there was a brittleness to her silence and he let it go. When she got out of the cab, she leaned over and gave him a peck on the cheek.

"You still want me to call tonight or should I leave you alone for a while?"

"No, call me. I'll probably be spooked now." She forced a smile.

"You look tired."

She forced another smile. "A friend of mine kept me up late." He laughed, relieved, and watched her go into the motel.

The car was ready. The mechanic, a slender Mexican named Joe, had put on a complete set of tires, explaining that the two good ones were too worn, that a car with new tires on only one side of the car would continually pull to the bad side. There was Freon in his air conditioning system now. Tires, Freon, labor and the tow came to $305.

"I'm having a bad week," he told the mechanic.

"Next week gonna be better."

He drove south to Fullerton, to the Lincoln Park Lagoon. He got out and walked, finally stopping beneath an enormous cottonwood that had to predate the park and most of the city. He sat there and had a cigarette and went over the night again, reveling in it, rehashing each glorious, surprising second of it, and after a while had to laugh at himself. With an effort, he made himself think of her brother. Some way or another it would be necessary to make an end of this search, to put some sort of answer together for her, if they were to have any chance together.

Then it struck him that the answer might end it. If Gerry Agee turned out to be the dark figure in Whelan's imagination, the animal who killed derelicts in a sick fury, then this thing with Jean Agee was over. And if Gerry was a corpse somewhere in someone else's morgue, then it was over, too. If the kid was dead, or if he turned out to be a killer, then the girl would go back to Michigan and, consciously or not, would do everything a normal person does to wipe out the recollection of evil. They might have a tearful last evening together, and promise to get together as soon as things calmed down, but Whelan knew enough of the human reaction to trouble to know he'd never see her again. He tried to look six months, a year into his future, and couldn't see anybody but Paul Whelan.

He finished his smoke and told himself that he had another job, that it was a good time to get busy.

He stopped back at his apartment for a quick turkey sandwich and left again. He drove the same streets, over and over, seeing the same knots of men standing on the corners, the same listless faces in the windows, same curtains knotted carelessly back to let in the breeze. Some of the faces stared back at him, some made him for a cop, others frowned, recognizing him, and he realized he'd cruised some of these isolated pockets of Uptown a dozen times.

He passed the Sal Army Center and saw J.B. blocking the entry of a very drunk young man. At a stoplight, two Puerto Rican girls in short skirts and tank tops waved at him and he realized he'd been staring at them.

He drove back to the building on Beacon. He parked his car down the street and sat there for a while listening to the radio and trying to think. It seemed to him that squatters normally took the lower floors of an abandoned building, and Sharkey was supposed to be up in years. But the apartment on Sunnyside had been on the second floor, and from where he sat he could see that the boards had been removed from the third-floor windows of an apartment. He looked up at the windows and sighed. A smart guy would wait till dark and have a chance of finding someone in the place. A smart guy would also then get his behind kicked in the rematch.

Well, I'm not a smart guy and I want to see what's up there. Now.

He went around the corner and entered the alley that ran behind the building. The backyard was a concrete courtyard. There were piles of trash and yellowing newspaper, and a large heap of scorched wood, presumably from the building's innards, and an ash-coated steel drum where street people had warmed themselves in harsher weather. Not that this weather wasn't just as harsh. The building cut off what little breeze came in from the lake and Whelan felt as if he'd entered a microwave. A small movement caught his eye and he found himself looking into a pair of dull yellowing eyes in a yellow face. A thin ragged man sat on the cement in the shade of the staircase and watched him. Whelan nodded slightly and looked away. Then he looked up at the third floor.

He thought of asking the old man who stayed on the third floor and decided it was pointless. He went quietly up the stairs, going slowly and listening for anything. At the curve between the second and third floors he looked up and went the rest of the way watching. The staircase led to two apartments on the third floor. On the porch outside the first he stopped and looked around. It appeared that squatters had begun the process of stripping the building for firewood. One railing was gone completely, making the far side of the porch a perilous place to be; the trapdoors leading to the roof were gone over both apartments, and the screen door was missing on the nearer one. The windows of this apartment were shut; the one farther from him had a window open, a kitchen window, just cracked a couple of inches or so but open nonetheless. He moved over to the door, put his hand noiselessly to the doorknob, took a breath, turned it and put a shoulder into the door.

It opened without resistance and he was hit by the airless heat within, by the dry smells of ancient wallpaper and crumbling plaster and rotting wood, and from beyond this kitchen, other smells, the rank smells of human life at the lowest rungs of existence: garbage and rotting food and human waste. He waited for a moment to listen, and became aware of a human presence: a man's sweat, the musty odors of old clothing, and he knew he wasn't alone. He took a step, heard linoleum crack and fought the sudden and powerful notion that he was going to die.

"Anybody there? I need to talk to somebody, that's all. Just a couple of questions."

He moved forward to the door of the kitchen, listening, holding his breath and feeling the sweat rolling down his back and neck. And then he just stopped.

He was standing at the door to what had once been a dining room, presumably a place where a normal happy family took meals, and in it was a human being. Whelan held his breath and his motion and suppressed his fear, and listened. The person in this room, whose existence was at that moment nearly palpable, was not moving, not breathing. He moved forward into the darker room and stooped down low and peered straight ahead to allow his eyes to adjust; a few feet beyond, he could see the empty living room, lit by the open window on the street side.

Gradually he could make out piles of trash in the corners of the dining room, fast-food containers and paper cups and what appeared to be a small pile of blankets. On the floor between living and dining room was a discarded coat. And in the center of the room, facing the front and the intruder as he'd done in life, was a dead man. He heard a pained voice, his own voice, saying, "Oh, Lord."

He walked over to the body and knelt down, knowing before he could actually make out the features that this was Hector. Hector Green, loyal friend and bodyguard and a hard man to cross.

He stooped down and put his hand to the floor for balance and touched something thick and wet and sticky. There was blood on his fingers, congealed blood, thickly clotted, more black than red, and there was more on the far side of the body. He pulled the man up by one shoulder and saw the surprised look on the face and, lower, the deep gashing across the stomach and chest. He'd been stabbed and slashed in several places. The front of Hector's old flannel shirt was matted, a shiny mass of blood, and Whelan thought he might be sick. You can never get used to it, he thought, and took a deep breath. He looked at the dead man's face and felt a rush of pain.

"Couldn't take you in a fight, old buddy, could he? I bet you were a good guy, Hector."

He looked around the room and felt a rush of frustration. I'm gonna find them all after they're dead.

He allowed the stiffened body to roll back to its original position and got up to have a look around, knowing it was useless. There was no sign of the hunted man called Sharkey who was somehow the explanation for all this. If Hector was dead, how far away could Sharkey be? Could he continue to survive without his bodyguard. Okay, he thought, now I'm looking for one old guy that can't move too fast. There was no blood that he could see in any of the other rooms, no sign that there had been violence at either of the doors, no second corpse. The front door wouldn't lock and it looked as though someone had put a shoulder into it, but that was as likely to have been Hector and Sharkey first getting in as it was their assailant.

He called Bauman from a public phone, got Rooney instead. Then he gave his news, heard the suspicion in Rooney's voice, the irritation at having to go out in the heat and tramp around in a boarded-up building.

Life's hard, Rooney.

"Bauman's in the can, Whelan. We'll be there in a couple of minutes. You stay there, you hear? You *stay* there." Rooney was muttering to himself when he hung up.

"A couple of minutes" proved to be twenty, and Whelan met them at the curb when they pulled up. A few seconds behind them a squad car rolled to a stop.

Bauman emerged from the car, hitching his pants up as far

as they'd go under his belly and squinting in the sunlight up at the building. He did not look at Whelan.

"Rooney said you'd be here as soon as you got out of the can. What were you doing in there, Bauman? Having a tender moment?"

Bauman turned slowly and stared as though he hadn't heard him.

"What? You got a problem?"

"It was just a joke."

Bauman stepped a little closer to him. "Oh, I wouldn't fucking joke, pal. We got two guys down inside of twenty-four hours and you were lookin' for 'em both, and we got your statement that you duked it out with the one and you discovered the other one." He studied Whelan for a second and then spoke under his breath. "Right now, I don't know you. Anybody asks, you're just a fuckup that thinks he's some kinda detective from the movies." He looked at Rooney, said, "Let's go," and then nodded curtly to the two uniforms. He gestured for Whelan to go first, and they all went around the back of the building.

Inside the apartment, Bauman bent down by the body as the other officers searched the place. Whelan saw the detective touch the dead man's forehead. Bauman nodded.

"Well, you're a pretty good detective, Whelan. You're a sharpie, all right. This is a dead guy, just like you said. There's blood and he's been stabbed."

"Have fun with me, Bauman. Enjoy yourself."

The detective shook his head and stood up, looking candidly at Whelan. "I ain't enjoyin' this. It ain't a *challenge* or any bullshit like that. And you know what's really putting a hair up my ass about this, Whelan?"

"I'm listening."

"I keep thinking maybe I'm wrong. I keep thinking it's gotta be one of us." He pointed at Whelan with the index finger, at himself with the thumb. "One of us, babe. And I know it ain't me." The smile now, bloodletter's smile.

"I didn't kill him, Bauman. Get serious. I didn't kill anybody."

Bauman shrugged. "I'm just a simple guy, Whelan. I gotta

add up the facts and see what I get, and right now what I get don't look good for you."

"You taking me in?"

Bauman tilted his head as though he hadn't thought of it. "Why not?"

He was taken to Area 6, a flat brown building on the exact spot where, as a boy, he'd visited Riverview Park, the last of the old-time amusement parks, with his parents. He met a lieutenant named Nichols, who seemed to go out of his way to give Bauman his head, and he was taken into a rectangular room with soundproofing across the ceiling. The air in the room was stale and smelled of cigarette smoke, and he knew it was no accident that it was the only place in the building that the air conditioning didn't seem to reach.

They questioned him for a while, Bauman and Rooney; Bauman asked most of the questions and Rooney chewed Rolaids nonstop and left the room half a dozen times. They were the standard questions, making him reconstruct his movements and regurgitate his story over and over again, each time from a different angle. And then he stopped answering.

Bauman leaned over him and blew cigar breath on him and stared into his eyes. "I asked you a question, Whelan. Answer it."

"I think I'll call a lawyer."

"Oh, yeah? Think you need one?"

"I think you're dicking me around and if I get an attorney here I can tie up your time for a while and return the favor. You don't have shit on me, Bauman. And I don't think you actually suspect me."

Bauman snorted in his face. "You keep lookin' for people and they keep turnin' up dead. People we want to talk to."

"You're connected to both of these dead men," Rooney said.

"So are you, as far as that goes. Come on, Bauman. What are you looking for?"

Bauman took a couple of steps back and put his hands into his back pockets. "Seems to me, you been a couple steps ahead of us lately."

"No. I've been playing hunches. Going to that building, that was a hunch. Nothing more."

"So maybe you got other hunches. Maybe you got something else I should know, maybe to keep somebody else from turning into a stiff."

"I don't know anything. I'd tell you if I did."

"Nothing? Come on, Whelan, think. Dig down, babe. Gimme something. This Sharkey, you got anything to tell me about him?"

He thought for a moment, then shrugged. "Another hunch."

"Let's hear it."

"I think he's got a record. That's what I think. This guy was on the run because of something he did, something in his past."

Bauman looked at him for a long time and then shrugged. "And that's all you got? A guess? That's it?" Bauman watched him for any sign of hesitation, any sign of deceit.

"That's what I've got. Now you've got it. Now let me out of here."

"Okay, Whelan. You can go," and he looked at Rooney. "But only 'cause Rooney's gotta eat dinner, right, Roon?"

"If you don't mind," Rooney said, and Bauman laughed.

It was evening when he returned to the neighborhood. His shirt stuck to his back like wet newspaper and he felt dirty. He was hungry, irritated that he'd had to pay for a cab back home and furious with Bauman.

He thought of calling Jean and decided not to push it yet. When a lady says, "Call me tonight" it doesn't mean ten after six.

He took a shower, then sat in his living room with the shades pulled down to fight the setting sun. He sipped at a can of pop and eventually made himself an omelet: green peppers, tomatoes, onions, a little monterey jack and a couple of sliced jalapenos. It broke when he flipped it but it was still good, and he ate it with gusto as he watched the evening news. It occurred to him that none of the local stations would be carrying stories of the deaths of Billy the Kid or Hector. Unimportant lives, unimportant murders.

After dinner he went out, drove to a liquor store and bought a six-pack, then drove over to the Wilson Men's Club Hotel. Wade Sanders was standing in front, watching traffic dull-eyed, rapping halfheartedly to women who refused to look at him, and when Whelan hit the horn, Wade looked up. Whelan waved him over to the car.

"Hey, Mr. Whelan."

"Get in, Wade. Let's go have a couple pops." He indicated the six-pack on the passenger seat.

Wade chuckled. "Sounds righteous to me, man." He hurried around to the other side and got in, grinning.

Wade smelled up his car but Whelan didn't mind. He drove to the park, stopped in the lot beside the bridge at Montrose, where the evening's traffic of make-out couples and underage drinkers was just beginning to assemble. Whelan made small talk, listened as Wade catalogued the jobs that might be coming down the pike for him soon, and Whelan found himself watching the young face intently, looking for a shred of promise. It was an open face, surprisingly without fear or hostility. A drunk's face. Genial and malleable and pitiful, and he knew this young man could be dead inside of two years.

"When you gonna put the brakes on, Wade?"

Wade stopped in mid-sip, looked at Whelan with surprise and shrugged. Disappointment came into the blue eyes.

"Yeah, I know. I never hassle you. Well, just this once, kid, just this one time let me hassle you. Go back to Ottawa, Wade. Or go someplace else."

Wade looked sullenly out the window. "Ain't nothing for me in Ottawa."

"Your ma 's there. See your ma. Then go somewhere else. Anywhere. Anywhere else is better than this."

Wade gave him a surprised look. "Better than Chi? This is a happening town, man. There's something going down every—"

Whelan leaned over and clapped a hand on his shoulder, hard. "Not for you. Maybe not for me either but I've got a house here. But there's nothing here for you. At least not as long as you suck those down all the time."

The boy looked at the beer can and opened his mouth to protest.

"I know, I know: you're gonna quit. Well, maybe you are, and maybe you aren't. But right now, in this town, you're going nowhere fast. You oughtta get out. Try someplace different, someplace smaller, maybe."

"Smaller? How'm I gonna find anything in a smaller place, man?"

"Beats the shit out of me, Wade, but I know it's easier to get lost in a big place. Easier to get swallowed up."

Wade watched him for a moment. "So what's this all about, man?"

"I was going to ask you a couple of things about this… this thing I've been working on and I guess I just got off on this other stuff. I like you. Always have."

He looked at the boy. Wade shifted uncomfortably in the seat, made a little shrugging motion and said nothing.

"And this week I saw two guys who were living like you, one of them your age, and they're both dead. Did you know Billy the Kid?"

He shook his head. "No. I knew who he was, though. Heard he got killed."

"But you knew Hector."

"Hector? Hector's dead, man?"

"Somebody stuck him, Wade. I found his body this afternoon." Wade stared out the window for a second, shaking his head. "I heard about Billy but I didn't know about ol' Hector. Hector was good people, man."

"And a week ago my friend Artie was killed, and he was a good guy, and he was a little like you, a little bit lost and a little too much of a drinker, and he is dead. Like you're going to be soon."

He couldn't believe he'd said it but he was glad. He could tell he'd made his point. Wade looked down at his beer, then took a sip just to be doing something.

When he could speak, Wade shook his head, still looking away, and said, "I dunno where to go."

"Go where you have somebody. Go home. Tell 'em you're in a little trouble. Tell 'em you booze if you have to. Force yourself, kid. Give yourself some room and some time. You know you'll be welcome at your ma's. You told me she can still tell your stepfather what to do, am I right?"

The shaggy head nodded, but Whelan wasn't convinced.

"Wade, Billy was your age, and nobody from his family is ever gonna see him again. They might not even find out what happened to him."

The boy looked over at the parked cars; when he spoke, his voice was thicker, and Whelan thought he seemed like nothing so much as a lost child.

"You're right, Mr. Whelan. Ain't doin' myself no good here. I just…Jesus, I don't wanna go shufflin' home like a bum, have everybody see me in the shit like this."

"Happens to us all, kid. Just do it in style, if you're gonna do it. I'll give you a few bucks, you can go back wearing decent clothes. Clean yourself up, go home, tell 'em you got sick of the big town and let the word out you're looking for work."

Wade laughed and sipped his beer. "You make it sound like a piece of cake. It ain't like that. It ain't no easy thing. And Ottawa, man, there's not a whole lot in Ottawa."

"I didn't say it would be easy. I just said that was how I thought you should do it. Maybe I'm wrong, but I think it's how I'd do it. Just go back for a while. What the hell, if it doesn't work out back there, you can always split again, try someplace else. What have you lost?"

This time there was no rebuttal and Whelan took a long pull at his beer. It tasted flat and cheap and made him want a cup of coffee.

"You got to get out of here, Wade. These guys are all dying. You can't tell because you're with them, but they're all dying, and it's a hard way to go. Go home for a while. Use the time to think about your next step. Maybe Ottawa isn't the place for you, maybe you'll think of someplace else. But if you stay here, you'll die here."

The boy nodded slowly and drained his beer. Whelan pulled another can loose and handed it to him. "C'mon, let's go for a little ride. The man fixed my air conditioner, so I should use it."

As they drove along the lake, Wade slumped down into the seat and made noises of contentment.

"Man, this feels sweet. This feels pretty boss to me."

Whelan laughed, and then a thought occurred to him. "Wade, what do you do at night when it's hot. Where do you go?"

Wade laughed. "I look for someplace with air-con and hope I don't get hassled. You know how it is, man. You get a little change, you go sit someplace cool and you make one cup of coffee last an hour."

"No, I mean at night. To sleep. When your room's too hot."

"Oh. Like the song says, man, 'Up on the Roof.' That's where I go. There's a door at the back of the third floor, leads right out onto the roof. I get up there with a blanket and my pillow and it's real nice, man. You get some breeze up there. That room's a fucking oven."

"You have the roof to yourself?"

Wade pursed his lips. "Mostly. Hardly ever see anybody else up there. I dunno why. It's pretty nice."

They stopped for a light at Ohio.

"Whoa, check it out, Mr. Whelan."

In the next lane, a young Latino couple in a powder-blue convertible were going at it, ten rounds of contact sport. Whelan watched them absently till the motorist behind him honked to tell him the light had changed. He was having trouble concentrating because he was remembering the two open trapdoors over the porch on Beacon. He leaned over and turned on the radio. "I need a little music. Okay?"

"Sure. Why not?"

They drove for a while and eventually returned to Uptown and the heat and grit of Wilson Avenue. He let Wade off in front of the hotel and told him to take the remaining beer.

"But go easy on this stuff, kid. You hear?"

Wade smiled at him. "I'll give anything a shot once."

"Good enough. I'll be talking to you. You think about what I said."

"Hey, thanks, man," Wade said, and went into the rooming house.

And Whelan drove away, nodding to himself. I'm gonna have to do more than just "chat" with you, kid. We're gonna get you out of here.

On a day when nothing else had gone right, it surprised him not at all that Jean had left her room. The desk clerk told him she'd stepped out for something to eat. This time, however, she'd left a message for him to call her later. He hung up, mollified by the message and amused at himself. A grown man, elated when the new girl tells him he has permission to call back.

He sat back and looked at the wall clock. He thought of the little derelict named Sharkey who had been the cause of so much death. He wondered how long Sharkey could stay on the run, how he could even survive without his bodyguard. How far can he get? And he thought about what Wade had told him and the more he looked at it, the more obvious it became.

I found him.

He thought of calling Bauman but held back, suddenly uncertain. He drove over to Beacon and parked at the corner and went around the back of the building. He stood in the alley just outside the back gate and studied the building for a long moment. There was no movement. The old man who'd been sitting beneath the staircase that afternoon was long gone now, probably scared off for good by the sudden onslaught of police cars and uniforms and potbellied detectives. A single bright orange street lamp illuminated a short span of alley. The outer edge of the glow just touched the back of the building, and the longer he stared at it, the more alien he felt.

He went up slowly and quietly, stopping at each landing and listening for twenty or thirty seconds. At the landing halfway to the third floor he stopped and took off his shoes. He climbed the remaining half dozen stairs in stocking feet and stopped on the porch and listened.

The steel rungs that formed the ladder to the trapdoor began three feet off the floor. He put his foot on a pile of boards to give himself a boost and went up the rungs; it was no easy climb and he couldn't see an older man doing it without a supreme effort.

At the top rung he paused, held his breath for a moment and then pushed his head slowly up into the opening. He looked around slowly, allowed his eyes to adjust to the darkness and then let out his breath. There was no more reason for stealth.

He pulled himself up onto the roof and stayed in a low crouch as he surveyed the roof. He was alone, except for the small dark form across the roof.

Sharkey had made it to the farthest corner of the roof, to the building's edge, and died there. Whelan stooped down and turned the body over gently. It was stiff but surprisingly light. Even in the darkness he could see that the face had been savagely battered, the nose broken, the eyes pounded shut. The old man's shirtfront was dark with blood, and when Whelan put his hand beneath the old man's head, he touched a mass of bloody hair. It was too dark to determine the precise cause of death but it was a good bet that this man had died of the beating.

He lay the head back gently and remained in a crouch, staring at the elusive old man named Sharkey. He'd get no answers to his questions from this man and his killer seemed farther away than ever. I find them all when they're dead. Anger and frustration welled up in him and he slammed the tar-paper roof with his fist.

"Goddamn!"

And then he heard the steps on the wooden porch below.

He got to his feet quickly, looked around for a place to escape and saw that there was a ten-foot gap between this roof and the nearest one. As he stared through the darkness at the trapdoor, a part of his mind told him that this must have been how the old derelict had felt just before he was killed.

He felt the pounding quicken in his chest and tried to calm himself, to keep his head clear. Advantages. Room enough to fight, time enough to get an angle on the man coming up through the trap. He rushed toward the trapdoor and got behind it, poised, ready to stomp barefoot at the head that came up.

A large heavy head came up even with the rooftop but no farther.

"You up there, Whelan?"

The breath went out of him and he watched the round face and crewcut of Bauman taking shape in the darkness. Bauman looked around, pulled himself up another rung and squinted into the darkness.

"C'mon, Whelan, quit fuckin' around. I saw you come up. Show yourself or I'll have an accident with my service revolver."

Whelan hesitated, then came around into Bauman's line of vision. Bauman paused, grinned maliciously, looked him up and down and then took in what he could of the rest of the roof. He squinted off in the direction of the body and then looked at Whelan, without a smile this time.

"Back off, Whelan. I'm coming up."

Whelan took a step back and watched the bulky body squeeze through the trap. Bauman walked over to the corpse, pulled out a pocket flash and had a long look at the dead man. Whelan saw him shake his head and then crouch down beside the body. He remained on his haunches for perhaps half a minute, examining the wounds and shaking his head. Then Whelan saw him touch the dead man's face, a quick but gentle movement.

Then Bauman turned slowly in Whelan's direction, and even in the darkness Whelan could read the urge to do someone some damage, lots of damage. Bauman stood up, came over to Whelan and put the flash in his face.

"You know 'im?"

"No, but I can guess."

"It's Sharkey. It's him, all right." Bauman kept the light in Whelan's face till he blinked.

"I know what you're thinking, Bauman."

"You're fulla shit," Bauman spat. "Nobody ever knows what I'm thinking."

"I didn't do this."

Bauman stared at him for a moment and Whelan realized the detective just wanted to see him squirm. Finally Bauman make a little snorting sound. "You took off your shoes. You thought there was somebody up here. If you killed him, wouldn't be any reason to sneak up. The body's cold, been dead a long time. If you were just comin' back to check, you wouldn't have taken off your shoes." He stared out at the lights of downtown Chicago in the distance. Whelan looked at the lights and thought they looked a lifetime away.

"This guy was already dead when we were here today, Whelan. Know that?" Without waiting for an answer, he turned to face Whelan. "How'd you know to come up here?"

"A hunch. I know a kid who lives in the Men's Hotel. He told me he goes up on the roof to sleep when it gets real hot."

Bauman nodded distractedly and looked around. "I don't think they come up here to sleep, though. This is where they hid out. I think the old guy couldn't get up and down that good." He pointed the flash at the corpse's legs. "See his ankles? All swole up. That happens with some guys when the ticker starts to go. He couldn't be runnin' up and down that ladder. I think they hid out in that apartment downstairs and got caught. And I think that Hector bought this guy some time to get up here."

Whelan thought about the dead man in the apartment below. "Makes you wonder. He was probably a better guy than either of us."

Bauman put the flash in his eyes again. "Speak for yourself, pal."

"So. You taking me in again?"

"The hell for? Rooney'd have a baby. We talked to you enough. You didn't do it."

Whelan waited a beat and then let it out. "Did you?"

Bauman took a step closer. "You got balls, fella. I'll give you that. No, I don't beat old men to death. Not my style. Sometime maybe I'll show you my style."

He looked over at the body. "Wonder if we'll turn anything up with his prints. I wanna know who this guy was. Gotta be a reason for all this." He looked at Whelan. "We ran a little check on the name. Only Sharkeys we found are dead; burglars, a whole family of 'em in New York. But dead. I'm thinking Sharkey ain't his name." He looked off at the night skyline again, then at Whelan again.

"You go home, Shamus. I need you, I'll be by."

"Fine with me," Whelan said, and walked toward the trapdoor.

"And don't forget your, uh, brogans, Mr. Whelan," Bauman said, and laughed.

He called her again and she was there, and he wanted to come down and be away from his life, from his world.

"Paul? I was wondering, could we go to your place? I just… this room is getting to me. I spend half my day and my whole night here. I just have to get out. And…I think I'm starting to get…you know, a little paranoid."

Warnings went off. "What do you mean, Jean?"

She laughed nervously. "I mean…it's really nothing, you know? I *know* it's nothing. I walk around and I think people are watching me or something." She laughed again.

"I'll pick you up in a half hour."

"Okay. Are you all right?"

"Not entirely. But it'll pass."

He was in his car in ten minutes, and five minutes after that he was doing sixty in the forty-five zone on the Outer Drive. He had no idea whether it was her imagination or reality, but he would take no chances with this girl.

They ordered Chinese food from the Hunan Express and he tipped the delivery man two bucks when he saw how nervous he looked.

"Thank you, sir," the man said, making three little bows. "Not good neighborhood. Not so good."

"I know, but I'm stuck here."

They watched TV and made small talk. In the darkest

recesses of his pantry he found a bottle of Chianti; he'd had it over a year and the wine seemed a little vinegary.

"I forgot I had this. You think it's turned?"

She sipped hers, winced, shrugged. "How would I know? I don't know anything about wine. In Michigan we make wine out of apples and, you know, boysenberries."

As they talked, it occurred to him that this place was no safer for either of them than her hotel room, that someone had already gotten in once. The sour wine took the edge off his fear and slowed the conversation. Eventually they stopped talking and made love on the floor to the drone of a late-night talk show, and when they went to sleep in his room, he lay awake for a long time, long enough for his contentment to leave him. In its wake was the image of a man nearing middle age, making a fool of himself over a girl just past school age, and he began to hope that he would soon find the trail of Gerry Agee, that the trail would lead south or west and they could follow it together and perhaps have an outside shot at something that might last out the year. But he didn't think so.

Twelve

He woke long before Jean and lay there indulging himself with the sound of her easy, slightly noisy breathing. He listened to her and watched her the way he had once watched Liz. He told himself he would trade a lot of things for the guarantee of a life just like this. Then he pulled himself out of bed. She got up on one elbow while he was carrying his clothes into the bathroom for a shower.

"What's your hurry, Mr. Detective?"

"I've got work to do. I want to finish this, all of it."

"Can I come with?"

He laughed. Mr. and Mrs. North. Nick and Nora. "No, you stay here. Or go shopping again. There must be a few places along Michigan Avenue that you missed."

She laughed. "A lot of them are so pricey that I was afraid to go in. Why don't you come with?"

"Can't. You go, I'll talk to you later. Just be careful, and when you're done, come on back here. I think it's…better."

She tilted her head to one side. "You think it's safer, don't you?"

"Yeah, a little."

She thought for a moment, then shrugged. "Maybe you're right."

When he left, he kissed her and let his lips linger, and told himself how good it felt to be leaving a woman in his house.

He had coffee and some toast at the New Yankee, bantered halfheartedly with Eva, the waitress, and watched the crowd, his real reason for being there.

He wanted to look at them again, all of them, see them through someone else's eyes. Some of them he'd seen many times, and in other places: working guys stalling before going in, old ones on Social Security or a pension, mashing their food into a pile in the center of the plate and nibbling at it to stretch the meal. At the bend of the counter, a sad-eyed man with a bruised cheekbone stared out onto the street; eyes red, hands shaky, trying to remember last night.

He watched them come and go, for a cup of coffee, cup of tea, plate of biscuits and gravy, day-old rolls, ice water, handout, use the washroom, start an argument, stand in the air conditioning, look for a woman who'd split. One of these? One of them *somewhere* out there. One of them had killed Artie Shears and four other men, all in the space of a couple of weeks, and he was still out there doing a fast dance, pretending to be something else. Someone he'd talked to. Yes, had to be. Someone he'd talked to.

He set his cup down and stared off into space, unaware that he seemed to be staring at Eva. She smiled at him, then saw that he wasn't really looking at her and busied herself at the coffee urn. He sat there and turned it over and looked at it as many ways as he could manage, and it all came up the same: the man he was looking for wasn't hiding in a basement somewhere. He was out on the street, he was no stranger. He was someone who was a regular on these streets, whose presence would go unremarked.

He sipped at his coffee and had a cigarette and went over the faces, the hangdog men in Captain Wallis's food line, the Indian men slurping soup at Dr. Ludwig's drop-in center, the men standing aimlessly outside the newsstand or waiting with Wade to turn in a day's work at the day-labor office. Who else?

He saw the angry red face of Bauman.

No. He refused to accept the simplicity of it all. Bauman hadn't killed all these men. No reason. No motive. He was sipping at his coffee when it struck him: no, Bauman hadn't killed *all* of them, but he could have killed one, maybe more.

"Oh, shit." And if he'd killed one, it was certainly possible that he'd killed them all, that there was no other killer to look for.

He remembered Bauman's face as he touched the dead man called Sharkey and refused to believe the cop had killed Sharkey. He tried to remember Bauman's face as he came up the ladder through the trapdoor: no, Bauman hadn't even known where to look for the body. No, there was a killer out there, a free man, man without a face.

Are you Gerry Agee? he wondered. Why can't I see your face? What am I overlooking? He decided to do it all over again, retrace his steps and talk to the same people again till something shook loose.

Abby was standing on the porch of the Indian Center, talking to a pair of very sunburned Indian boys. She asked Whelan if he wanted to become an Indian and he laughed. They made small talk for a few minutes but she had nothing to tell him: nothing new, no funny behavior, no newcomers, no one acting strangely, no one who'd dropped out.

Same story at the Sal Army, where J.B. gave him a quizzical look and Captain Wallis smiled patiently.

"Anybody acting strangely, huh?" He raised his blond eyebrows and looked at the guard.

"They all be acting strange," J.B. said.

At the door, he stopped and turned. "I'm really sorry about Billy, captain."

The captain made a gesture of futility with his hands. "It's what I always thought would happen to him. I just wanted to prevent it."

The clerk at the hotel told him Wade had gone out with a work crew from Readymen, and his Public Aid contact was in the field. He caught up with Woodrow outside the Burger King on Sheridan and gave him a buck for a hamburger, but Woodrow had nothing for him.

"No, nothin' out of the or'nary. Least, not for here, ya understand?"

"Yeah, I do. I really do."

At the Way Mission he pushed open the door and was met by the most hostile pair of blue eyes he'd seen in years. They belonged to a trim white-haired man whose face seemed to have been shaved and scrubbed pink and who hadn't had an extra calorie in ten years. There were no wrinkles on him, no smudges on his gleaming black shoes, no hair out of place. He was tall and slender and the picture of conservative taste in white shirt, blue slacks and a narrow blue tie. The man turned slightly and Whelan saw that he'd been standing over Don Ewald. The boy was sitting in a chair in the little waiting room. He was red-eyed and his nose was slightly swollen. There was a scratch along his neck. He was wearing his usual blue shirt and dark pants, and at his feet was a small black suitcase. He looked up, noticed Whelan and looked down quickly.

"May we help you, sir?" the white-haired man asked.

"You must be the Reverend Roberts."

"And you are…"

"That's Mr. Whelan, the detective," Don offered.

The older man took a step closer to Whelan, his face flushing. "So you're the gentleman responsible for my people having ludicrous notions about 'investigating' when they're supposed to be about something quite different. And you see the results."

He gestured toward Don.

"Sorry, I don't understand what you're talking about."

"Look at him," the man commanded.

"What happened to you, Don?"

The boy looked up, blinked, and a tear squeezed its way out of one eye. He shrugged. "I wanted to see if I could help you. I stayed out on the street last night, asking people questions. I thought if I waited till it was dark, there might be different people out." He shot a frightened glance at the Reverend Roberts. "I thought it would help my ministry, too."

"Oh, Donald," the Reverend said.

"Anyway, I was getting ready to leave and I tried to take a shortcut down Racine to get to the bus stop, and three men were standing in a vacant lot and they started to walk after me. I walked faster but they caught me and…they took my wallet and they took…my medallion." He pointed to the scratch on his neck. "And they beat me up."

"You hurt bad?"

"Not really. I had a bloody nose. But they got my medallion. It was a gift from my parents."

"Are you happy, sir?" The Reverend Roberts put his hands on his hips and thrust his face out toward Whelan.

"Now what do you think? You think I wanted him hurt? You have rocks in your head, Reverend?"

"You will not talk to me in that tone, sir. This isn't much of a place but it is a chapel. We pray here."

"I'll calm down if you will."

Reverend Roberts stared for a moment, then seemed to relent all at once. "I'm sorry. Forgive me. It...I just got very angry over this. My people run enough risk in their ministry, so they don't need to be taking unnecessary chances playing at detective after their day is done."

"I didn't think he'd go out asking questions at night."

"Well, he did. And now he's going home for a time."

"You're sending him home?"

"We're...he's not certain this work is for him. Are you, Don?"

Young Ewald shook his head, looking at his scuffed shoes. "I don't seem to be any good at it. I'd like to come back but...I seem to mess things up."

"He's never been quite comfortable up here, have you, Don?" The boy shook his head and the Reverend shrugged. "He's a fine young man and he'll find his place, but not everyone is cut out to preach on the streets." He seemed to lose himself in thought for a second and then gave his head a little shake.

"And another of my young men got himself into some danger last night."

"Tom," Don Ewald said.

"Tom Waters? What happened to him?"

"*He* was mugged in his neighborhood. Some young boys asked for his money and he resisted. He fought them."

"That's pretty stupid."

"Of course it is. Especially since we are not sympathetic to violent responses in anyone. He should not have fought back. It was unnecessary and foolhardy. It…it is a problem with Mr. Waters."

"And how's he?"

"He has a shiner and a fat lip and his watch is gone."

"A hard night for the street ministry."

"You might say that. Don is leaving, Tom is still spouting pugnacious nonsense and I have another young man out with a mild case of food poisoning." He stared out at Broadway for a moment and then smiled, and the smile grew into a grin.

"What's so funny?"

"Oh, it's just that I've got myself a street ministry in one of the toughest neighborhoods I've ever known, and I have almost no budget for anything, and I never thought for a second that any of it would be easy, so what am I getting so upset about? This is about what I expected." He smiled. "I have no wife or family, just this work, which is exactly what I thought it would be. Now how many people can say that?"

"Not many at all," Whelan said, deciding that he liked the Reverend Roberts. He looked at Don Ewald. "Can I do anything for you, Don?"

The Reverend looked at the boy and smiled gently. "He's too shy to ask, but I believe he'd like very much for someone to drive him to the Greyhound Bus station downtown. He could take the el but I know he'd like company."

"I can give you a ride, Don. What time's the bus?"

The young man looked up shamefacedly. "There's a bus at one and another one at three. Or there's one at six this evening if you're too busy—"

"No. I'm not busy. I'm just spinning my wheels this morning. Want to go now?"

He nodded. "Thanks, Mr. Whelan."

Whelan and the Reverend exchanged a quick amused glance at Don's obvious relief that he wouldn't have to be standing alone on el platforms, his suitcase and facial expression announcing to the world that here was another rube who couldn't handle what the Big Town had to offer.

The minister gave Whelan a thoughtful look. "I hope I

don't seem unfeeling. I understand that your investigation has to do with the, ah, death of a friend. Have you had any success, Mr. Whelan?"

"Nothing I could put into a resume."

"Well, if there's anything I can do…"

As an afterthought, Whelan drew out the picture of Gerry Agee. "I'm still looking for this one."

The minister held it out at arm's length and squinted, then shook his head. "No. I remember faces. Haven't seen this one."

"Well, thanks anyway. Should we get going, Don?"

Don Ewald stood, held out his hand to the Reverend Roberts. "Thank you for everything, sir. I'm sorry I didn't do much of a job for you."

"You weren't working for me, son. You were working for the Lord, and I'm sure he knows how hard you tried. Perhaps after you've had some time to think, talk things over with your parents, you'll arrive at a more suitable ministry for yourself."

The boy hung his head and appeared to be on the verge of tears. "I'm just real…real embarrassed right now. I don't even want to face my father."

The Reverend Roberts surprised Whelan by laughing, a loud, surprisingly hearty laugh, and he clapped the boy on the shoulder.

"I was sent home from *my* first ministry in total disgrace. I got into a fight with a local boy who heckled me while I preached to passersby. And there was…some trouble with a young lady and her parents." The minister colored slightly and Whelan smiled.

"And the gentleman for whom I worked said I didn't so much preach the gospel as harangue people—his very word, 'harangue.'"

Don looked at the minister with a beatific smile and Whelan knew the Reverend Roberts had just gone from respected supervisor to cherished hero. The kid might be back after all.

He drove east to the Drive and left the boy to his thoughts. Don stared out the window as they left Uptown and his expression was unreadable. Whelan tried to concentrate on his driving, but in his mind was the picture of Jean Agee in his bed, watching him undress, her brown shoulder nestled against his pillow, leaving her scent everywhere in his bed. For a moment he fancied that he still had her smell in his nostrils, and for a time the neighborhood and this poor country boy and the string of brutal killings shrank in importance. He cruised the Drive at fifty and turned on the radio.

Bob Seger was singing "Night Moves" and reminiscing about summer romances in Michigan twenty years ago and Whelan realized that in all his adult life he'd never had one. To his left, people rode gracefully along the bike paths or walked along the beaches; in five minutes he was nearing the Loop and the lake to his left was dotted with sailboats. He was heading into what he'd always believed to be the most beautiful stretch of city in all of America. A little dishonest, a little misleading to the visitor, for it gave no hint of the urban horrors growing through the cracks a mere mile to the west, but it was breathtaking, nonetheless, and he felt sorry for the boy staring out the window, who wasn't having a summer romance and was going to be sitting moodily on a crowded bus in a few hours, breathing body smells and filtered air and exhaust and trying to figure out his life.

"You ought to think of it as a vacation, Don."

"What? I ought to what, sir?"

"You ought to stop calling me 'sir,' for starters. I said you ought to think of it as a vacation. It's the only way. When you get out of one thing and you don't have a clear notion of what you'll do next, you have to think of it as a vacation, as a breather for yourself. A man gets laid off from a factory or fired from an office, he has to think of it as a period of readjustment, a time when he's getting a line on what's available to him. If you think of it as a time when you've…failed, well, you're a failure. And it shows. People will sense it when they talk to you. You won't impress anybody."

He looked ahead as he spoke, occasionally glancing at the swimmers and sunbathers, and then he realized the boy was staring at him. He shot a quick look at Don and saw that the kid was grinning.

"Okay, I sound like I'm bughouse, right?"

"No, I thought it was great. I never heard anything like that. Do you really believe that?"

"Yes," he said without hesitation. "Yeah, I really do. I think everybody screws up now and then. Everybody changes jobs, loses jobs, loses ability or interest and has to find something to do with himself. We live in a pretty tough society, Don: nobody realizes it, but we do. Just ask any guy who's been laid off how his community treats him, how it looks at him. So, what you want to do now, if you don't mind all this curbside advice, is to look at this as an opportunity to scout around and find something better for yourself. Maybe you'll find a ministry that'll he better suited to you—that, I don't know anything about. But don't go home thinking you're a failure, which is what you're thinking right now. All right?"

Don laughed. "All right. I'll try that."

"Okay, but the time you'll have to remember that is when you face your folks, okay? You didn't fail: it just didn't work out."

The boy seemed to be visualizing the impending meeting with his parents, then nodded slowly. Whelan stole a glance at him. A baby-faced boy, his naivete clear to anyone. A thought struck him as he turned off the Drive and headed into the Loop, a thought he'd had once or twice before but for mere seconds, and he went fishing.

"So tell me: is Tom gonna last out there on the street?"

"I think so. He's not like me, Mr. Whelan. He's pretty tough. He's a country boy but these people on the streets, they don't intimidate him at all, the the teenagers, they don't bother him. If anything..." and he looked out the window.

"What were you going to say?"

"He gives it right back to them. If somebody tries to scare Tom, he gets hostile. You should see him, Mr. Whelan. These two Southern boys were making fun of us one day and Tom told them to get lost, and one of them said something about, you know, taking care of Tom, and Tom's face just changed completely. He went after that boy and both of them ran. And for a while after that, he was really tense and I think it was because he didn't get his hands on that boy. He wanted to fight."

Whelan looked at him, then had to hit the horn as a cabbie cut him off crossing Michigan.

"If you come back to this town, kid, don't drive in it." He hit the brakes as another cabbie tried to shoehorn himself into Whelan's lane.

"You're sweating, Mr. Whelan."

"It's what I do when I'm frightened, Don." They waited while a semi squeezed painfully out of an alley onto Randolph and put traffic on hold.

"Did Tom ever seem to have particularly strong feelings about the derelicts?"

He could sense the boy's hesitation. "Oh, I don't know…"

"Did he ever say anything?"

Don looked at him. "It's just that he's not used to them, that's all. He doesn't understand how they could let their lives go so far downhill."

"He doesn't have any use for them, huh?" Don nodded slightly and looked away. "And he's a pretty streetwise boy, in his way. He's been doing this a lot longer than you, I guess. Am I right?"

Don looked at him with embarrassment. "Oh, no. That's the…that's the thing that really gets me. I've been here almost a year. It'd have been a year in September. Tom just got here in April. He's only been here a few months and he's pretty much at home already. He's a…you know, a natural." The envy in the boy's voice was clear.

Whelan was thinking about the damage a muscular, streetwise young man with a hostile nature and a hatred for derelicts could do. He tried the picture of Tom Waters pacing in a room at the YMCA and snarling at ghosts and he felt a growing nausea.

He pulled in front of the Greyhound Bus Station and felt a pang of nostalgia, saw a younger Paul Whelan coming home from Vietnam by bus after his plane had been rerouted to Detroit.

"Well, here we are, Don."

"Thank you for everything, Mr. Whelan."

"My pleasure. Good luck, Don. I think you'll do just fine." He held out his hand. Don took it eagerly.

"I hope so, Mr. Whelan. And I'm gonna tell everybody in Bakersfield that I worked with a private detective." Whelan laughed and watched Don Ewald enter the cavernous bus station, escaping from Chicago.

He used a corner phone to call Reverend Roberts. Tom Waters hadn't come back from an early errand. He was less than a mile from the Estes, so he drove over to see if Jean was back yet.

He went directly to the room. A maid was cleaning it. He stuck his head in, asked if anybody was home and got a suspicious look for his pains. Uncertain, he went across the street to Grant Park and sat for a while, watching a group of Texas tourists in Stetsons and cowboy boots and a group of Japanese businessmen taking pictures of each other. After half an hour and three cigarettes, he went back to the Estes, struck out again and left.

He drove back to the Way Mission but a sign on the door told him it was lunchtime. It was dark inside. He went back to his office, took in the mail and deposited all of it in the wastebasket. He called his service.

"Well, Mr. Romeo Whelan."

"Hi, Shel. What's happening?"

"Apparently you're happening, hon. So this Miss Agee is now something more than a client?"

He felt himself blushing and Shelley gave him her great whiskey-throat laugh.

"You suggesting I've been unprofessional?"

"Baby, I'm suggesting you've been lucky. She called twice. Said to tell you 'Jean' called. No more 'Miss Agee.'"

"An operative occasionally gets to know his clients on a first-name basis."

"I guess. She still sounds young."

"She is. But I'm in no position to be fussy. What did she say?"

"First she called to see if you wanted to meet for lunch around noon. But then she called and said she'd be home around four or five. And she says maybe she'll let you take her out to dinner. Also, she says to tell you she bought you something." Shelley laughed again.

"Wonderful. I love presents from women. Anybody else?"

"That dinosaur you been running around with. Officer Friendly."

"Bauman. What'd he want?"

"Your ass, I think. He wants you to call him right away at Area Six. Right away, Paul. He called twice, too, and he wasn't nice."

"He's not nice, most of the time."

"I'd whip him into shape."

"Somebody ought to. Well, thanks, Shel."

"Good luck tonight, hon," she said, and she was laughing as she hung up.

"Bauman."

"Nice telephone manner. Whelan here. What's up?"

"Well, Mr. Invisible. Where you been, Whelan? Keeping the streets safe?"

"I had to drop somebody off in the Loop."

"That little piece you been chasing?"

"No, somebody else," he said, irritated. "So, you called me. What's up?"

"Well, now," Bauman drawled, playing with him. "I got something. Got an FBI report right here in front of me, very interesting report. Dunno what it all means yet, but it's interesting."

"Come on, you got an I.D. on the prints already?"

"Hey, what rock you been living under? I put in a Code One, they get me a report on prints in eight, ten hours max. Yeah, I got an I.D. Name wasn't Sharkey, like I was sayin'. The guy's name was Albert Becker. Ring any bells, Whelan? Set off any alarms?"

"Not yet. Should it?"

"I dunno. Maybe not. I just thought maybe you'd know something, maybe you know more than you let on. This Becker, he's actually somebody. He was in the papers once. Nineteen sixty-nine."

"I was in Vietnam in 1969. What did this guy do?"

"Embezzlement. He was a banker. Hotshot banker at a little savings and loan on the Northwest Side. You know, one of those dinky little banks, all their clients were Loogans or Polacks. Anyhow, this Becker, he pretty much took this bank down. He split one day with a quarter million bucks. They investigated, found out he'd taken out a lot more than that over a five or six-year period. He'd been milking that bank, setting up phony loans that went directly into his pockets, having them write off the loans. And he spent it all. Seems the guy liked to play the ponies and pretend he was a big shot. Played the trotters, played the parlay cards, you name it. Anyhow, the shit hit the fan and this Becker went South. Took his money and got the hell out. He was never found. Left his wife and kids and a bungalow on a nice quiet street and went underground."

Whelan said nothing. Now he had it all, though there were still connections to be made. He had the killer and things were falling into place. A thrill of anticipation went through him. Then he saw the anxiety-ridden face of Art Shears and told himself not to take too much pleasure in his accomplishments.

"Whelan? You still there?"

"Yeah, I'm here. I was just thinking."

"That's good, 'cause I was thinking, too. We got something here. Somewhere in this guy's life is what we're looking for. His killer. We got his killer now, Whelan."

"You think?"

"Oh, yeah, I think. We find out who took the flak at the bank and I think we got a pretty good idea who whacked him."

"Maybe you're right," he said, but he was thinking that there were shortcuts.

"Think about it, Whelan. I'll be in touch."

"This mean I'm not a suspect anymore?"

Bauman snorted. "You ever work for a bank?"

"They wouldn't have me," he said, and laughed.

Tom Waters was exactly where Whelan had first seen him, on Broadway just down the street from Leland, speaking to a pair of aged drunks and looking as though he alone knew the way to the truth. Whelan parked under the tracks in the bus stop and walked across the street.

The drunks were beginning to walk away and Waters was looking frustrated, forcing himself to smile and continue to talk to them. Whelan heard him mention "the apostle Paul," something about a hard-living man who knew when to turn his life around. He stopped in midsentence, aware of someone behind him.

"Oh. Hi, Mr. Whelan."

"Tom. Nice eye."

Waters looked embarrassed. It was indeed a nice eye, swollen partly shut, a deep purple, doing nothing for his ministry. The left side of his lip was slightly enlarged and there was a cut visible just where lip met teeth. Whelan nodded to him.

"You got tagged a couple good ones, huh?"

Tom Waters shrugged and his hand went to the eye. "Yeah. I guess I let 'em catch me off my guard."

"Don't be embarrassed. He was pretty good. I went a couple rounds with him and he left a few marks on me, too."

The young man's face showed confusion. He frowned. "You know these boys? The ones who—"

"I don't know any boys, Tom. I know Hector, though. I *knew* him, at least. I fought him in an empty apartment, just like you did. And he was pretty good. You had an edge, though: you had a knife, so you won yours and I lost mine."

He heard the slightest quaver in his voice and felt a dull rage growing, a solid pressure in his chest. Waters's eyes were distressed and he took a step backward.

"I'm not following you, Mr. Whelan. I don't have a knife. And this had nothing to do with Hector..." He looked at

Whelan for a moment, wet his lips and said, "Have you been drinking, Mr. Whelan?"

"No. No, I haven't. It's a little early for me, Tom."

Tom Waters scratched his cheek, gave his head a little shake and tried again.

"I think we're talking about two different things. This happened in my neighborhood, just some teenagers who came out of a gangway, there were no knives or anything like that. I guess I was pretty lucky about that."

Whelan held his stare to make the boy squirm. Tom Waters simply stared back in obvious confusion and Whelan realized he hadn't prepared for this reaction. For a moment he considered popping the kid a quick one, just to get a rise out of him. Tom Waters watched him, his face full of concern, and it was obvious that he wasn't going anywhere and he wasn't going to say anything more.

"Tell me, Tom, where'd you spend the afternoon? Packing? You must be just about ready to split, huh?"

Waters looked surprised. "No, I wasn't packing. I'm not going anywhere. Oh, you're talking about Donnie. He left. I didn't even get a chance to say goodbye."

"Yeah, I know all about Don. I drove him."

"Well…I'm not leaving, Mr. Whelan, unless Reverend Roberts gets rid of me for my stupidity. I wouldn't leave on my own, though. I *love* this work." He thought for a second. "And I spent part of the afternoon in a *police* station. I've never been inside one before. It was really interesting." Waters was grinning, Whelan said nothing.

"They found the boys who jumped me. I got one of 'em." He chanced a small, prideful smile. "I broke his nose. It was a right, I think."

Whelan looked at him for a long moment. "Would you be willing to go back to the police station with me? To prove your story?"

Waters frowned, then sighed. "I don't know what any of this is about and I don't know why I have to prove anything but…sure. The boys are all being held. The one I hurt went to an emergency room to have his nose looked at and they got him there." He studied Whelan's face, misread it and shook his head.

"I know you don't think much of us, Donnie and me—I didn't even want to get involved with your work because I thought you'd just laugh at us. You probably don't even have much use for the Reverend Roberts, he probably seems a little silly to you with his storefront church, but he's a great man. I've never met a man like him. I've seen him take a person off the street and turn him into a man of Christian fiber."

"He seems to be a fine man."

"But you think Donnie and I are a couple of hicks, right? I know I make mistakes, and the Reverend seems to think fighting back last night was another one, but I'm not afraid of any of these people. I'm here to help and I can't be pushed around. I fight back and then I go out and do my work."

The little oration seemed to relax the boy, and he settled back on his heels, hooked his hands into his back pockets and watched Whelan.

Whelan realized with disappointment that he believed him, and that he probably liked him as well. Out of place, this boy was, out of his league, maybe, but cornfed and stubborn and ornery and honest.

"A lot of times we…we get a little suspicious of people who are different from us. I don't think you're a fool; you're different. Different from me, at least. I don't understand you. My problem, not yours. I owe you an apology. A man was killed sometime yesterday and I thought he might have left a few marks on whoever killed him, the kind of marks you're wearing."

Waters shook his head. "You live in a violent world, Mr. Whelan. You've seen more death than you should, it seems. Don't you ever want to leave it all?"

"Sure. Sometimes. But escaping is something very few people do successfully. Cities are full of people who'd like to escape and never get around to trying it."

"But your work—"

"My work is sorting out other people's troubles, and sometimes there is violence in it. Believe me, I try to keep it to a minimum." He smiled. "I'm sorry. I was…I got carried away."

"It's all right, Mr. Whelan."

"I owe you lunch."

"Okay," Tom Waters said.

He went back to his car. There was a ticket under the wiper. "Oh, outstanding."

He got in, put on the seatbelt and started the Jet, and thought for a moment. Maybe Tom Waters wasn't out of the woods yet. It would be a bizarre coincidence for a killer to be mugged on the streets of Chicago after killing someone, but just bizarre enough to happen. He thought about it for a second. No.

He went back to his office, thought of calling Jean but forced his mind back to his work. He needed to have the whole story, to have at least what Bauman had but he was in no mood to talk to Bauman. He swore softly to himself: it meant a trip to the library and working with the accursed microfilm machines, but there was no other way.

The Hild Regional Library had the Chicago papers and the *New York Times* on film. It took him time to find what he needed. It took several attempts to thread the thing properly—on his first try, he turned on the machine and the microfilm pulled itself loose, treating the entire viewing room to the *whack-whack-whack* of loose film slapping against the table. Behind him he heard an attendant snicker, but he politely refused her offer to thread it for him.

The index told him he was looking for papers from June and July of 1969 and eventually he had the spools on correctly and the film threaded into the viewer and went whirring through life in Chicago in 1969. It gave him an eerie feeling to see these papers for the first time: he'd been in Vietnam and had seen no hometown news. A surprising amount of space was devoted to the meteoric performance of the Cubs, in first place all summer and pounding lumps on all comers, giving no hint of the awful collapse that would bring summer to an end for baseball fans all over the city. There were many stories on Vietnam, grandstand plays by politicians on both sides of the political fence, allegations by both newspapermen and congressmen that the military were distorting the news from the front, inflating the body count, using dead cattle and domestic animals in the count, anything to convince an increasingly skeptical public that we were beating Charlie's ass. He laughed at a story that an underground student newspaper at De Paul had given the "Mandrake the Magician" award to the Viet Cong for having been killed off in their entirety at least a dozen times by the Pentagon's count but still continuing to fight.

There were the usual murders and robberies and fires and swindles and revelations that aldermen were running their wards like medieval barons, and finally, in the second week of July 1969, there was the amazing story of Albert Becker. It was all there, in both the *Tribune* and the *Sun-Times,* pretty much the same story and treatment, a classic story with familiar scenes and players. A man respected by coworkers and neighbors, a solid member of his community, the archetypal successful American family man: a wife, two kids, a bungalow on the Northwest Side half a mile from the bank where he'd worked since it opened in 1952. A safe, sane existence on the surface, bearing almost no resemblance to the life he led on the sly. The story was basically as Bauman had outlined it except that the numbers were slightly more interesting: it was only a guess that Becker had taken a quarter mil with him. There was evidence that he'd skimmed, over the years, up to four hundred thousand dollars beyond that, and blown much of it through his gambling, but no one knew for sure. Predictably, both papers insisted on running the same picture of Albert Becker: it was a little blurred and the man in it, who only faintly resembled the corpse on the Uptown roof, was smiling and looked like something of a nebbish. Neither paper had any kind of edge in the information provided and the angles in coverage were pretty unimaginative.

It wasn't until he hit the follow-up stories that it came together for him. In a front-page article that took second billing to a major North Vietnamese advance, the *Tribune* reported that Mrs. Francine Becker, wife of the fugitive banker, had taken her own life. Despondent over her abandonment by her husband, shaken to her heart's core by the knowledge that he'd led a double life and humiliated before friends and neighbors, the tormented woman had asphyxiated herself in the garage after carefully making arrangements for the children to be at her sister's. Whelan shook his head. What a waste, what an unnecessary death.

The *Sun-Times* carried a similar article but with one difference, a picture. A family portrait, taken in presumably happier times. It was a standard type of portrait, generic middle-class photography from some storefront studio, with beaming parents and stiffly smiling children. And it was all there. Whelan felt the breath go out of him, felt a dull ache behind his eyes. He sank back in the chair and sucked in air and felt the churning in his chest and stomach. He stared up at the ceiling for a moment, then composed himself and reexamined the photograph.

Becker had been an unprepossessing man, even in his better days, but there was nothing in the face to suggest the criminal urges that apparently directed his life. Francine Becker was a sweet-faced woman, fleshy, perhaps a few pounds overweight. But it was the children in the portrait that riveted Whelan's attention. The girl was older, perhaps ten when the picture had been taken, and the little boy was a couple of years younger, and it was not the features, indistinct at best in the blurry microfilm of the photograph, that caught his eye, but rather something in the facial expression of the boy, and in the girl, a smile and the faintest tilt of the head. He'd seen them, these traits, and he'd seen these two children as adults, had in fact just driven one to a bus station and had the night before made love to the other, and for a moment, for just a sliver in time Paul Whelan felt perfectly alone in the world.

He shut off the viewer and sat back for a moment. What was the con game called that they'd worked on him? A variation of the Big Store, maybe. Did it matter? He suppressed the urge to leave, forced himself to think the thing through carefully and see the true issues rather than the personal ones. There was, of course, the issue of his bed, of his love affair, of his physical and emotional dependence on the girl he'd just taken into his life, and there was the issue of friendship, of offering "aid and solace" to a boy in distress.

But other things were, on a very primal level, more important and he had to do something about those. He drove back to his office, oblivious to the growing traffic of late afternoon. At the office he had a cigarette and stared out his window at the traffic on Lawrence, at people with simpler lives heading home, leaving to endure stifling subway cars and stop-and-go traffic and hot apartments, and he wished his life was, just for this one day, one of those. At five o'clock he thought of calling Jean Agee. He called Bauman.

They put his call in to Violent Crimes and a flat voice told him Bauman was out having something to eat.

"I need to leave a message, then. It's important. Tell him to call Paul Whelan at the office. Tell him it'll make his day."

"All right, sir," the dead voice said.

Twenty minutes later Bauman called. "So you got a lead, huh? Hey, we're cooking down here, Whelan. I got guys workin' on half a dozen things."

"Figured you would," he said, and hoped Bauman would do it all and say it all and make the rest of the call unnecessary.

"Yeah. I got people out talking to one of the bank officers, a V.P. that got left holdin' the bag when Becker went South, and we found the president, he's retired now and livin' in Sarasota, so I got local people down there goin' out to talk to him…"

He heard Bauman ticking off several other leads and shook his head. A lot of nothing.

"I got something for you, Bauman," he said, cutting the detective off in midsyllable.

"Yeah? Like what?"

"I've got it all. I've got your killers."

"Killers, huh? You make it more than one."

"Yeah, more than one. I got the killers, I got the motive, I got the whole shot."

There was a momentary pause at the other end.

"You sound pretty sure."

"I am."

"You don't sound so happy. How come?"

"I'm just tired."

"You're a pretty smart fucker, Whelan."

"No. I'm not. Not nearly as smart as I used to think."

"Whatever you say. Be right over."

"Don't bring Rooney. He depresses me."

Bauman was laughing as he hung up.

He put the phone back and turned his chair back to the window. For ten minutes he stared out over the street and smoked and went over and over in his mind the events of the past week and a half, looking for the one incontrovertible hole in his thinking that would tell him it was all a mistake, that his gut was right and the picture was a fluke. He picked up the phone and called her.

"It's Paul."

She laughed. "Oh, I know who it is, you don't have to be so formal. Want to come down and have dinner? I'll show you what I bought. And I got you something."

"I got your message. Good shopping trip?"

"The best!" she said breathlessly. "Stores like this are just a new experience to me. I'm not even sure they have stores like this in suburban Detroit where all the fancy houses are. Paul, I...I just let myself go and spent hundreds of dollars. I used two different charge cards to get it all in." She laughed. "I'll be paying for it for the next year but it was worth it." She stopped for breath.

"I can't make it for dinner. I'm tied up," he said, and hoped he had punctured the mirth.

"How come? Something with your case?" She paused and added, "Anything about...Gerry, Paul?"

"The first one. I don't have anything on Gerry. Listen, I can come down a little later, maybe."

"Okay. Come on down later. You don't have to call, just come down. We can get burgers someplace or something."

"Sure."

Another hesitation. "You don't sound good. Are you all right? Do you want to make it another night?"

"No, I'm just a little...out of it. Preoccupied. I'll be down between seven and eight."

They said goodbye and he hung up and sat at his desk waiting. About ten minutes later there was a knock and he could see the heavy form of Bauman tensed outside his door.

"Come on in. Since when do you stand on ceremony?"

Bauman pushed the door out of his way and stopped just inside.

"Traffic's a bitch. Accident at Lawrence and Ashland, got a bus stalled in the middle of the street. So, you got something good now, Shamus?" He grinned, then squinted at Whelan. "You don't look so good, Whelan."

"I feel worse."

Bauman took a few steps into the office. "So, whaddya got for me?"

"I got stories for you, Bauman. Sit down. I got stories for you."

THIRTEEN

After he talked to Bauman he went home and sat for a time in his living room. His wall clock told him he'd never make seven, that he'd be lucky to make it by eight, but he sat in the old stuffed chair and focused on street noises and tried not to think about it. Eventually he pushed himself out of the chair and got ready, changing shirts and washing up. Just like a date, he told himself.

Bauman called just before he left.

"No luck at the bus station. Coulda gone anywhere," he said, biting off the ends of his words and wheezing into the phone. Whelan could almost hear him sweat, and could picture the detective's fat fist squeezing the life out of the phone.

"He'll turn up. Or she'll tell us where to find him."

"*I* know he'll turn up. And we're checking your broad out now, we'll check out her address and then we'll find him. We already talked to people in Michigan and California." There was a pause. "This ain't the way to do this thing."

"Yeah, it is. It's the natural way."

"Natural's got nothin' to do with it. We should just go in and pick her up like any other scuz and throw her ass in the wagon and go down to Six to book her."

"You can wait a few minutes. It's not going to kill anybody. I just want to do this my way."

"Okay, fine," Bauman said, and it was anything but fine.

The sky over the lake was bleeding its colors and he thought he caught just a whiff of autumn, the cold lake smell that would eventually usher in winter.

She opened the door on one knock and her perfume caught

in his nostrils, and when he just stood there like a man who's knocked at the wrong door, she laughed and clasped her hands behind his neck and kissed him open-mouthed and greedily. He could hear her husky breath and his own panting, and then gently peeled her off.

"Let's go inside. I'm shy."

She grinned and pulled him in by the hand, the way a girl in college had once tugged him reluctantly onto a dance floor. She closed the door with a dainty movement of her foot and pushed him into a chair, then eased herself into his lap, snuggling till she was comfortable.

"So how'd it go?"

"What?"

"Your…you know, your work, dummy."

"All right. I…I did all right. I got what I was looking for." He looked away. She ran a finger across his upper lip and he could smell the soap. She had just showered, and he wished he could stand mindless in a stream of scalding water.

"So," he said. "So you grew up here, huh?"

He felt the faintest start but she smiled and blinked.

"Me? No, I'm not from here. We lived in Detroit when I was little but I don't even remember it. The whole neighborhood's torn up now. We moved to Hope—"

"Now, how, exactly, did you set this up?"

She did a double take, blinked comically and shook her head. "Set what up? What are you talking about?"

"I'll tell you what I think, Jean, I think you came into town with old Don and you did legwork for him, that's what I think. You were his 'operative' till he found out I was involved. The police had very little and he figured he didn't have to worry about them. They weren't going to put everything else aside and jump on this business. He was counting on them not being able to put a lot of manpower into a couple of dead bums. Then he ran into me."

He looked at her and held his stare. She shrank back and shook her head again.

"Paul, you're just…just rambling and you're not making any

sense. Have you been drinking? You don't smell like it, but—and who's Don?"

"Don is your little brother, darlin'."

Now she moved as though frightened, slipping quickly off his lap and putting space between them. She stood a few feet away with her hands on her slender hips and let him get a good look at her.

"You'd better go. Call me tomorrow when you're...when you feel better. I'm not mad or anything, Paul, but you're making me...uncomfortable."

Whelan laughed, surprised that he could still see humor in anything. *"You're* uncomfortable? How do you think I feel, knowing you've been jerking a little chain for a week and a half and it had me on the other end?" He sat back, put his hands behind his head and watched her.

"Don is your brother. Not Gerry. Don. I was kind of surprised about that, using your real names, but you didn't think anybody'd ever see the two of you together to make a connection. Hell, the people in the old neighborhood probably don't even remember your names. It's been fourteen years. No, old Don was working the street and he found out the guy he killed in the alley behind Broadway and Leland was somebody's friend. My friend. So when I started showing up on the street every day asking questions he probably made it a point to meet me sooner or later—I think he actually tried to break in one night. Then he needed somebody to let him know what I found out. Somebody to keep him posted. And that was you." He pointed a finger at her. "I just never would have believed how far you'd go to get information. And...what was going to happen if you found out I really had something? Were you going to help him kill me?"

She began to shake her head slowly. "You've got to stop this, this is, *crazy*, Paul. I think you're losing your mind or something."

"Aw, knock it off, lady." He leaned forward in the chair suddenly and she gave a little cry of fear.

"I saw the picture, Jean. I saw you and Don and your mother and father. I saw the family portrait. The Becker family of Chicago."

She breathed through her mouth and said nothing. She ran her hands up and down the sides of her jeans, looked off for a moment to compose herself, and nodded.

"Okay. You know about it, then. You saw the picture, but you don't know everything. You don't know how it was for us, how we lived, how it felt when my mother killed herself."

"No, I don't. You're right."

"He killed her. He just killed her. He swindled all those people who liked him and trusted him, and then he left us all, and it killed her. And it made…it made Donnie a little bit crazy. It really did."

"Did he understand? Wasn't he a little too young to put it together?"

"At first, yes, but…he was really a bright little kid and it didn't take long for him to understand what had happened. And later, when he realized that…that his father was still alive somewhere, he became obsessed by it."

"So you—what? You searched for him?"

"Oh, no, not at first." She smiled at him. "I was trying to be normal. I didn't even want to think about it and I think I blocked it out for a long time, for years. We went to live with my aunt in Michigan and I wanted a normal life, I wanted to have friends and go to school and go out with boys."

"What changed it?"

"For me? Nothing changed it for me. But *he* called one night. He called to talk to my aunt and she asked him to talk to me. He was drunk and blubbering and talking about how much he missed us—" She was looking past him as she spoke, eyes narrowed. She said nothing for a moment, then looked at Whelan. "We talked about it all the time after that. Donnie was— we just started looking for him. Hooked because it seemed like something that ought to be done. Donnie made it a full-time job. He went out West looking for…for *him*. Denver first, then he tracked him to San Diego, found out he was calling himself 'Sharkey' and traced him to Bakersfield." She stared down at the floor.

Whelan watched her and felt somehow off-balance, and wondered if he really had this thing put together yet.

"I need the whole thing, Jean. Keep talking."

"Eventually he found out that my…my father had been living in a little rooming house in Bakersfield and somebody told him that my father got tired of the West Coast, that he needed money and thought he could get his hands on some back here. So Donnie came to Chicago."

"And did some poking around, right? Stayed at the Lawson YMCA for a couple of months."

She stared for a moment, then nodded. "Yes. He wanted to ask around, find out where men like my father would be likely to end up. He went to your Skid Row area—"

"Not much of that left now."

"And he looked around where he was staying, hung around in that little park where a lot of crazy people are?"

"Bughouse Square, everybody calls it."

"And then he started looking around in Uptown."

"How did he get a job as a minister's assistant?"

"It's something he's done before. He's really clever, he can talk people into a lot of things. He had done some carpentry work for a storefront minister in San Diego, knew the names of a few little churches out in California—"

"And put together a little resume for himself, huh?"

"Yes. He thought it would be a good way to look, talk with people without attracting attention."

She held out her hands to him and her face grew red and tears welled up in her eyes. She came forward slowly, shaking her head.

"But I never thought he'd kill anybody, I never thought he could do that, Paul. Oh, I'm so sorry."

And without knowing how or why he was off the chair and holding her, trying to calm her, contrite and confused and on the point of panic.

"All right, all right," he heard himself repeating over and over. "It's all right, take it easy…" and when she'd calmed down, he led her to the edge of her bed and sat her down.

"Do you know where he is now?"

She shrugged. "I think he'll go to Detroit. He has some friends there who'll put him up. After that, I don't know."

"He was here?"

She nodded.

"Why didn't he take you with?"

She shook her head. "I wouldn't go after I realized what he'd done. I was so shocked—"

"But what did he tell you he needed from me all this time? Didn't you know what was going on?"

"No. That he was out there killing people?" She sniffled and got up, crossed the room to the small dresser to get Kleenex, their came back to the bed and sat.

"He just told me he thought you knew where my father was."

He thought about what he'd told her. "No, Jean, I told you all along what was going on."

"I didn't really think that was what you were doing. You didn't seem to be finding anything, so I thought maybe you really were after my father for some reason."

"But I told you about the killings."

She gave him a puzzled look. "Why would I connect those killings with my brother? Why should I think he was out there killing winos?"

"And now?"

"Now I know it's all true." Her whole body seemed to sag. "It hit me last night. I started putting things together, things he'd said, things you'd told me, and how certain things seemed to happen after I'd talked to him, and then I knew."

"Last night—did you ask him?"

"Yes. He said he killed them all and it was no big deal."

"No big deal, huh?"

She nodded. "That's what he said. They were all bums and drunks like our old man, so it was no big deal."

He took out the photo of "Gerry Agee." "So who is this turkey, anyway?"

She looked at Whelan and laughed. "That's the guy I took to my senior prom. Fooled you, huh?" She smirked and laughed again, and Whelan nodded, wondering at her easy lapse into mirth.

"But I scared you, darlin'. When I went back to the YMCA and asked around."

"I didn't think you would do that and I was afraid you'd show them the picture."

"It never occurred to me to flash the picture. Everybody admitted Gerry Agee'd been there. You…you didn't like what I found out there, did you?"

She began to shred the Kleenex in her hands. "No. I knew there was something wrong with Don but those stories of yours, about him pacing his room and making strange sounds and talking to himself, I never thought it was that bad." She shuddered.

"So why did he kill them all?"

"To get to my father. He told me he caught an old man in an alley and tried to get some information but the old man died when Don hit him."

"Hit him? He beat him to death. It was an old derelict named Shinny." She stared at him open-mouthed. "And Art Shears?"

"He made a mistake. He thought your friend knew something. He was wrong. He even listened to his tape to see if he had anything on it. Nothing."

"Your father made Don, didn't he? He recognized him?"

"I think so, or somebody told him someone was asking around about him. Don said Sharkey just disappeared, along with that poor man Hector."

"And Billy the Kid?"

"Don said he got in the way. I don't know what he meant."

"He meant Billy saw him kill Art Shears."

"Right. You told me somebody saw Billy the Kid running away from the alley or something."

"Not exactly. Somebody saw the killing, and saw Billy watching it go down. Billy was watching the killer, your brother."

Her eyes narrowed. "Somebody saw the killing?" She gave a little shake of her head.

"Yes. Somebody saw it," he said, and held his breath.

He watched the color drain from her golden complexion till she had a sickly look and his stomach churned. "You didn't know we had a witness for all this, huh?"

She smiled a little but her eyes were unfocused.

"It doesn't make any difference, does it? Now now."

"No, I guess not. You pretty much told me what the police would want to know. But I still need to know. Why? Why did he want to find your old man, anyway? To kill him?"

"I guess."

"I suppose he figured the old man owed you something. And this was his way of taking out his share, huh?"

"Yes." She wiped her nose with the tattered Kleenex.

"And in all fairness, he did owe you something." He watched her.

"He sure did. He owed us a lot more than…than anybody could realize."

"And what about the money?" he asked casually.

She shot him a quick glance, sudden and alert. "The money?"

"The money he ran off with. What'd he do with it?"

She shrugged. "I never thought about it."

"Probably blew it all pretty fast. Gambled it away, maybe. That was one of his problems, right?"

She looked away and seemed to be thinking about something else. "Yes, one of his many."

"Wonder why he came here, why he came back."

She looked at him. "I don't know. To get money, I guess."

"Did Don have some notions about that?"

She hesitated, then nodded. "He thought, you know…He thought there might be money here. Somewhere."

"Where?"

"I don't know."

"Why would a derelict live like an alley cat for fourteen years and then come back to pick up money he had all along?"

"It's not so farfetched, Paul. I've heard stories about people stashing their money away for years and coming back to it when they thought nobody was looking for it anymore."

He wanted to laugh. "So you came to Chicago to make the

big score, huh?"

"The big what?" She smiled. "What are you talking about?"

"Your papa's money. That's what you were after. That and a pound of flesh. I think you convinced each other that the money was still around somewhere and that the old man was going to lead you to it. I think old Don came here to kill him and you came here looking for money. That's it, isn't it?"

She said nothing but stared at him.

"Do you know how badly I wanted to believe that crock of shit you were handing me? The poor worried little lady with the crazy brother. But I like your style: you were prepared. I'll give you that. You had one story in case I believed you, and you had another one in case I didn't, and in both of them you're just the innocent bystander."

"I'm not telling you any story, I'm telling you the truth."

"No. It's all a crock and I'm an idiot for trying to believe any of it. Your brother was out there on the streets killing people and it didn't even make you blink. I'm not even sure you were surprised by the tales I came back from the Y with. You knew he was whacko. You knew he'd kill whoever he had to and you were willing to accept that. And all along, through it all, you were hanging onto my every word, anticipating every move I made, passing information along to him. Setting me up."

She stared at him unblinking, and he knew it was almost over.

"And sleeping with me."

She made a little shrug. "That wasn't part of it. That part I enjoyed. Donnie doesn't tell me when to get involved with somebody." She surveyed the room with a bored look. "You're the first man I've been to bed with after a steady diet of schoolboys, Paul." She smiled slowly and he felt his heart chill.

"Let me tell you what else I think, Jean. That night at the park, when Billy and I had our little encounter—I thought Billy slashed my tires, just to make sure I got the message. And now I think Don did it. I think he was hoping Billy'd take me out for him, and he may have even been thinking about doing it himself. But he was there, the same time I was. He was there and I felt him watching me, but I had no idea who it was."

He looked down. "The worst part is, I led him to Billy and I think I probably helped him find Hector and…your father."

"He would have found them anyhow. One way or another, sooner or later, he would have found them."

"But he learned about Billy from me." She said nothing. "And I probably led him to the building he found your father in. Did he tail me, Jean?"

She shrugged and frowned, as though she was irritated.

"Jean, do you understand that you're a murderer?"

"No. That's crazy—"

"You're responsible. You knew."

"Oh, come off it! I didn't do a thing except sleep with a stranger. A stranger I've become very fond of." She gave him a head-on look and confidence came into her eyes.

"Sorry, darlin', but as they say downtown. I've got motive, opportunity, method and a confession."

"What confession?"

"The one you just gave me."

"I didn't give you anything."

Whelan allowed himself a harsh laugh. "There's the understatement of the decade."

She came forward, looking him in the eye, and hunkered down beside his chair. She put her hands on his leg and he was conscious of her scent, and he tensed.

"Let me just ask you one thing, Paul. What difference does it all make now? Donnie's crazy, sure, and he did everything you said, but those were dead men already, Paul. They were the walking dead and they just died a little sooner. They were just… wasted lives. They were wasted lives already."

He laughed again and she looked startled.

"That's what Mengele said about the Jews. That prick that killed children for his experiments, that's what he said. Did you know that? That was his justification. No, Jean, they weren't dead yet and whether they were wasted lives is not yours to say. Jesus, one of them was about nineteen years old. And one was my friend."

She lowered her head. "I'm sorry about him, Paul. I

really am."

He sighed. "Oh, I really doubt it." She looked up at him and he stared around the room, admitting the pain he felt that he couldn't unmake this, talk it all away, lie to the world. He let his glance fall on each object in the room, taking it all in and knowing he'd never set foot in the Estes Motel again.

"What I can't get over is how stupid I feel."

"You're smart enough. Donnie thinks you're really smart. He was getting a little nervous there for a while." She bit her lip and forced a slight smile. "Come with me."

"Where?"

"Anywhere you want. Let's just leave, go somewhere, get out of…this place. I hate this city."

"You haven't done a thing for it, either, kid. No, we can't go. I sure couldn't."

"Why not?"

He laughed. "Are you kidding? I couldn't trust you for ten minutes at a stretch. Be like sleeping with a scorpion." He caught a flash of anger in her eyes and got to his feet. "You never did call the Jacobsen Agency, did you?"

She smiled stiffly. "Sure I did. They recommended you and a couple of other investigators." She shrugged. "It was a bonus. It just sounded better to say you were recommended."

"So you guys had your story down from the get-go, huh? Pretty sharp for a couple of kids abandoned by their father. Too bad you didn't find his money, for all your hard work." He began walking to the door.

"Oh, Paul—"

He turned. "You know, what I can't figure out is why you stayed behind. Was that to convince me, make it look like you had nothing to do with Donnie? Pretty smart. And when were you gonna leave? Next week, maybe, when you got tired of me?"

She stared at him. Her look was a mixture of fear and hostility and she looked much older now.

He smiled. "So, when were you planning to catch up with Donnie?" Something came quickly into her eyes and passed just as quickly, but he'd caught it. It was the look of privileged information, of what she knew and he didn't, and his breath caught in his chest.

"Oh, shit. Am I a sharpie or what? He hasn't gone anywhere. I dropped him off at the Greyhound Station but I didn't see him get on a bus. He's still here. You guys aren't through yet. Which is it, the money or me?"

She put her hands on her hips and looked down at the floor.

"Maybe both, huh? Old Donnie does think I'm smart. Where? Not here, the room's registered to you." He studied her for a moment. "I'll bet I can guess. I think I have a houseguest. He's been there before, too. Phew, old Donnie puts in a long day."

She looked as if she'd protest and he held up a hand to silence her. "Save it, kid." He went to the door, opened it and looked at her one more time. "I should have known. A guy like me and a little co-ed from a small town." He shook his head and smiled. "By the way, the money's gone, Jean. There's nothing here."

"How do you know that?" There was new interest in her eyes.

"I just do. It's the only thing I'm sure of. He pissed it all away a long time ago. Trust me." And as he stepped out into the hall, Whelan said over his shoulder, "Listen, Jean. Remind me: I've got somebody I want to introduce you to," and he slammed her door.

The gray Caprice was parked directly in front of the lobby doors and Bauman was having a routinely hostile conversation with the liveried doorman, who apparently couldn't see the need to block the way of ritzier automobiles with an unmarked police car.

"You lookin' for some kinda trouble, pal?"

"No, man, I jus' got to keep this space open for the limos an' shit."

"Well, this is my limo. Your boss got a problem with that, send him out and I'll take him over to Eleventh and State. You can come, too." The doorman, looking wonderfully out of place in a red-and-green costume that would have been outrageous at

Waterloo, stepped back, shaking his head, causing his lime-green top hat to topple to one side.

Whelan walked over to the Caprice. Rooney was behind the wheel, looking disinterestedly at the Michigan Avenue traffic.

"Out making new friends already, huh, Bauman?"

Bauman made a growling sound. "Wants to tell me where I can park. A guy in a clown suit wants to tell me where I can fucking park."

"Just as long as you're having a good time. Hey, are we keeping Rooney up?" The older detective gave Whelan a look of distaste, then stared across the street at the park.

"She still up there, Whelan?"

"Yeah. My guess is she's packing, real fast."

Bauman nodded and looked genuinely uncomfortable. "Okay," he said pointlessly. He cleared his throat, played with his collar, nodded again.

"Go on up, Bauman."

"Yeah. We got word out on the brother. A.P.B. everywhere from here to Windsor, Canada, and every place from here to L.A. He's history."

"Hope so. He's not contributing to our society. I gotta go. Talk to you later."

"Yeah. C'mon, Roon. Let's go."

The detectives got out of the car and motioned to a squad car parked farther down the block. Whelan walked briskly down Michigan Avenue, down the most beautiful street in Chicago, and hated the noise and the light and the warm night air. He lit a cigarette and took a deep drag. It tasted hot and dry and turned his stomach slightly. He wasn't comfortable with what he was doing: if it went wrong, the kid would be on the street, but probably not for long. He wanted badly to see his face. He wanted to see Don "Ewald" face to face.

He parked at the corner and sat in his car for twenty minutes, watching his house, studying the street, investigating the shadows and the night shapes. It wasn't late but there was no one moving on Malden, as though word had gone out. Eventually he told himself it was time to go in. Don was in his house.

He got out of the car, heart racing and conscious of sweat rolling down his sides under the loose-fitting shirt. White shirt—if Donnie-boy is at the window, he's made me already.

He closed the car door quietly and forced himself to breathe slowly, and remembered with breathtaking clarity another day when he feared he was about to die. He remembered crawling out into a clearing, remembered thinking how incredibly hot it was, crawling and hearing the gunfire and the incessant screaming of the wounded boy, and he remembered cursing to himself at the noise the boy was putting up, and thinking "It's my time" over and over, "It's my time," and then reaching the kid and pulling him by his shirt and feeling rather than hearing the round that took him in the thigh and pulling and wondering why it was taking so long.

He walked around to his trunk, opened it and rifled casually through his disordered tool kit, and came up with a small hammer. He slipped it under his shirt in back and tucked it into his belt. He rooted around for a second more, pretended to be searching for something, then shut the trunk and walked slowly toward his house.

He took the steps at a normal pace, shuffled his feet noisily on the warped wood of the old porch, fished around in the rusted mail box and came up with nothing. He fumbled for his keys, looked around at the porch. On summer nights when he was a boy, impervious to the heat like all small boys, he would sit out here with his father, listening to him spin tales of the old days, and then it struck him.

After all this animal has done, after everything else, the killing and the plotting, this lowlife sonofabitch is in my house. They invaded my life and now they're in my house!

Got something for you, Donnie.

He turned the key and flung the door open as he had five thousand other times. He tossed his keys on the hall table, slammed the door behind him and walked into the living room. He could smell him.

You can smell the guy who's waiting for you, an old cop had told him once. People don't notice, but it's there. You can smell his sweat or his deodorant or his gum or the liquor he drinks or his lunch, but everybody's got a smell.

He could smell the man waiting to kill him. It was faint, just an acrid trace in the stale air of the living room, but there, nonetheless, the street-smell of clothes worn in the sun all day, a mixture of body odors and the windblown dirt of the city.

He stood at the outer edge of the living room until he was certain the boy was not in the room. Then be reached back with one hand to touch the hammer and walked over to turn on the lamp in the front window. He stood still for a moment, listening, thought he heard a floorboard creak somewhere in the back of the house and held his breath. He heard nothing more.

Where would he be? In the back of the house, farthest from the door, or somewhere Whelan was more likely to go as soon as he came in? Bathroom, where there would be no room for either of them to move? No. He looked across the room at the dark doorway to the bedroom, the room he would pass on his way to any other part of the house.

He was in there.

Yeah, he was in the bedroom. Whelan looked around his living room, fought a momentary urge to run, told himself that a house is a collection of defensive weapons, wondered how to enter the bedroom without leaving himself open, and finally blew it all off. Let's do it.

"Come on out of there, Donnie, darlin'. That's where your sister and I romped and frolicked while you were out stomping winos. Come out and get a piece of me, babe."

He took a couple of steps toward the bedroom, stopped beside an old wooden chair and hooked his thumbs into his back pockets. With his right hand he carefully slid the hammer out from his belt and rested it against the back of his leg.

There was a subtle rustling from within the darkened bedroom and then footsteps and something moved to the left of the doorway and Donnie Agee emerged, moving fast, and Whelan's heart came as near as it ever would to bursting.

The being that came bounding out from the darkness was no man. Red-faced, eyes bulging, head thrust forward so that he looked up at Whelan from beneath his brow, Donnie came out in a crouch, not a fighter's stance so much as the prelude to a pounce. His young face was contorted with all the anger of his barren life and his mouth worked, and in one hand he held a knife, a small, wood-handled knife that Whelan recognized as his own.

Whelan made a sudden move to his left and Donnie shuffled forward, knife held low where Whelan would have trouble holding it off.

Whelan beckoned. "Come on, Donnie. We don't have all night."

Donnie waded in, made a swiping motion with the blade, moved forward two shuffling steps, his weight forward, body tense. Whelan could see the veins pulsing in his neck and temple. A grenade ready to go off.

He moved to his right, closer to the chair, and the point of the blade followed his movement. He watched Donnie and wondered if his own face was bathed in sweat like the boy's, realized his whole body was wet. He made a jerky movement to his left and the boy matched it effortlessly. Don was undoubtedly quicker than he was, and he knew if he backed up, he was finished.

Hands still behind his back, he switched the hammer to his left.

"C'mon, asshole, let's get it on. You killed anybody face to face lately? You killed anybody that wasn't asleep, or a drunken old man? C'mon, halfwit, come get a piece of me."

The boy's lips were wet and a froth of saliva appeared on his upper lip, hanging down like a fang. He seemed to be on the point of saying something.

"Trouble with you, kid, is you want a fair fight out of me," Whelan said, and in one motion picked up the wooden chair in his right hand and swung it up into Donnie's face. He let the chair go and swung the hammer, a straight overhand blow, felt the cast iron hit bone and heard Donnie groan, and then the kid was down.

His swing took him off-balance and he teetered slightly to his left; he tried to recover his balance and Donnie was up on one knee and slashing, and the blade tore into Whelan's calf, then into his thigh and he staggered against a table. Donnie bounded up at him, blood streaking his face, and Whelan fought panic and bounced the hammer off the kid's head again. It was a glancing blow that caught him just above the ear and Donnie let out a high-pitched keening noise. He slashed out at Whelan again with the knife and Whelan jumped back. He swung the hammer one last time, putting shoulder into it and this time he caught the boy across the nose. Whelan felt the blood spray him and then Donnie was staggering across the room, attempting to run, holding on to his face and making a strangled screaming sound, and as he got to the front hall the door seemed to explode against the wall and Detective Albert Bauman of the Chicago Police Department thrust his bulk into the narrow hallway.

Whelan watched as Bauman caught Donnie under the chin with one hand and began to squeeze, and he saw the knife move before be could call out. Bauman stopped the knife with his free hand, took the blade in the center of his palm, closed his fist around it and squeezed the blade, then literally lifted the boy off his feet by the throat. Don's face went violet and his eyes bulged till Whelan thought they'd pop from the sockets, and the boy's legs kicked spastically at Bauman. There was a gurgling sound, and he could see blood dripping from Bauman's hand around the knife. Whelan lurched toward the hall, heard himself yelling, "Bauman, don't kill him, don't—"

And he heard the detective's booming, outraged voice.

"YOU!"

Bauman shook him and stared into the kid's purpling face and squeezed, and Donnie tried to free his knife and the detective's voice shook walls.

"YOU...HAVE THE RIGHT TO REMAIN FUCKING SILENT."

And gradually, as he gave the kid letter-perfect Miranda, his voice went from a bellow to a monotone, and he lowered the boy to the floor, relaxed his grip on Donnie's windpipe and let him go. He pulled the bloody knife from his hand and tossed it onto the hall floor.

The boy collapsed in a sobbing heap on the floor, moving back and forth on hands and knees like a hurt child, and Bauman got on top of him and cuffed him. Then he looked at Whelan.

"Whaddya call this? You fuck-up. He kills you, and he's out on the street again."

"I'm sorry. I wanted a piece of him."

Bauman looked down at the battered figure on the floor. "Looks like you got it."

Whelan sank onto the ruined carpet. The cut in his calf stung but the longer, deeper one in the thigh bled freely and bathed him in searing pain. He squeezed at the skin around the cut and looked at Bauman.

"What are you doing here? How—" Bauman looked at him, a little half smile on his face, and Whelan gave a short laugh.

"You followed me."

"I don't trust anybody, Whelan. I watched you. You were movin' like a guy that's got someplace to go. And the broad cinched it for me. She asked where you were and then she says, 'Hope he went straight home.'"

He gave Whelan an odd look, almost paternal. "Got it outta your system now?"

"Think so."

"Good. Now watch him while I make the call. How bad you cut?"

"I've had worse but it hurts like a sonofabitch."

"We'll get you all fixed up. You'll be dancing again in no time." At the door he paused, dripping blood from his hand. "Where, Whelan? Where'd you get worse? That time with Kozel."

"In the Delta."

Bauman nodded. "And you were, what? A medic?"

"Yeah."

"Tommy was a medic. My cousin Tommy."

"He come back?"

"Fuck, no. We grew up together. He lived a couple blocks

from us."

"So who'd you vote for?"

Bauman flashed him a look of amused malice. "That guy McGovern. After Tommy, I voted for McGovern. Do it again, too. You see, Whelan? I'm just a fat old peacenik at heart," he said, and went out to use the radio.

"Oh, I'll bet," Whelan said to himself.

EPILOGUE

Wade was standing out in front of the Wilson Men's Club Hotel and smiled uncertainly when Whelan got out of his car. Whelan walked stiff-legged over to him.

"Hey, Mr. Whelan. How's the leg?"

"They think I'm going to live." He handed Wade the envelope. "You know what to do with this, right?"

Wade took it in both hands and looked uncomfortably at Whelan.

"Yeah, man. I do."

"Buy clothes, get a train ticket, use the rest to get yourself started down there."

"I'll pay you back, man."

"I don't care if you do. But you can if you want. See you around, Wade. Drop me a line, maybe."

"You're good people, Mr. Whelan."

"So are you, Wade. Get out of town," he said, and smiled.

He stood in front of the A&W, perfectly aware that he looked like a lost puppy. He looked at the sign and then cupped both hands against the window to peer in, looking for some sign that it was all some kinky Persian joke, but the evidence was obvious, complete, unmistakable. It was closed. Counters were clean, supplies and equipment were carefully put away just as if the two madmen were coming back later in the morning to open up. He looked at the sign for the third time and said, "Shit."

It was, in its way, a marvelous sign, a sign that could only have been composed by Gus and Rashid:

CLOSD. THIS ONE NOT OPEN NO MORE
WE GOING TO CALIFONIA TO MAKE BIG MONEY
GOD BLESS PRESIDNT REGAN AND USA

He started to laugh. Gus and Rashid were about to be turned loose on California.

Californians, save yourselves!

Whelan wondered what ethnic heritage they would claim for themselves in California. When they'd arrived on Lawrence, they'd called themselves Egyptians, and during the worst of the Iranian crisis they'd told anybody who'd listen that they were Israelis offering cuisine from the Holy Land. "Food that Jesus would like." What would they be on the coast? Mexicans? Hondurans?

A large shape in a green jacket appeared beside his reflection in the window.

"Hey, sleuth. So these guys boogied, huh? Whaddya think, maybe they poisoned somebody and had to leave town?"

He looked at Bauman. "No, if my guess is right, they decided to go out to the Coast, become entrepeneurs, stare at the blond girls in the little tiny bathing suits and enjoy the American dream. They'll fit right in." He glanced down at Bauman's bandaged hand. "How's the injury?"

"It's no big deal," Bauman said, a little testily. "So how's your leg?"

"Thirty-eight stitches. Three in the little cut, thirty-five in the big one. Had to toss my ma's old rug, too."

Bauman looked around the street, eyes coming to rest on a pair of plump young Puerto Rican girls squeezed into halter tops and jeans made for their little sisters. He shook his head, looked slightly flustered when he saw Whelan watching him, then smiled.

"I'd even be willing to learn the language. Any language they want." He watched the girls enter Sam's Carniceria.

"He won't stand trial, that little fucker. You figured that, right?"

"Yeah, I figured. Spend some time in a hospital, I hope?"

"Oh, a long, long time, Whelan. He's growlin' and hearin' voices, talking like he's different people. I think they'll want to keep him in just to study all his moves." He shot an uneasy glance at Whelan.

"What about her, Bauman?"

Bauman kept his eyes trained on traffic as he spoke. "She's gonna stand trial. She don't hear no voices, Whelan."

"No voices, maybe, but isn't she something?"

Bauman looked at him. "That's a hard little number, there, Whelan."

"Yeah."

"All these poor fuckers dead…you know she still thinks her old man had a stash somewhere?"

"She say that?"

"Yeah. I told her she got all these people killed for nothing and she just gives me this little smile and says, 'What you don't know would fill a book.'"

Whelan looked up at the sky and blocked her out. A cloud mass was forming to the west. Rain, maybe. He had calls to make, people to talk to: he would need to talk to Marie Shears to tell her that Art's killers were in custody. She probably knew already, but she'd have a thousand questions. More than that, she'd need a listener. And he wanted to talk to Captain Wallis again, to talk about the hapless boy known as Billy the Kid. He dreaded both conversations and was suddenly very tired of it all, sick to death of his neighborhood and the people he knew and his life.

"Bauman, I need a long, long ride on a train."

"Yeah, I bet."

"You ever want to be finished with it all, Bauman? Just take off somewhere and leave it all to somebody else?"

Bauman watched the street. "Nah. This is all I got, Whelan. It's all I got." He cleared his throat and took out one of his nasty little cigars. "C'mon, you wanna go get a cup of coffee?"

"Why not."

"Let's go down to this joint under the tracks. You can tell me all about being a private eye," and he laughed.

"I'll have to fit you into my schedule," Whelan said, and they walked up Lawrence to the coffee shop. The wind was picking up from the west, a hot wind that lifted dirt and grit and loose paper from the street and sent it sailing. The reigning odors of the street were car exhaust and grilled onions, and somewhere somebody was cooking with chilies, and there was salsa music booming from a third-floor window.

Whelan shrugged and told himself to worry about somebody else's troubles.

MORE FROM MICHAEL RALEIGH

A BODY IN BELMONT HARBOR

The body of a small-time drug dealer washes up in Belmont Harbor among the yachts of Chicago's wealthy. Convinced that this murder connects to her husband's suicide two years prior, wealthy widow Janice Fairs hires private eye Paul Whelan to investigate.

Whelan's investigation takes him into the rarefied air of the wealthy, where he begins to discover unlikely connections between the two men in the harbor. But Whelan isn't the only one snooping, and he discovers himself an unwitting player in a game of cat-and-mouse, with deadly consequences.

THE MAXWELL STREET BLUES

Chicago private eye Paul Whelan is hired by an elderly jazz musician to find a missing street hustler named Sam Burwell. As Whelan delves into Burwell's past, the world of street vendors and corner musicians, he uncovers old enmities and love affairs, but his search for Burwell comes up empty. That is, until Burwell is found murdered.

Soon Whelan is swept up into a whirlwind of old feuds, dark pasts, unlikely romances...and a killer hiding in plain sight.

KILLER ON ARGYLE STREET

Chicago Private Investigator Paul Whelan takes the case when an elderly woman asks him to look into the disappearance of Tony Blanchard, a young man she'd taken in after his parents died. Instead, Whelan discovers a string of murders, all tied to a car-theft ring.

All the evidence suggests that Tony is dead as well, but Whelan keeps digging until he finds himself surrounded by a dangerous maze of silent witnesses, crooked cops, and people willing to kill to keep the truth from surfacing. When a friend from Whelan's past emerges—a friend Whelan thought long dead—his investigation takes a dangerous turn; one that brings him no closer to Tony, and a lot closer to his own demise.

THE RIVERVIEW MURDERS

Margaret O'Mara's brother disappeared thirty years earlier, so when his last known associate is found murdered, O'Mara hires Chicago PI Paul Whelan to investigate.

Whelan makes the rounds through seedy bar and dilapidated apartment buildings where he discovers connections to a long-gone Chicago amusement park where another murder took place forty years prior.

Soon, Whelan finds himself navigating his way through dark pasts, deep secrets, and a mystery that may cost him his life.